Unicorn Selfies

Another
Phoebe and Her Unicorn Adventure

Complete Your Phoebe and Her Unicorn Collection

Phoebe and Her Unicorn

Dana Simpson

Unicorn on a Roll

Another Phoebe and Her Unicorn Adventure

Dana Simpson

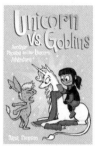

Unicorn Vs. Goblins

Another Phoebe and Her Unicorn Adventure

Dana Simpson

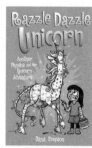

Razzle Dazzle Unicorn

Another Phoebe and Her Unicorn Adventure

Dana Simpson

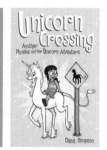

Unicorn Crossing

Another Phoebe and Her Unicorn Adventure

Dana Simpson

Phoebe and Her Unicorn in The Magic Storm

Dana Simpson

Unicorn of Many Hats

Another Phoebe and Her Unicorn Adventure

Dana Simpson

Phoebe and Her Unicorn in Unicorn Theater

Dana Simpson

Unicorn Bowling

Another Phoebe and Her Unicorn Adventure

Dana Simpson

The Unicorn Whisperer

Another Phoebe and Her Unicorn Adventure

Dana Simpson

Camping with Unicorns

Another Phoebe and Her Unicorn Adventure

Dana Simpson

Virtual Unicorn Experience

Another Phoebe and Her Unicorn Adventure

Dana Simpson

Unicorn Famous

Another Phoebe and Her Unicorn Adventure

Dana Simpson

Unicorn Playlist

Another Phoebe and Her Unicorn Adventure

Dana Simpson

Unicorn Selfies

Another
Phoebe and Her Unicorn Adventure

Dana Simpson

Andrews McMeel
PUBLISHING®

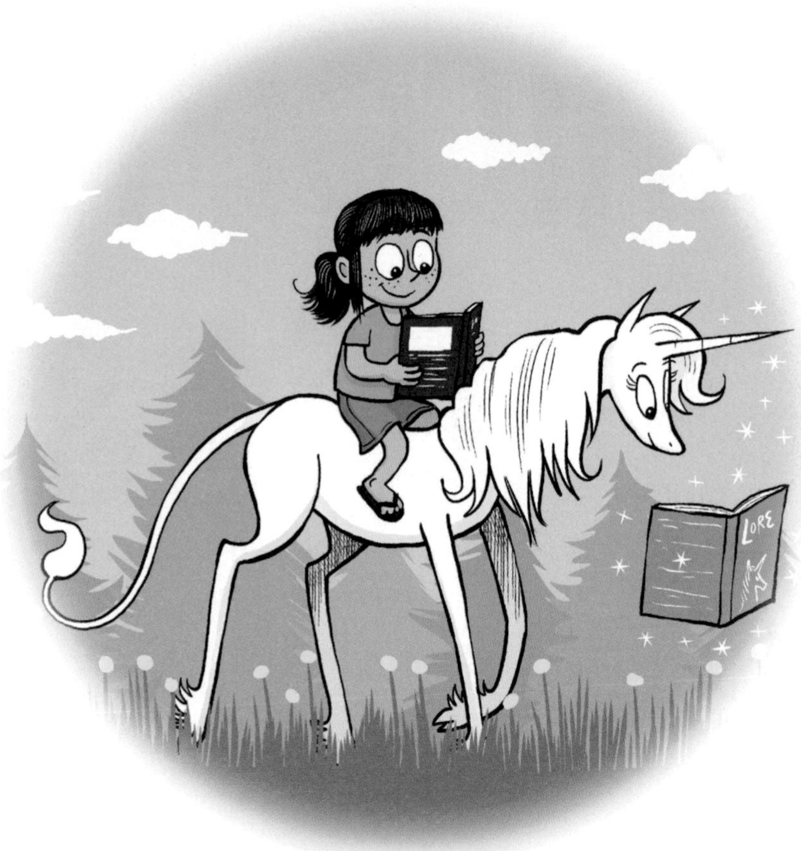
LORE

Hey, kids!

Check out the glossary starting on page 173
if you come across words you don't know.

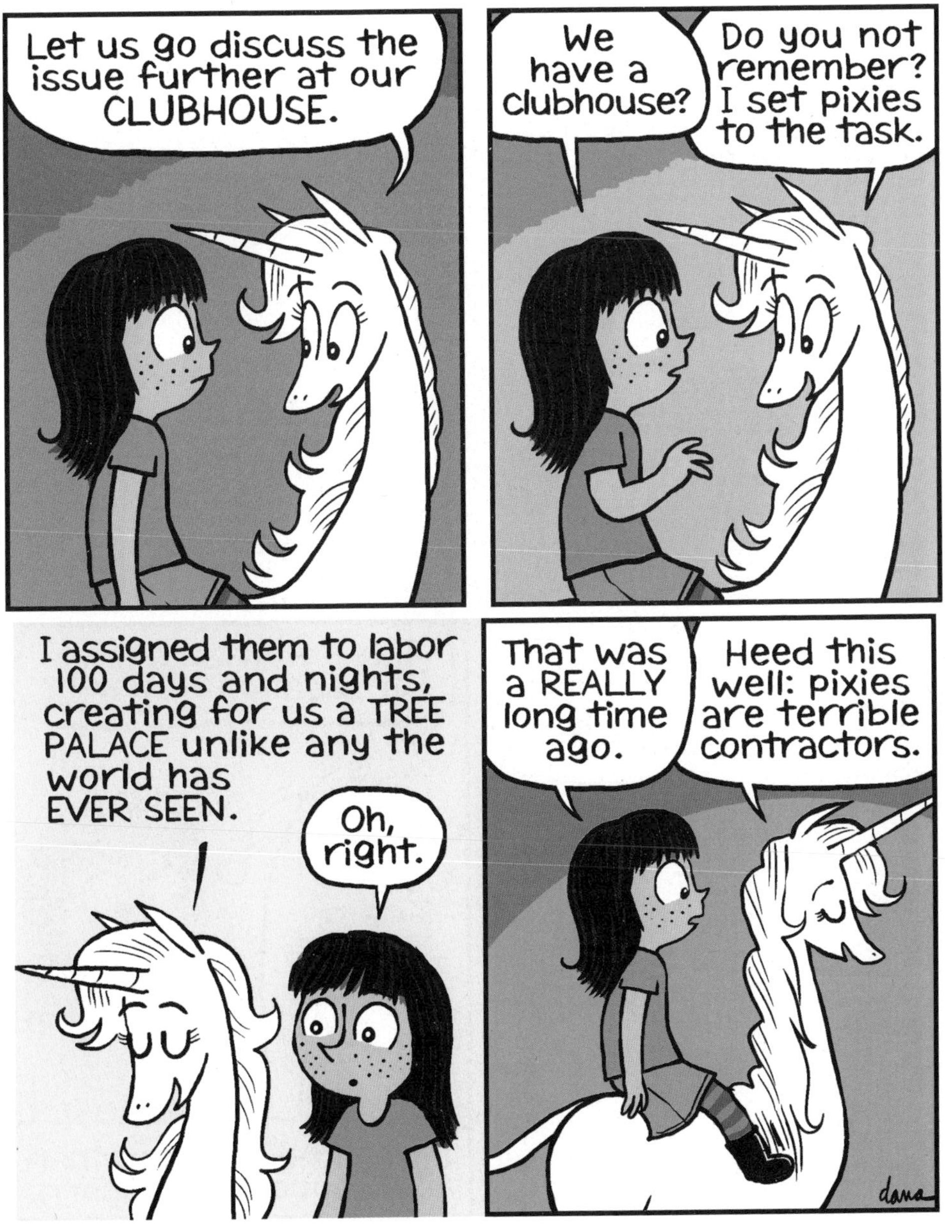
Let us go discuss the issue further at our CLUBHOUSE.
We have a clubhouse?
Do you not remember? I set pixies to the task.
I assigned them to labor 100 days and nights, creating for us a TREE PALACE unlike any the world has EVER SEEN.
Oh, right.
That was a REALLY long time ago.
Heed this well: pixies are terrible contractors.
dana

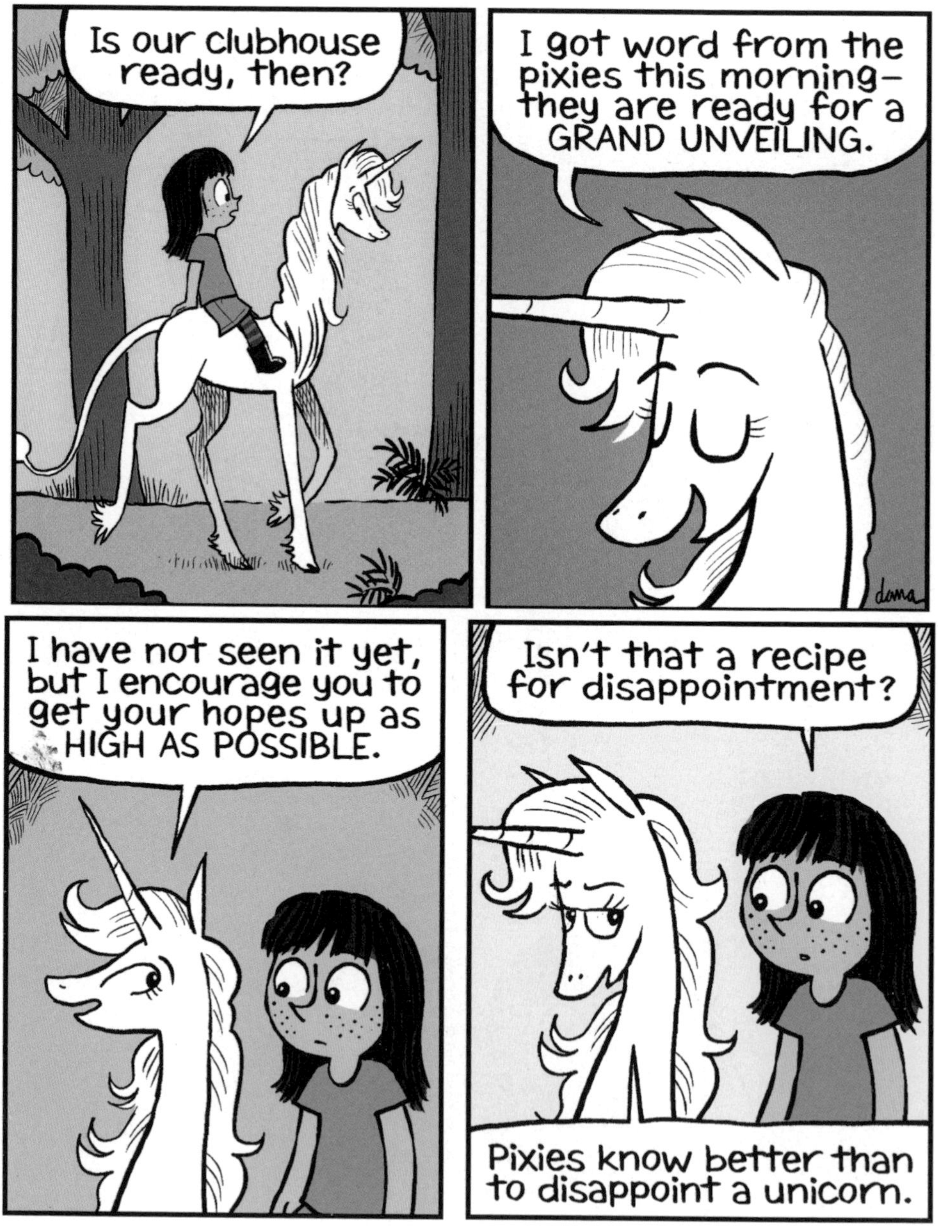
Is our clubhouse ready, then?
I got word from the pixies this morning— they are ready for a GRAND UNVEILING.
dana
I have not seen it yet, but I encourage you to get your hopes up as HIGH AS POSSIBLE.
Isn't that a recipe for disappointment?
Pixies know better than to disappoint a unicorn.

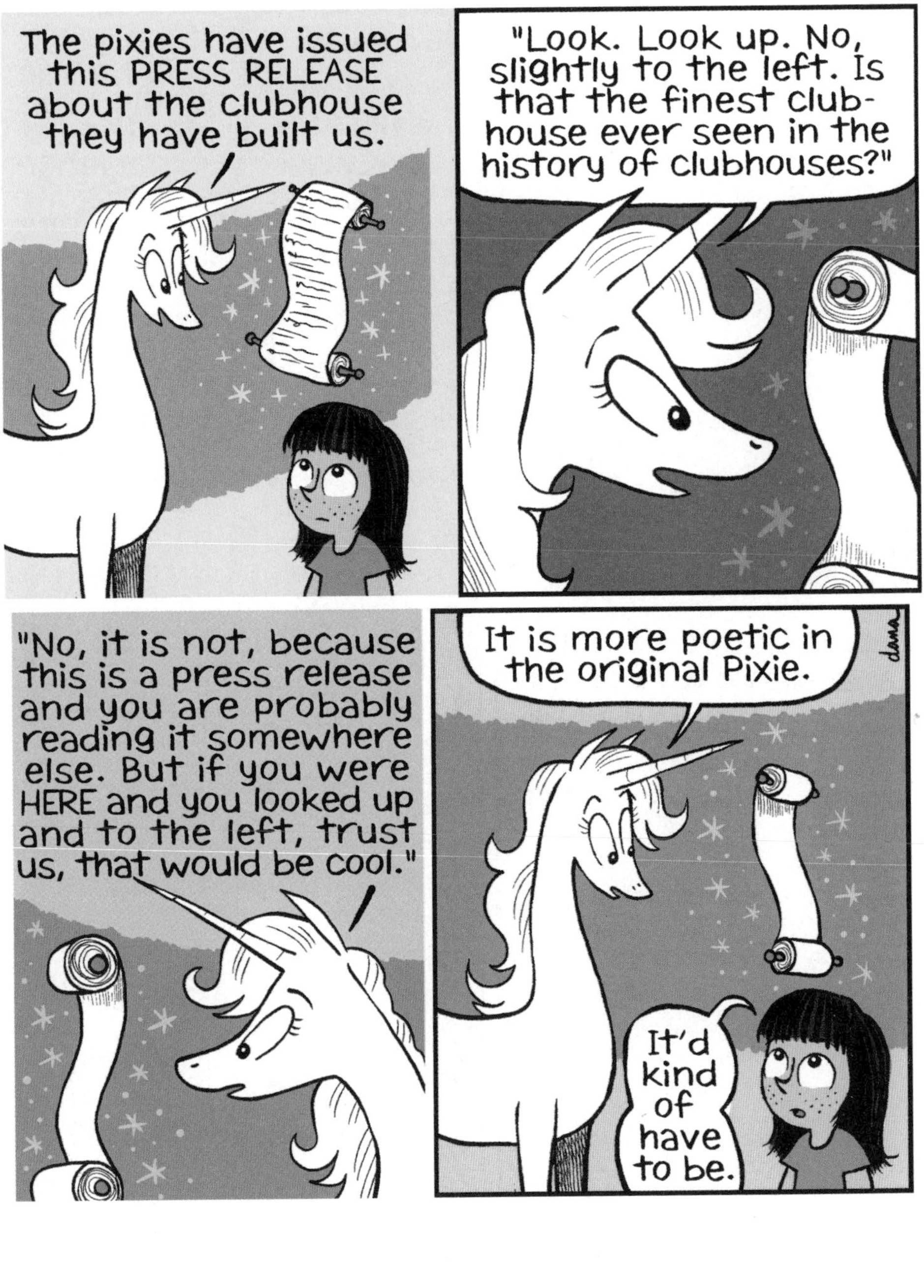
The pixies have issued this PRESS RELEASE about the clubhouse they have built us.
"Look. Look up. No, slightly to the left. Is that the finest clubhouse ever seen in the history of clubhouses?"
"No, it is not, because this is a press release and you are probably reading it somewhere else. But if you were HERE and you looked up and to the left, trust us, that would be cool."
It is more poetic in the original Pixie.
It'd kind of have to be.
dana

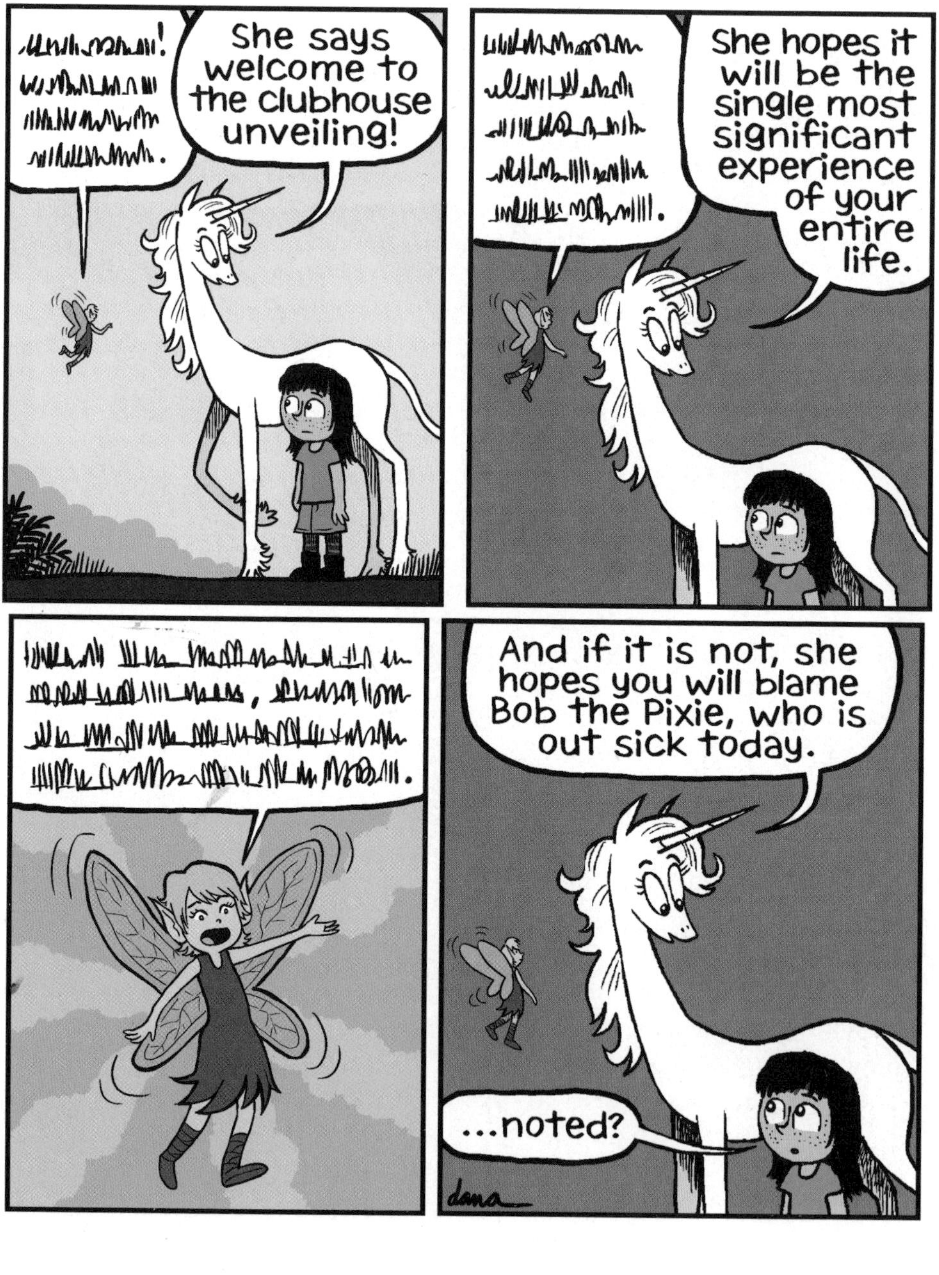
She says welcome to the clubhouse unveiling!
She hopes it will be the single most significant experience of your entire life.
And if it is not, she hopes you will blame Bob the Pixie, who is out sick today.
...noted?
dana

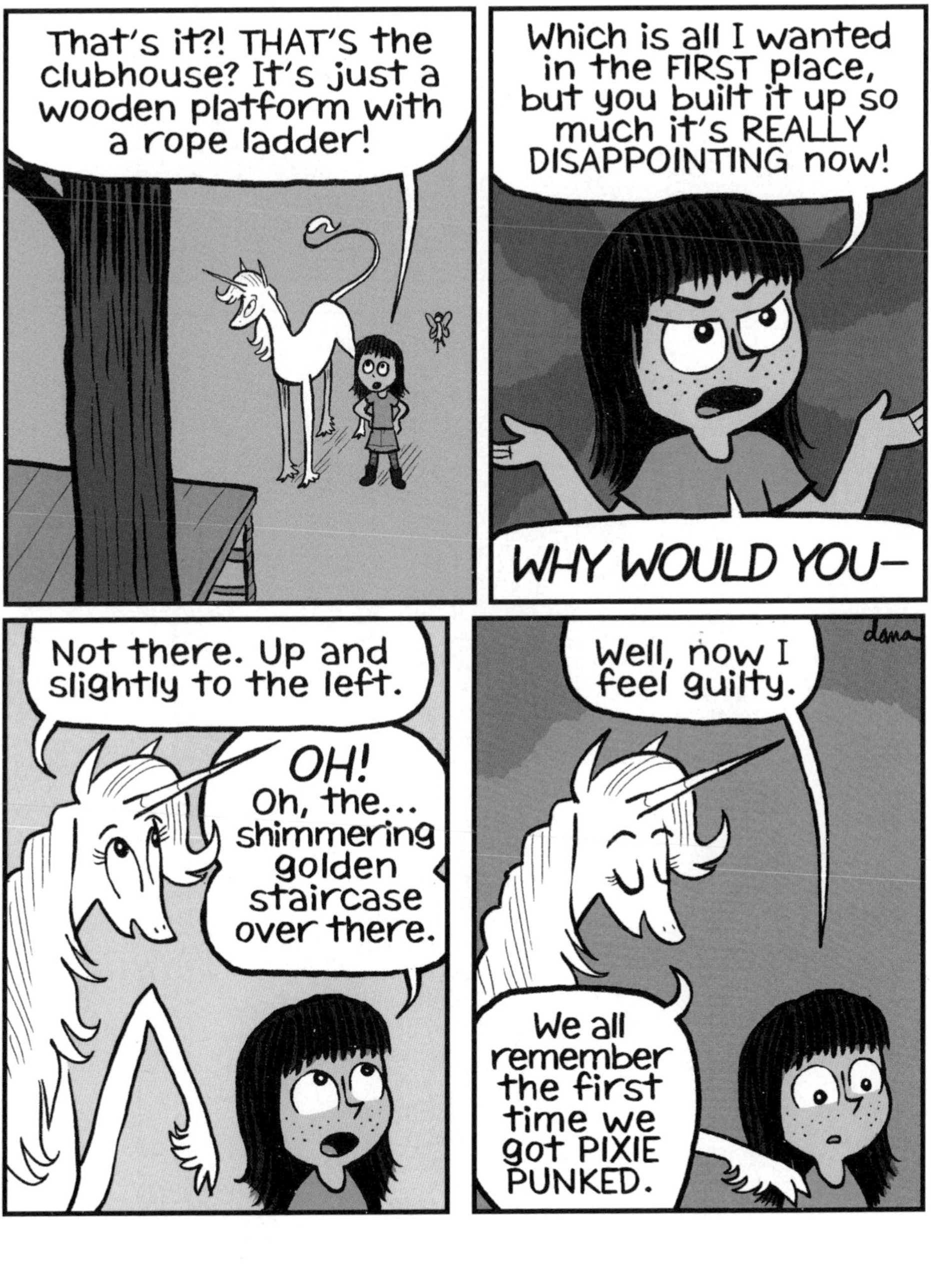
That's it?! THAT'S the clubhouse? It's just a wooden platform with a rope ladder!
Which is all I wanted in the FIRST place, but you built it up so much it's REALLY DISAPPOINTING now!
WHY WOULD YOU–
Not there. Up and slightly to the left.
OH!
Oh, the... shimmering golden staircase over there.
dana
Well, now I feel guilty.
We all remember the first time we got PIXIE PUNKED.

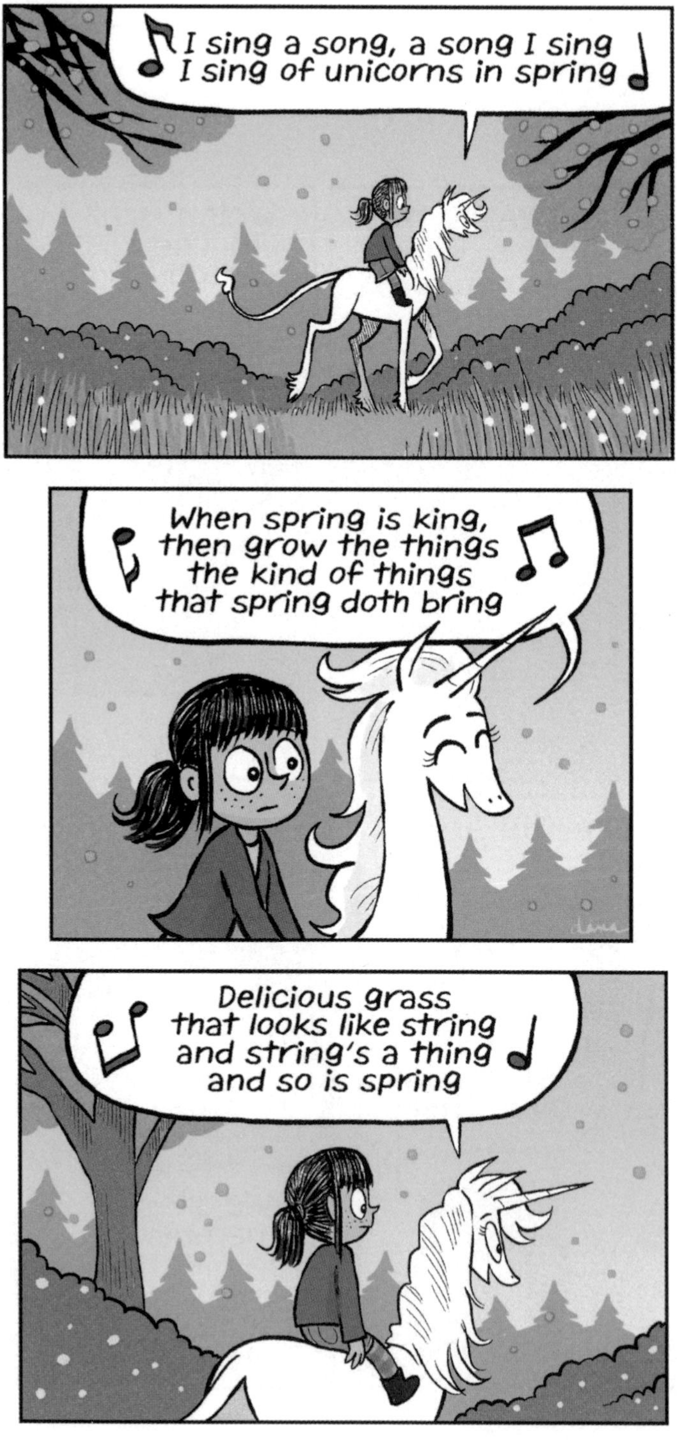
I sing a song, a song I sing
I sing of unicorns in spring
When spring is king, then grow the things the kind of things that spring doth bring
Delicious grass that looks like string and string's a thing and so is spring

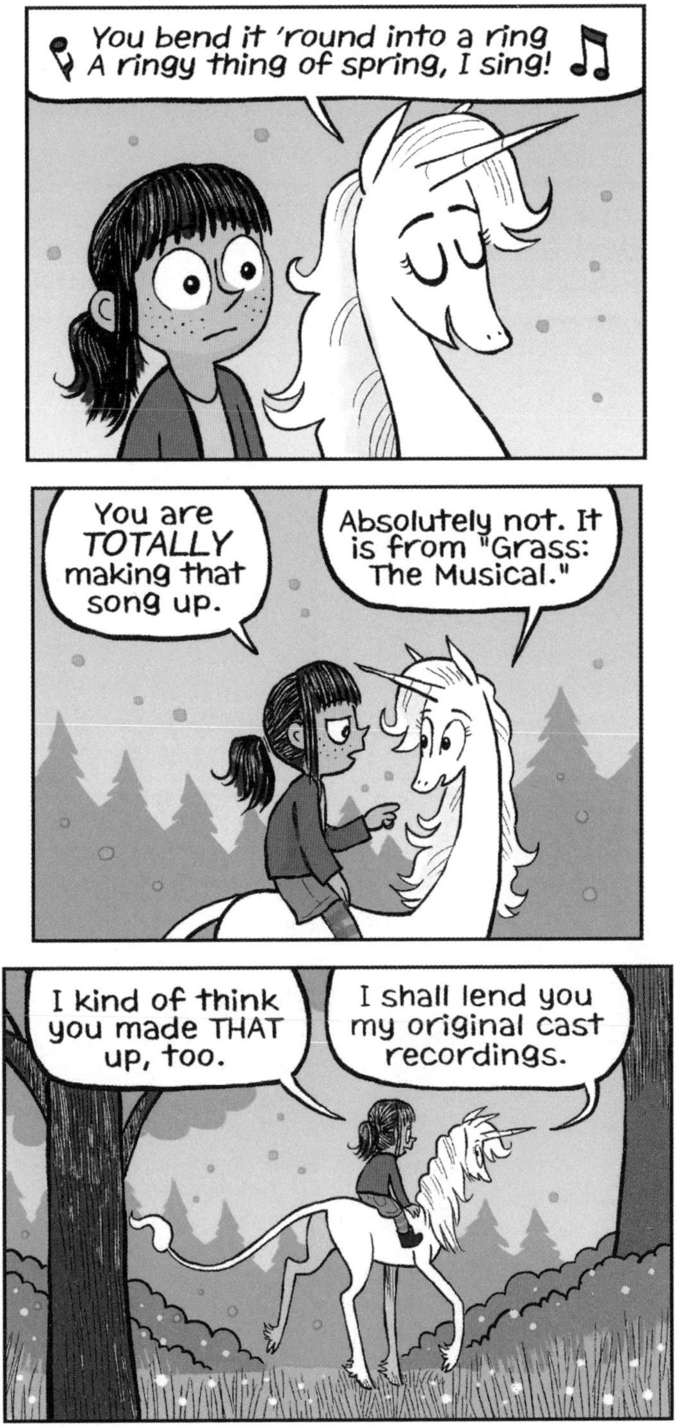

You bend it 'round into a ring
A ringy thing of spring, I sing!
You are TOTALLY making that song up.
Absolutely not. It is from "Grass: The Musical."
I kind of think you made THAT up, too.
I shall lend you my original cast recordings.

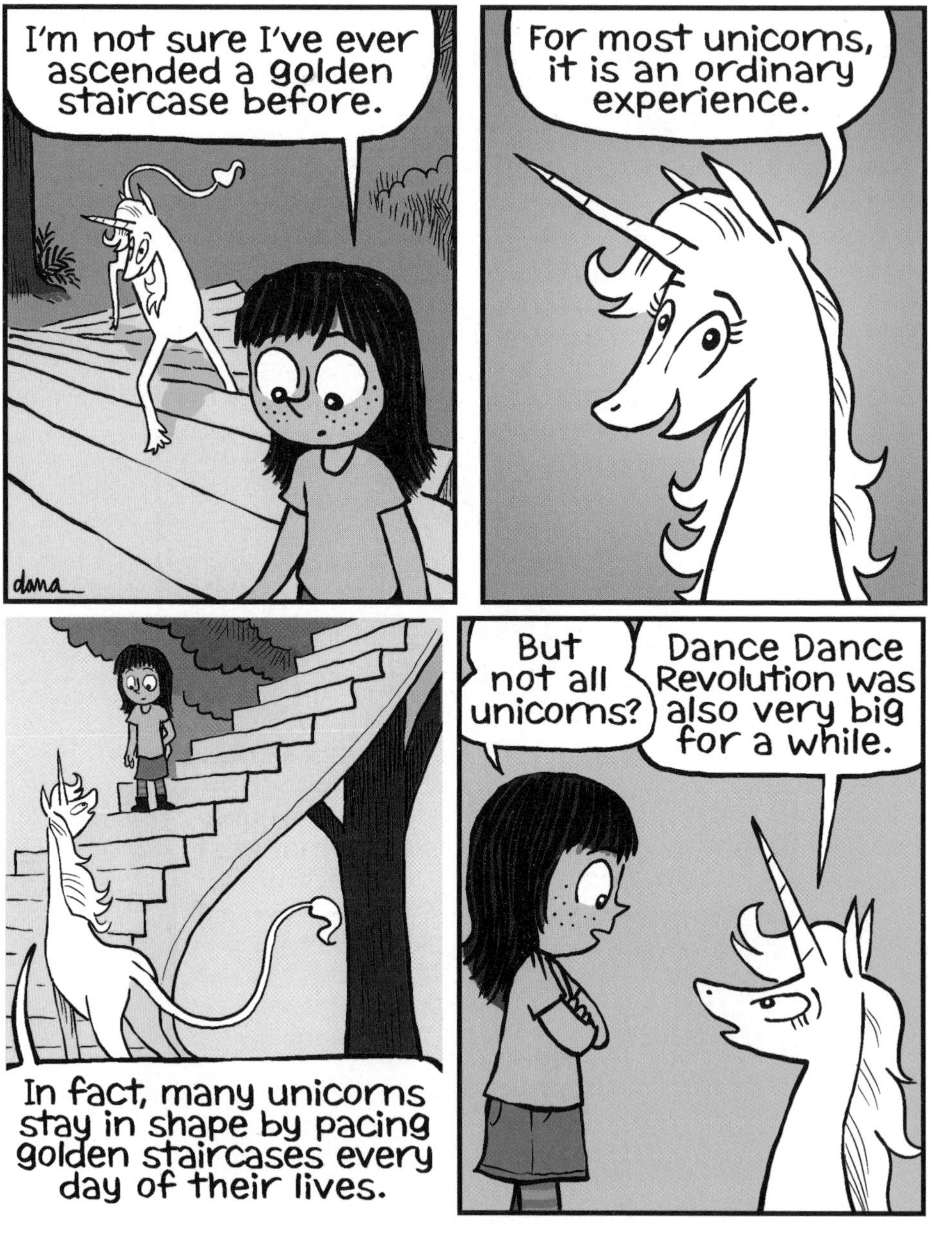
I'm not sure I've ever ascended a golden staircase before.
dana
For most unicorns, it is an ordinary experience.
In fact, many unicorns stay in shape by pacing golden staircases every day of their lives.
But not all unicorns?
Dance Dance Revolution was also very big for a while.

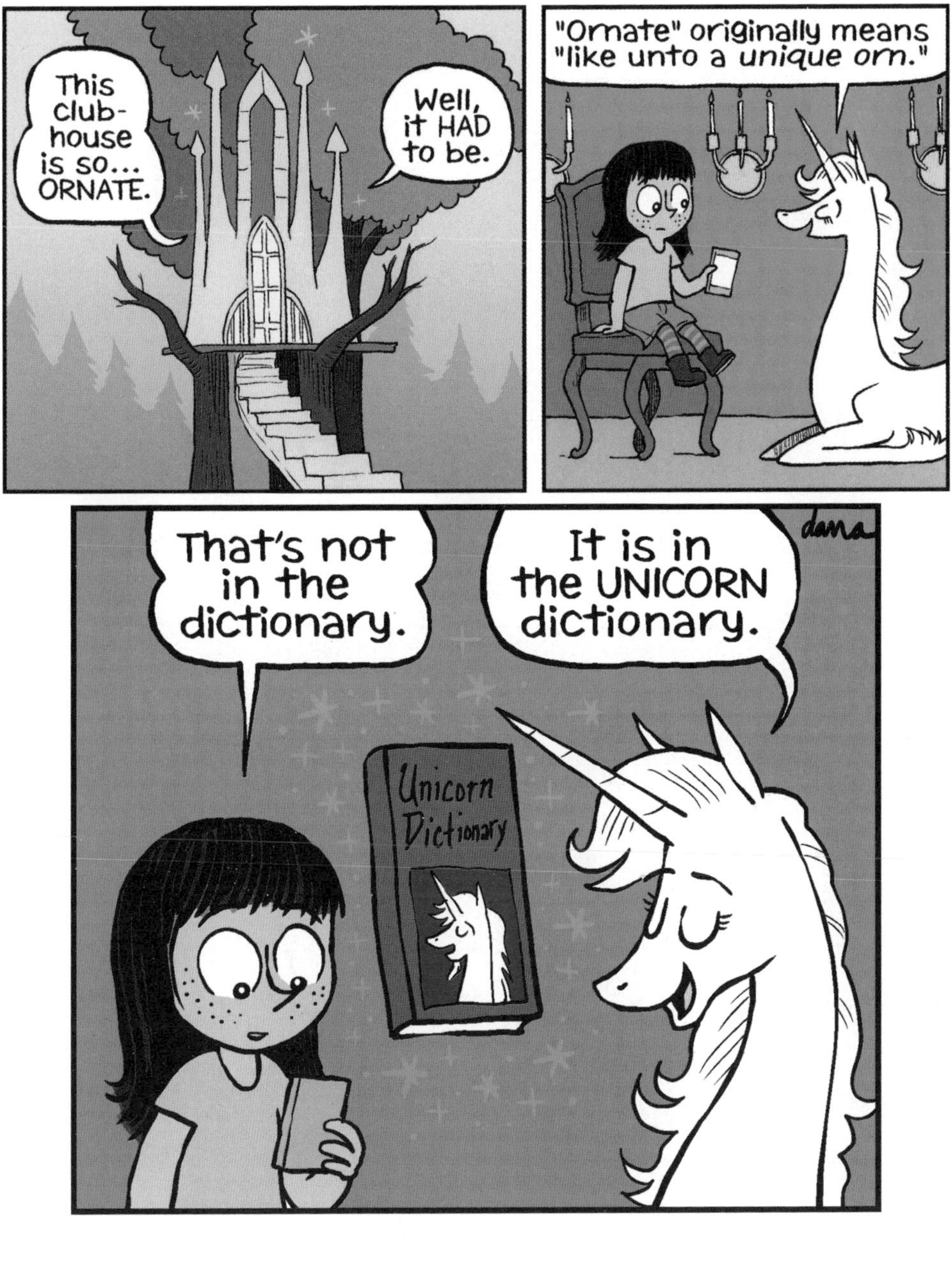
This club-house is so... ORNATE.
Well, it HAD to be.
"Ornate" originally means "like unto a *unique orn*."
That's not in the dictionary.
It is in the UNICORN dictionary.
Unicorn Dictionary
dana

Now that we have an amazing clubhouse, we should think about what kind of club we're going to be.
I'm fine with it being a "making weird intense faces" club.
I will explain.

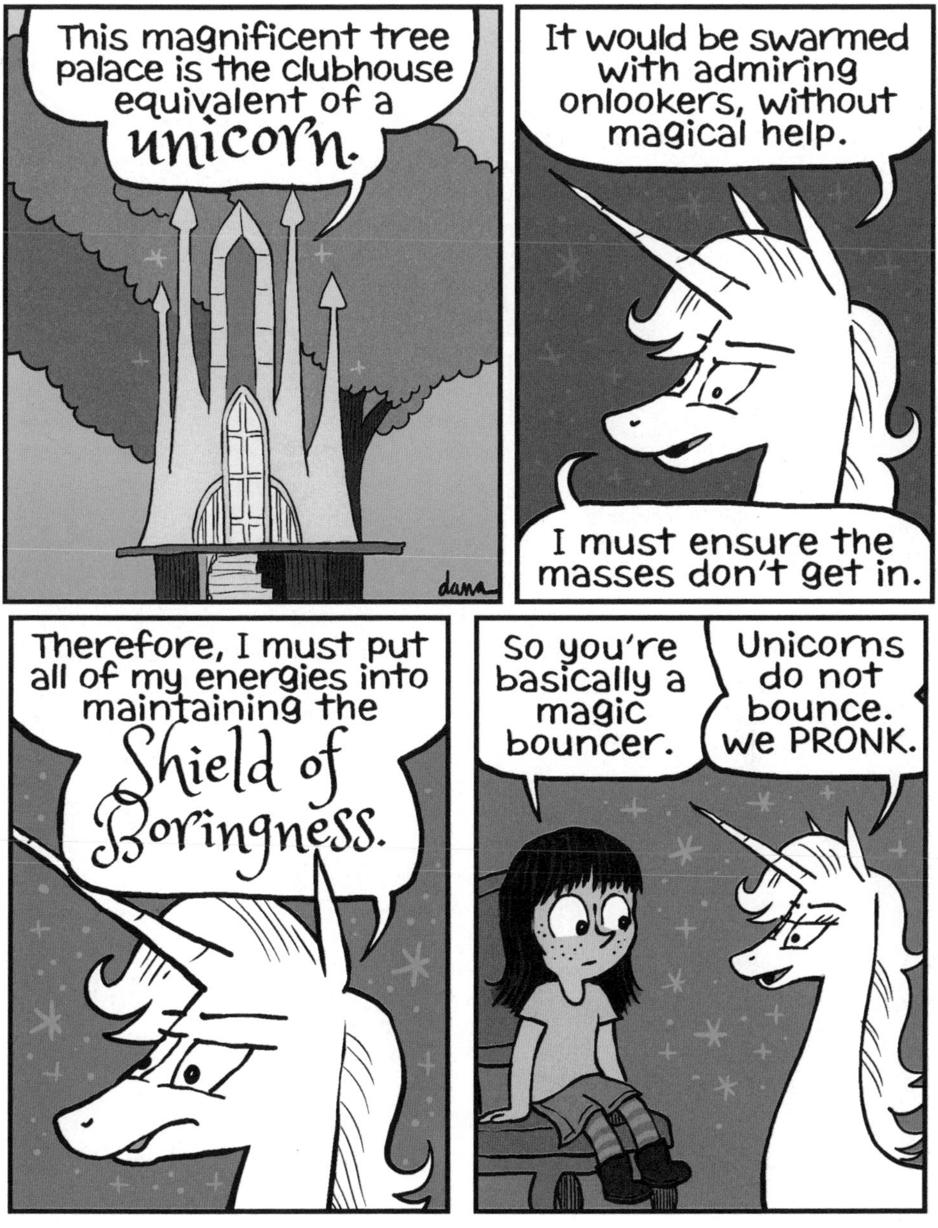
This magnificent tree palace is the clubhouse equivalent of a unicorn.
dana
It would be swarmed with admiring onlookers, without magical help.
I must ensure the masses don't get in.
Therefore, I must put all of my energies into maintaining the Shield of Boringness.
So you're basically a magic bouncer.
Unicorns do not bounce. we PRONK.

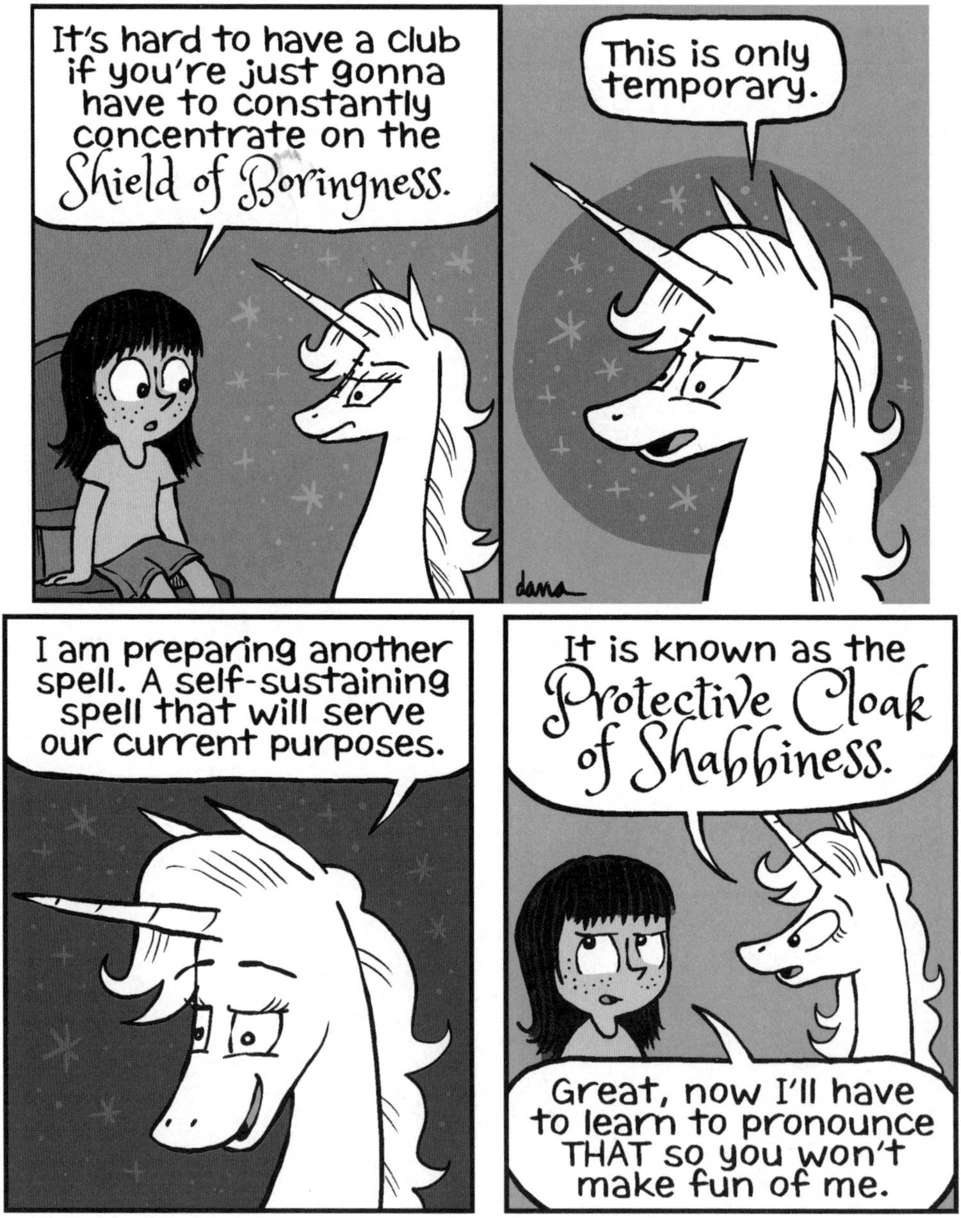
It's hard to have a club if you're just gonna have to constantly concentrate on the Shield of Boringness.
This is only temporary.
dana
I am preparing another spell. A self-sustaining spell that will serve our current purposes.
It is known as the Protective Cloak of Shabbiness.
Great, now I'll have to learn to pronounce THAT so you won't make fun of me.

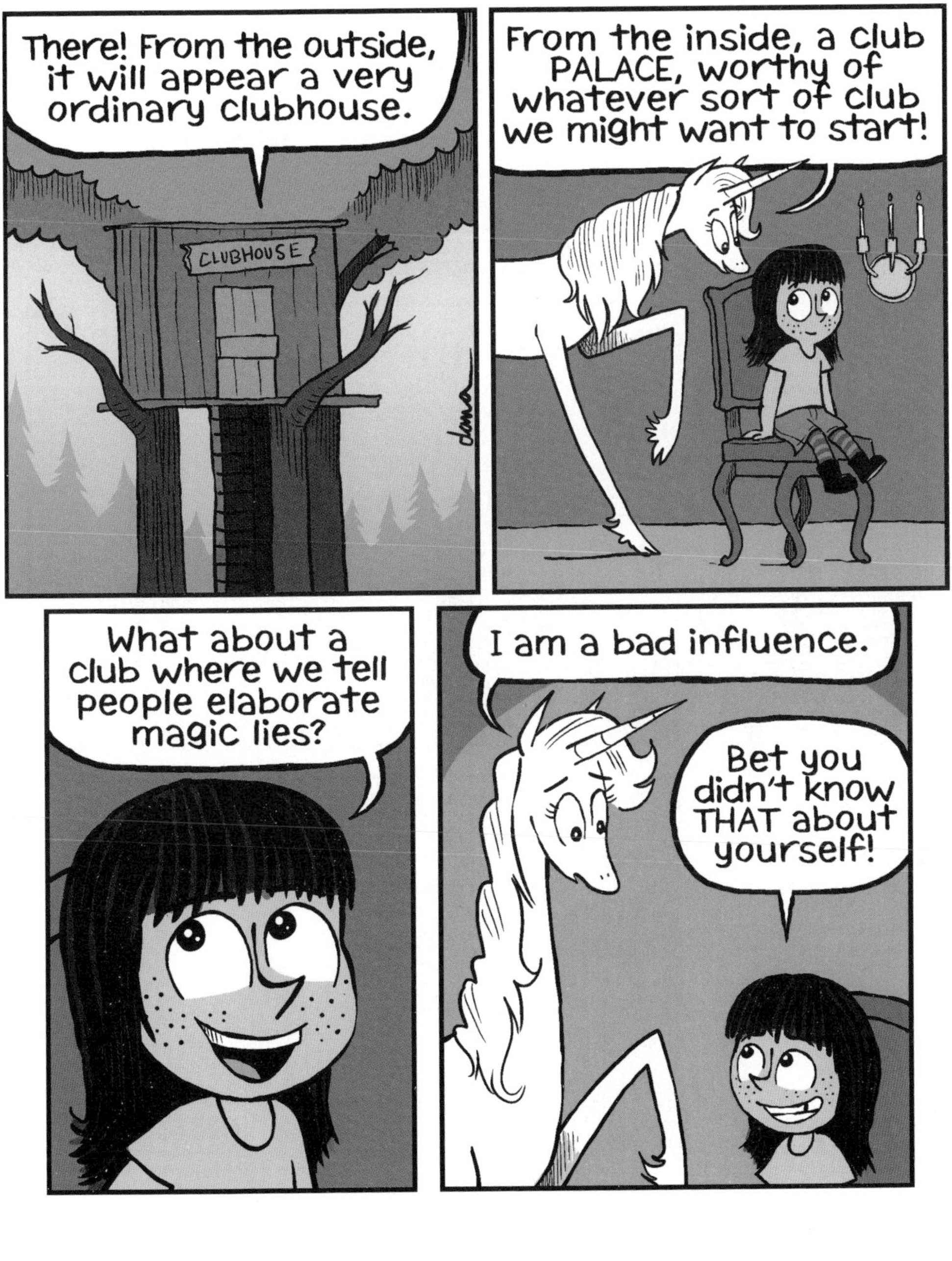
There! From the outside, it will appear a very ordinary clubhouse.
CLUBHOUSE
From the inside, a club PALACE, worthy of whatever sort of club we might want to start!
What about a club where we tell people elaborate magic lies?
I am a bad influence.
Bet you didn't know THAT about yourself!

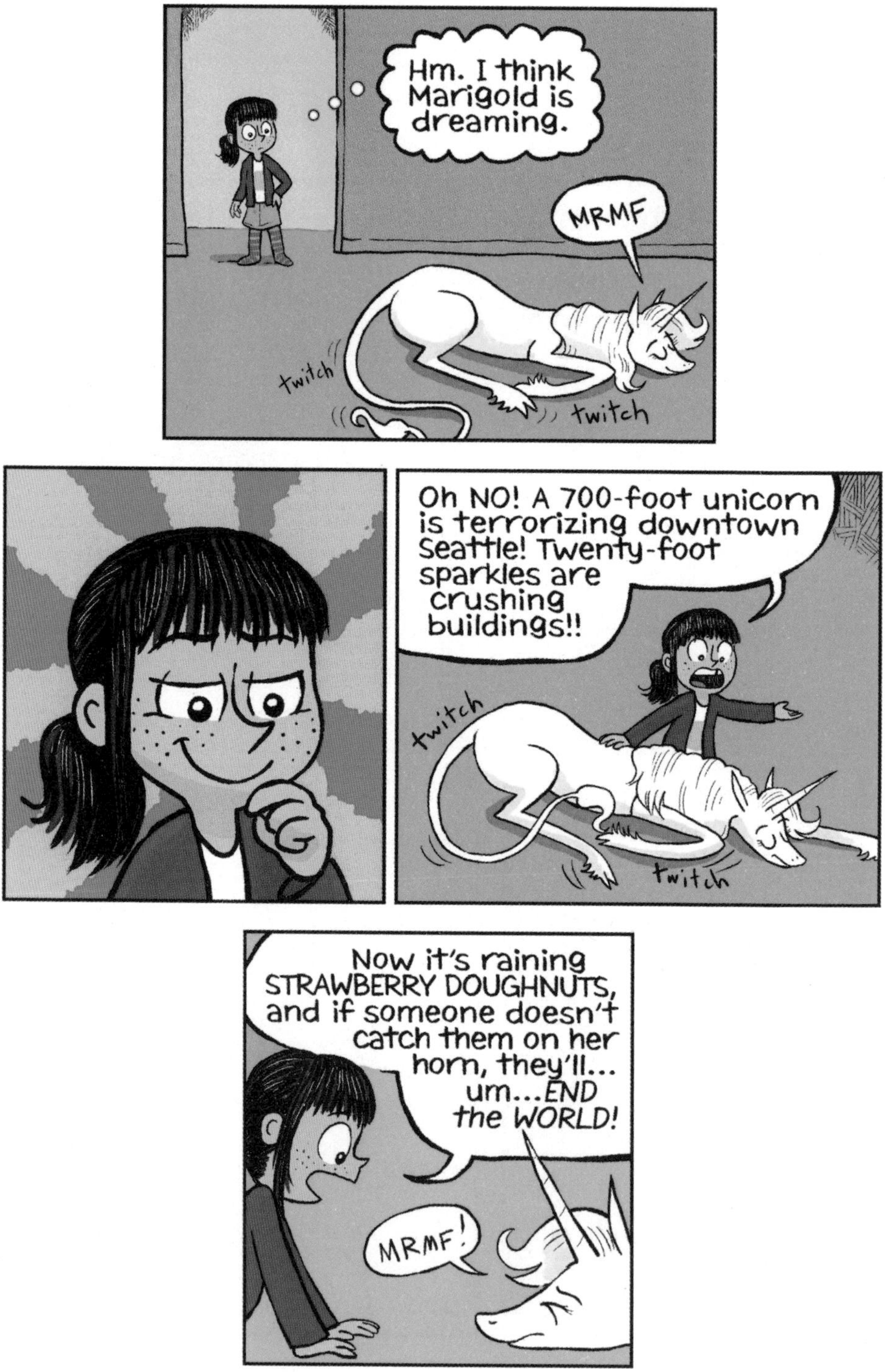
Hm. I think Marigold is dreaming.
MRMF
twitch
twitch
Oh NO! A 700-foot unicorn is terrorizing downtown Seattle! Twenty-foot sparkles are crushing buildings!!
twitch
twitch
Now it's raining STRAWBERRY DOUGHNUTS, and if someone doesn't catch them on her horn, they'll... um...END the WORLD!
MRMF!

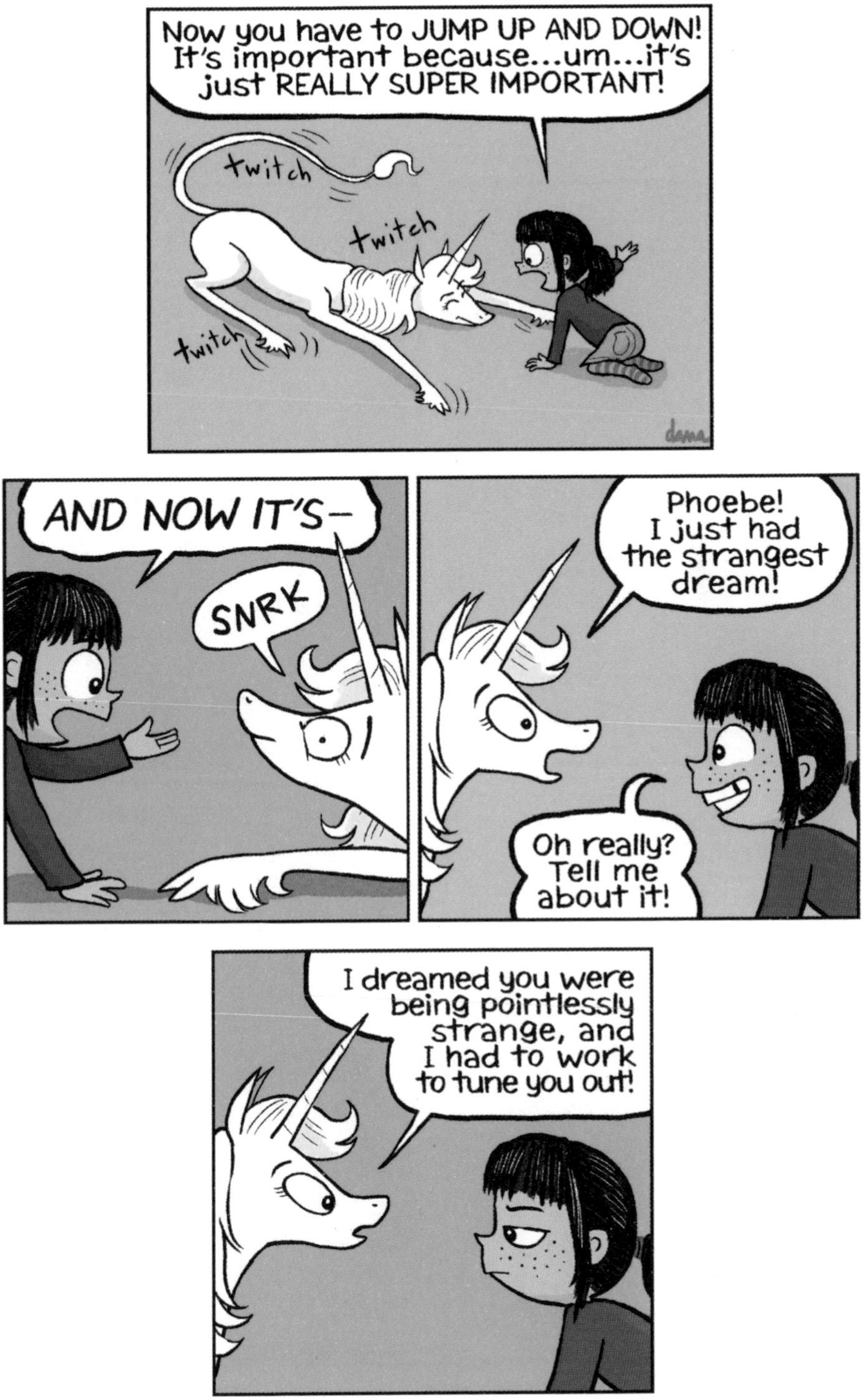
Now you have to JUMP UP AND DOWN! It's important because...um...it's just REALLY SUPER IMPORTANT!
twitch
twitch
twitch
dana
AND NOW IT'S—
SNRK
Phoebe! I just had the strangest dream!
Oh really? Tell me about it!
I dreamed you were being pointlessly strange, and I had to work to tune you out!

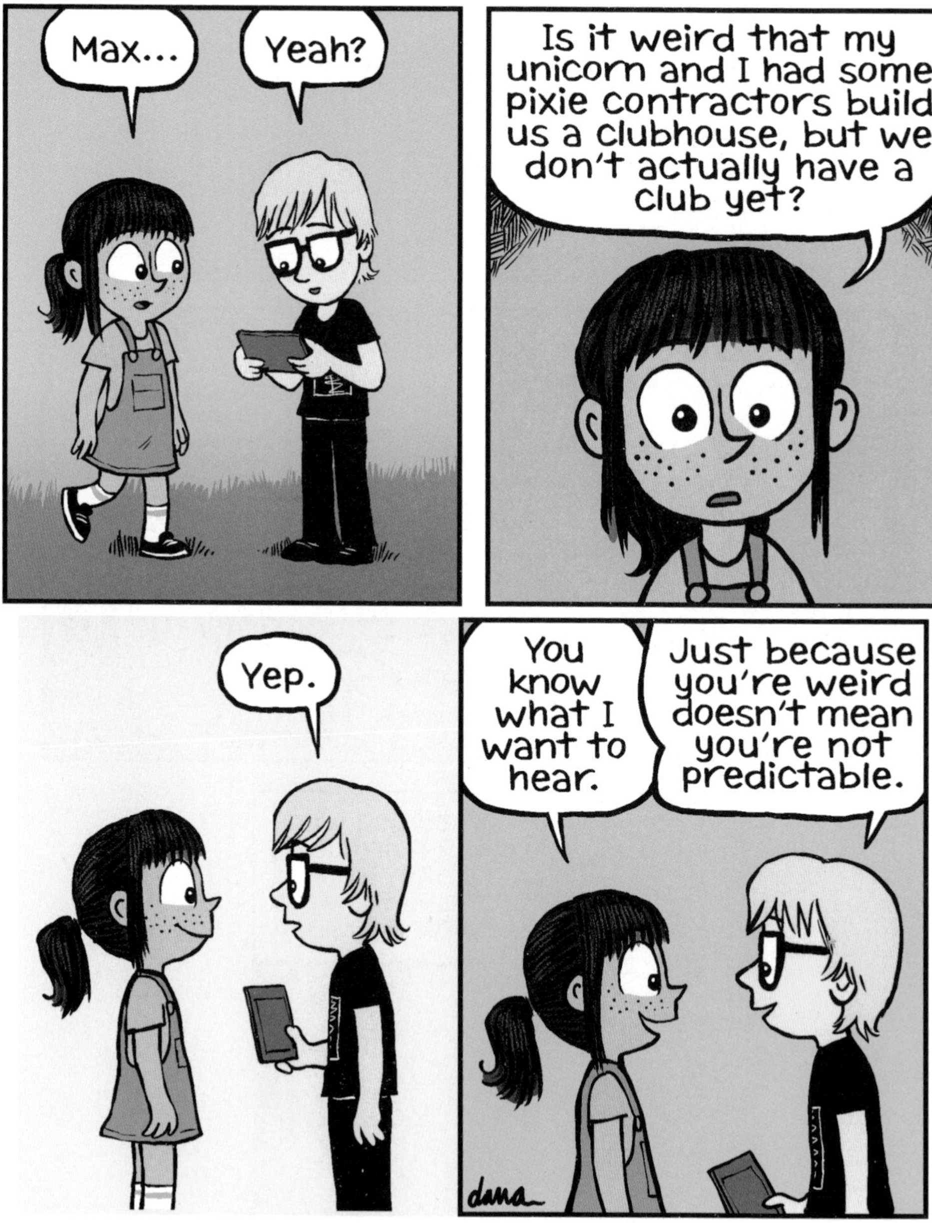
Max...
Yeah?
Is it weird that my unicorn and I had some pixie contractors build us a clubhouse, but we don't actually have a club yet?
Yep.
You know what I want to hear.
Just because you're weird doesn't mean you're not predictable.
dana

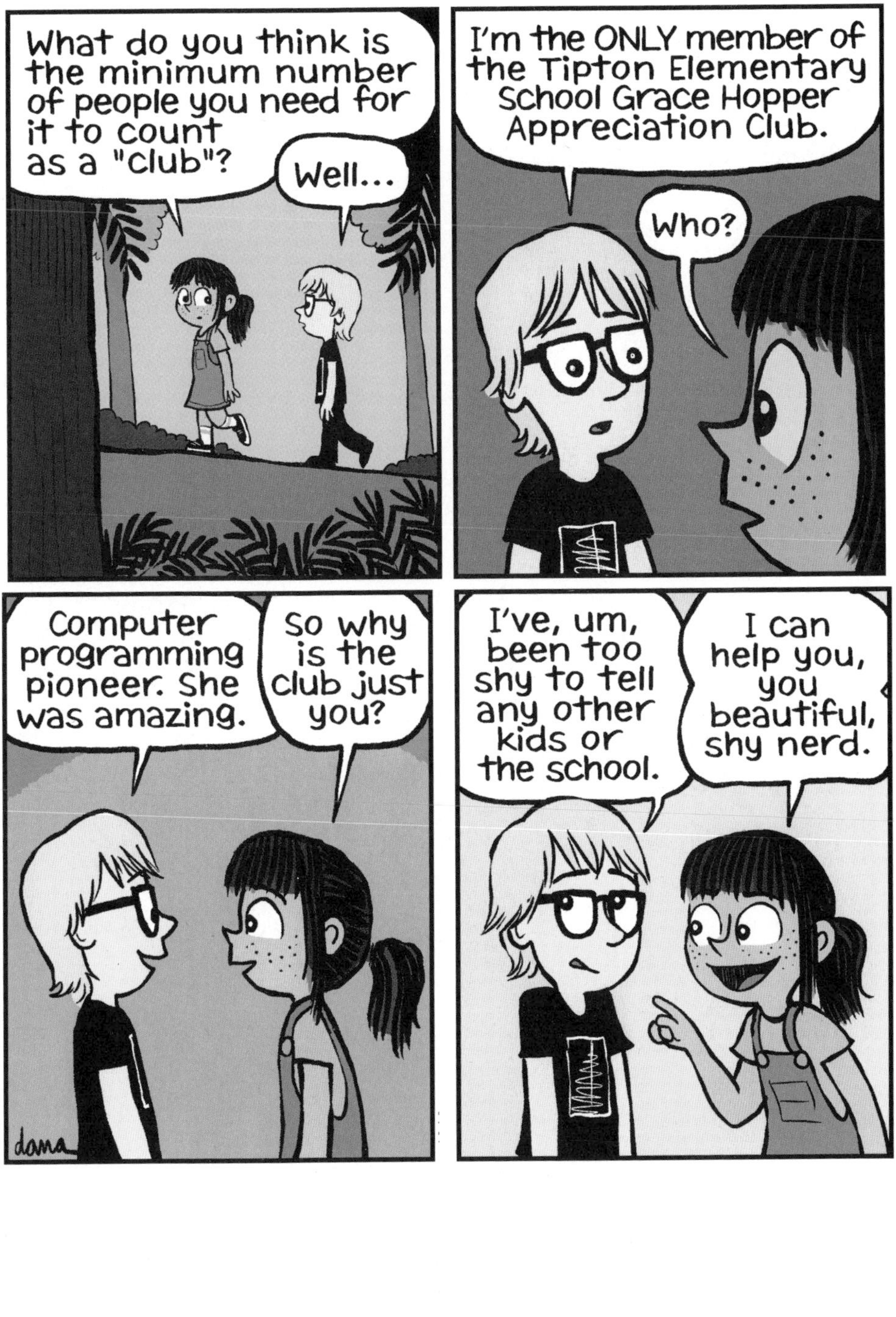
What do you think is the minimum number of people you need for it to count as a "club"?
Well...
I'm the ONLY member of the Tipton Elementary School Grace Hopper Appreciation Club.
Who?
Computer programming pioneer. She was amazing.
So why is the club just you?
I've, um, been too shy to tell any other kids or the school.
I can help you, you beautiful, shy nerd.
dana

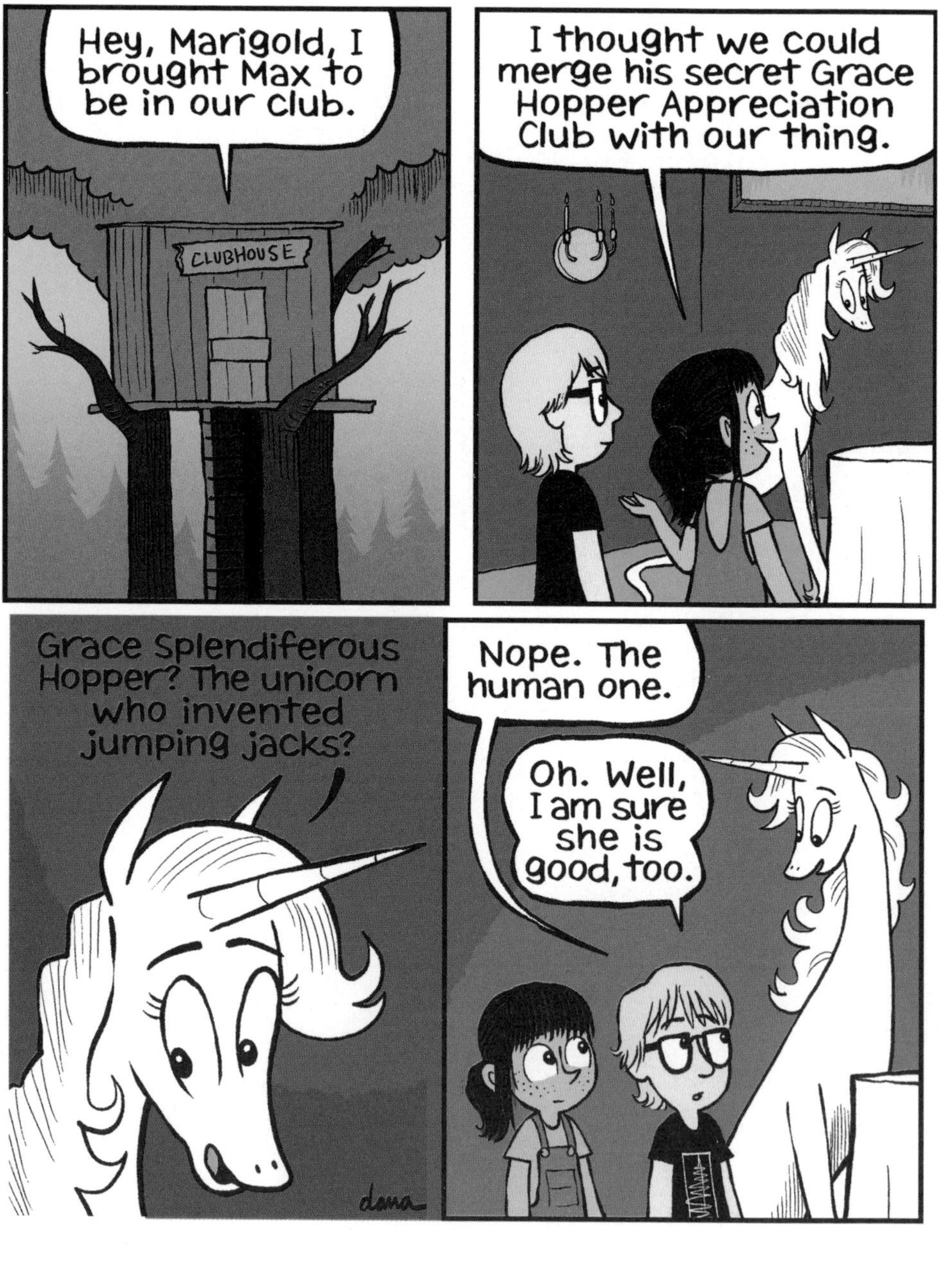
Hey, Marigold, I brought Max to be in our club.
CLUBHOUSE
I thought we could merge his secret Grace Hopper Appreciation Club with our thing.
Grace Splendiferous Hopper? The unicorn who invented jumping jacks?
dana
Nope. The human one.
Oh. Well, I am sure she is good, too.

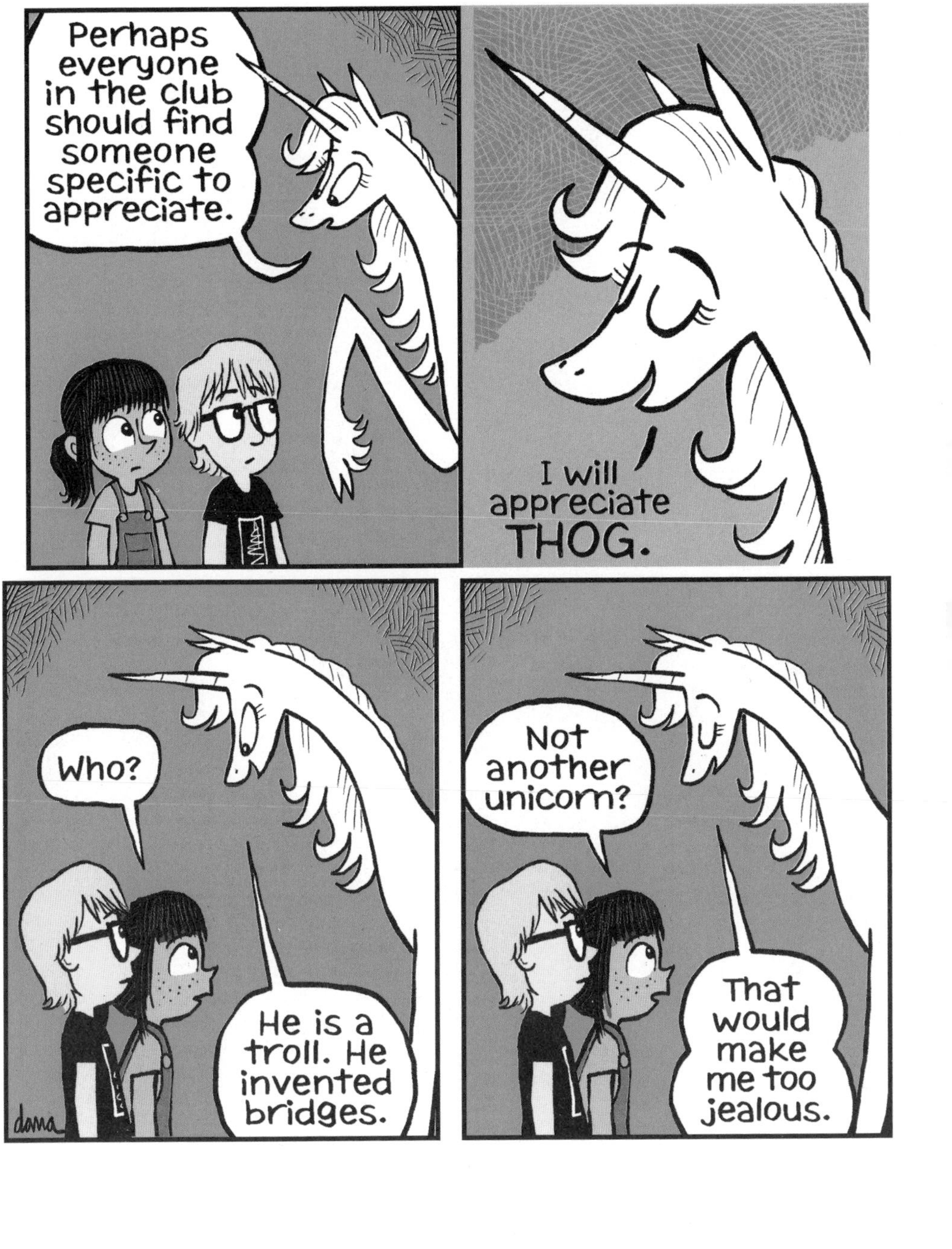
Perhaps everyone in the club should find someone specific to appreciate.
I will appreciate THOG.
Who?
He is a troll. He invented bridges.
Not another unicorn?
That would make me too jealous.
dana

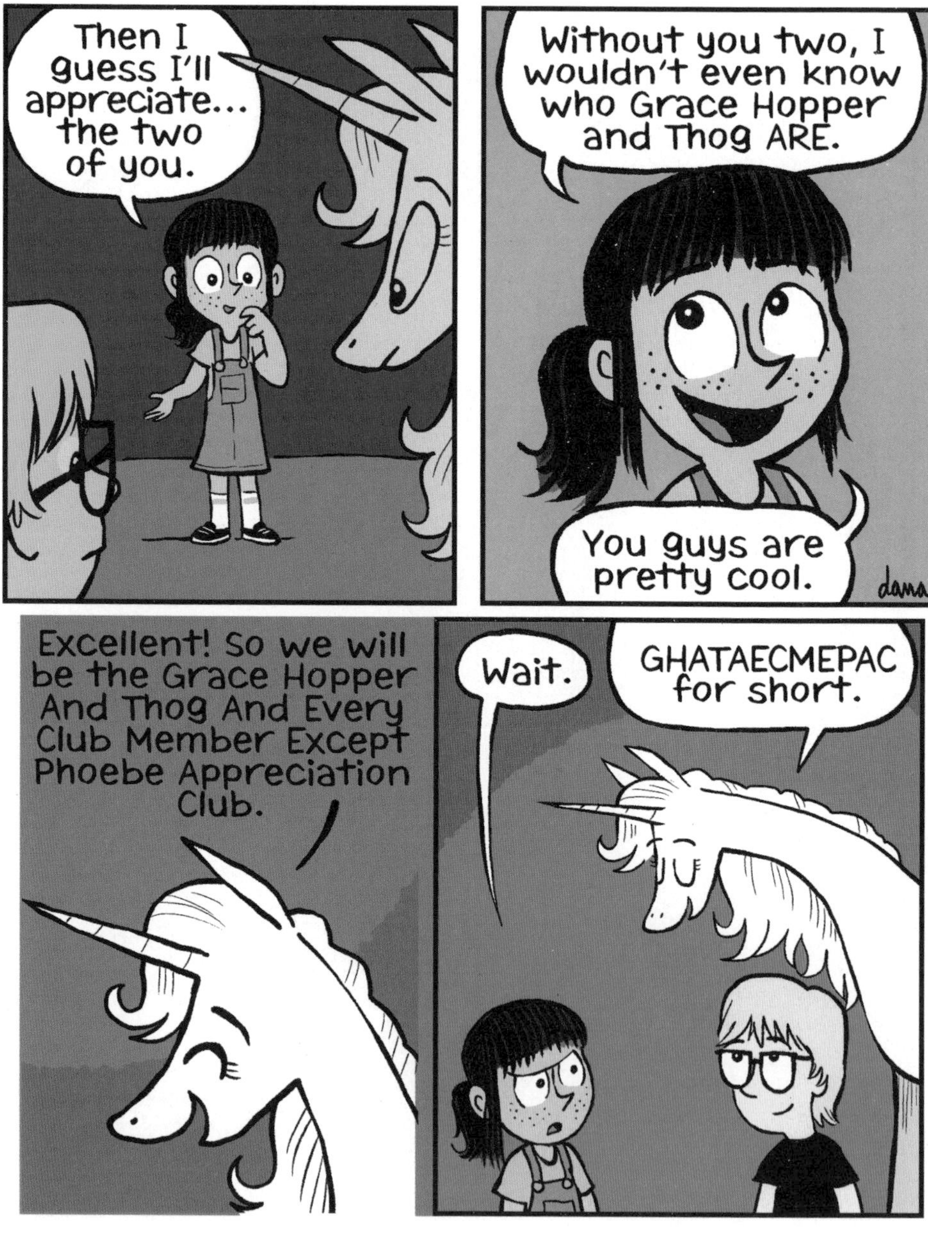
Then I guess I'll appreciate... the two of you.
Without you two, I wouldn't even know who Grace Hopper and Thog ARE.
You guys are pretty cool.
dana
Excellent! So we will be the Grace Hopper And Thog And Every Club Member Except Phoebe Appreciation Club.
GHATAECMEPAC for short.
Wait.

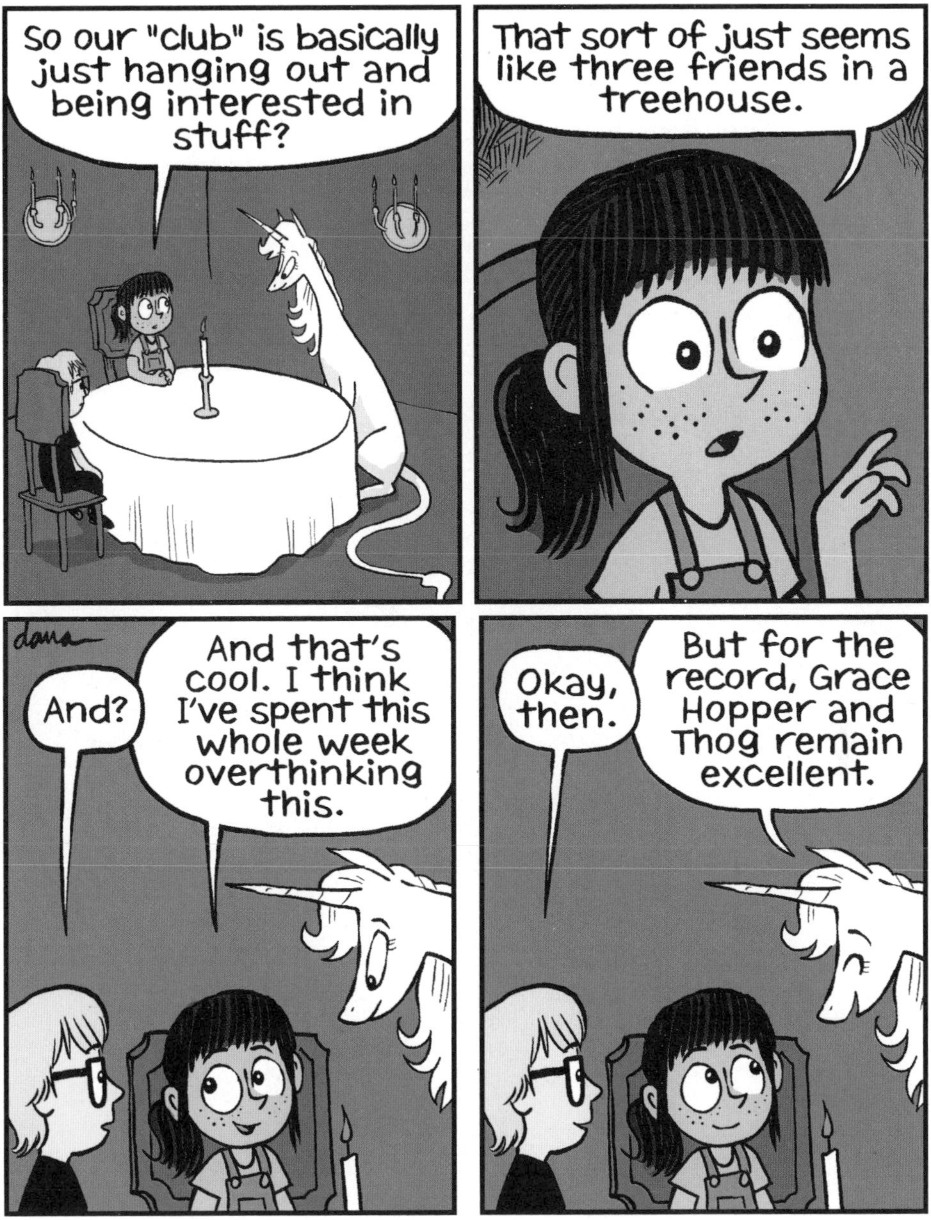
So our "club" is basically just hanging out and being interested in stuff?
That sort of just seems like three friends in a treehouse.
dana
And?
And that's cool. I think I've spent this whole week overthinking this.
Okay, then.
But for the record, Grace Hopper and Thog remain excellent.

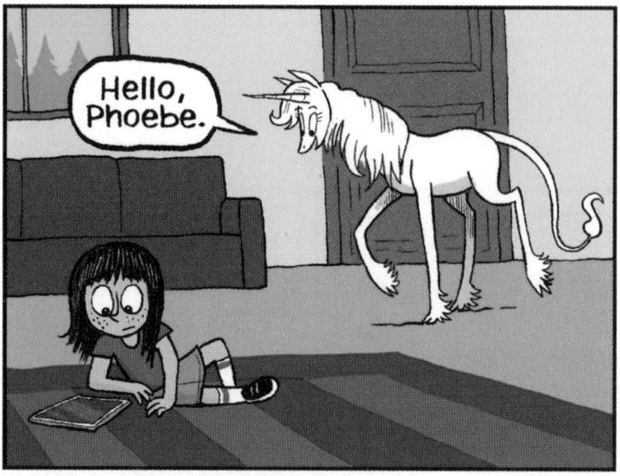
Hello, Phoebe.

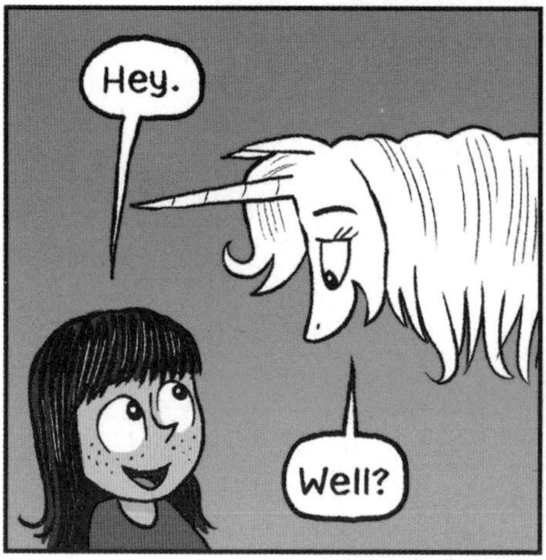
Hey.
Well?

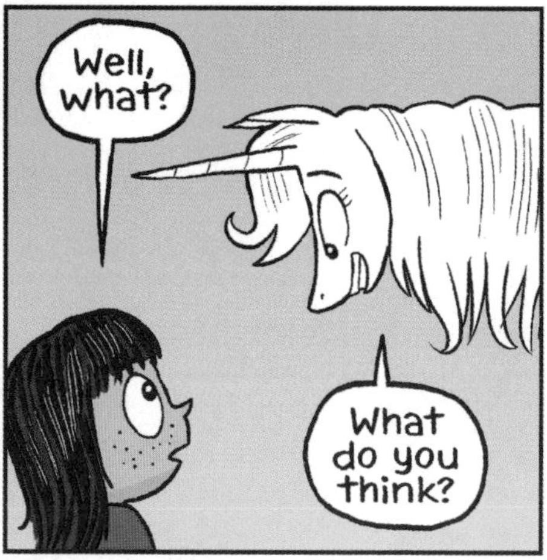
Well, what?
What do you think?

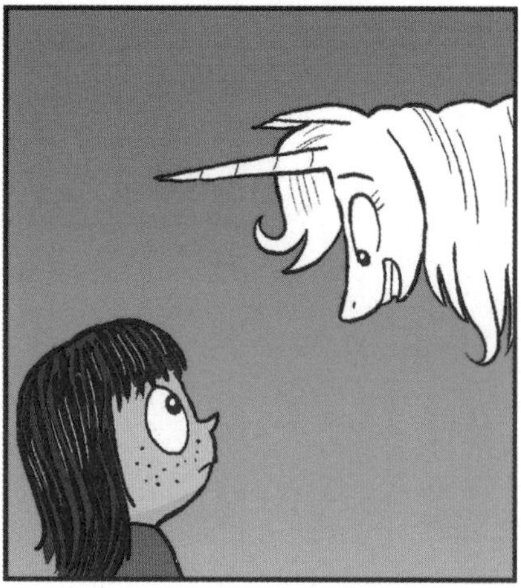

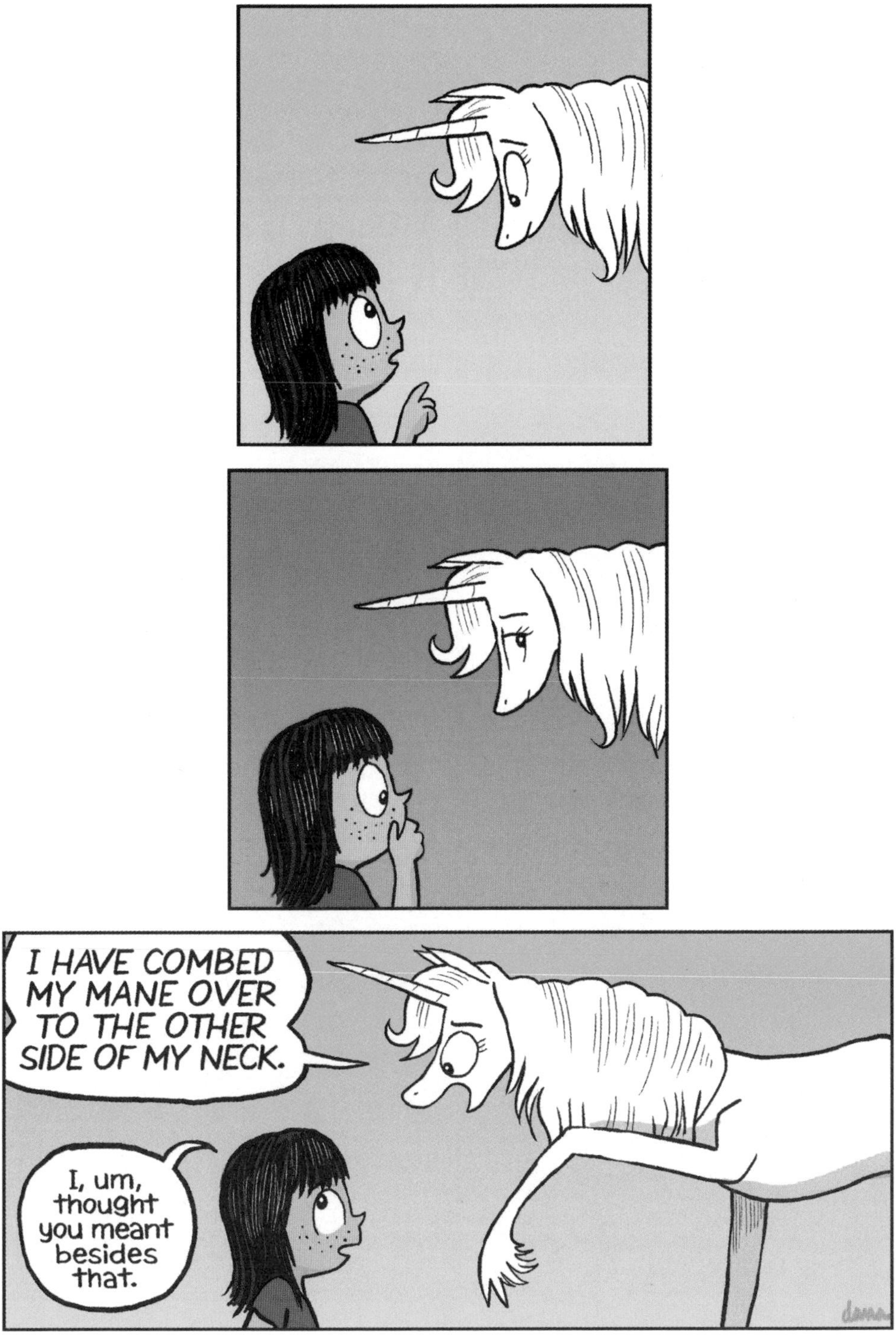
I HAVE COMBED MY MANE OVER TO THE OTHER SIDE OF MY NECK.
I, um, thought you meant besides that.

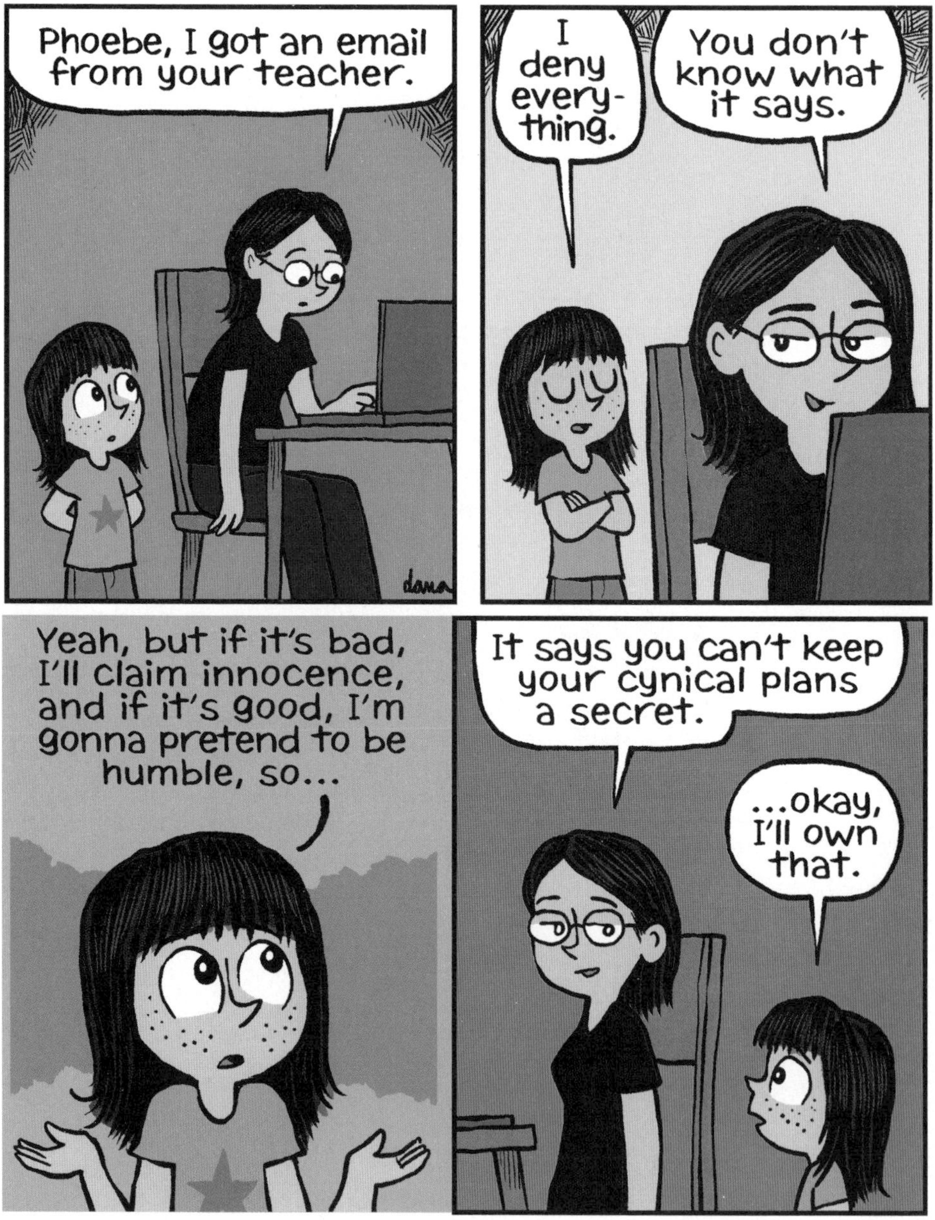
Phoebe, I got an email from your teacher.
I deny every-thing.
You don't know what it says.
Yeah, but if it's bad, I'll claim innocence, and if it's good, I'm gonna pretend to be humble, so...
It says you can't keep your cynical plans a secret.
...okay, I'll own that.
dana

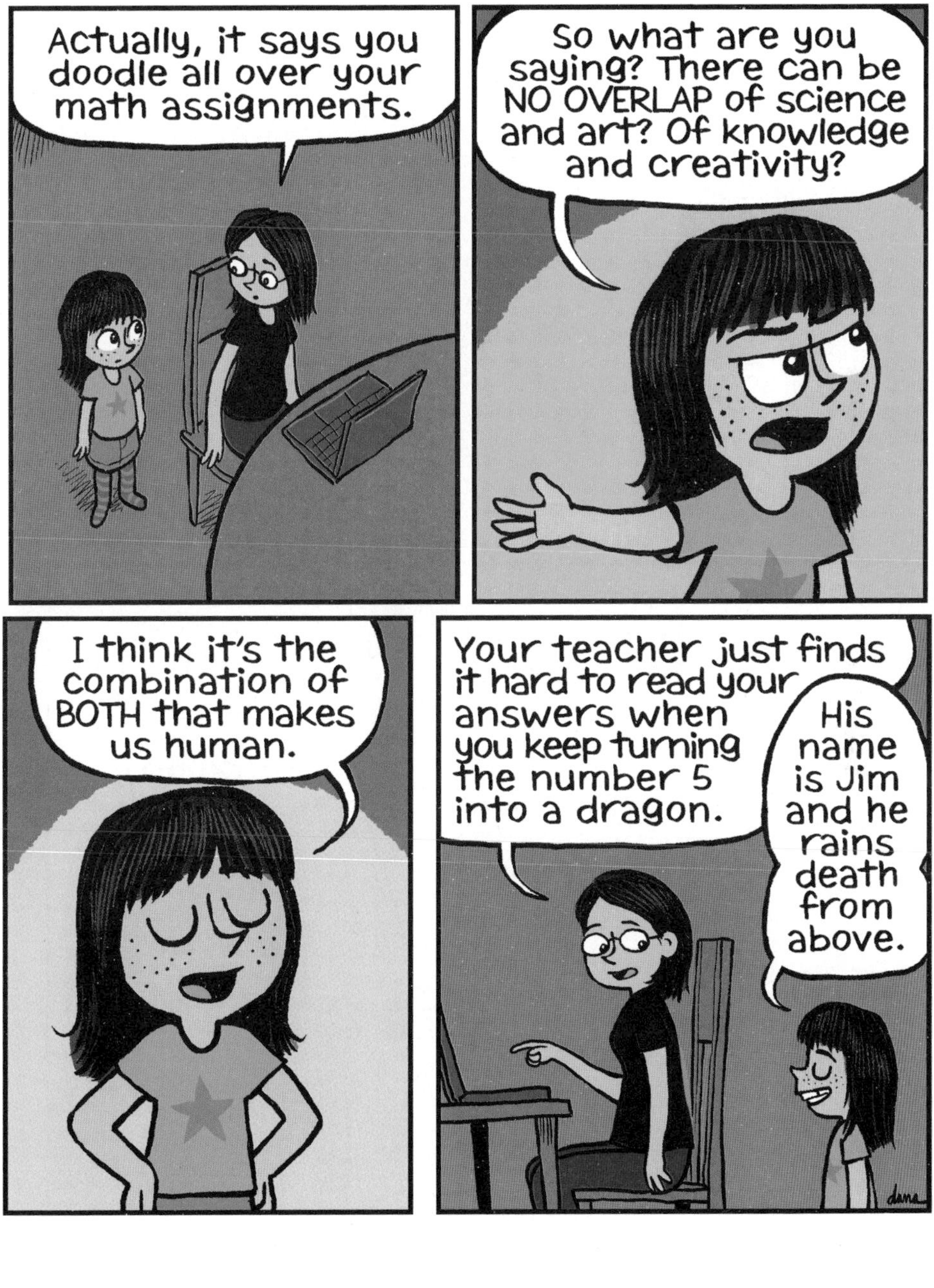
Actually, it says you doodle all over your math assignments.
So what are you saying? There can be NO OVERLAP of science and art? Of knowledge and creativity?
I think it's the combination of BOTH that makes us human.
Your teacher just finds it hard to read your answers when you keep turning the number 5 into a dragon.
His name is Jim and he rains death from above.
dana

I actually don't care if you doodle on your math assignments.

Good, 'cause I like it, and, really, what's the harm?

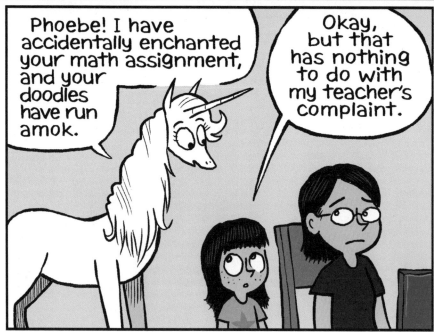

Phoebe! I have accidentally enchanted your math assignment, and your doodles have run amok.

Okay, but that has nothing to do with my teacher's complaint.

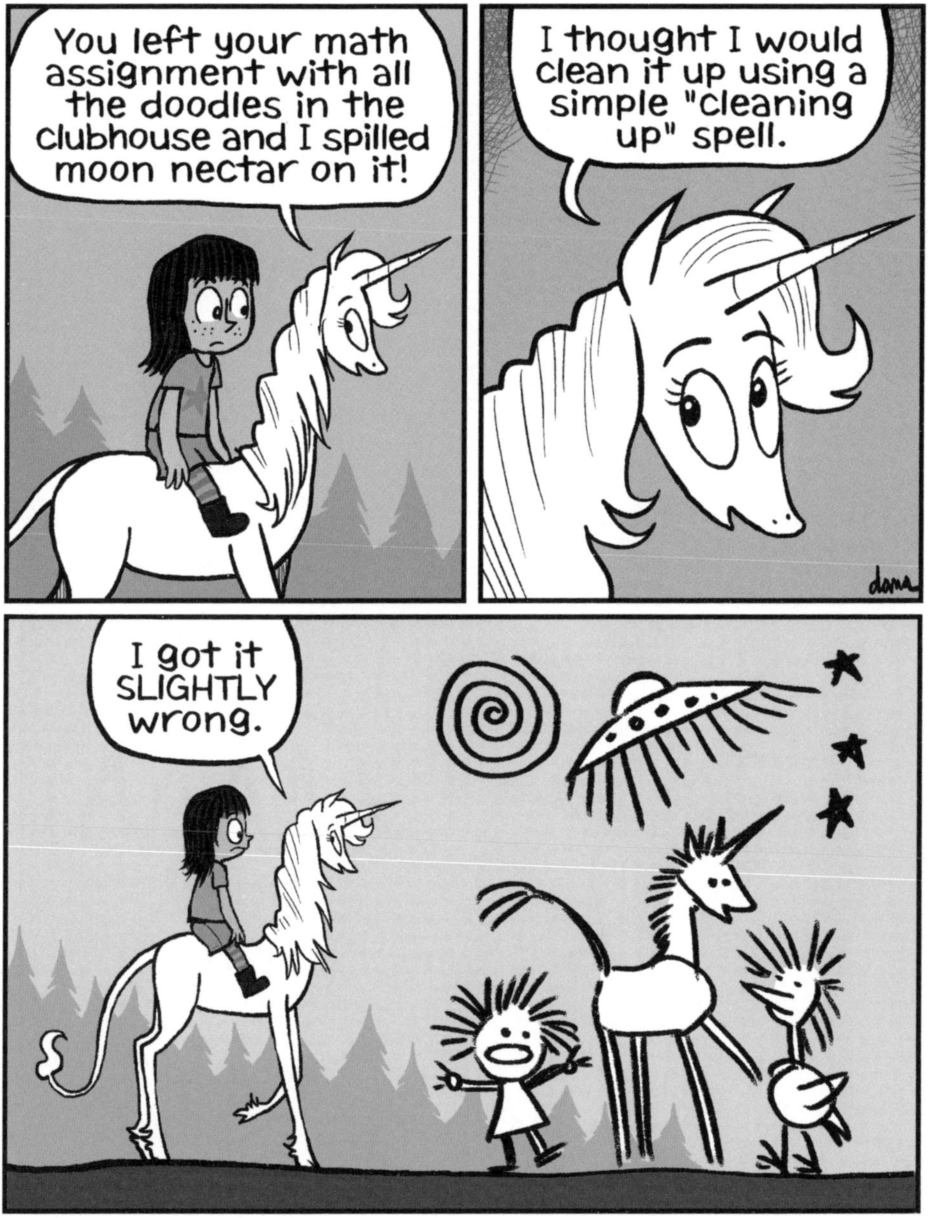
You left your math assignment with all the doodles in the clubhouse and I spilled moon nectar on it!
I thought I would clean it up using a simple "cleaning up" spell.
I got it SLIGHTLY wrong.

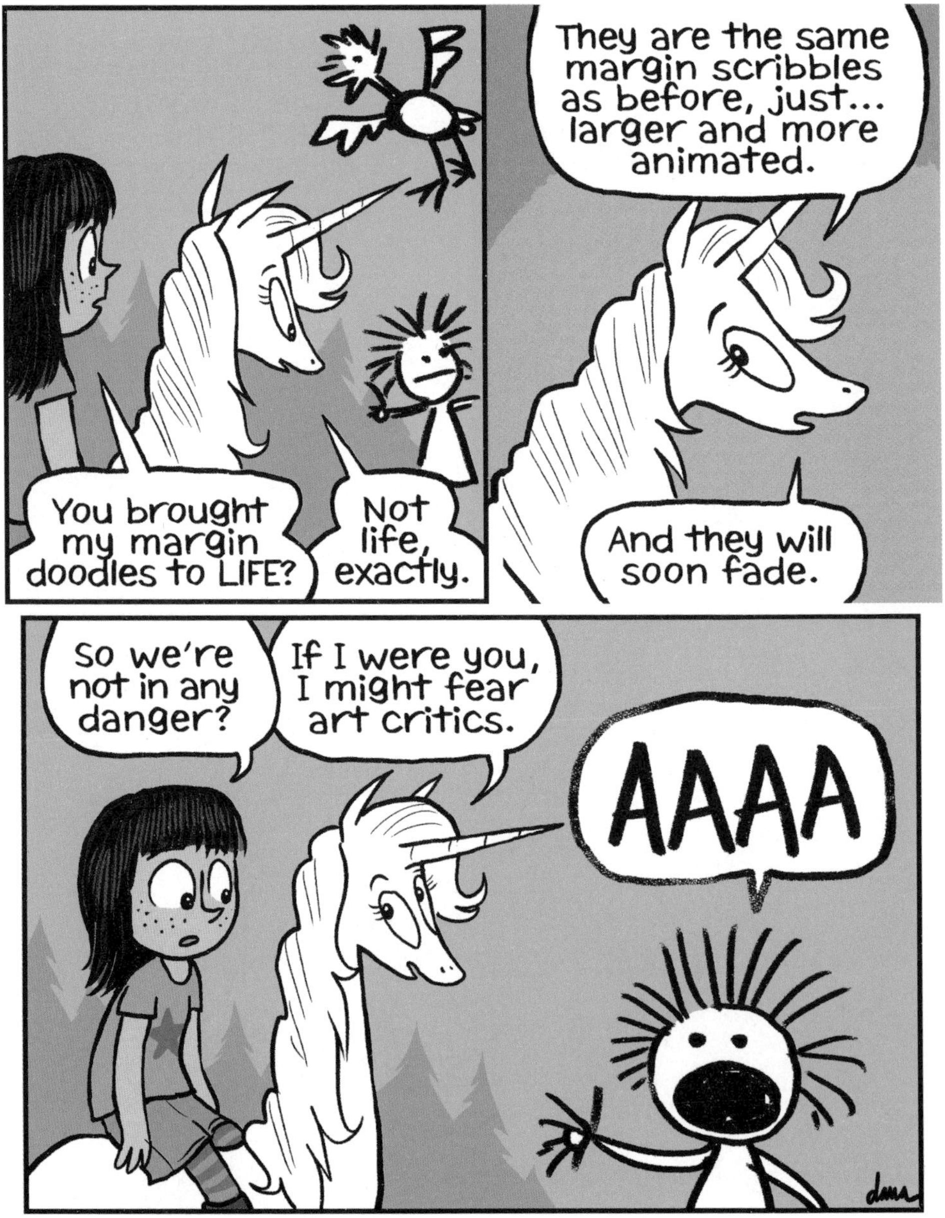
You brought my margin doodles to LIFE?
Not life, exactly.
They are the same margin scribbles as before, just... larger and more animated.
And they will soon fade.
So we're not in any danger?
If I were you, I might fear art critics.
AAAA
dana

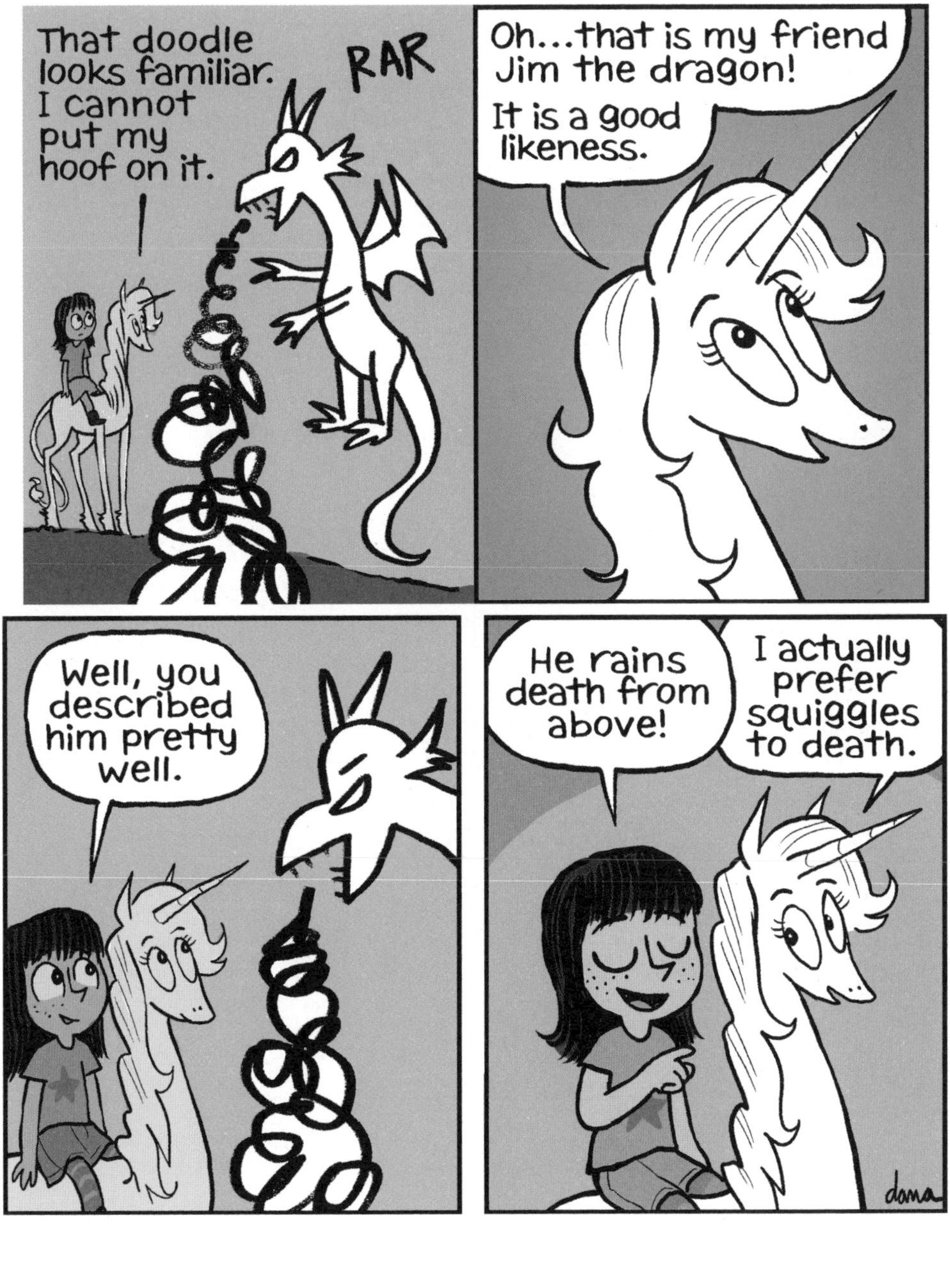
That doodle looks familiar. I cannot put my hoof on it.
RAR
Oh...that is my friend Jim the dragon!
It is a good likeness.
Well, you described him pretty well.
He rains death from above!
I actually prefer squiggles to death.
dana

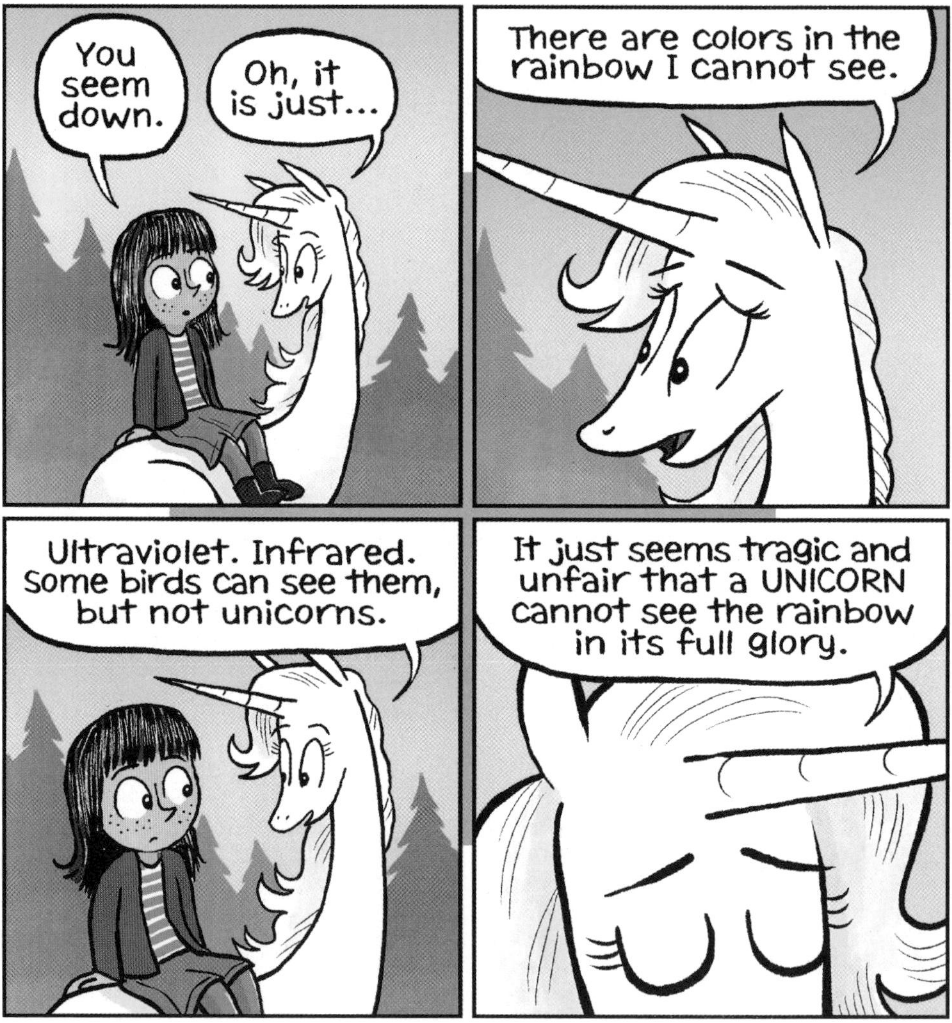
You seem down.
Oh, it is just...
There are colors in the rainbow I cannot see.
Ultraviolet. Infrared. Some birds can see them, but not unicorns.
It just seems tragic and unfair that a UNICORN cannot see the rainbow in its full glory.

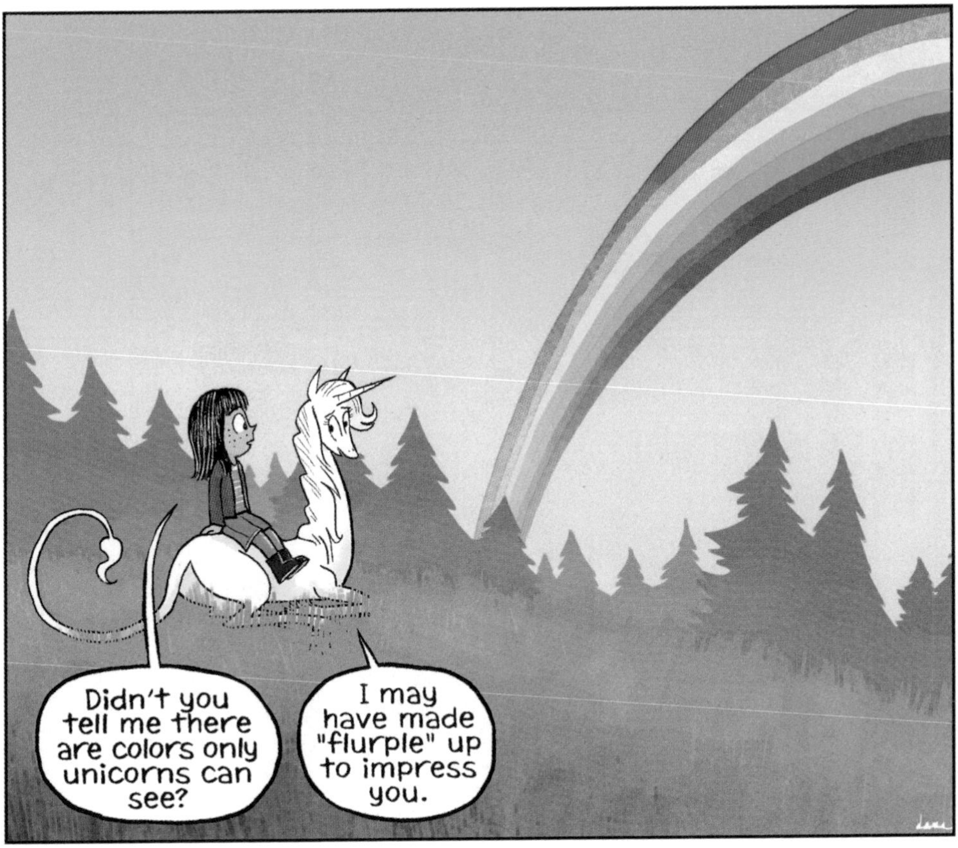
Didn't you tell me there are colors only unicorns can see?
I may have made "flurple" up to impress you.

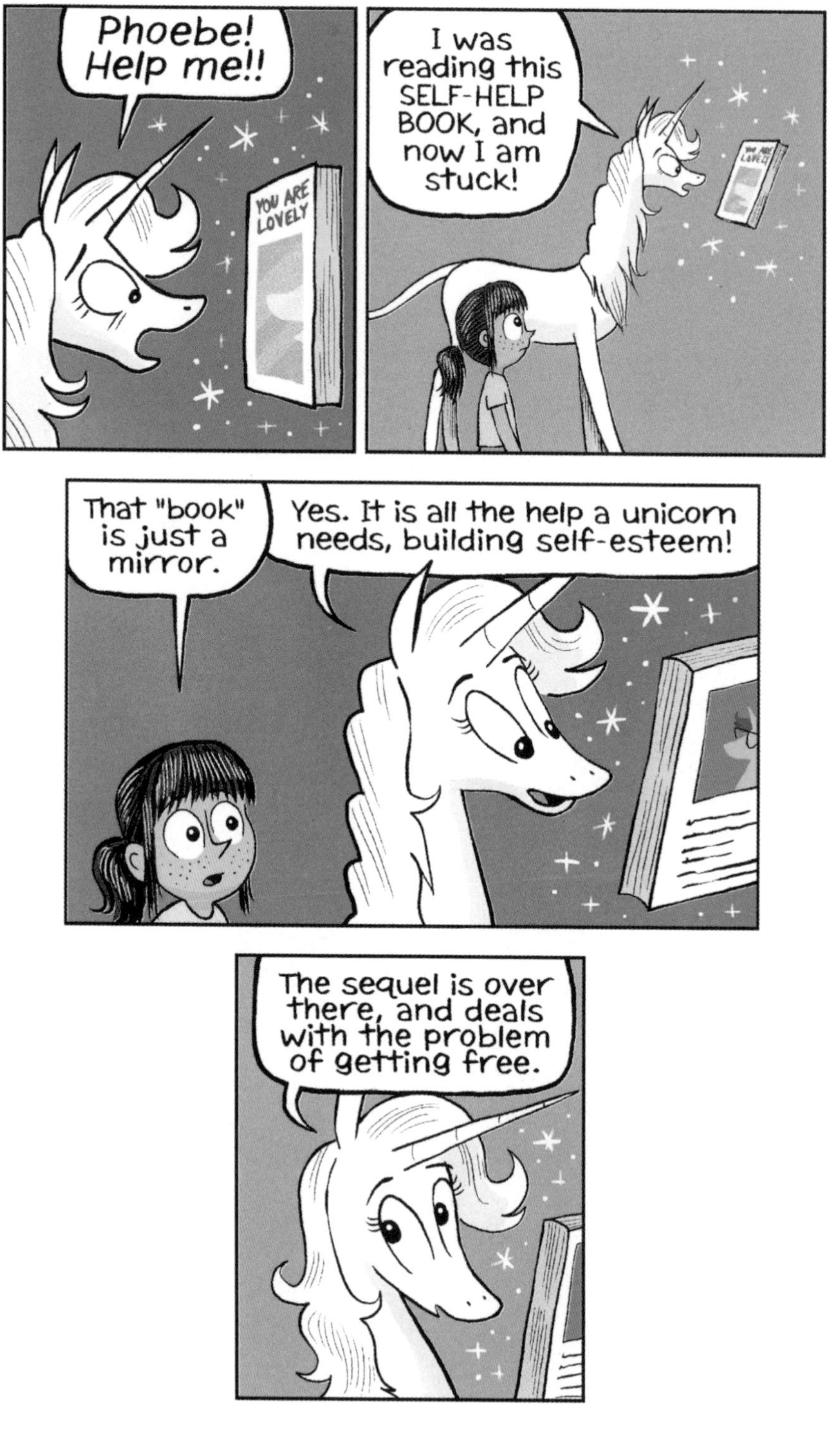
Phoebe! Help me!!
YOU ARE LOVELY
I was reading this SELF-HELP BOOK, and now I am stuck!
That "book" is just a mirror.
Yes. It is all the help a unicorn needs, building self-esteem!
The sequel is over there, and deals with the problem of getting free.

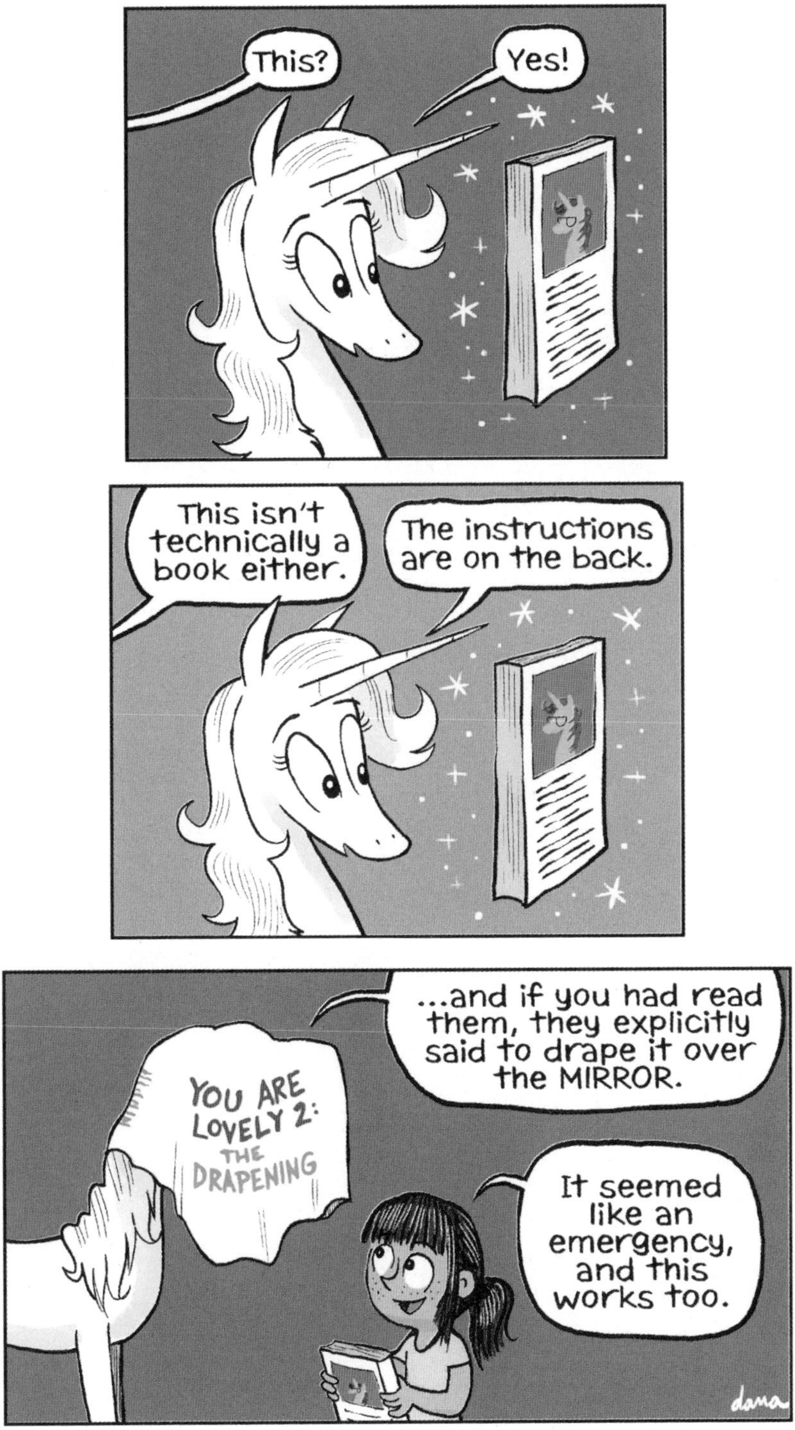
This?
Yes!
This isn't technically a book either.
The instructions are on the back.
...and if you had read them, they explicitly said to drape it over the MIRROR.
YOU ARE LOVELY 2: THE DRAPENING
It seemed like an emergency, and this works too.
dana

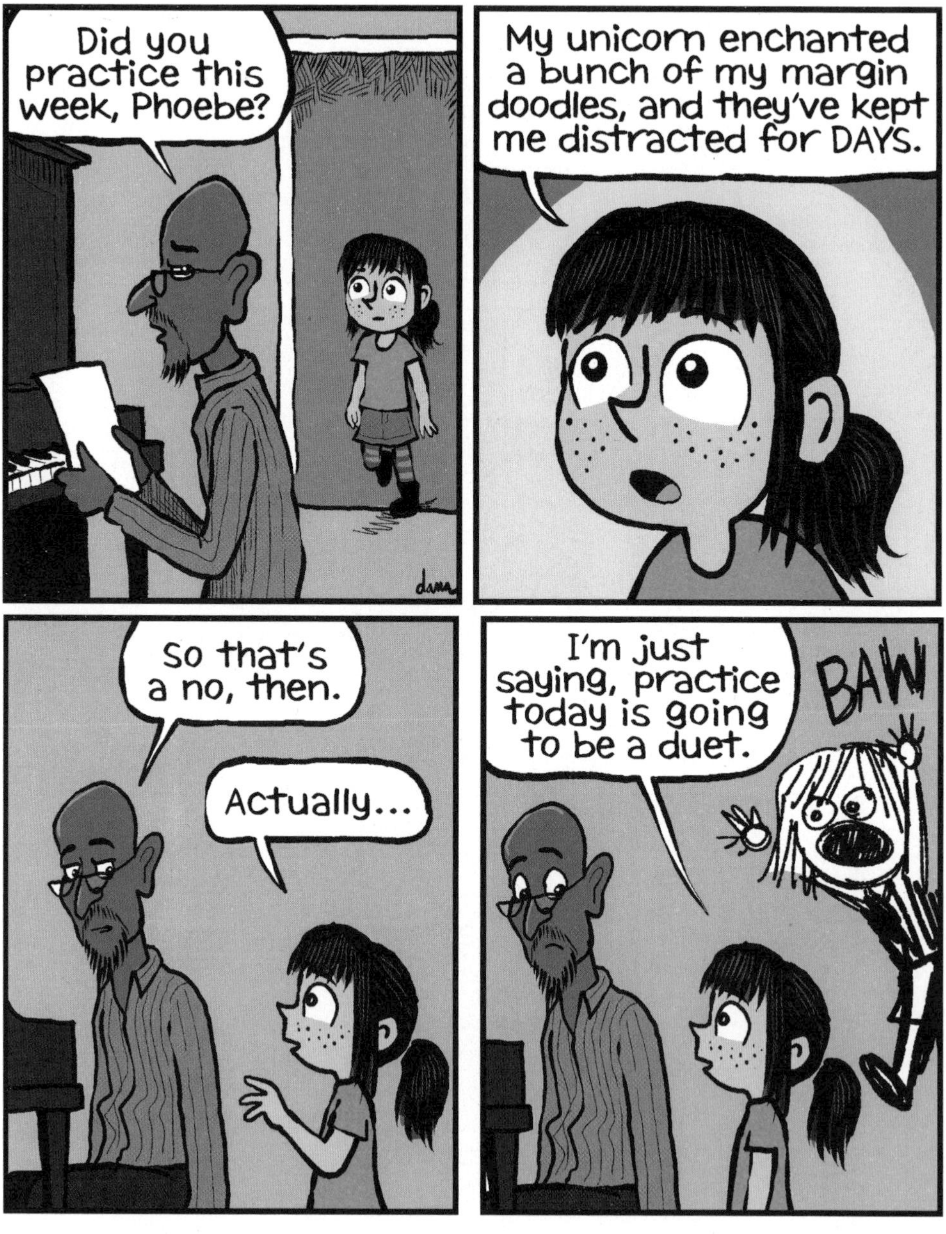
Did you practice this week, Phoebe?
My unicorn enchanted a bunch of my margin doodles, and they've kept me distracted for DAYS.
So that's a no, then.
Actually...
I'm just saying, practice today is going to be a duet.
BAW

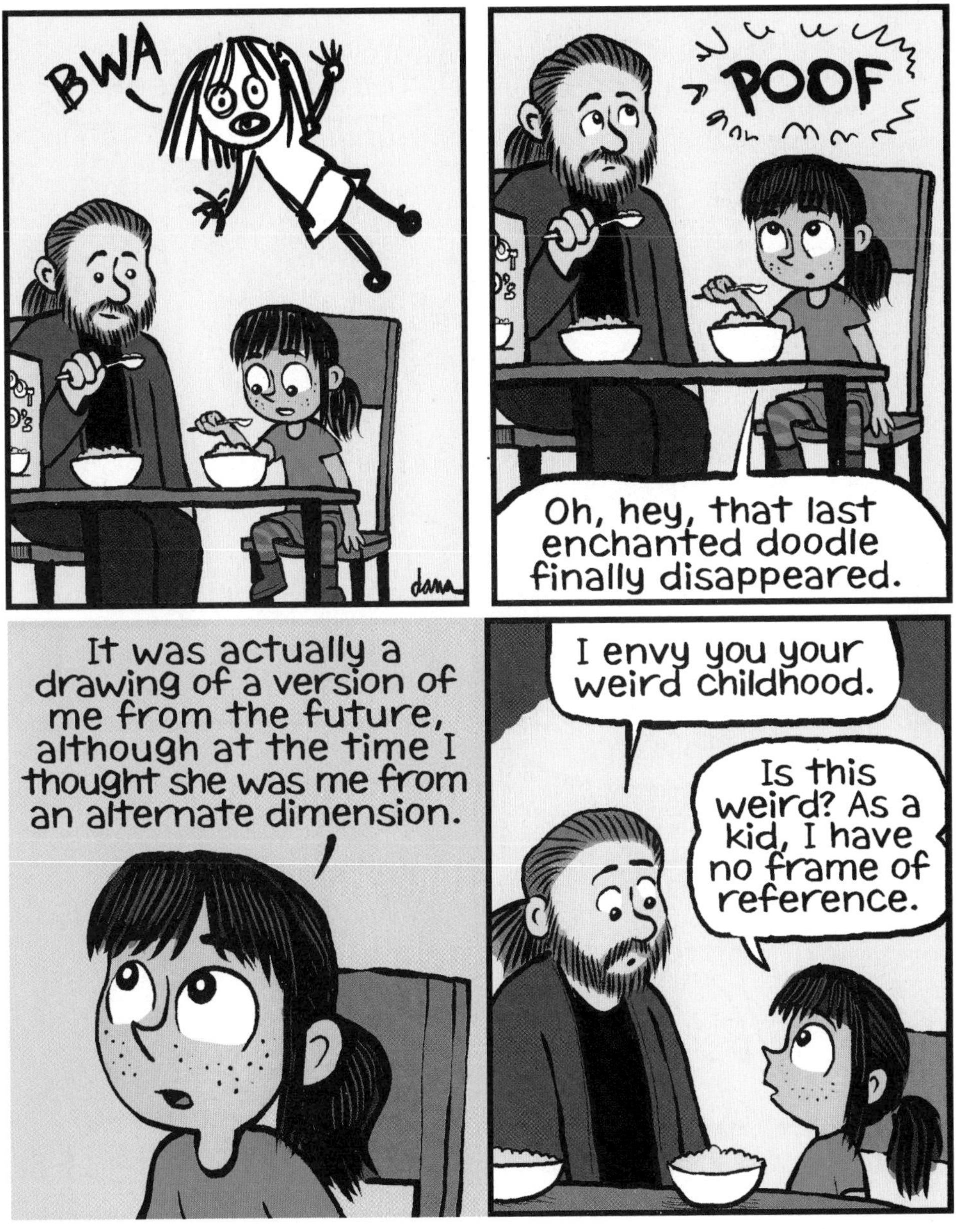
BWA
POOF
Oh, hey, that last enchanted doodle finally disappeared.
It was actually a drawing of a version of me from the future, although at the time I thought she was me from an alternate dimension.
I envy you your weird childhood.
Is this weird? As a kid, I have no frame of reference.

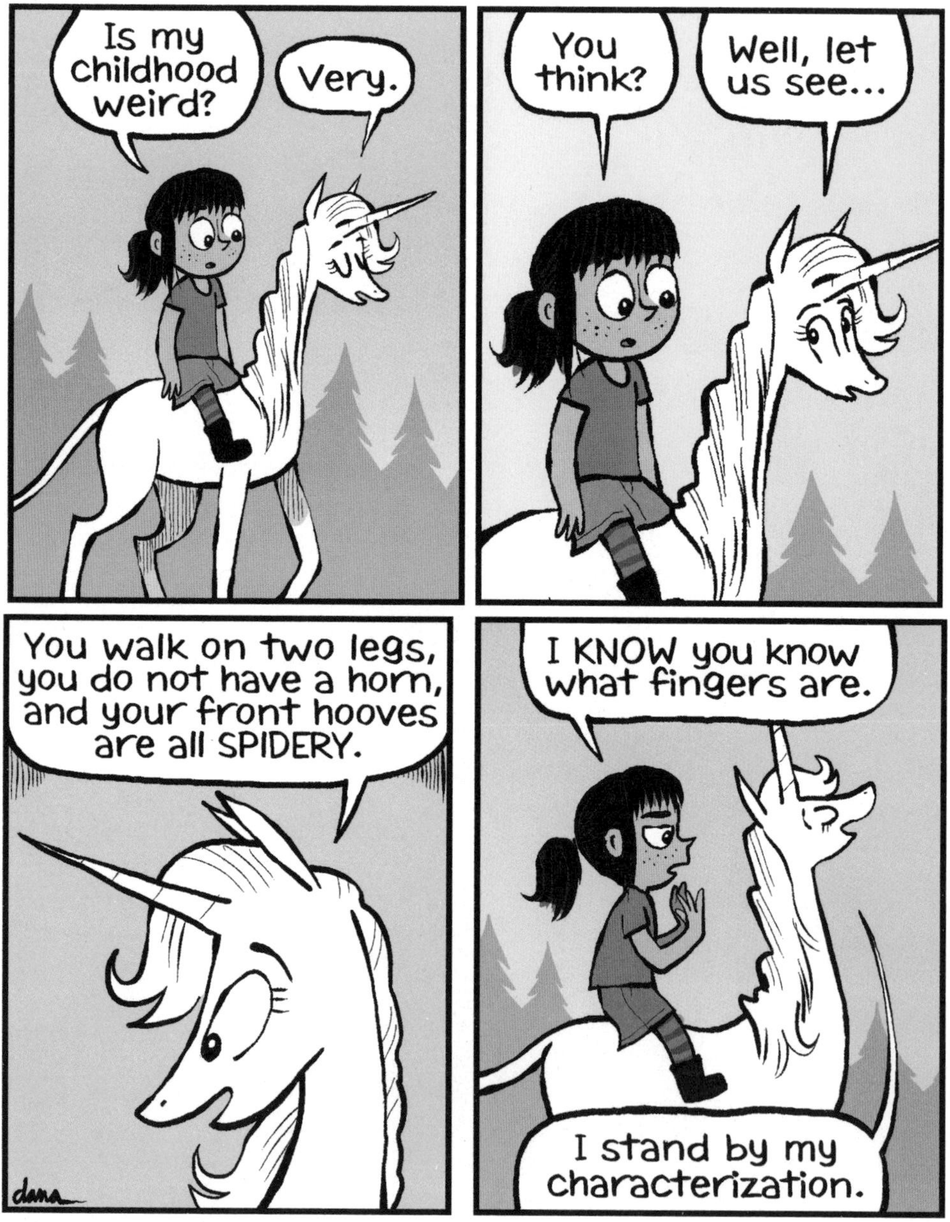
Is my childhood weird?
Very.
You think?
Well, let us see...
You walk on two legs, you do not have a horn, and your front hooves are all SPIDERY.
dana
I KNOW you know what fingers are.
I stand by my characterization.

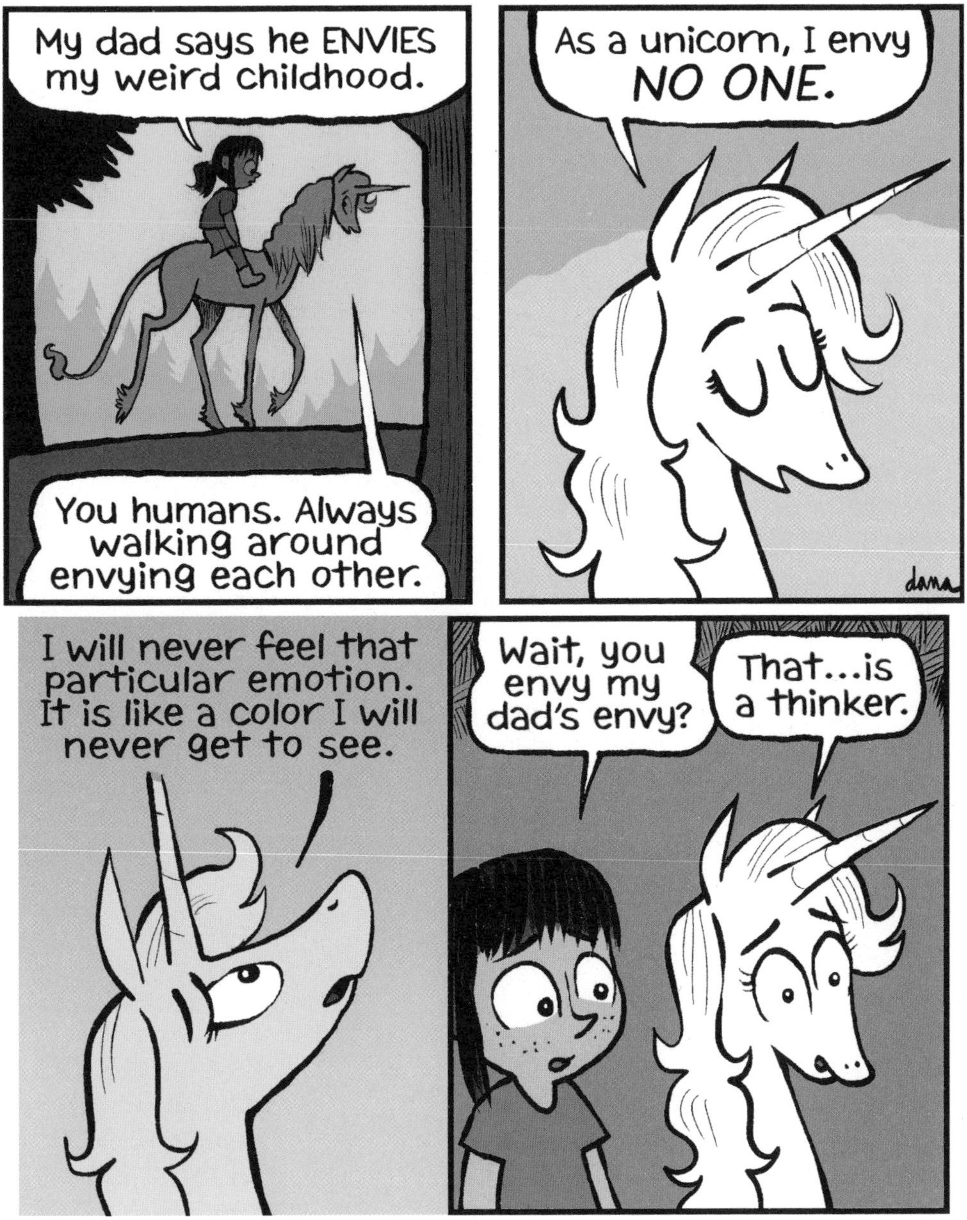
My dad says he ENVIES my weird childhood.
You humans. Always walking around envying each other.
As a unicorn, I envy *NO ONE.*
dana
I will never feel that particular emotion. It is like a color I will never get to see.
Wait, you envy my dad's envy?
That...is a thinker.

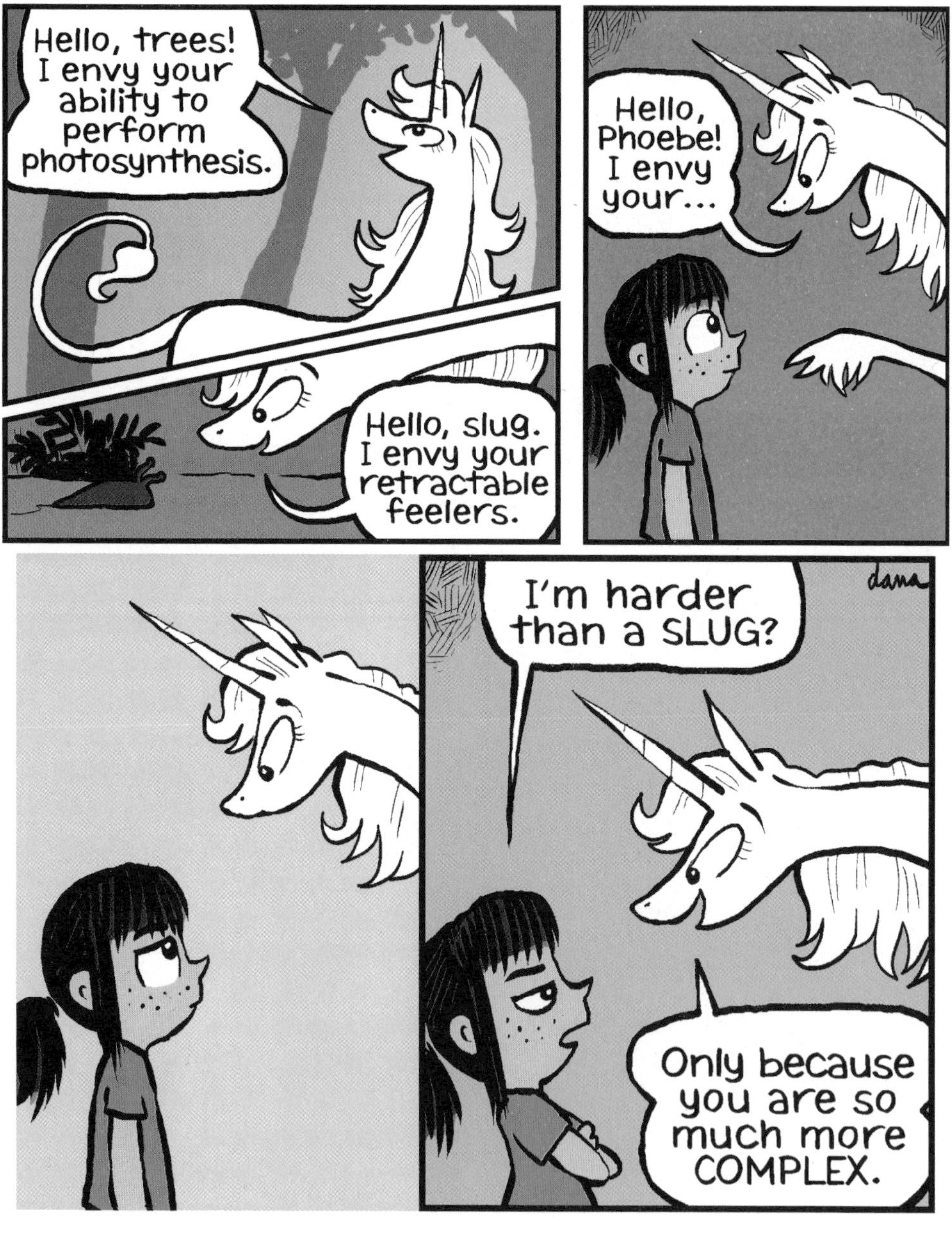
Hello, trees! I envy your ability to perform photosynthesis.
Hello, slug. I envy your retractable feelers.
Hello, Phoebe! I envy your...
dana
I'm harder than a SLUG?
Only because you are so much more COMPLEX.

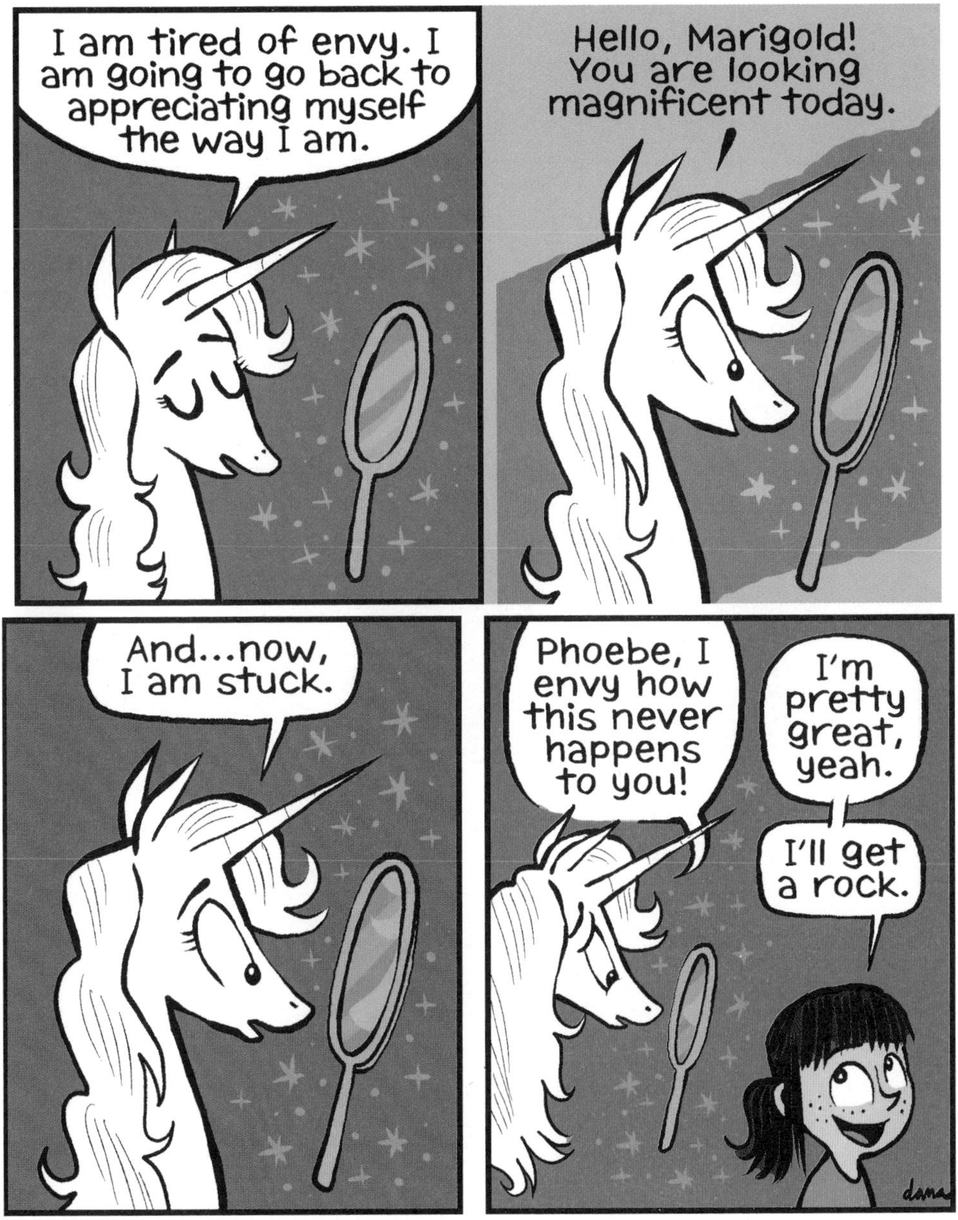
I am tired of envy. I am going to go back to appreciating myself the way I am.
Hello, Marigold! You are looking magnificent today.
And...now, I am stuck.
Phoebe, I envy how this never happens to you!
I'm pretty great, yeah.
I'll get a rock.

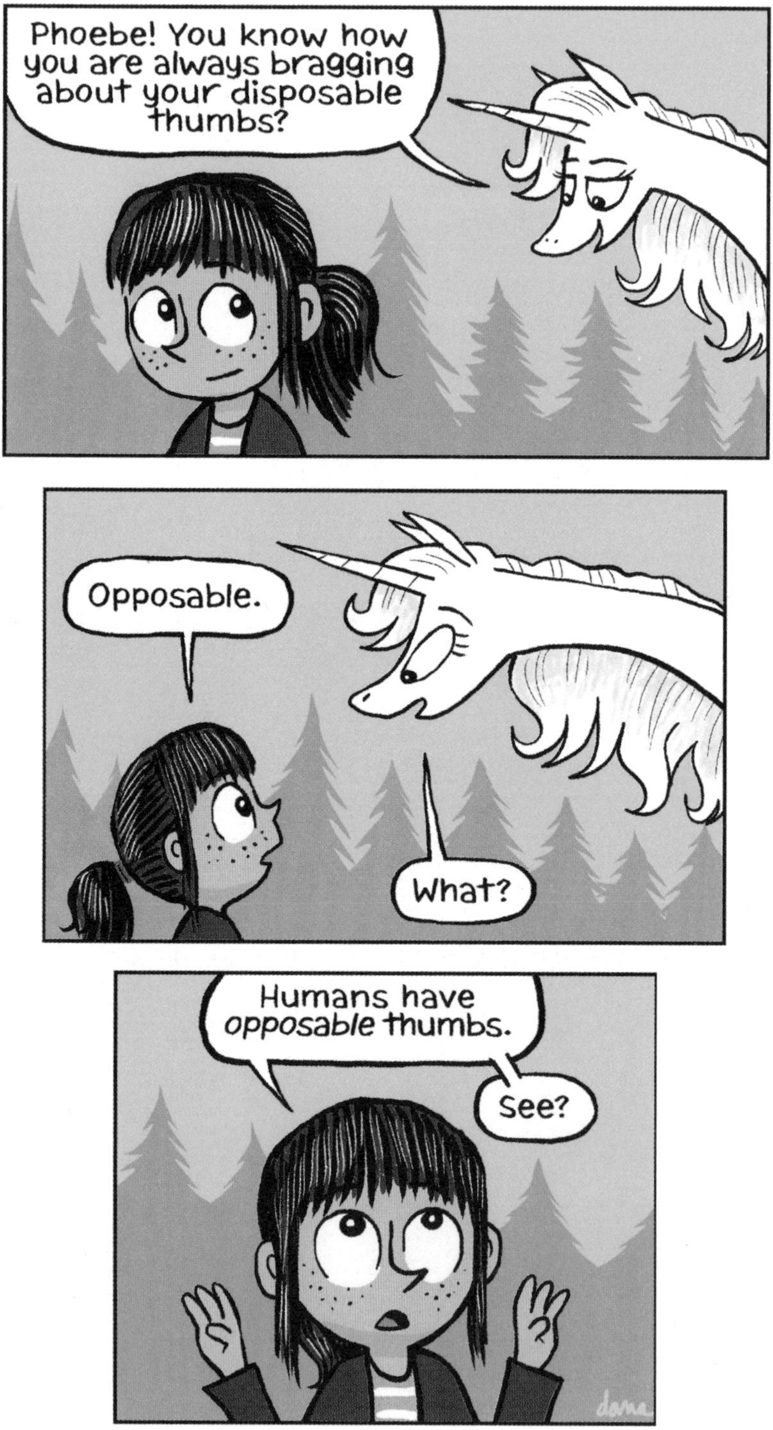
Phoebe! You know how you are always bragging about your disposable thumbs?
Opposable.
What?
Humans have *opposable* thumbs.
See?
dana

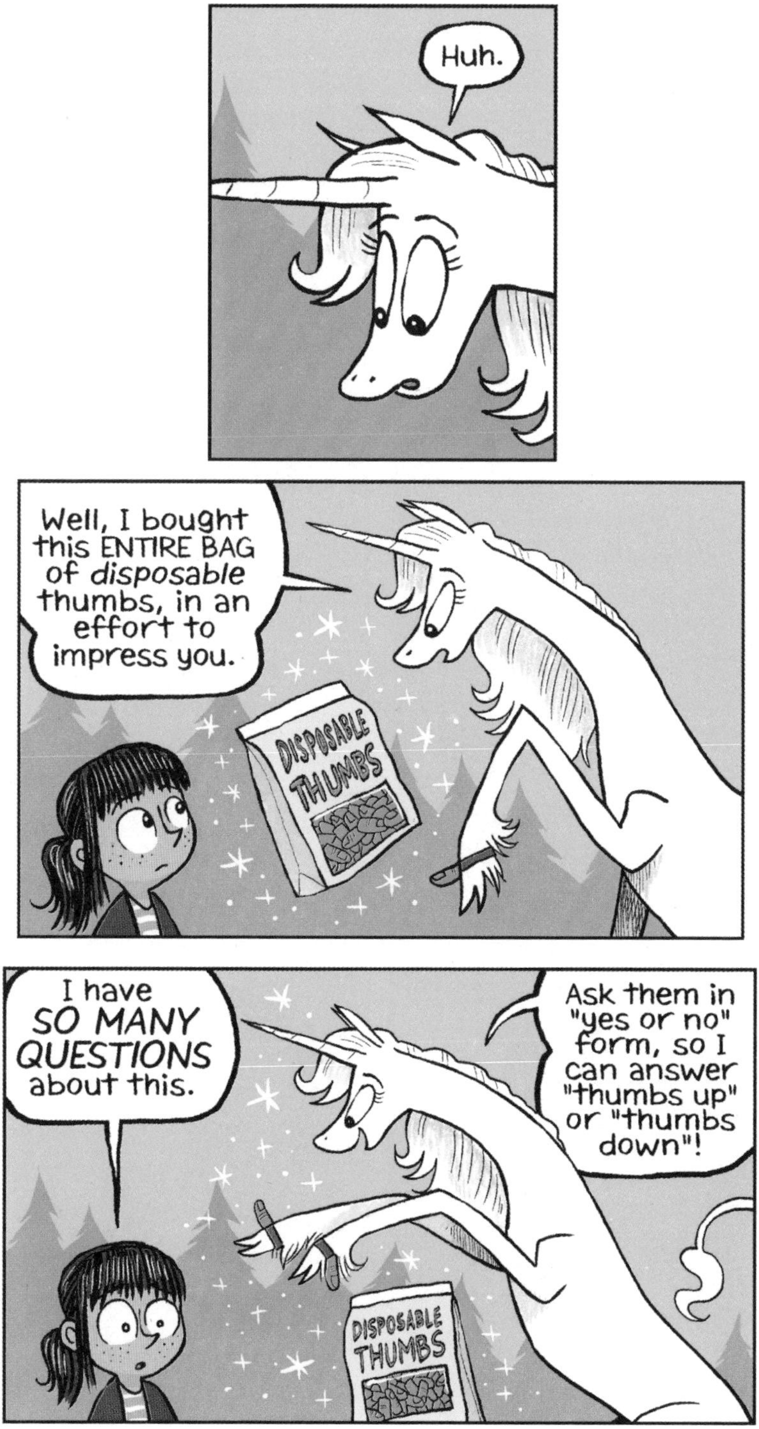
Huh.
Well, I bought this ENTIRE BAG of *disposable* thumbs, in an effort to impress you.
DISPOSABLE THUMBS
I have **SO MANY QUESTIONS** about this.
Ask them in "yes or no" form, so I can answer "thumbs up" or "thumbs down"!
DISPOSABLE THUMBS

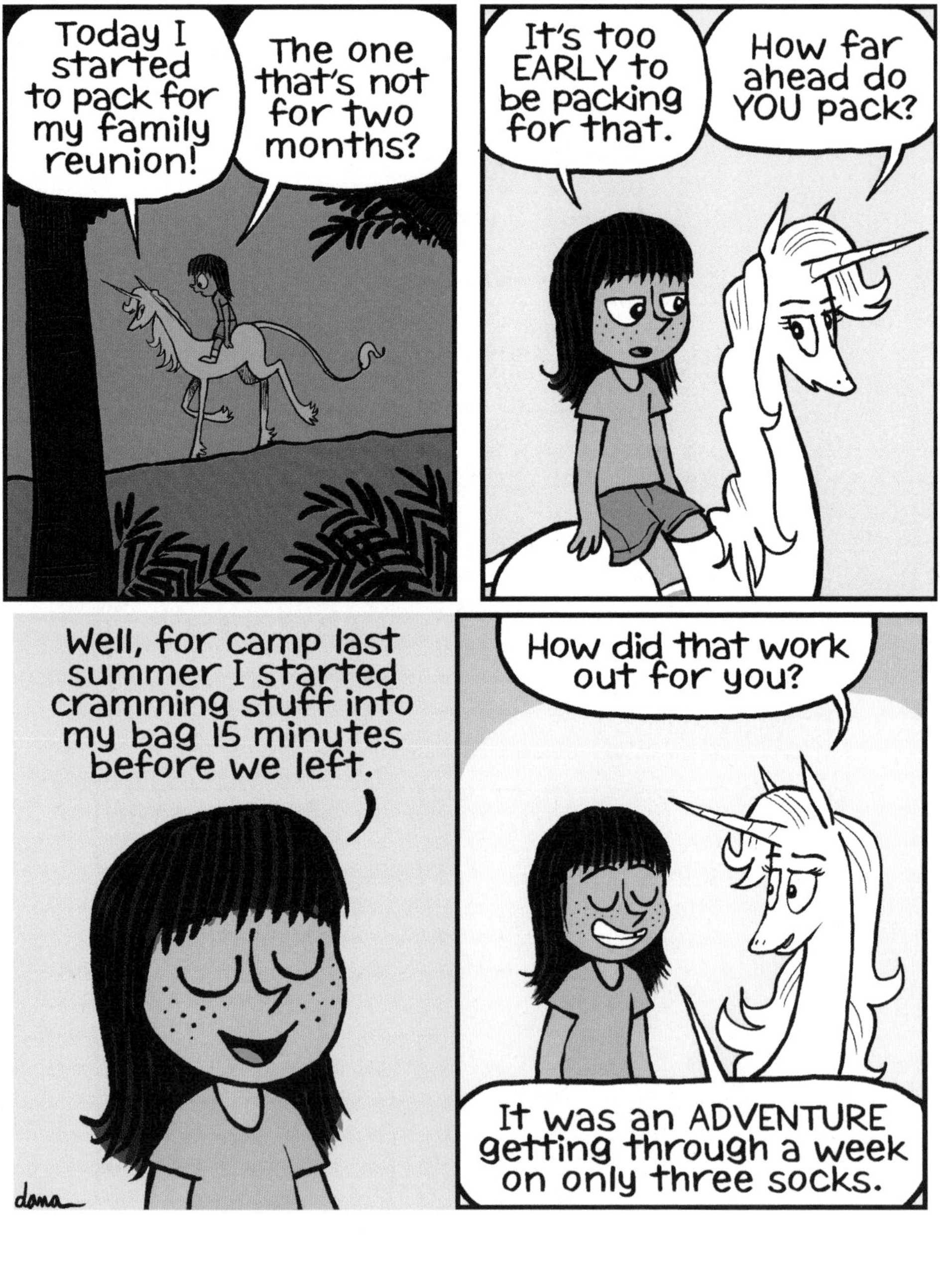
Today I started to pack for my family reunion!
The one that's not for two months?
It's too EARLY to be packing for that.
How far ahead do YOU pack?
Well, for camp last summer I started cramming stuff into my bag 15 minutes before we left.
How did that work out for you?
It was an ADVENTURE getting through a week on only three socks.
dana

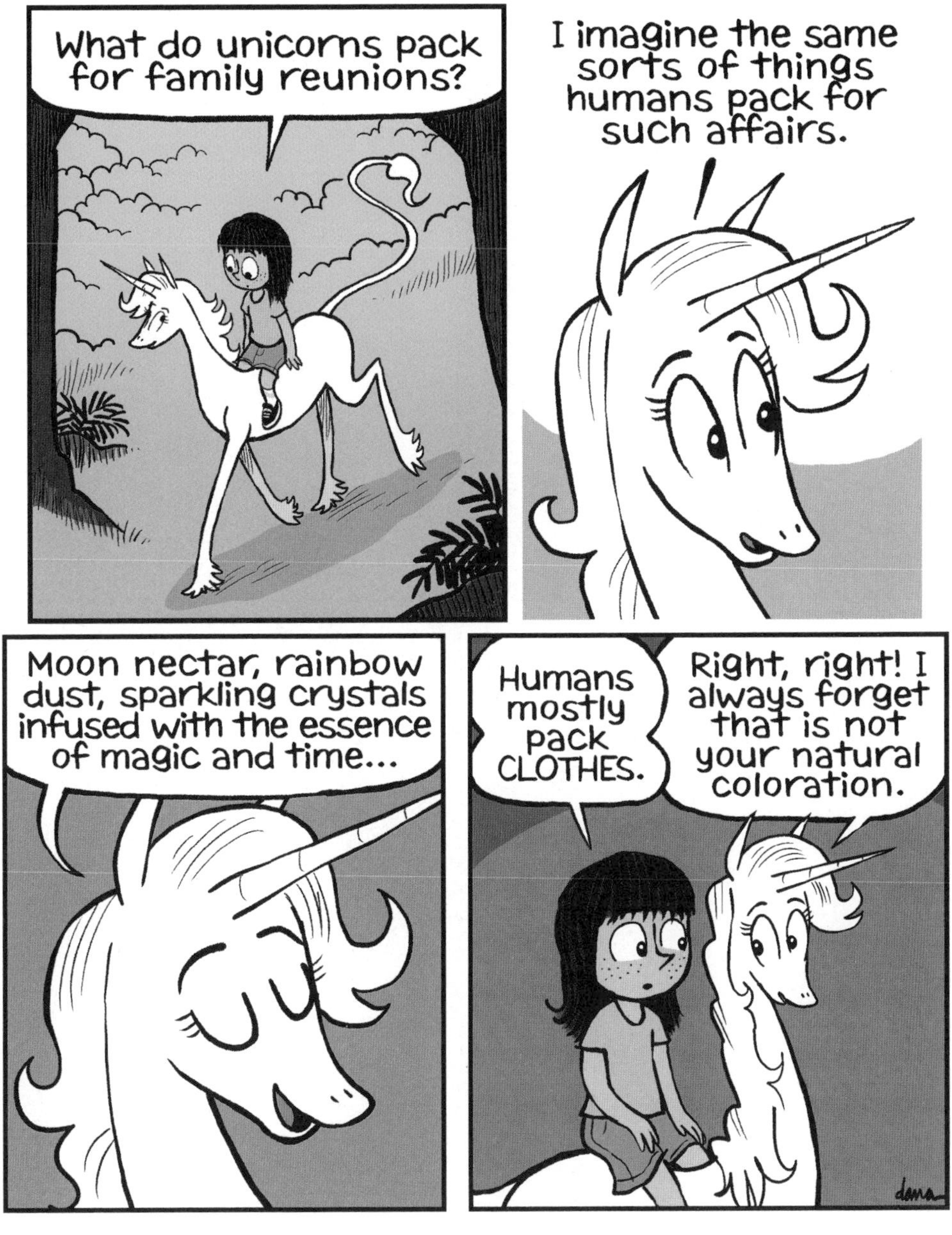
What do unicorns pack for family reunions?
I imagine the same sorts of things humans pack for such affairs.
Moon nectar, rainbow dust, sparkling crystals infused with the essence of magic and time...
Humans mostly pack CLOTHES.
Right, right! I always forget that is not your natural coloration.
dana

The truth is...I am packing for my family reunion so early because I am nervous.

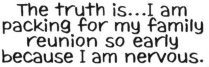

It is one thing to impress the world, and quite another to impress my RELATIVES.

I know how it is.

My cool older cousins call me "Phoebe the Freebie," because nobody would ever pay for one of me.

That is not actually very cool.

Hey, it's NOT, is it? I'm actually somehow disillusioned.

dana

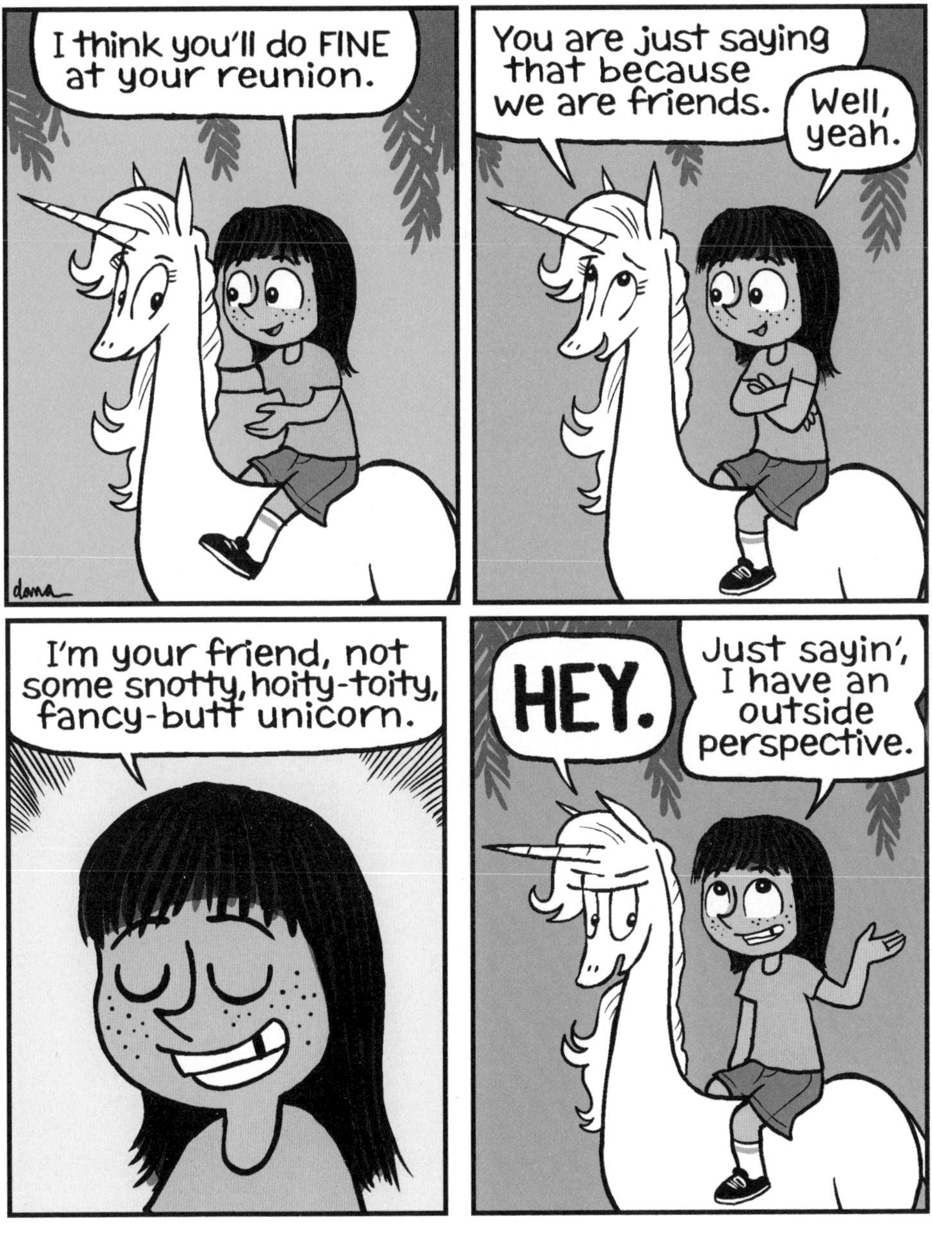
I think you'll do FINE at your reunion.
You are just saying that because we are friends.
Well, yeah.
I'm your friend, not some snotty, hoity-toity, fancy-butt unicorn.
HEY.
Just sayin', I have an outside perspective.
dana

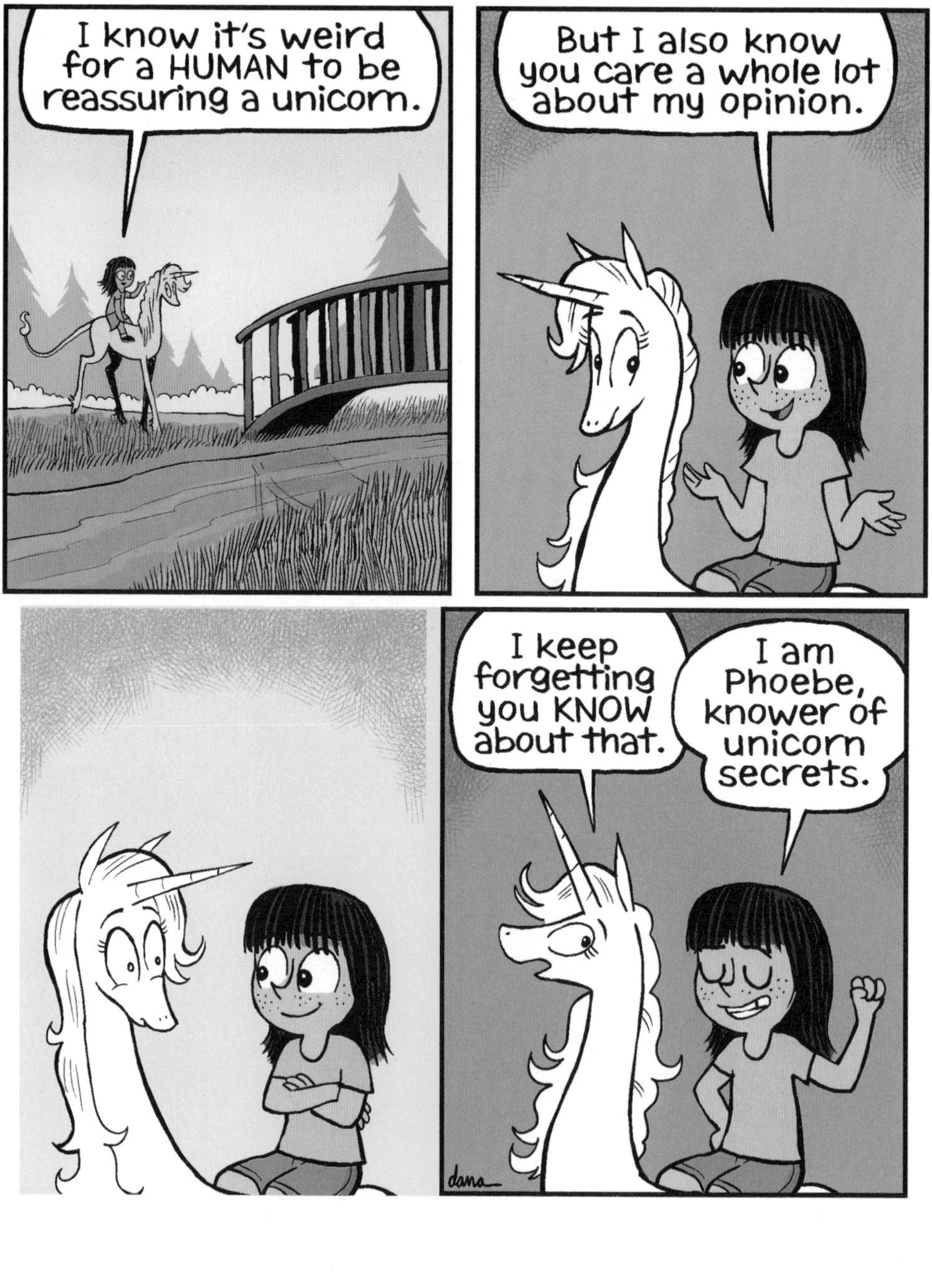
I know it's weird for a HUMAN to be reassuring a unicorn.
But I also know you care a whole lot about my opinion.
I keep forgetting you KNOW about that.
I am Phoebe, knower of unicorn secrets.
dana

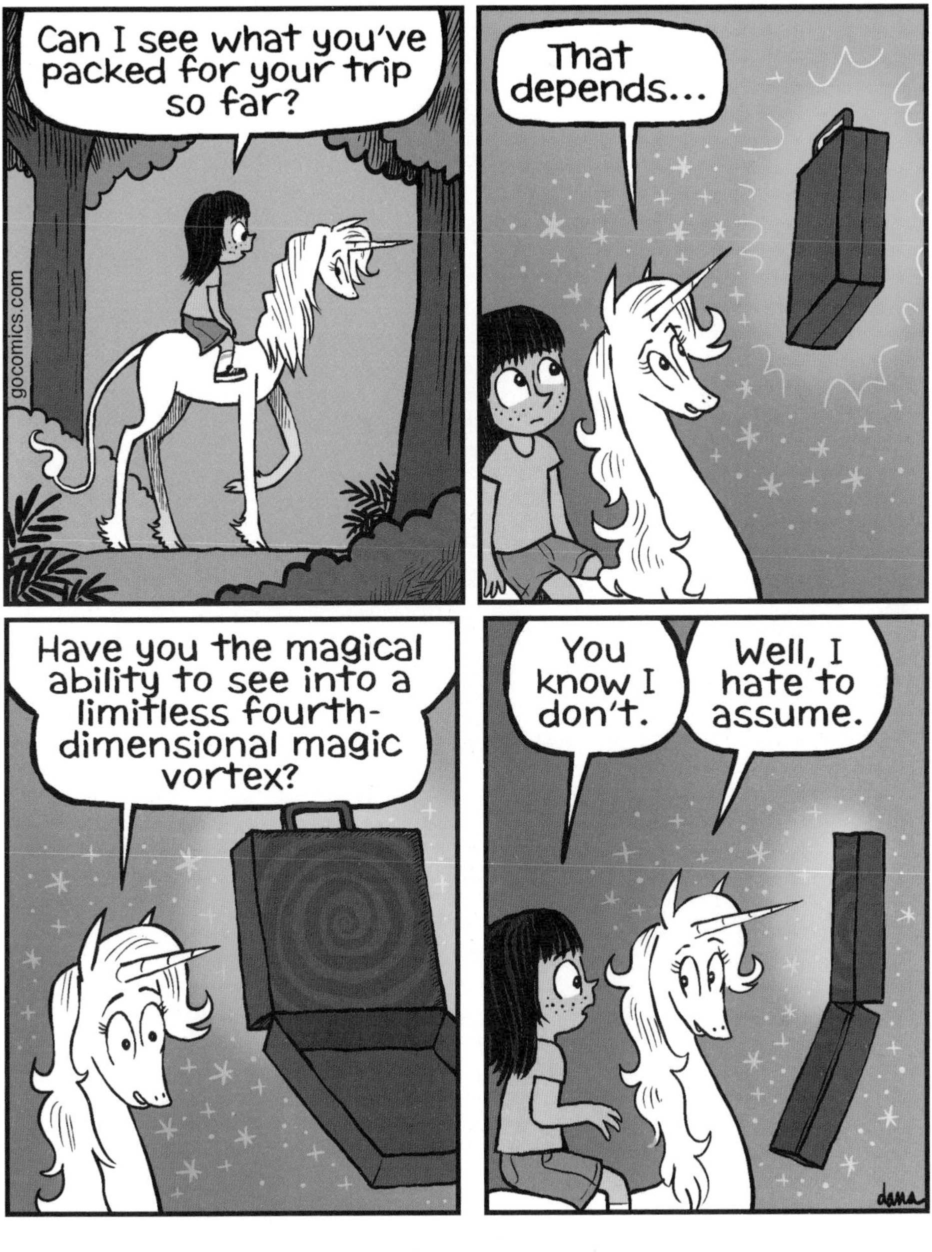
Can I see what you've packed for your trip so far?
gocomics.com
That depends...
Have you the magical ability to see into a limitless fourth-dimensional magic vortex?
You know I don't.
Well, I hate to assume.
dana

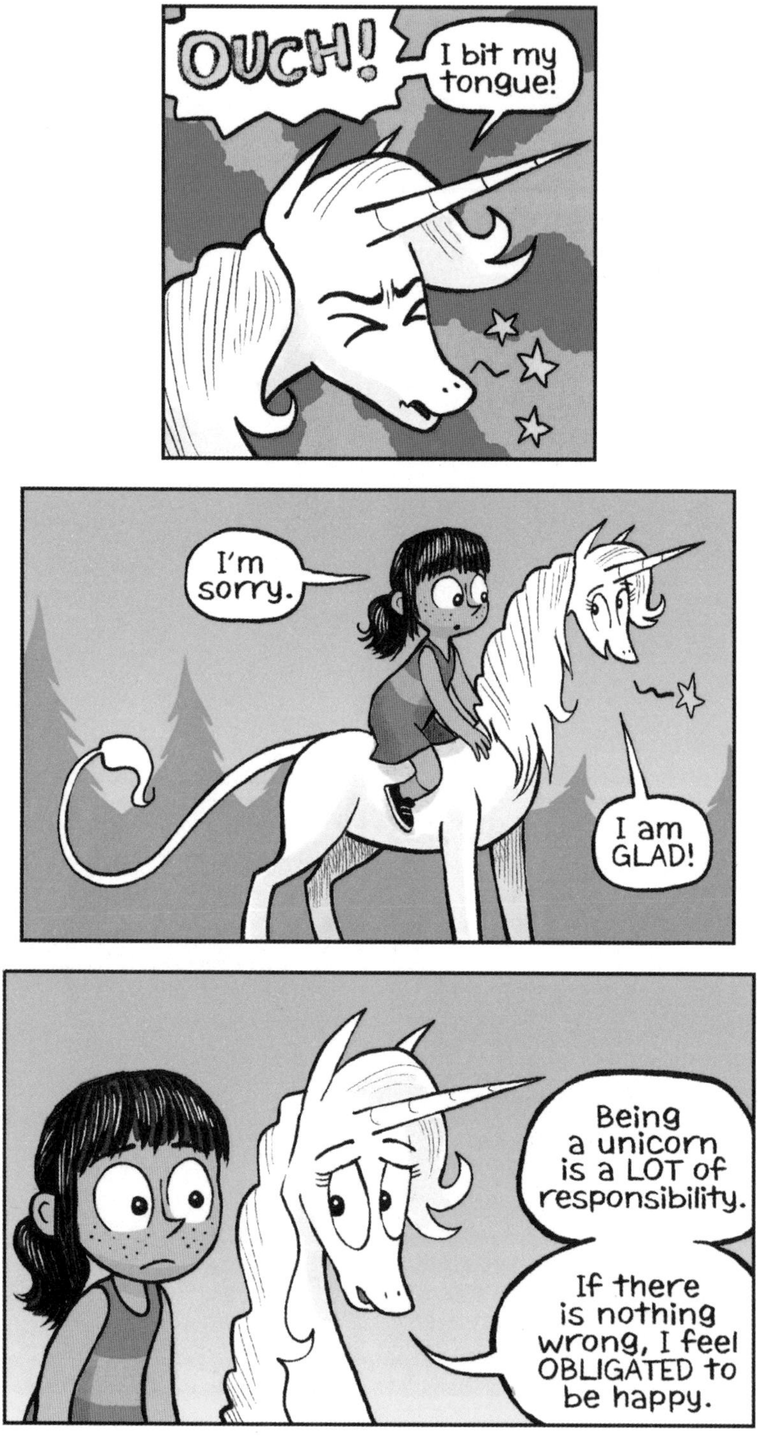

OUCH!
I bit my tongue!
I'm sorry.
I am GLAD!
Being a unicorn is a LOT of responsibility.
If there is nothing wrong, I feel OBLIGATED to be happy.

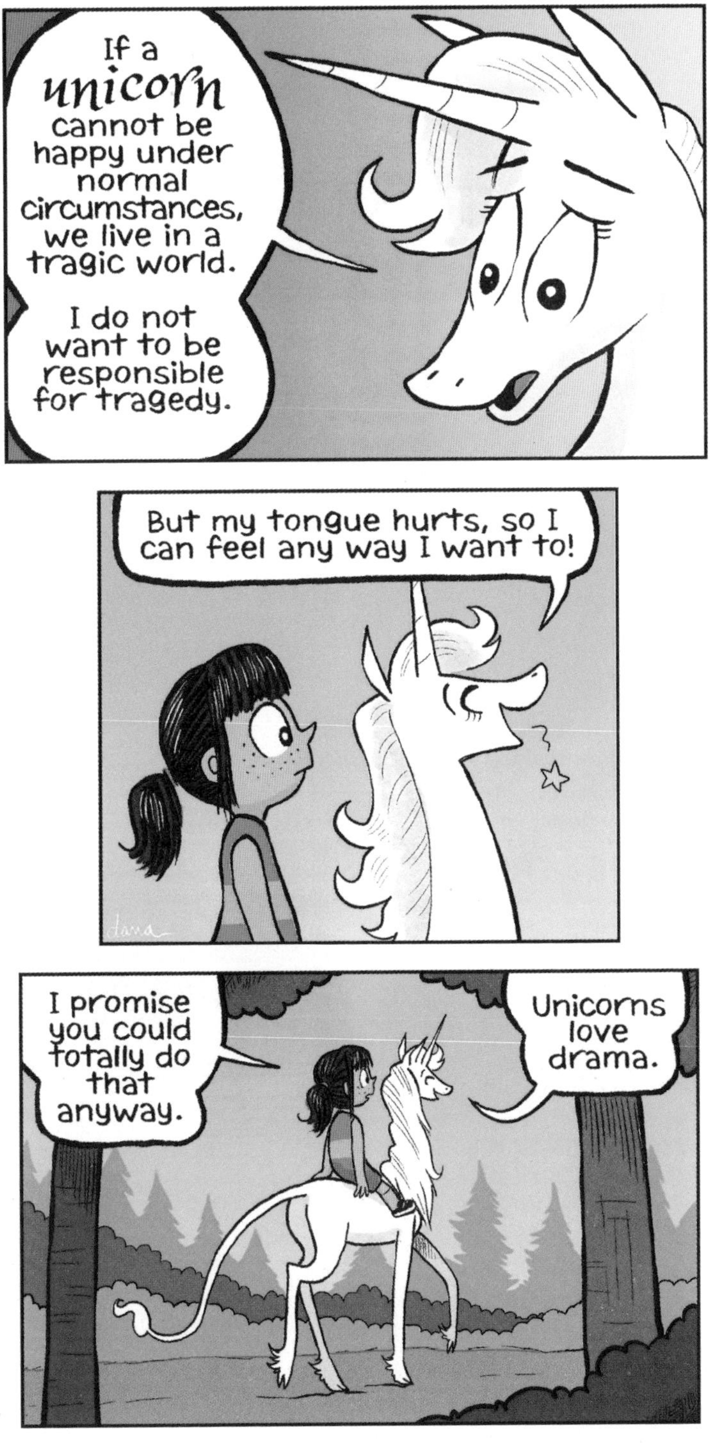
If a *unicorn* cannot be happy under normal circumstances, we live in a tragic world.
I do not want to be responsible for tragedy.
But my tongue hurts, so I can feel any way I want to!
I promise you could totally do that anyway.
Unicorns love drama.

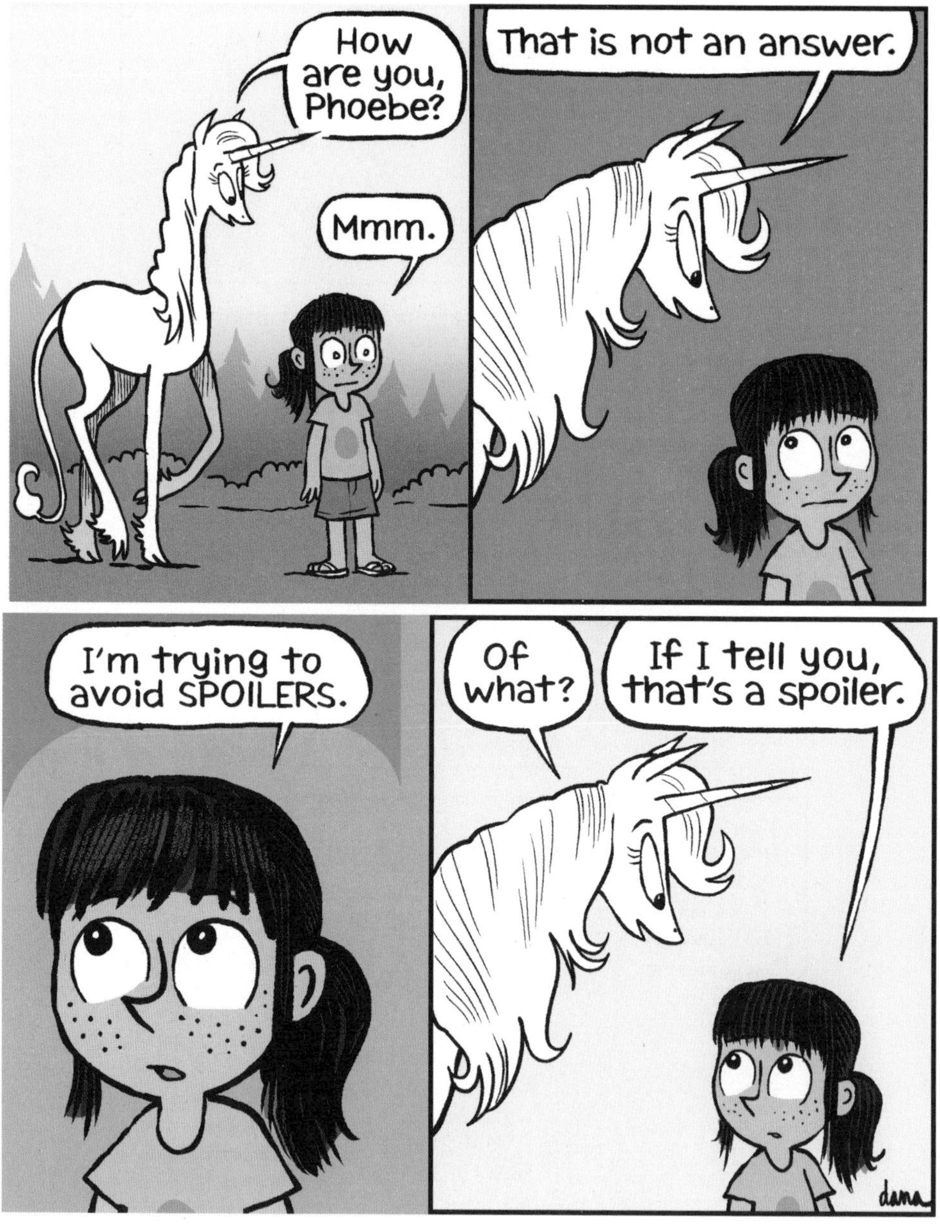
How are you, Phoebe?
Mmm.
That is not an answer.
I'm trying to avoid SPOILERS.
Of what?
If I tell you, that's a spoiler.
dana

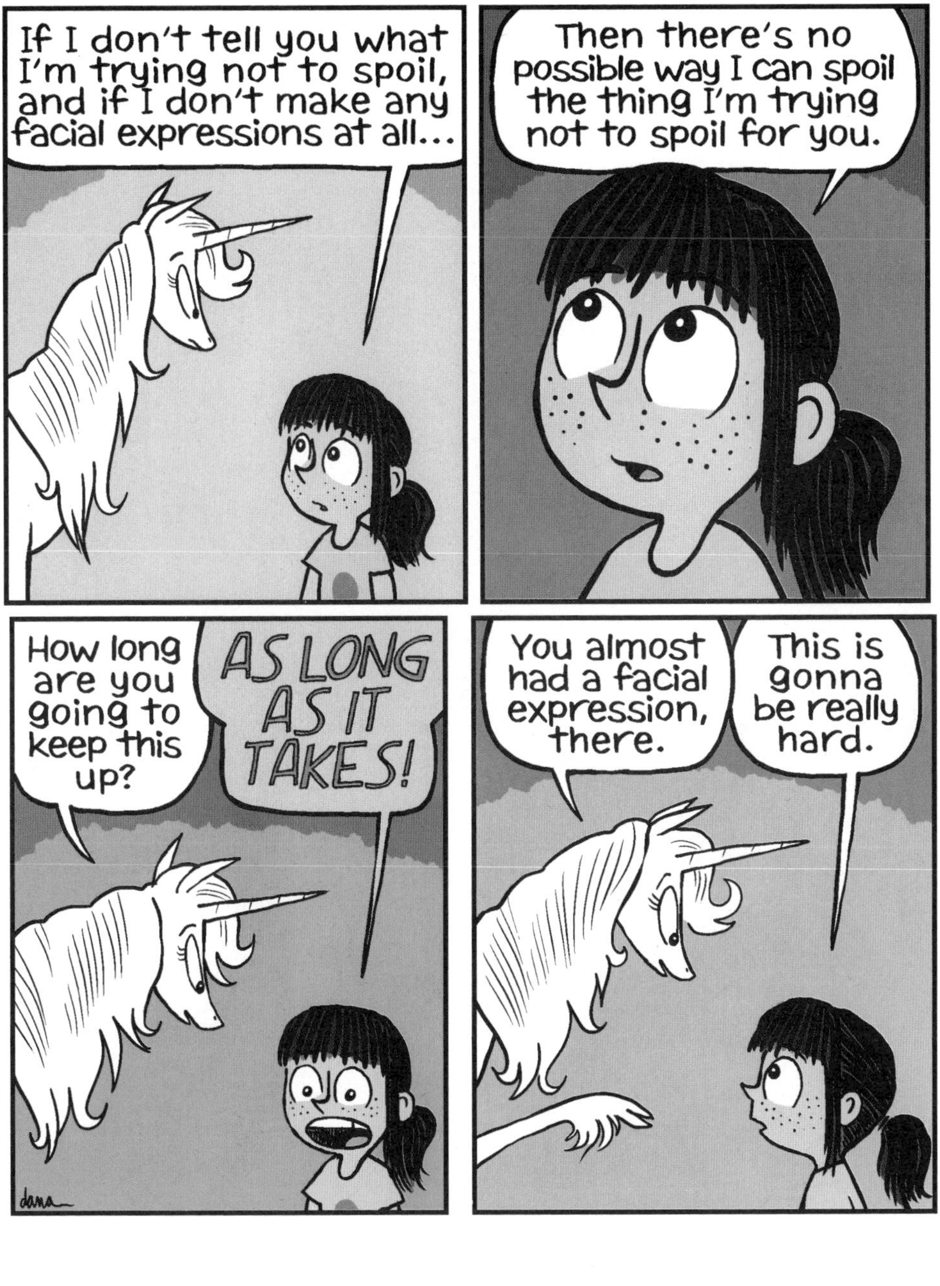
If I don't tell you what I'm trying not to spoil, and if I don't make any facial expressions at all...
Then there's no possible way I can spoil the thing I'm trying not to spoil for you.
How long are you going to keep this up?
AS LONG AS IT TAKES!
You almost had a facial expression, there.
This is gonna be really hard.
dana

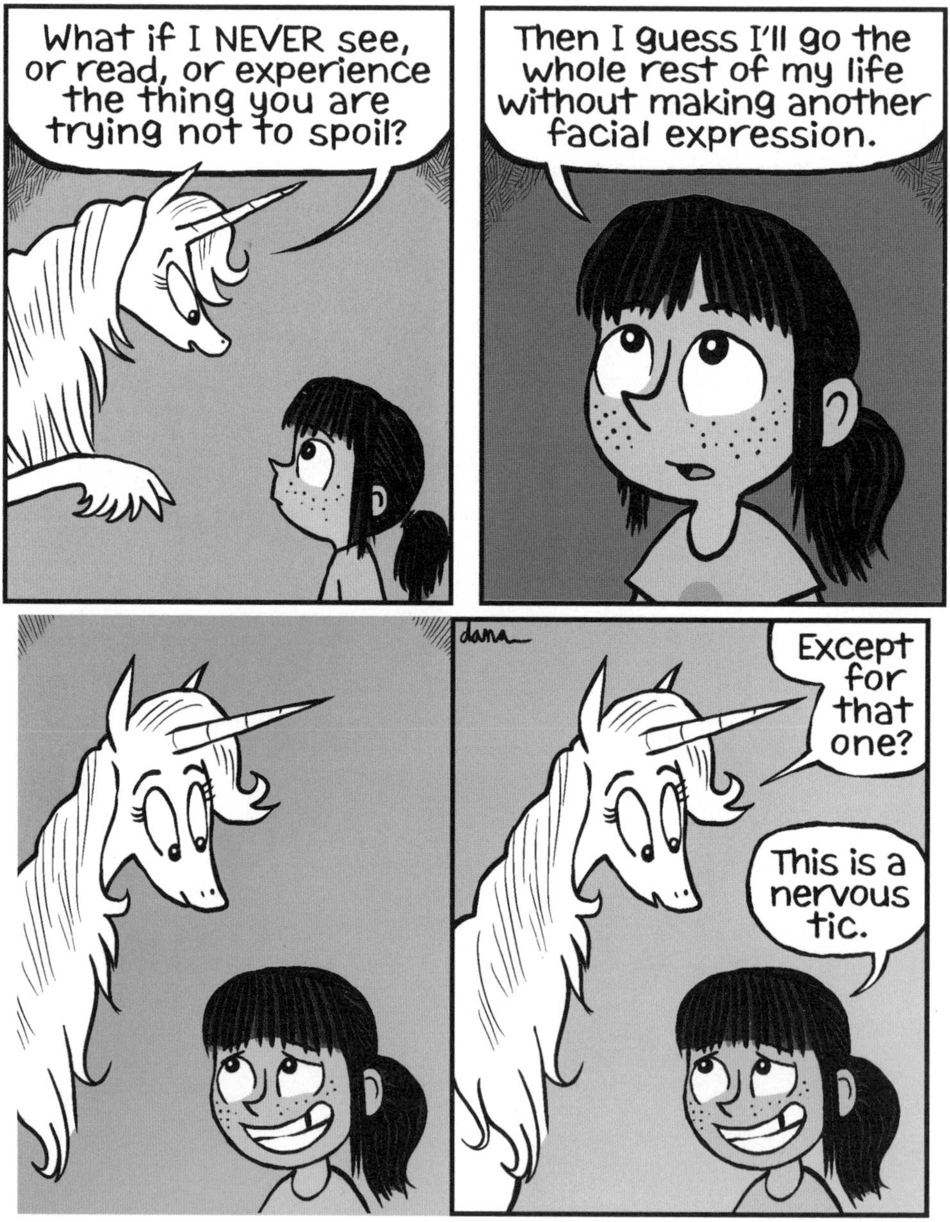

What if I NEVER see, or read, or experience the thing you are trying not to spoil?
Then I guess I'll go the whole rest of my life without making another facial expression.
dana
Except for that one?
This is a nervous tic.

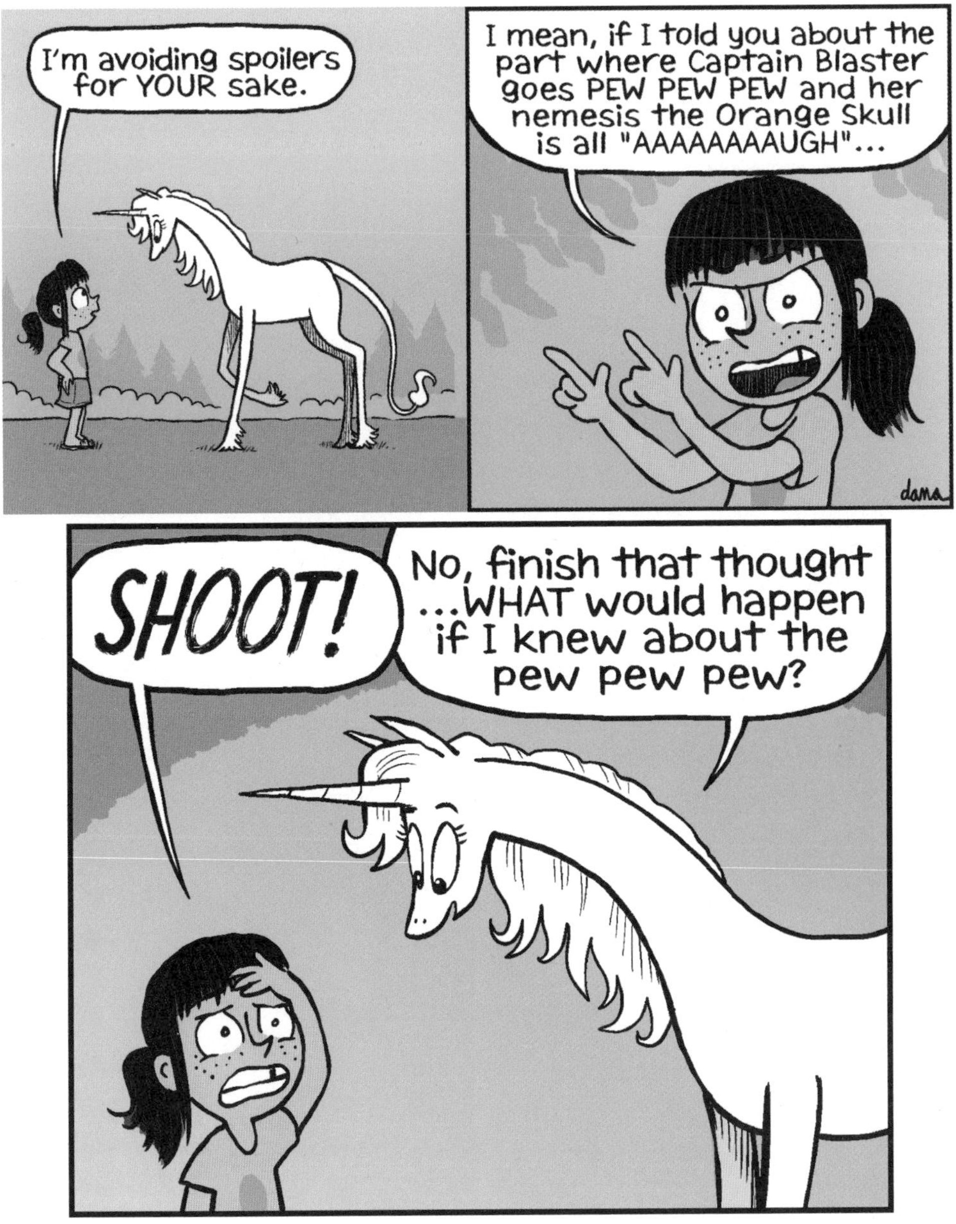
I'm avoiding spoilers for YOUR sake.
I mean, if I told you about the part where Captain Blaster goes PEW PEW PEW and her nemesis the Orange Skull is all "AAAAAAAAUGH"...
dana
SHOOT!
No, finish that thought ...WHAT would happen if I knew about the pew pew pew?

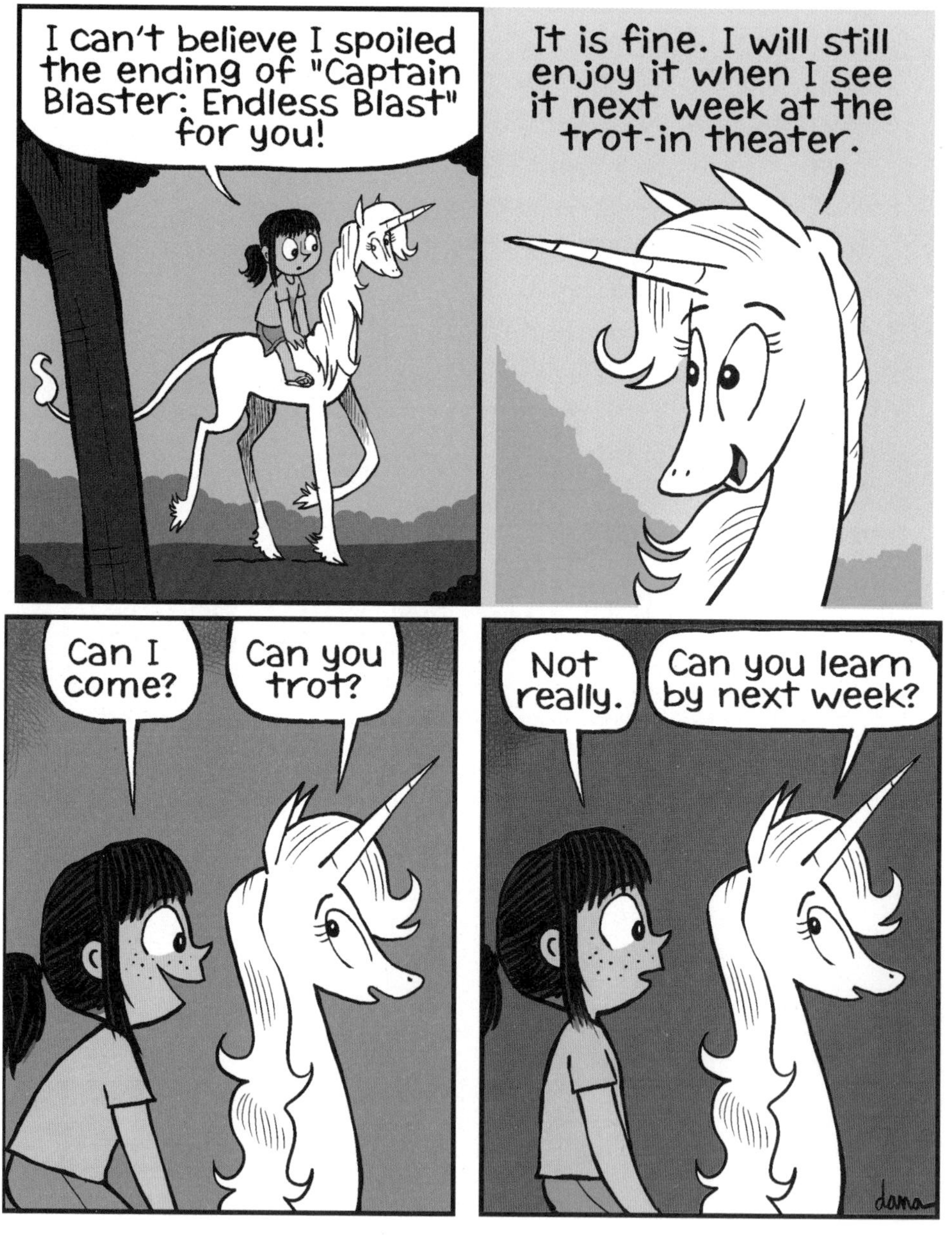
I can't believe I spoiled the ending of "Captain Blaster: Endless Blast" for you!
It is fine. I will still enjoy it when I see it next week at the trot-in theater.
Can I come?
Can you trot?
Not really.
Can you learn by next week?
dana

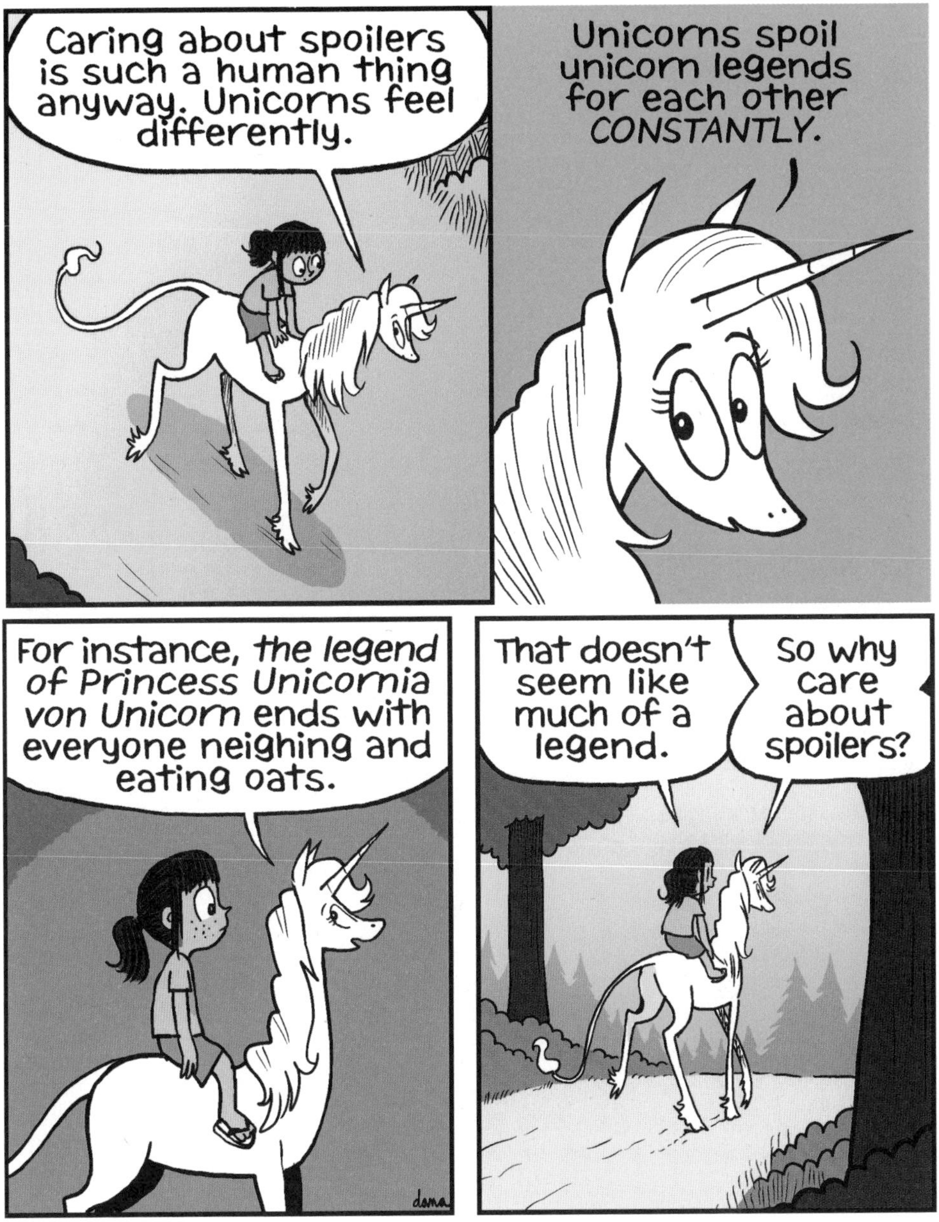
Caring about spoilers is such a human thing anyway. Unicorns feel differently.
Unicorns spoil unicorn legends for each other *CONSTANTLY.*
For instance, *the legend of Princess Unicornia von Unicorn* ends with everyone neighing and eating oats.
dana
That doesn't seem like much of a legend.
So why care about spoilers?

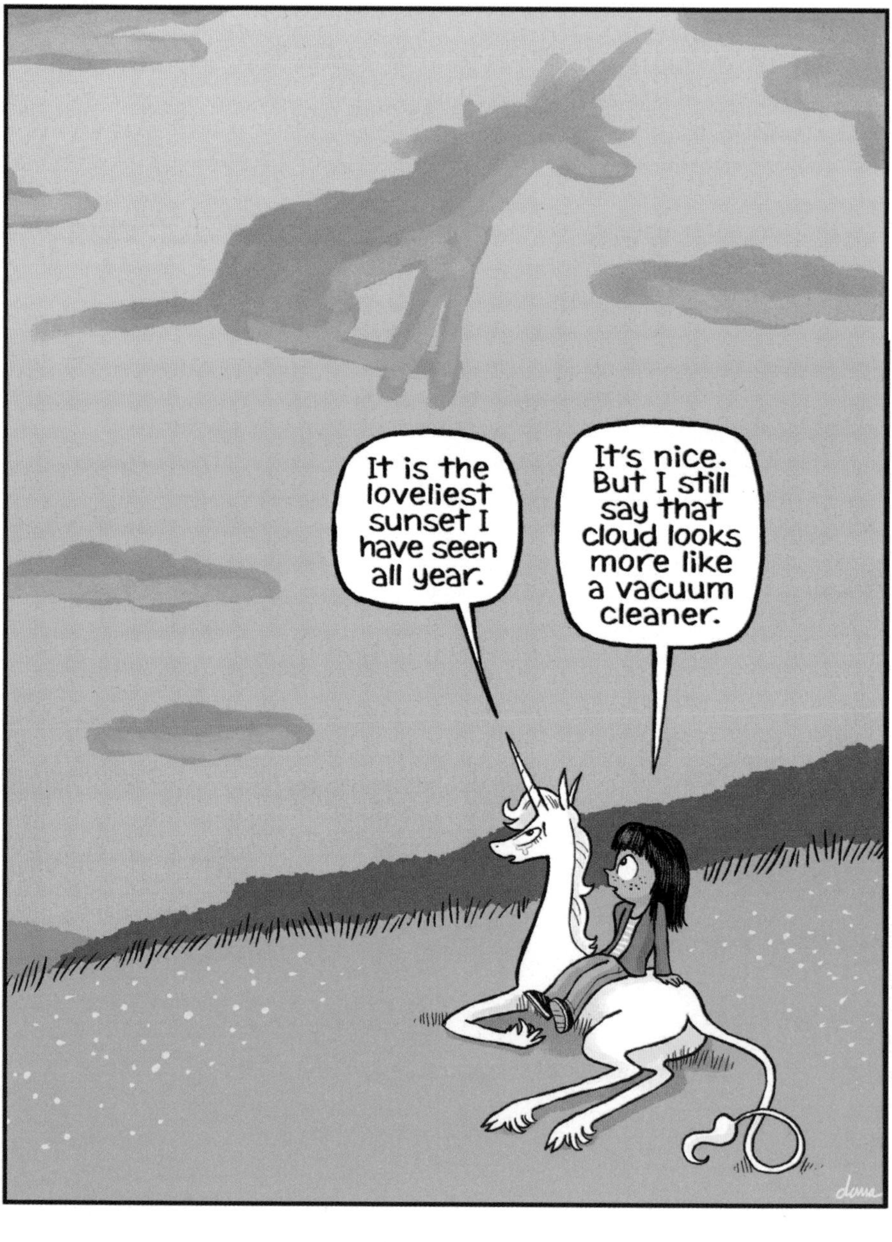
It is the loveliest sunset I have seen all year.
It's nice. But I still say that cloud looks more like a vacuum cleaner.

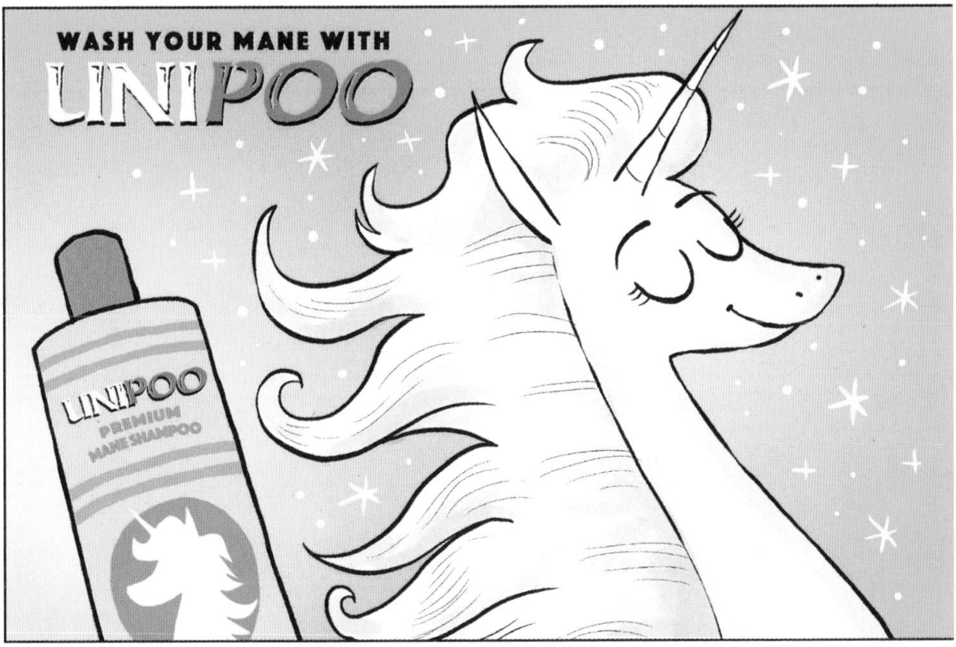
WASH YOUR MANE WITH
UNIPOO
UNIPOO
PREMIUM
MANE SHAMPOO

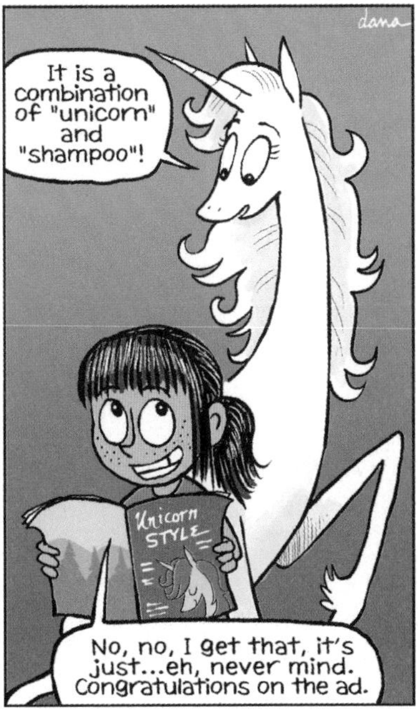
dana
It is a combination of "unicorn" and "shampoo"!
Unicorn STYLE
No, no, I get that, it's just...eh, never mind. Congratulations on the ad.

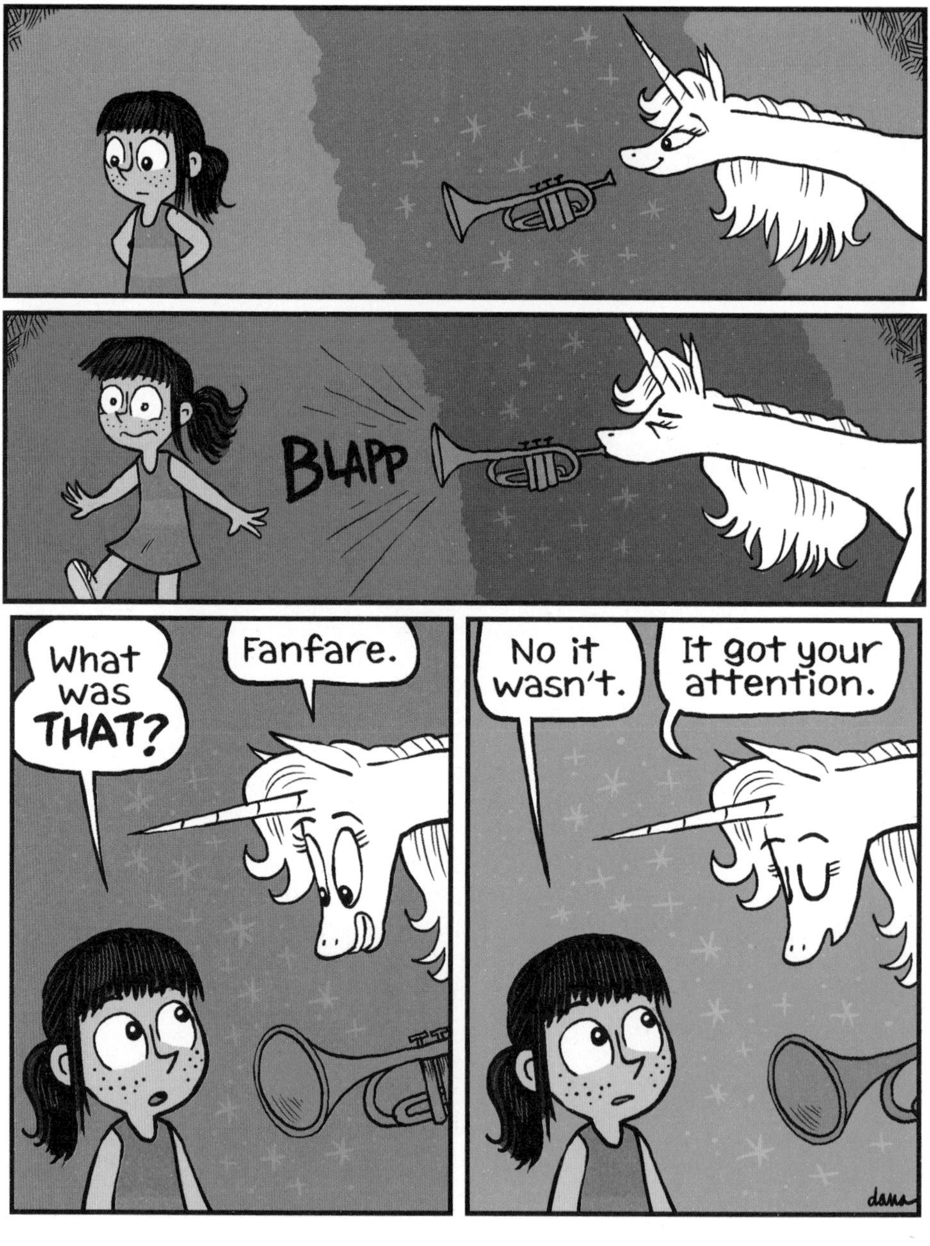
BLAPP
What was THAT?
Fanfare.
No it wasn't.
It got your attention.
dana

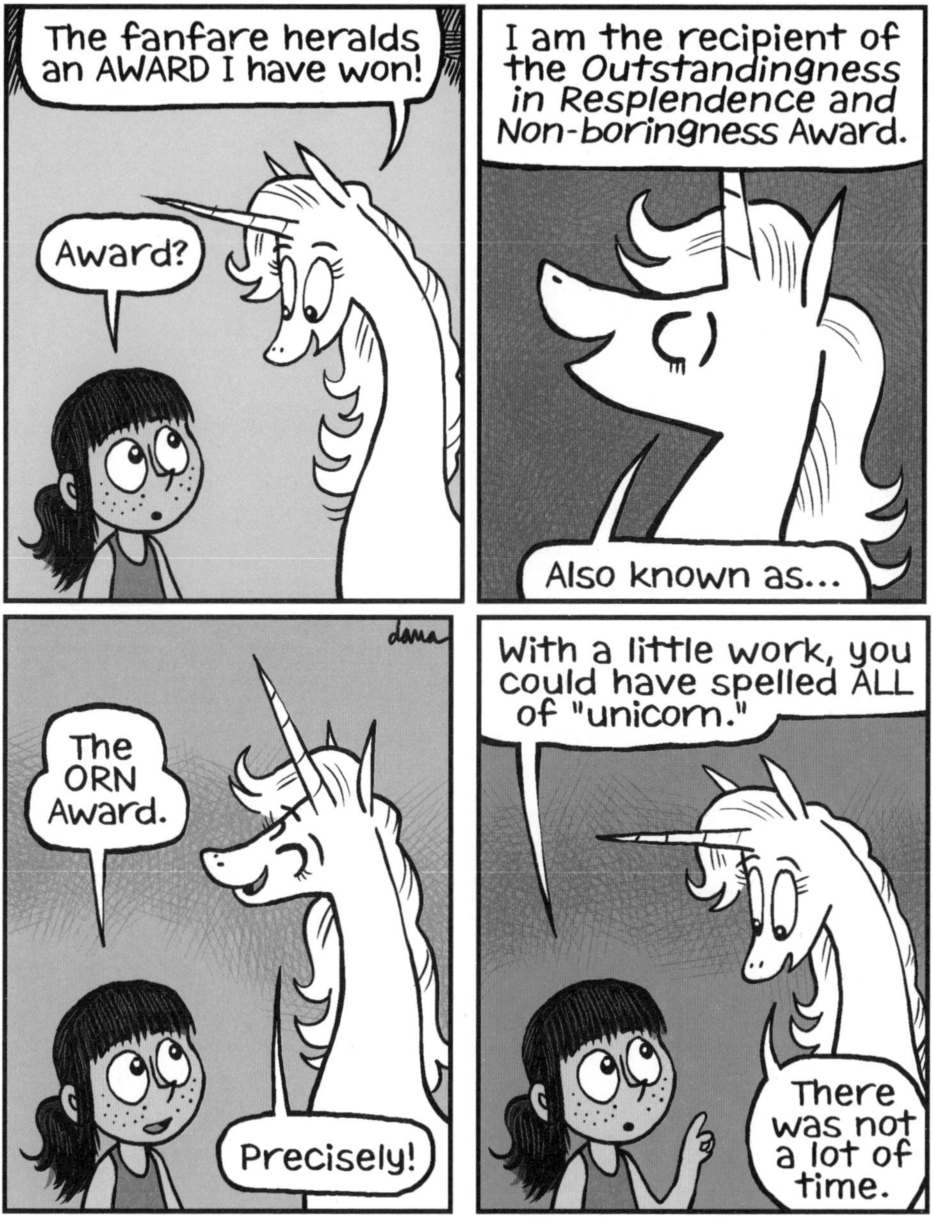
The fanfare heralds an AWARD I have won!
Award?
I am the recipient of the *Outstandingness in Resplendence and Non-boringness* Award.
Also known as...
dana
The ORN Award.
Precisely!
With a little work, you could have spelled ALL of "unicorn."
There was not a lot of time.

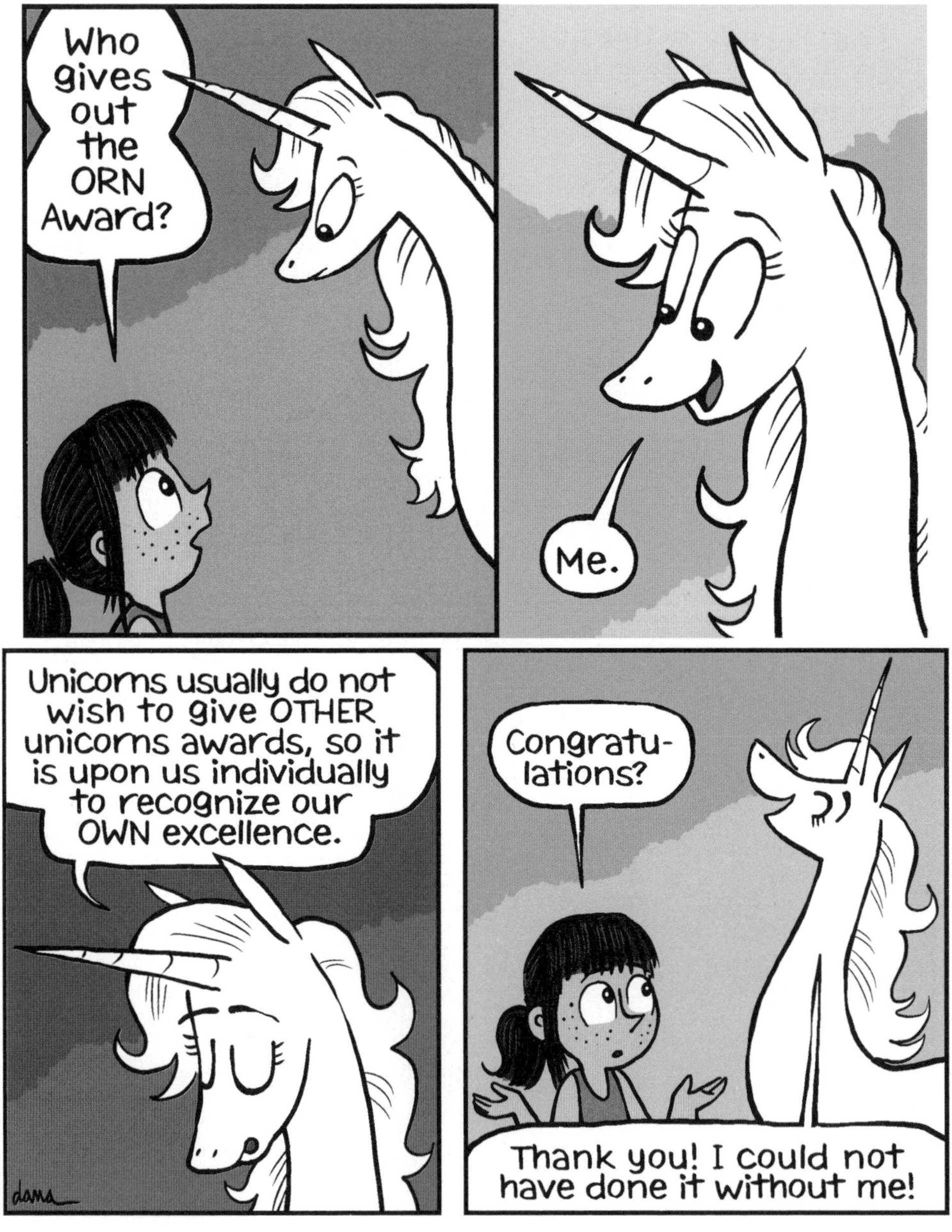
Who gives out the ORN Award?
Me.
Unicorns usually do not wish to give OTHER unicorns awards, so it is upon us individually to recognize our OWN excellence.
dana
Congratulations?
Thank you! I could not have done it without me!

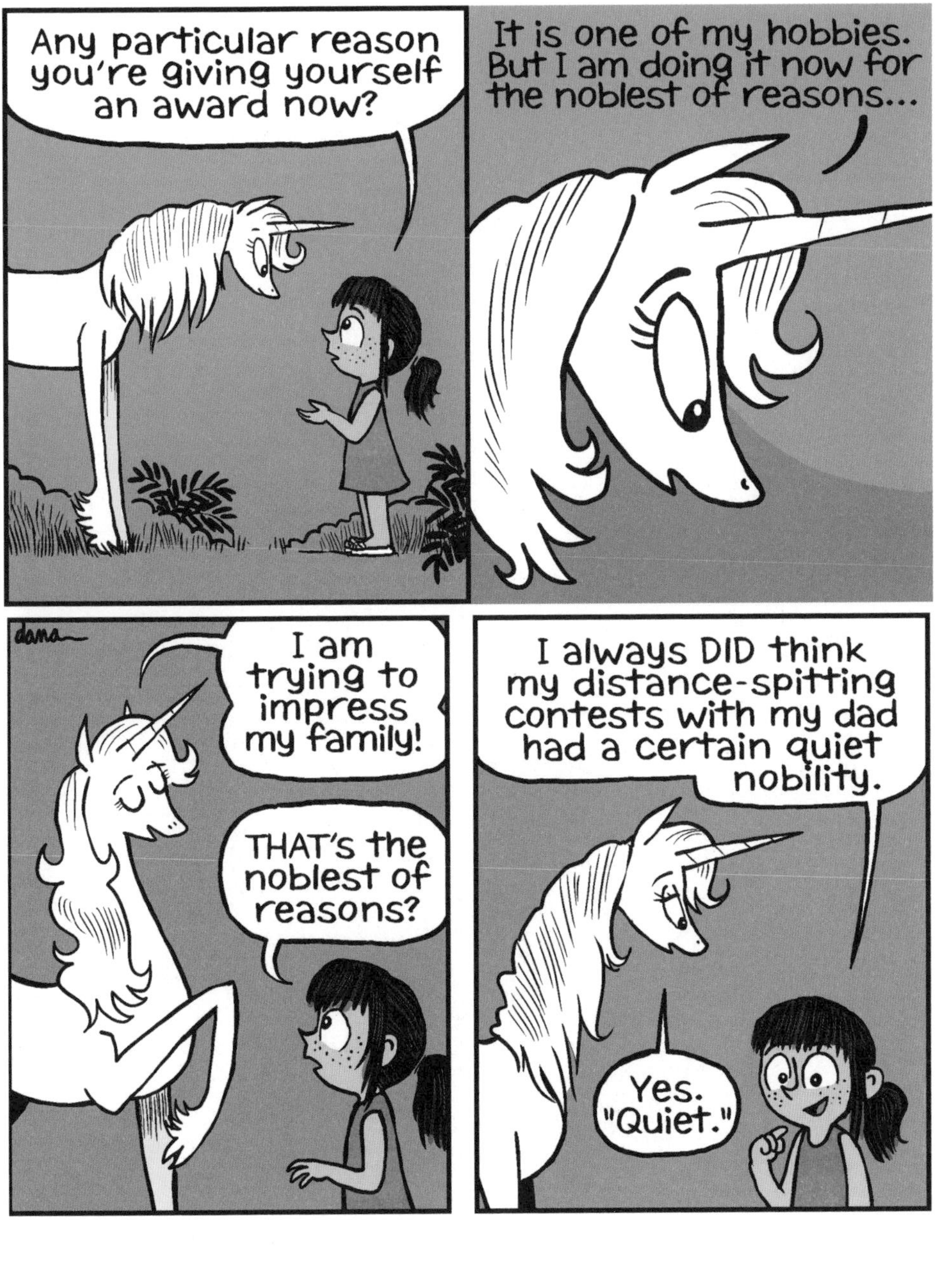
Any particular reason you're giving yourself an award now?
It is one of my hobbies. But I am doing it now for the noblest of reasons...
dana
I am trying to impress my family!
THAT'S the noblest of reasons?
I always DID think my distance-spitting contests with my dad had a certain quiet nobility.
Yes. "Quiet."

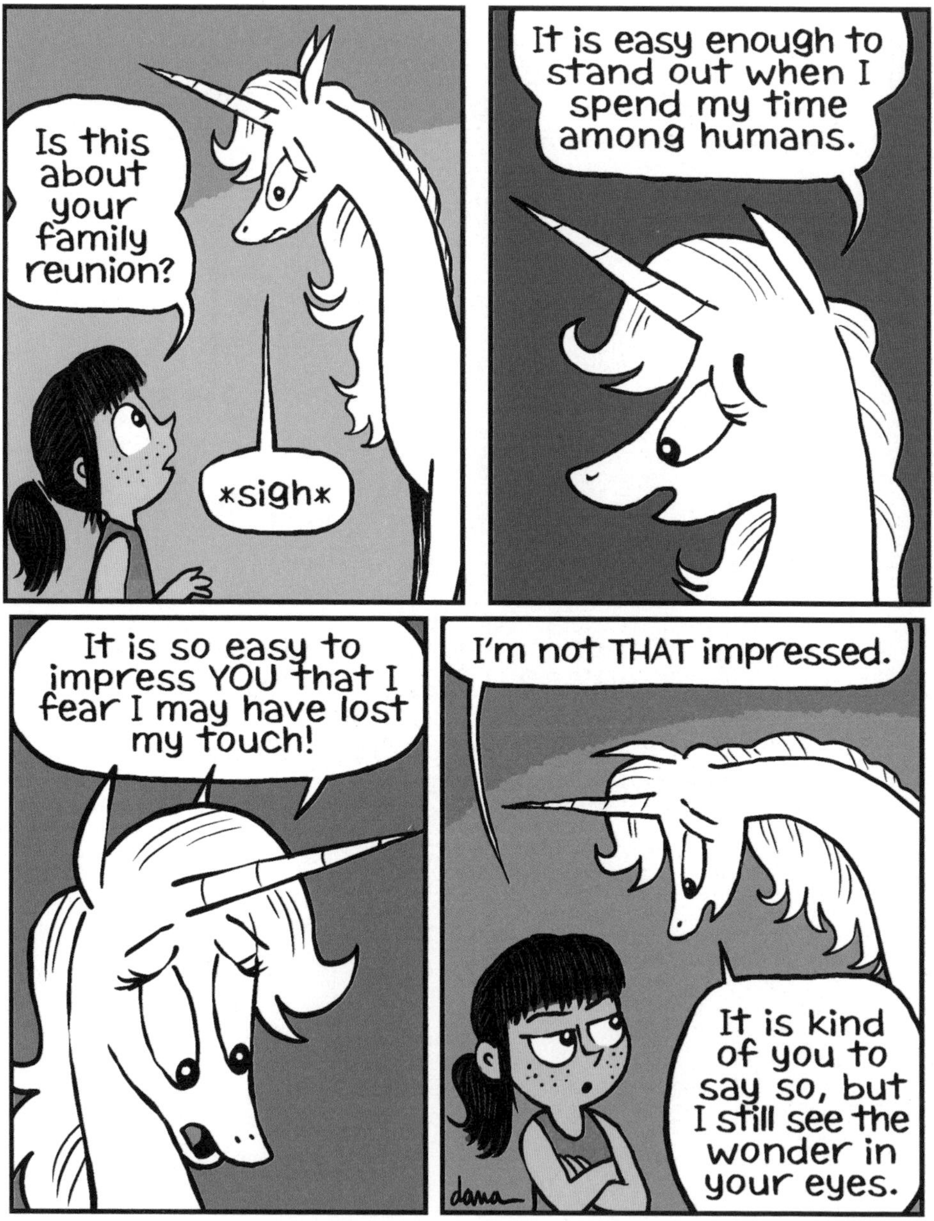
Is this about your family reunion?
sigh
It is easy enough to stand out when I spend my time among humans.
It is so easy to impress YOU that I fear I may have lost my touch!
I'm not THAT impressed.
It is kind of you to say so, but I still see the wonder in your eyes.
dana

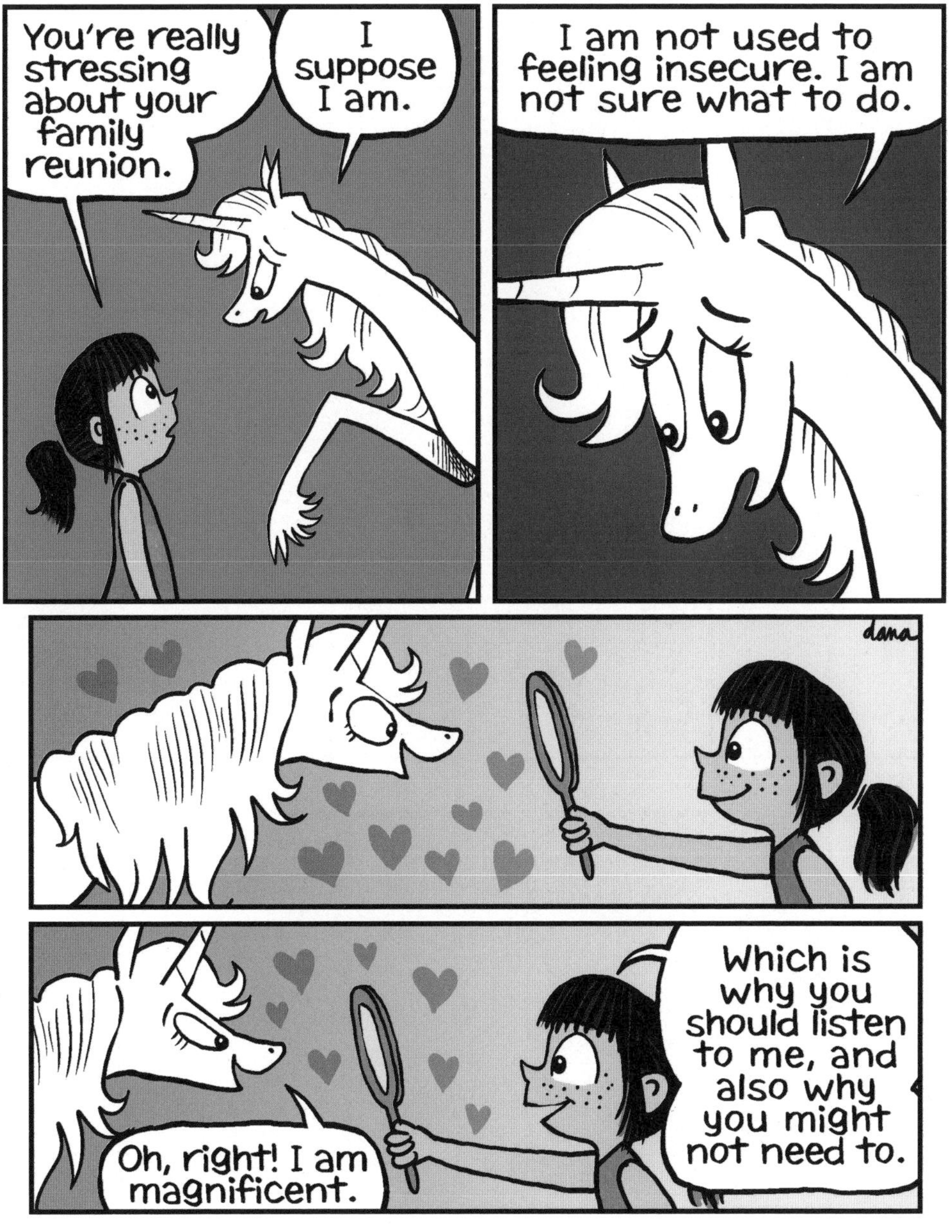
You're really stressing about your family reunion.
I suppose I am.
I am not used to feeling insecure. I am not sure what to do.
dana
Oh, right! I am magnificent.
Which is why you should listen to me, and also why you might not need to.

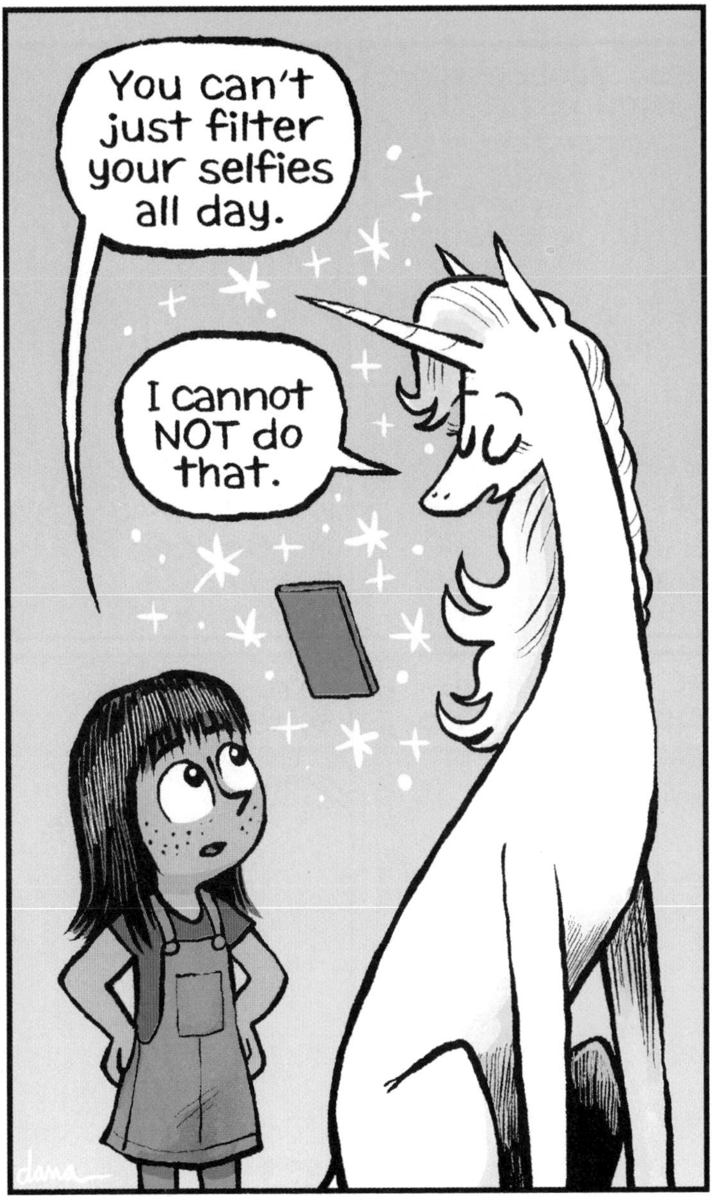
You can't just filter your selfies all day.
I cannot NOT do that.
dana

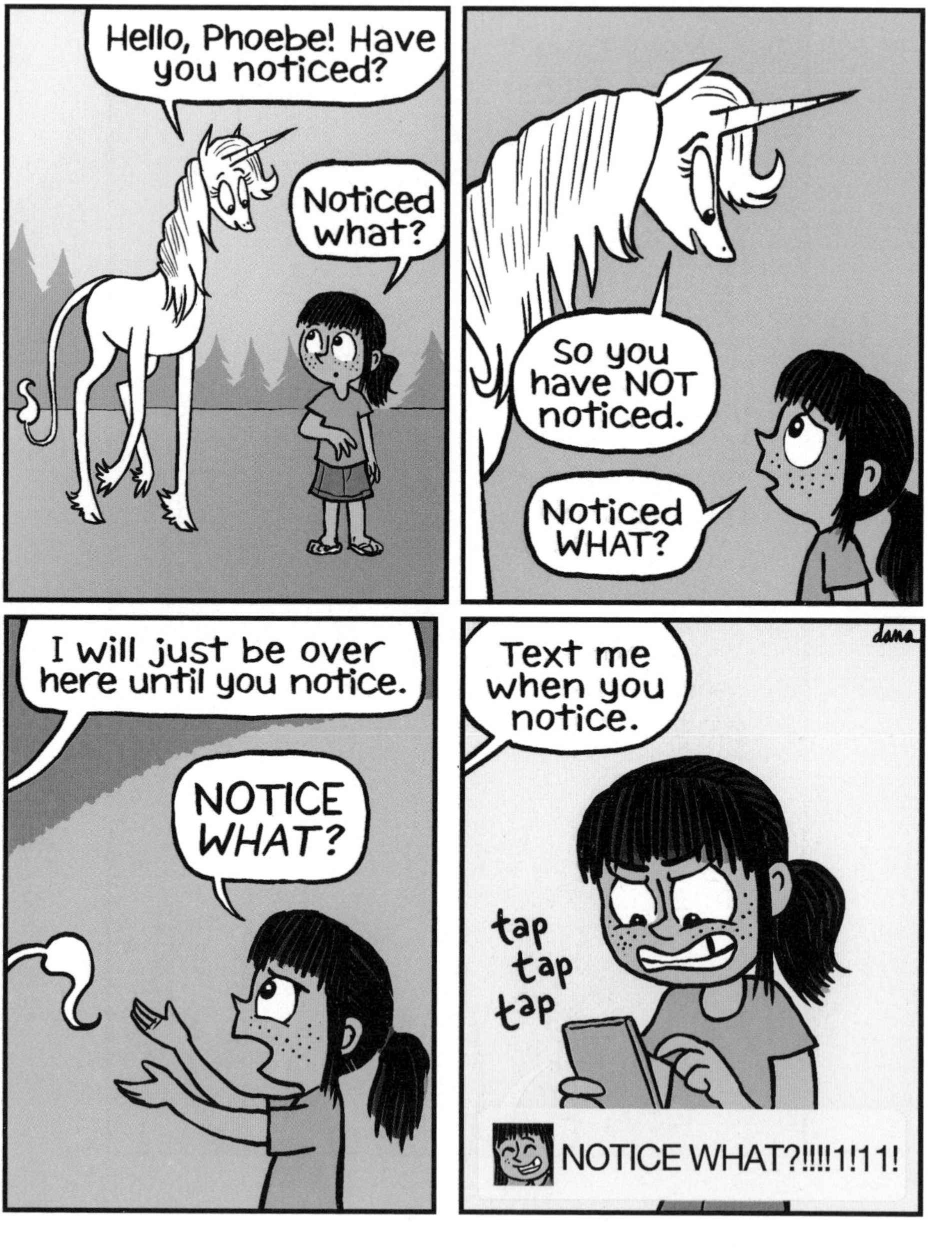
Hello, Phoebe! Have you noticed?
Noticed what?
So you have NOT noticed.
Noticed WHAT?
I will just be over here until you notice.
NOTICE WHAT?
dana
Text me when you notice.
tap tap tap
NOTICE WHAT?!!!!1!11!

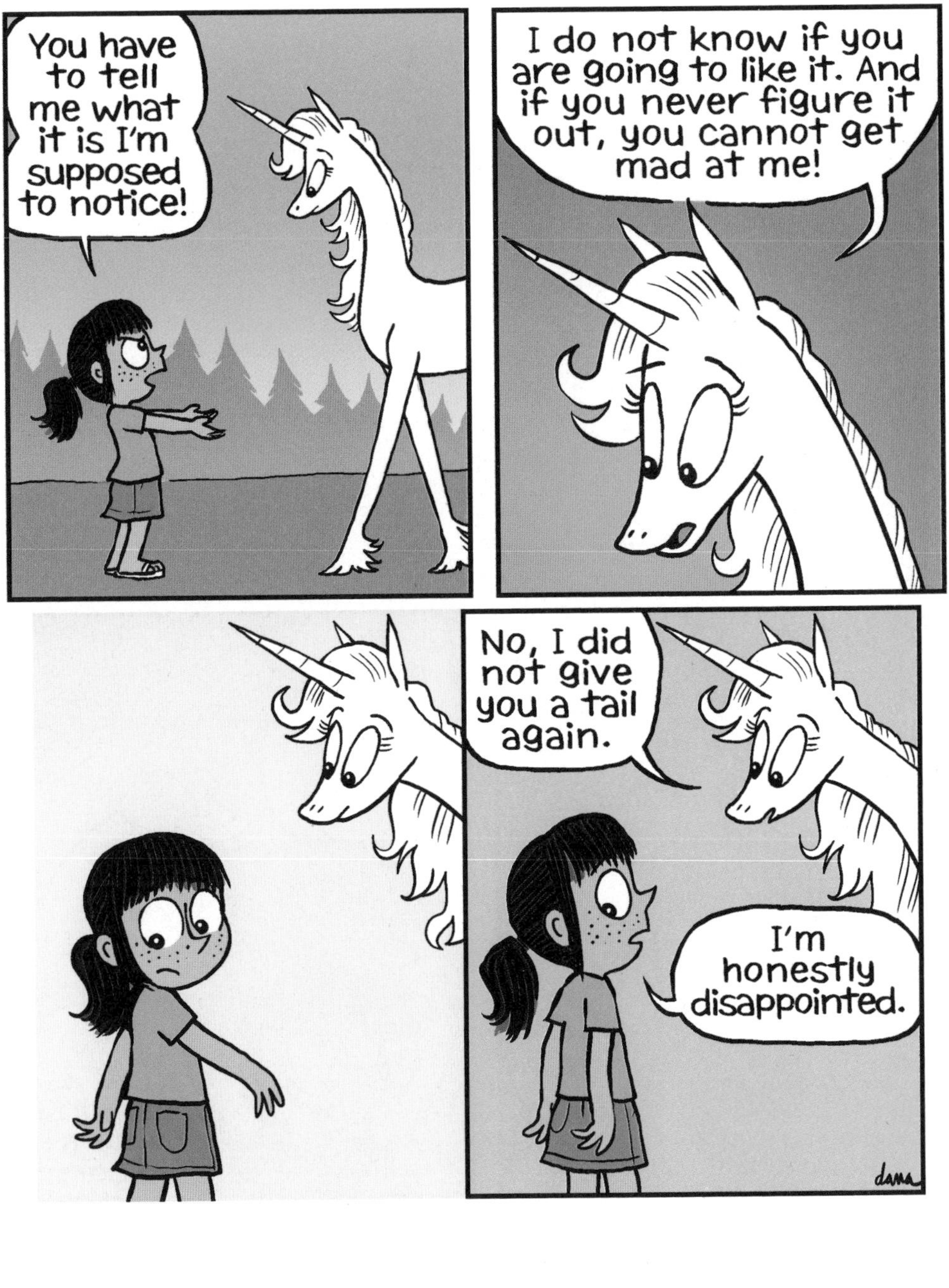
You have to tell me what it is I'm supposed to notice!
I do not know if you are going to like it. And if you never figure it out, you cannot get mad at me!
No, I did not give you a tail again.
I'm honestly disappointed.
dana

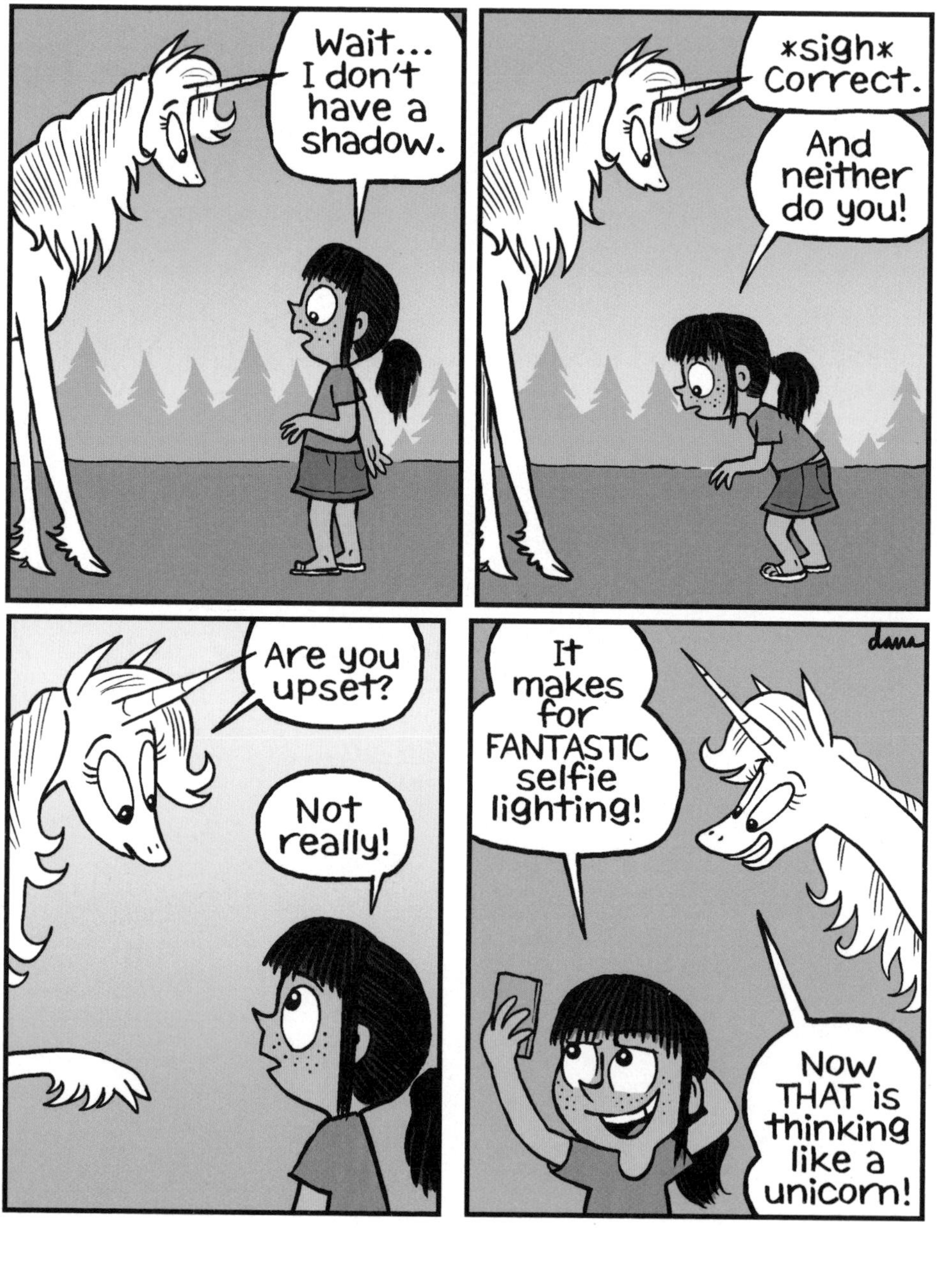
Wait... I don't have a shadow.
sigh Correct.
And neither do you!
Are you upset?
Not really!
It makes for FANTASTIC selfie lighting!
NOW THAT is thinking like a unicorn!

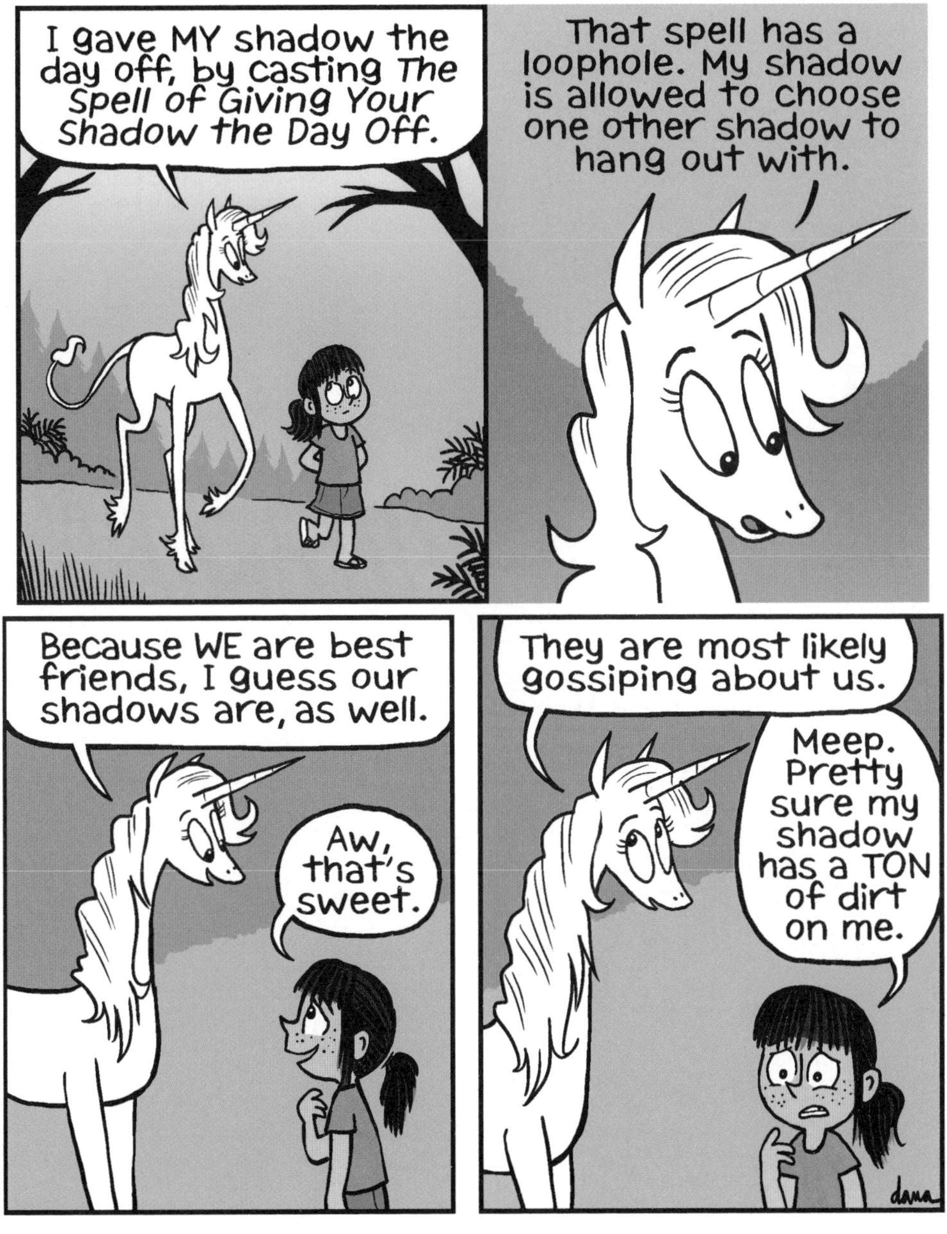
I gave MY shadow the day off, by casting *The Spell of Giving Your Shadow the Day Off.*
That spell has a loophole. My shadow is allowed to choose one other shadow to hang out with.
Because WE are best friends, I guess our shadows are, as well.
Aw, that's sweet.
They are most likely gossiping about us.
Meep. Pretty sure my shadow has a TON of dirt on me.
dana

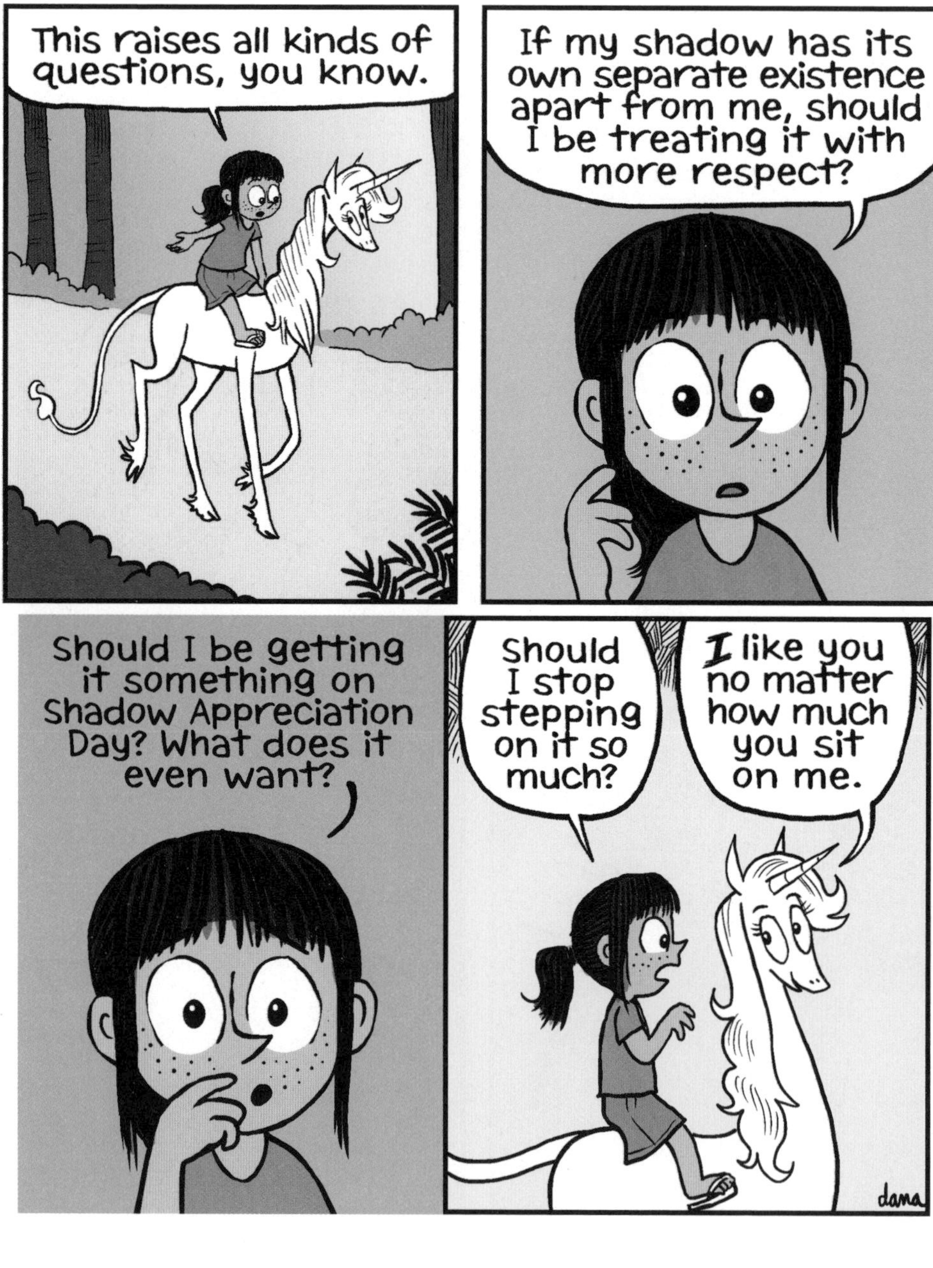
This raises all kinds of questions, you know.
If my shadow has its own separate existence apart from me, should I be treating it with more respect?
Should I be getting it something on Shadow Appreciation Day? What does it even want?
Should I stop stepping on it so much?
I like you no matter how much you sit on me.
dana

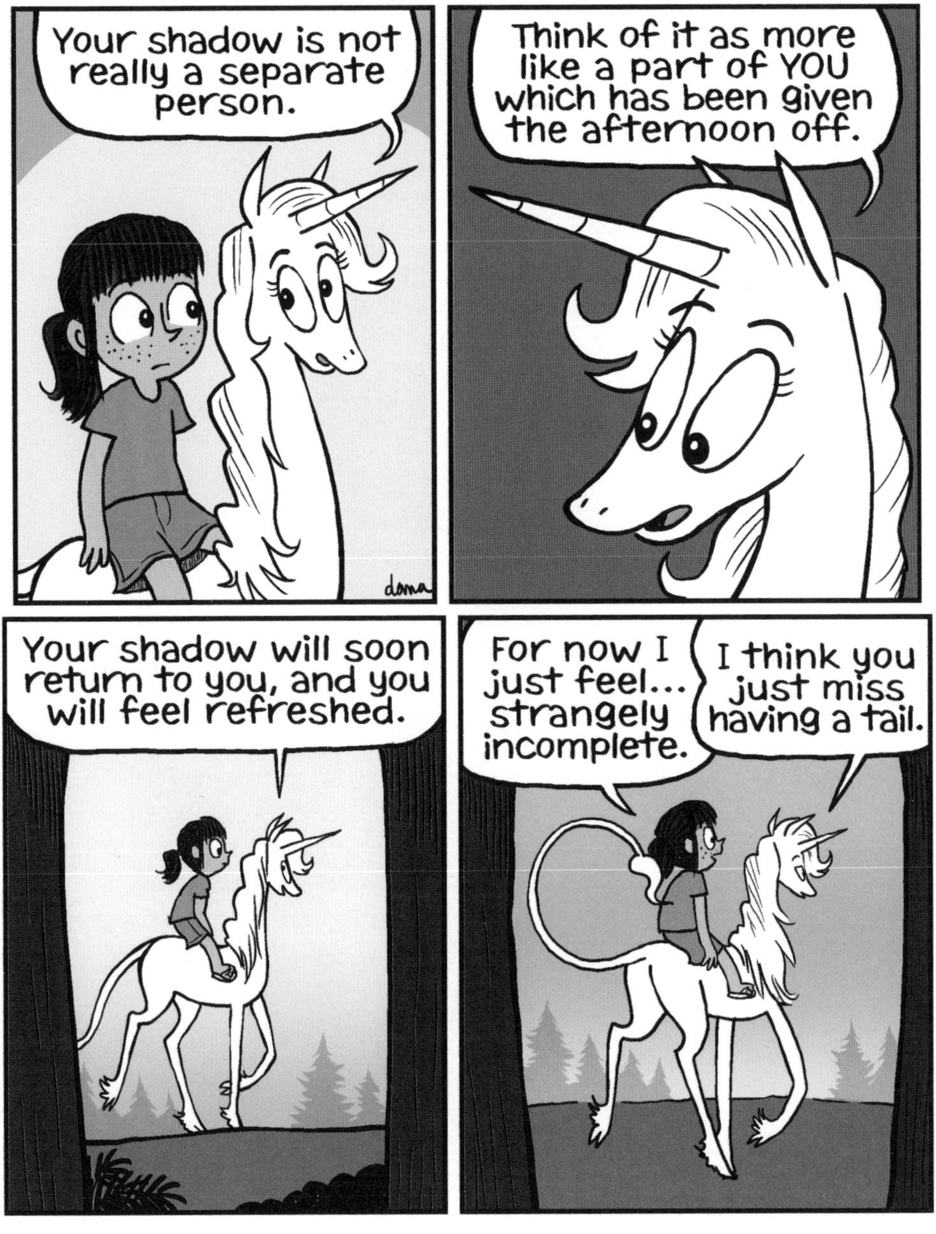
Your shadow is not really a separate person.
dana
Think of it as more like a part of YOU which has been given the afternoon off.
Your shadow will soon return to you, and you will feel refreshed.
For now I just feel... strangely incomplete.
I think you just miss having a tail.

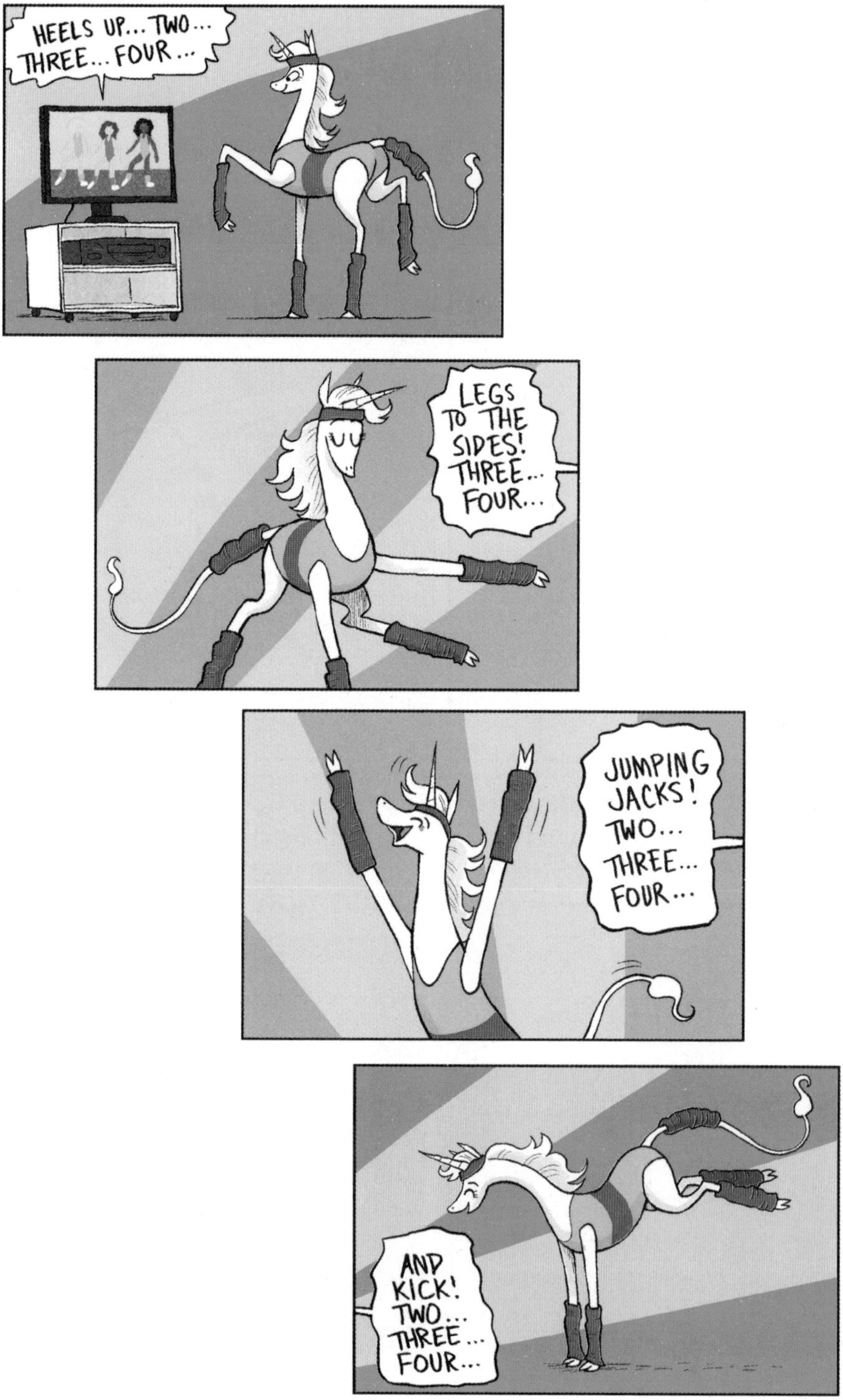
HEELS UP... TWO... THREE... FOUR...
LEGS TO THE SIDES! THREE... FOUR...
JUMPING JACKS! TWO... THREE... FOUR...
AND KICK! TWO... THREE... FOUR...

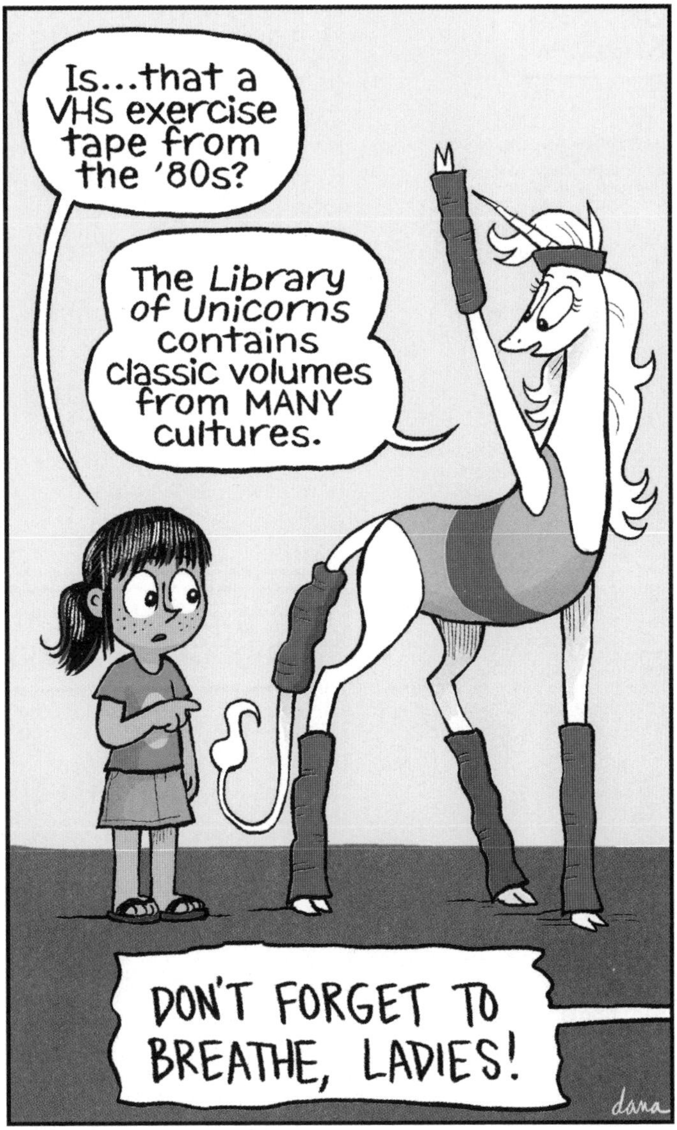
Is...that a VHS exercise tape from the '80s?
The *Library of Unicorns* contains classic volumes from MANY cultures.
DON'T FORGET TO BREATHE, LADIES!
dana

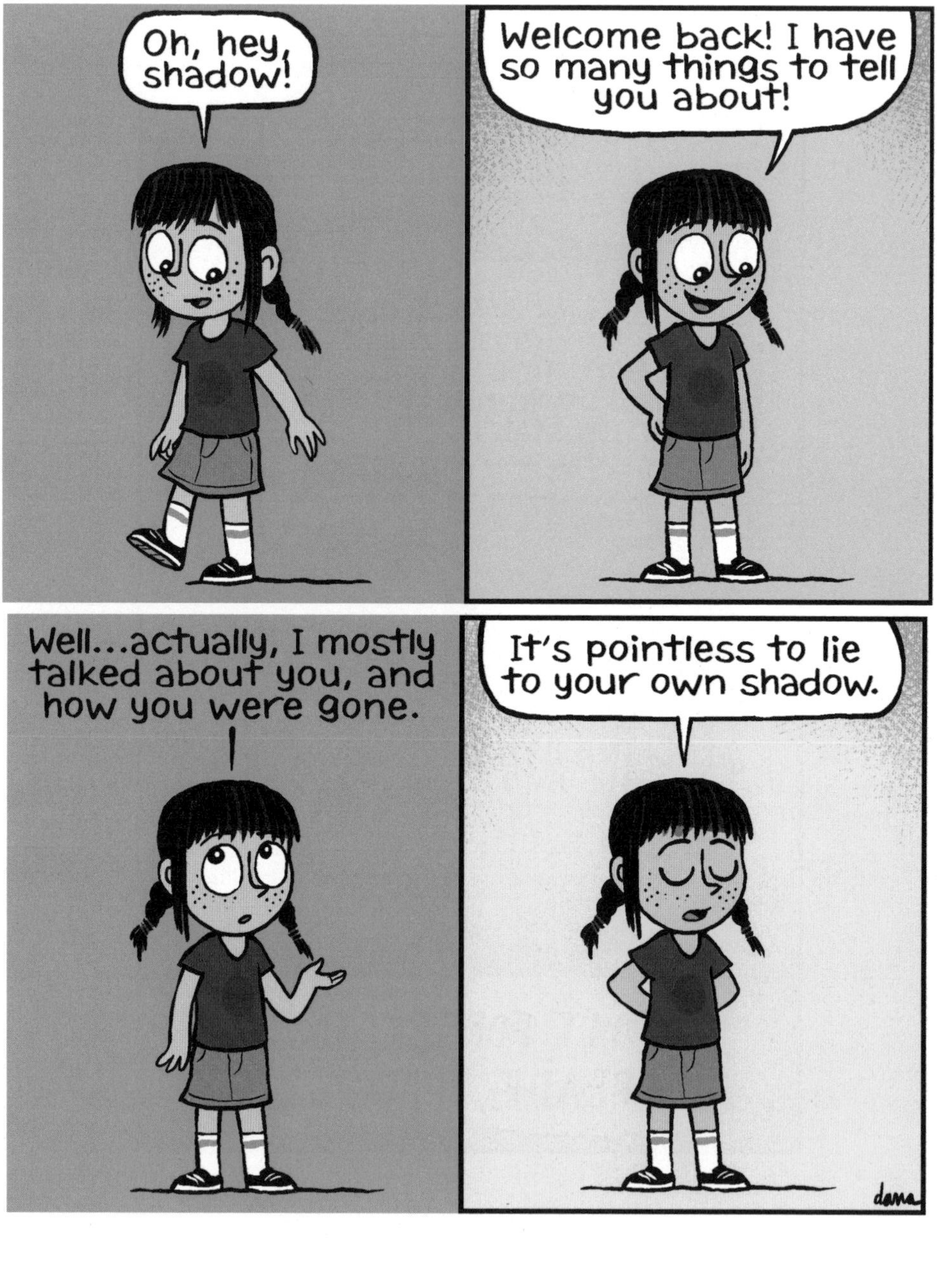
Oh, hey, shadow!
Welcome back! I have so many things to tell you about!
Well...actually, I mostly talked about you, and how you were gone.
It's pointless to lie to your own shadow.
dana

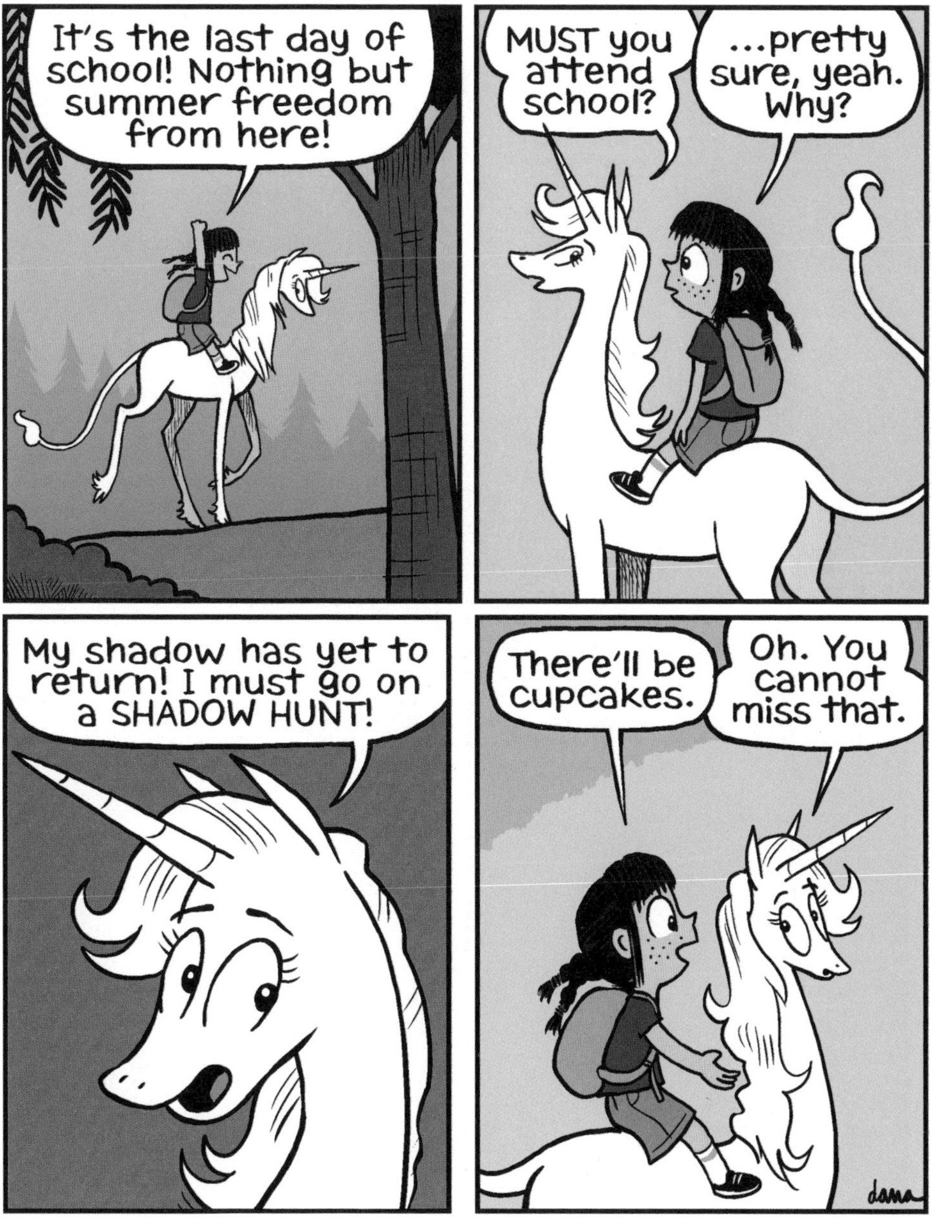
It's the last day of school! Nothing but summer freedom from here!
MUST you attend school?
...pretty sure, yeah. Why?
My shadow has yet to return! I must go on a SHADOW HUNT!
There'll be cupcakes.
Oh. You cannot miss that.
dana

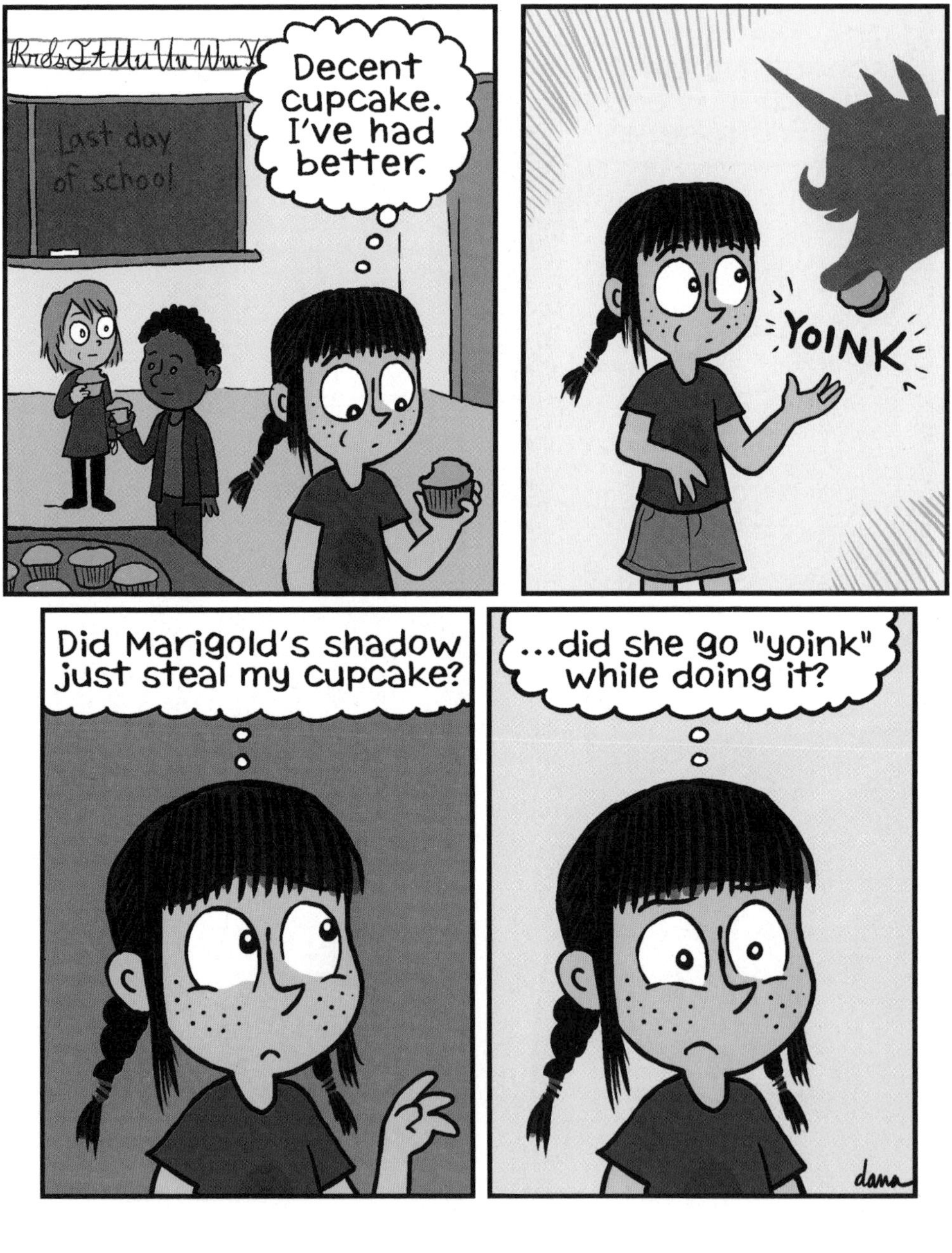
Last day of school!
Decent cupcake. I've had better.
YOINK
Did Marigold's shadow just steal my cupcake?
...did she go "yoink" while doing it?

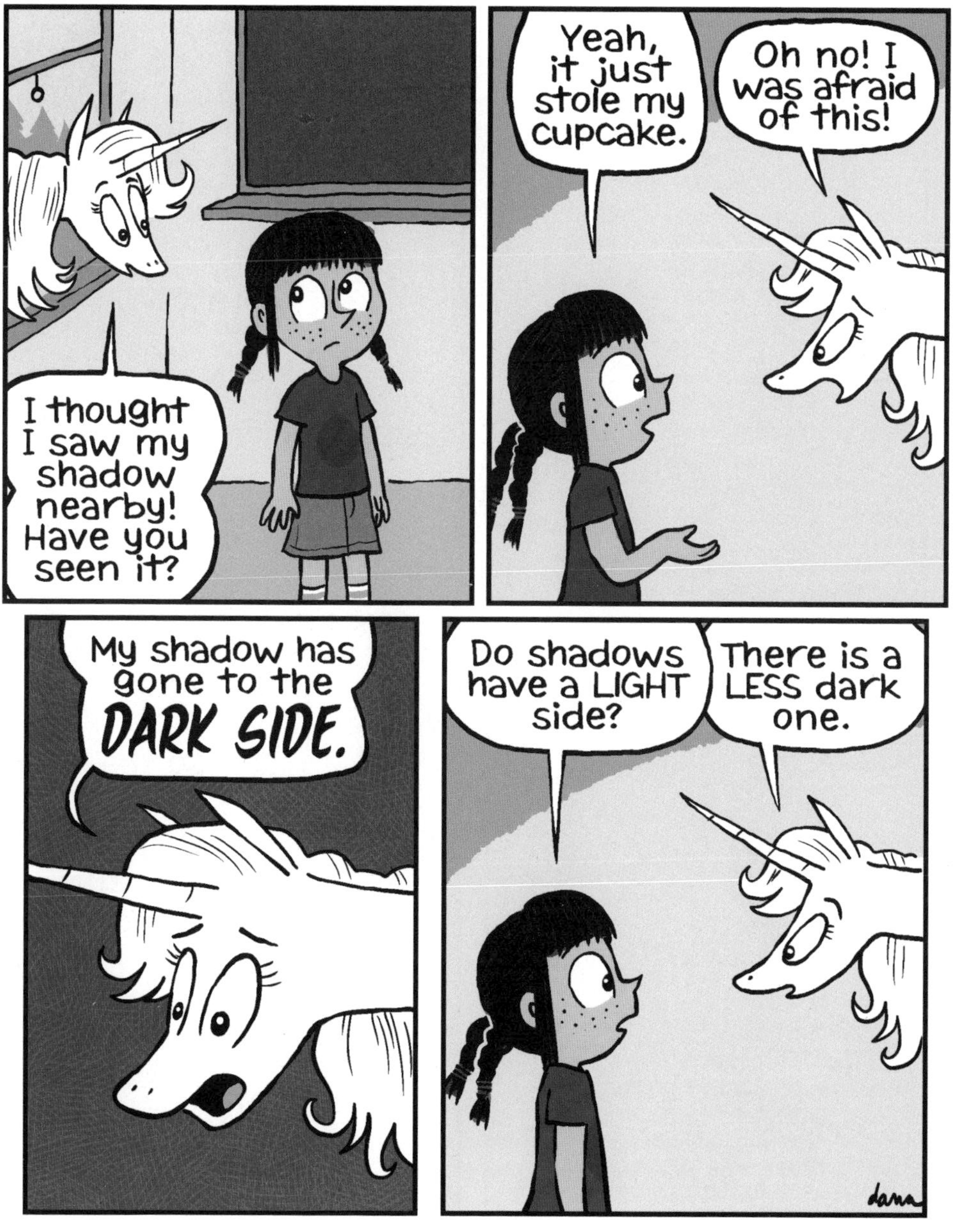
I thought I saw my shadow nearby! Have you seen it?
Yeah, it just stole my cupcake.
Oh no! I was afraid of this!
My shadow has gone to the DARK SIDE.
Do shadows have a LIGHT side?
There is a LESS dark one.
dana

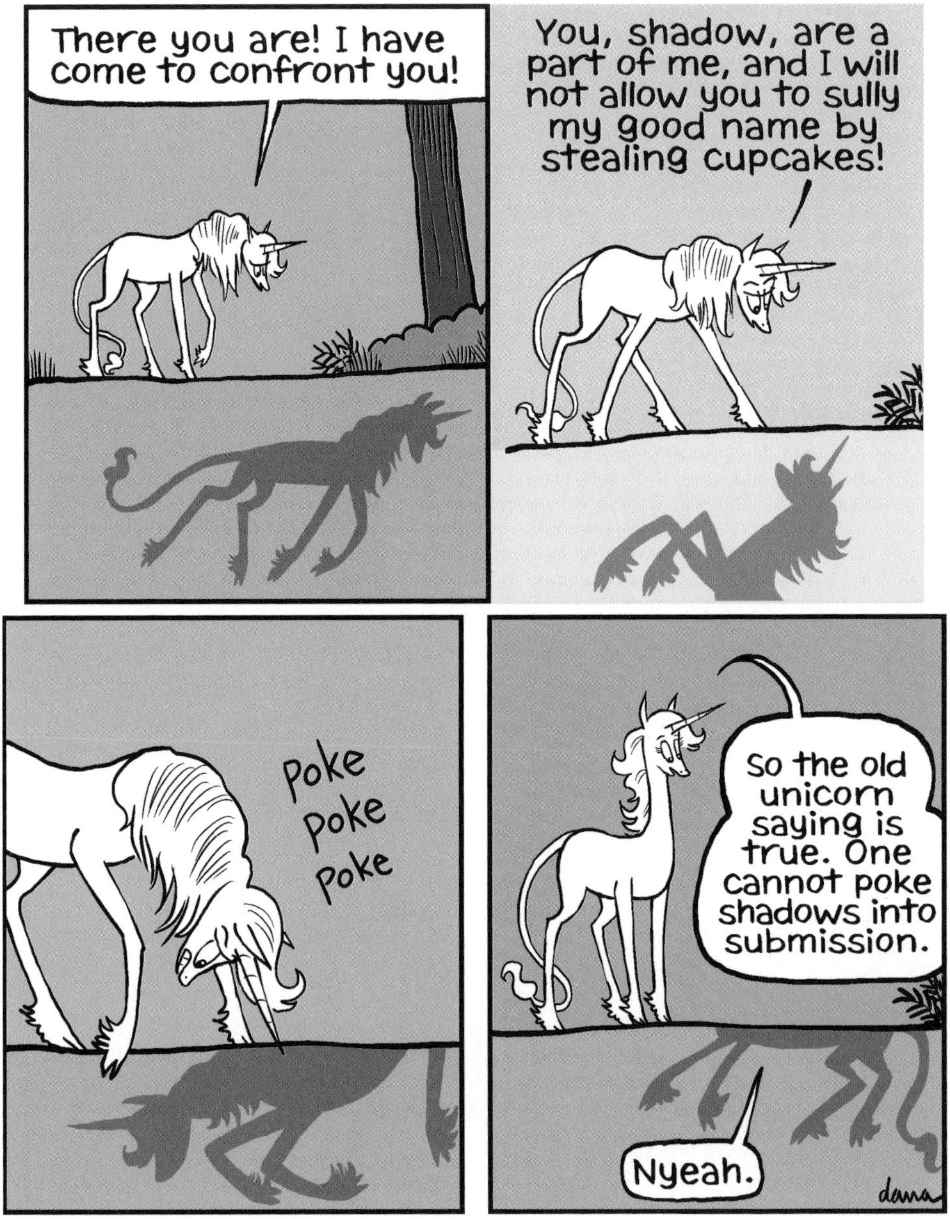
There you are! I have come to confront you!
You, shadow, are a part of me, and I will not allow you to sully my good name by stealing cupcakes!
poke poke poke
So the old unicorn saying is true. One cannot poke shadows into submission.
Nyeah.
dana

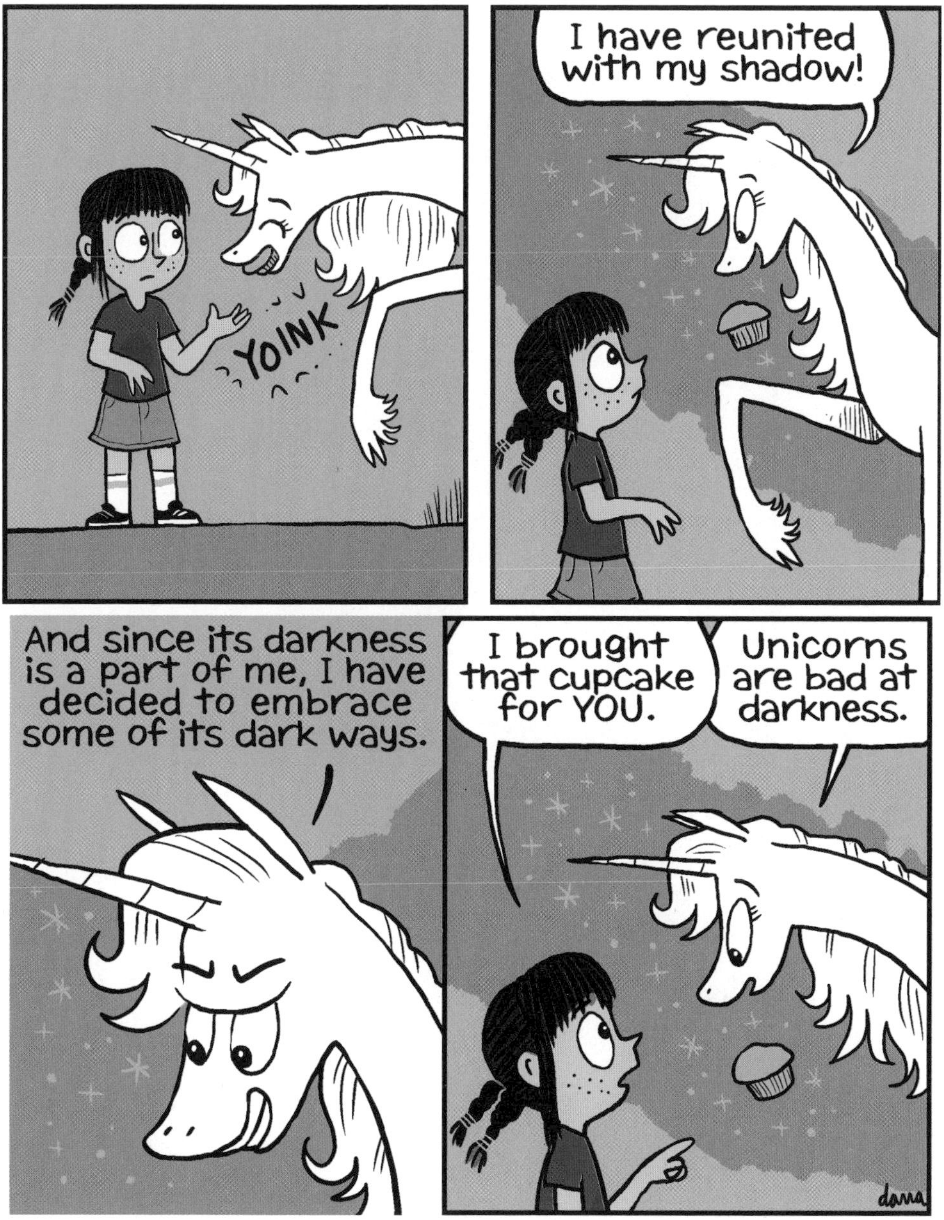
YOINK
I have reunited with my shadow!
And since its darkness is a part of me, I have decided to embrace some of its dark ways.
I brought that cupcake for YOU.
Unicorns are bad at darkness.
dana

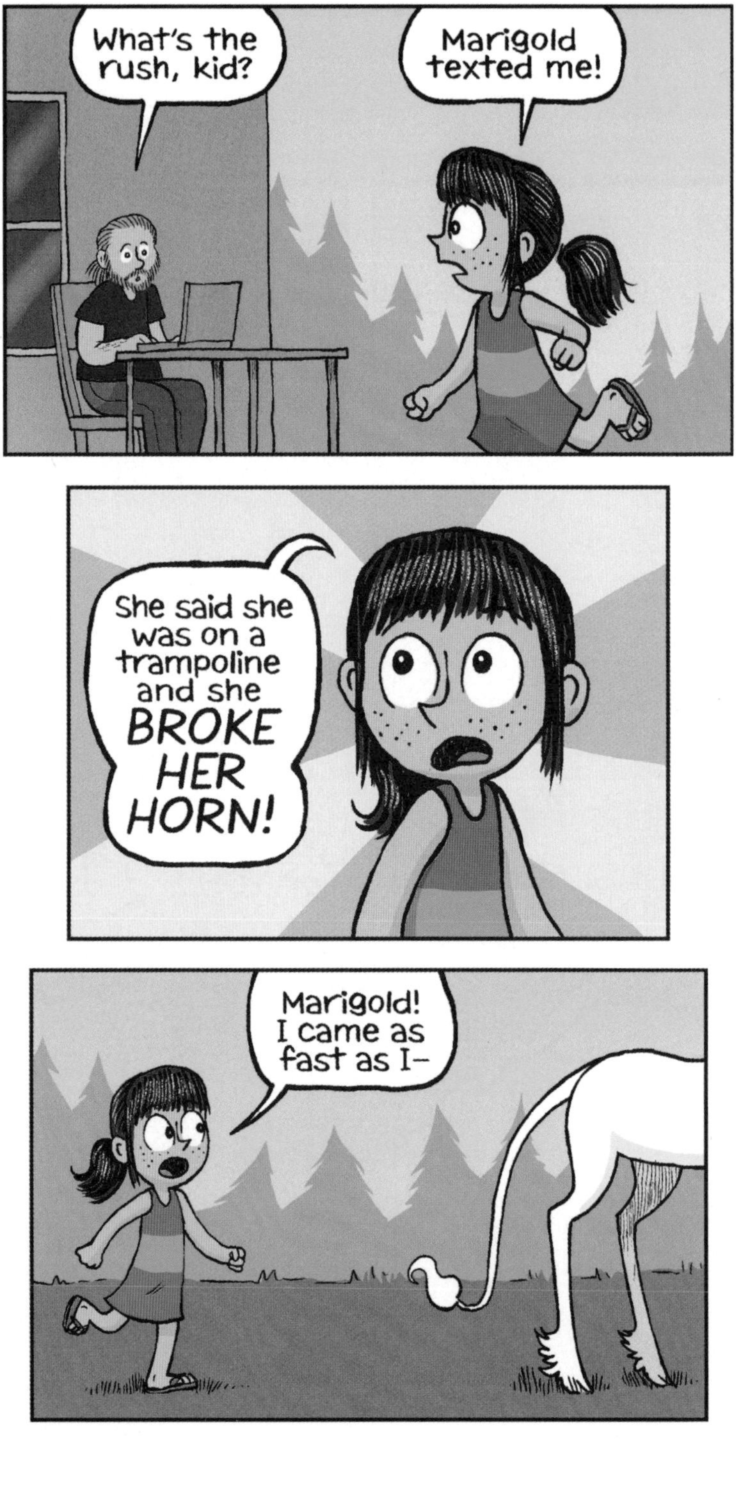
What's the rush, kid?
Marigold texted me!
She said she was on a trampoline and she BROKE HER HORN!
Marigold! I came as fast as I-

You didn't say it was a FRENCH horn.
It must have slipped my mind.
I don't know what question to ask first.
As if YOU have never played a French horn concerto while jumping on a trampoline.

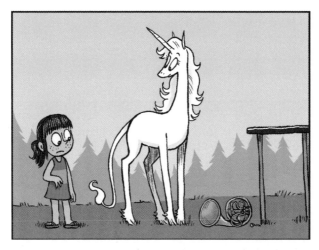

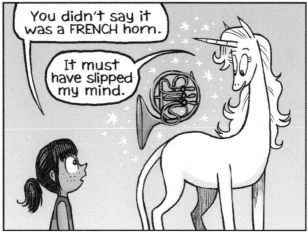

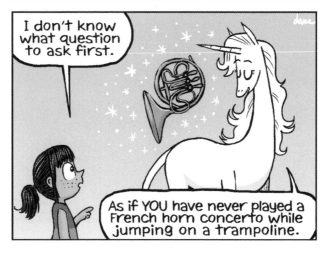

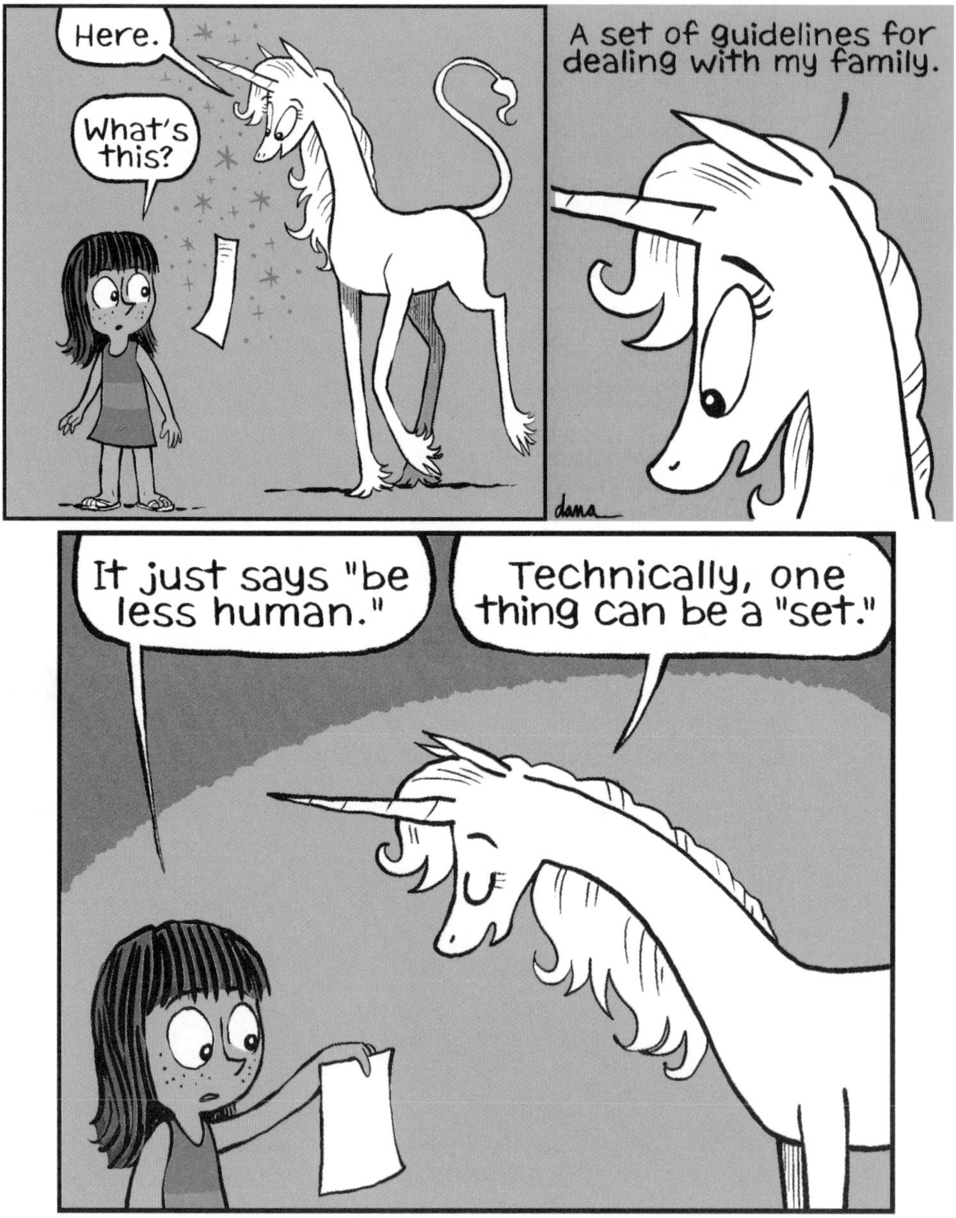
Here.
What's this?
A set of guidelines for dealing with my family.
dana
It just says "be less human."
Technically, one thing can be a "set."

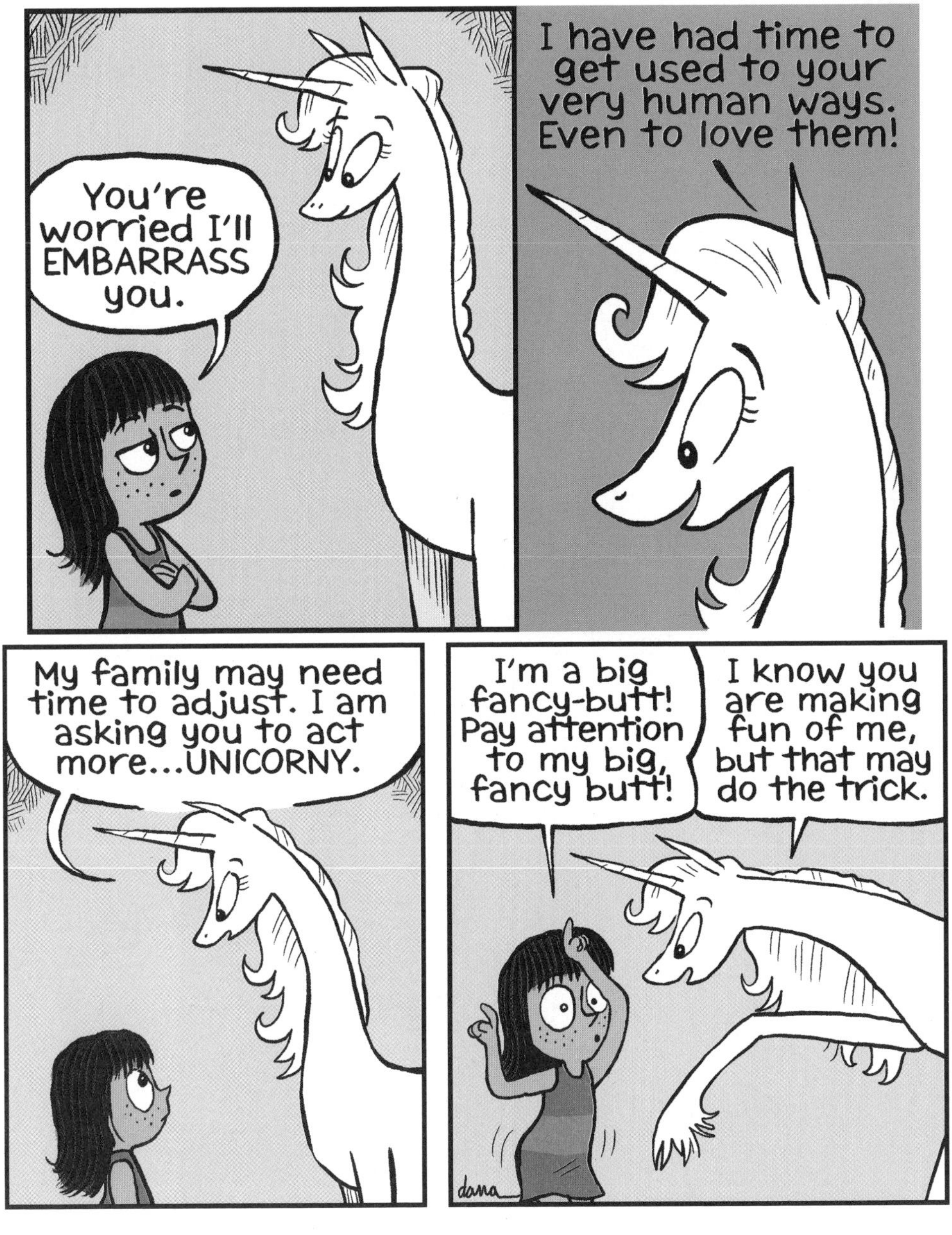
You're worried I'll EMBARRASS you.
I have had time to get used to your very human ways. Even to love them!
My family may need time to adjust. I am asking you to act more...UNICORNY.
I'm a big fancy-butt! Pay attention to my big, fancy butt!
I know you are making fun of me, but that may do the trick.
dana

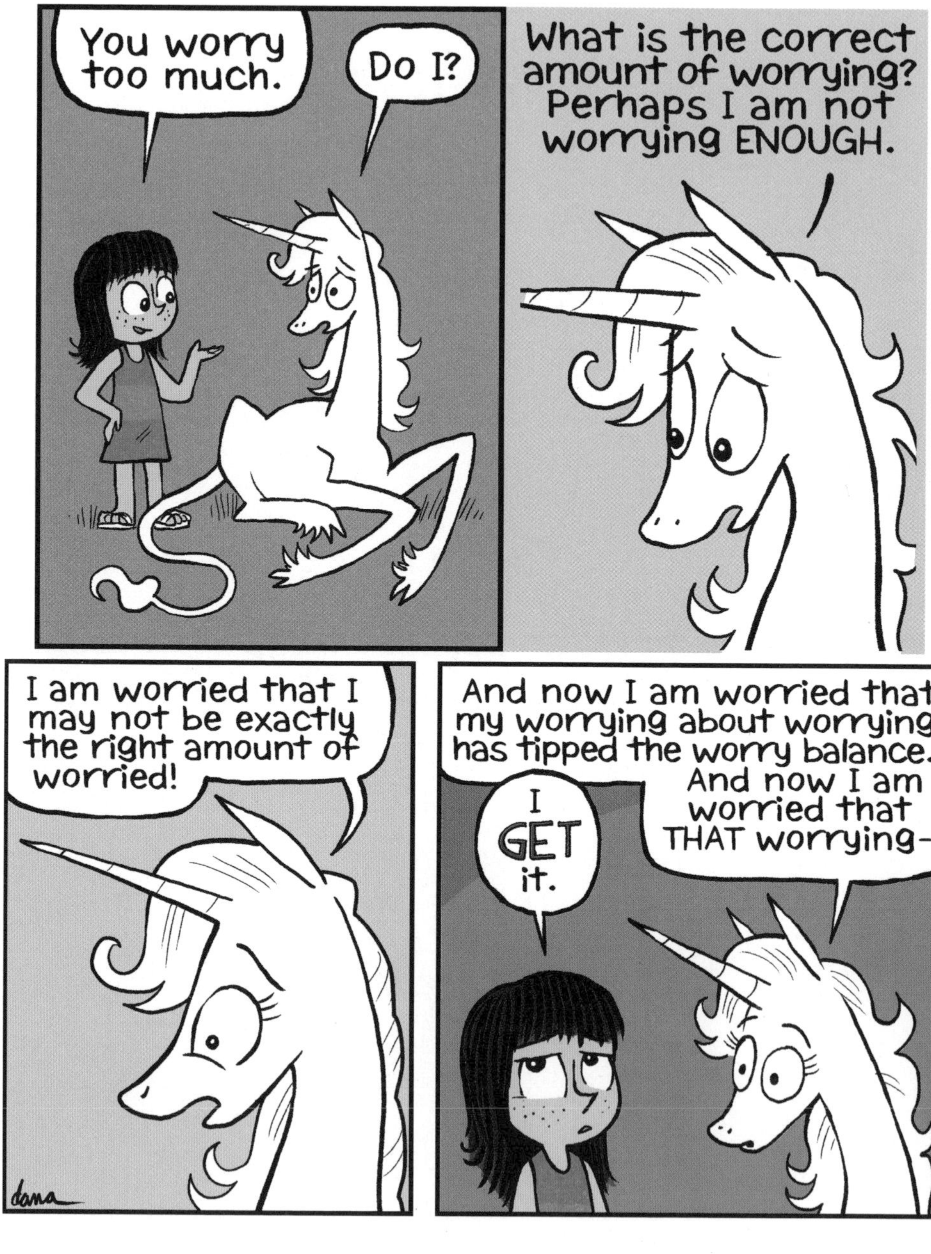
You worry too much.
Do I?
What is the correct amount of worrying? Perhaps I am not worrying ENOUGH.
I am worried that I may not be exactly the right amount of worried!
dana
And now I am worried that my worrying about worrying has tipped the worry balance.
And now I am worried that THAT worrying-
I GET it.

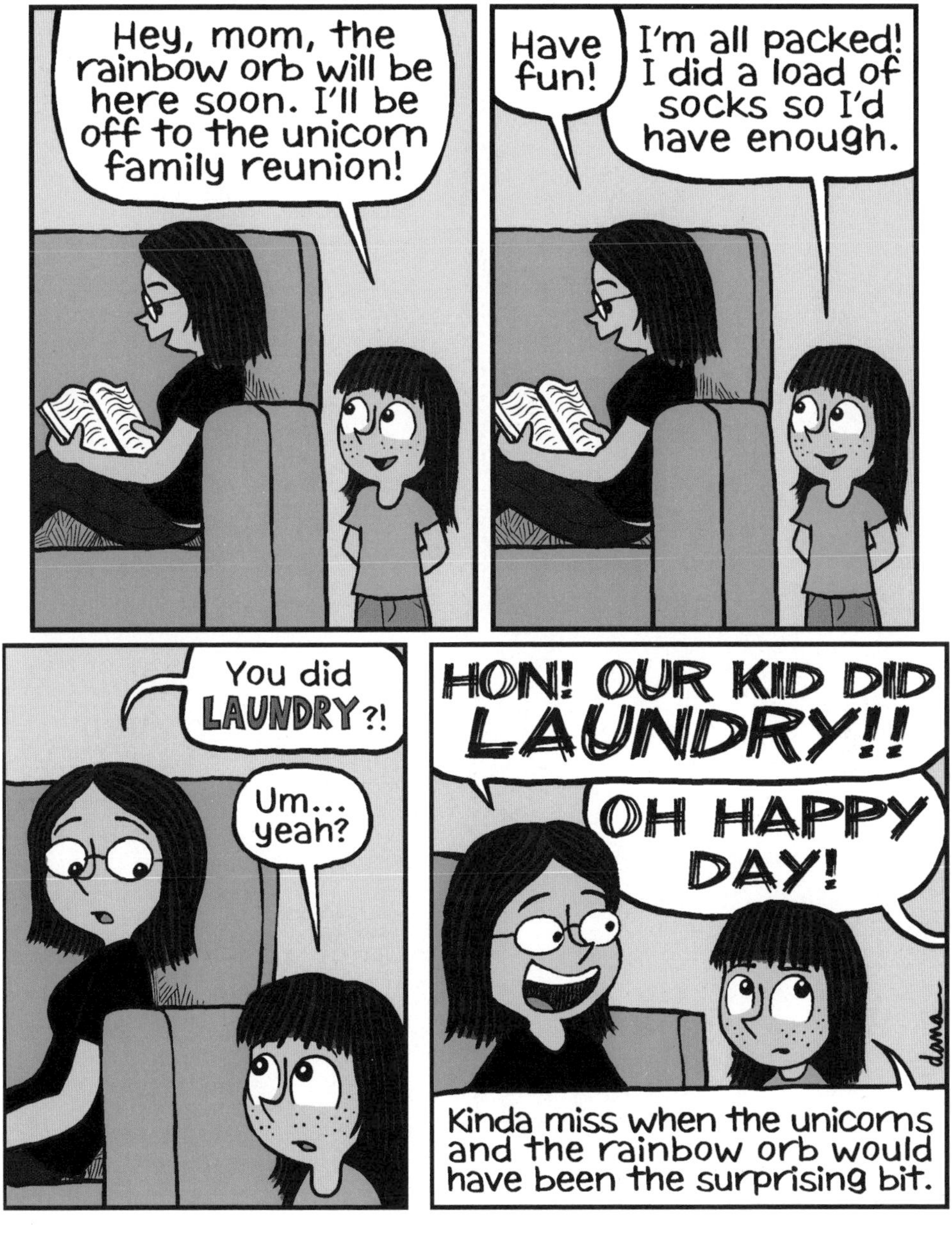
Hey, mom, the rainbow orb will be here soon. I'll be off to the unicorn family reunion!
Have fun!
I'm all packed! I did a load of socks so I'd have enough.
You did LAUNDRY?!
Um... yeah?
HON! OUR KID DID LAUNDRY!!
OH HAPPY DAY!
dana
Kinda miss when the unicorns and the rainbow orb would have been the surprising bit.

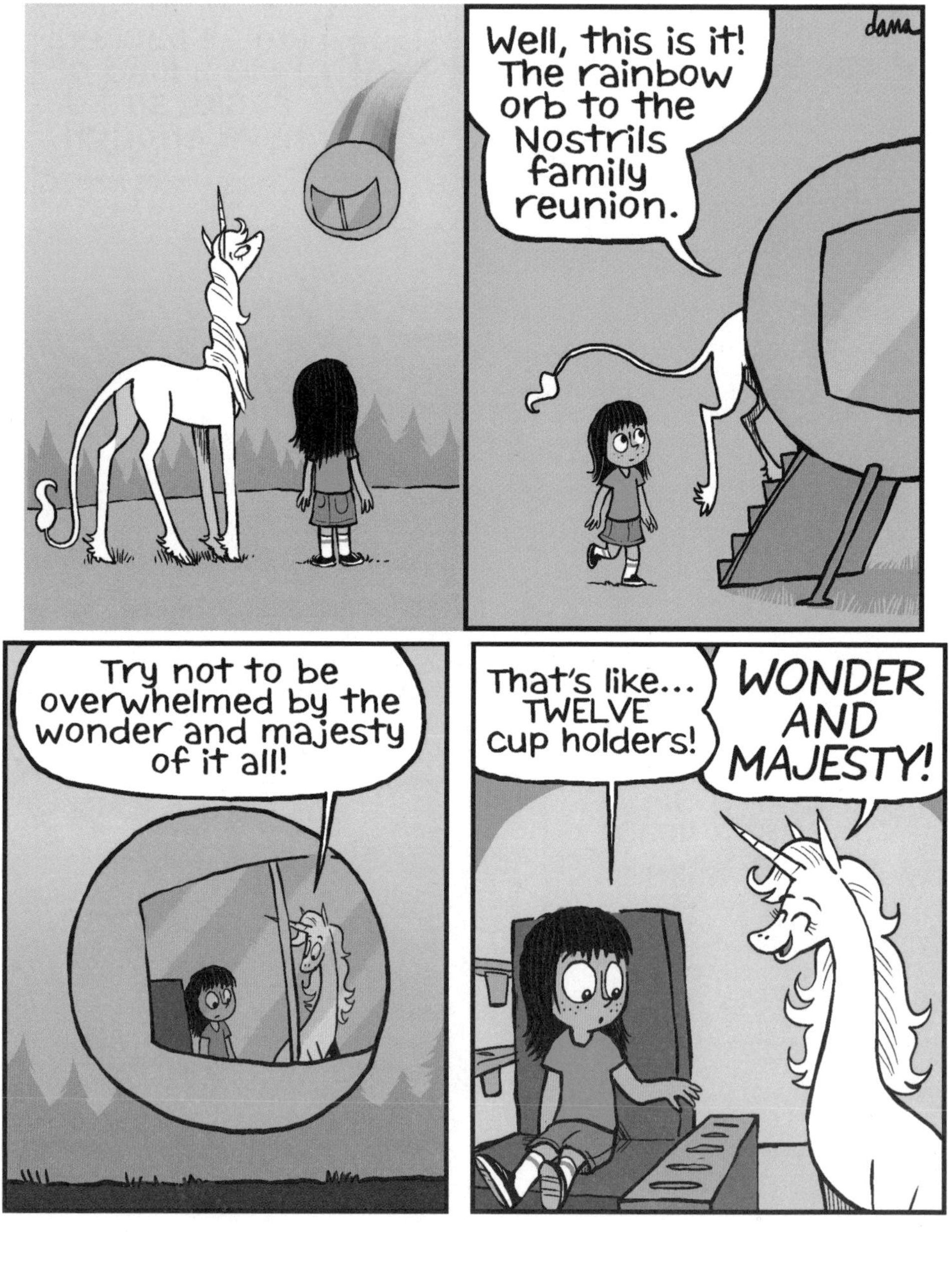
dana
Well, this is it! The rainbow orb to the Nostrils family reunion.
Try not to be overwhelmed by the wonder and majesty of it all!
That's like... TWELVE cup holders!
WONDER AND MAJESTY!

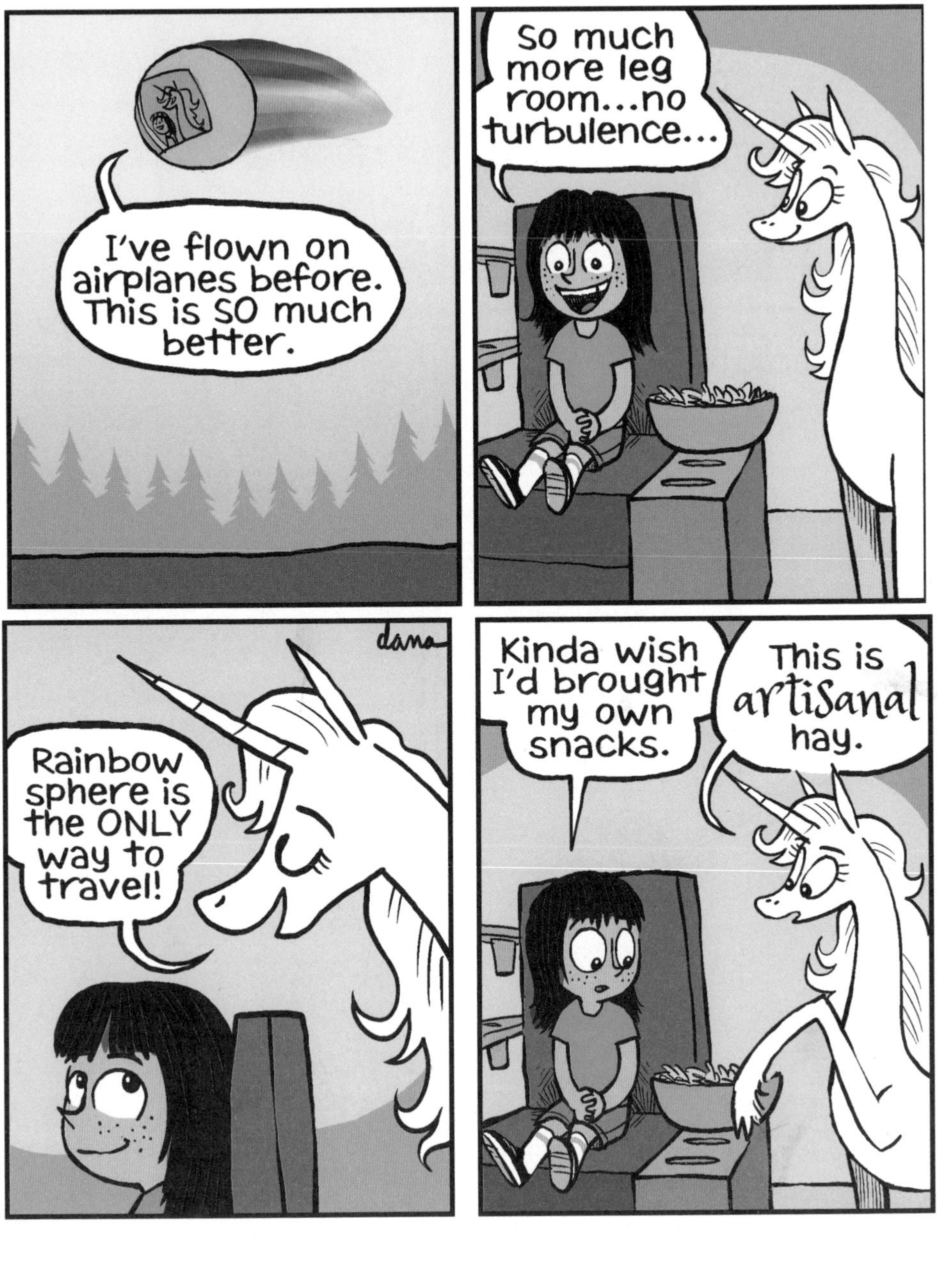
I've flown on airplanes before. This is SO much better.
So much more leg room...no turbulence...
dana
Rainbow sphere is the ONLY way to travel!
Kinda wish I'd brought my own snacks.
This is artisanal hay.

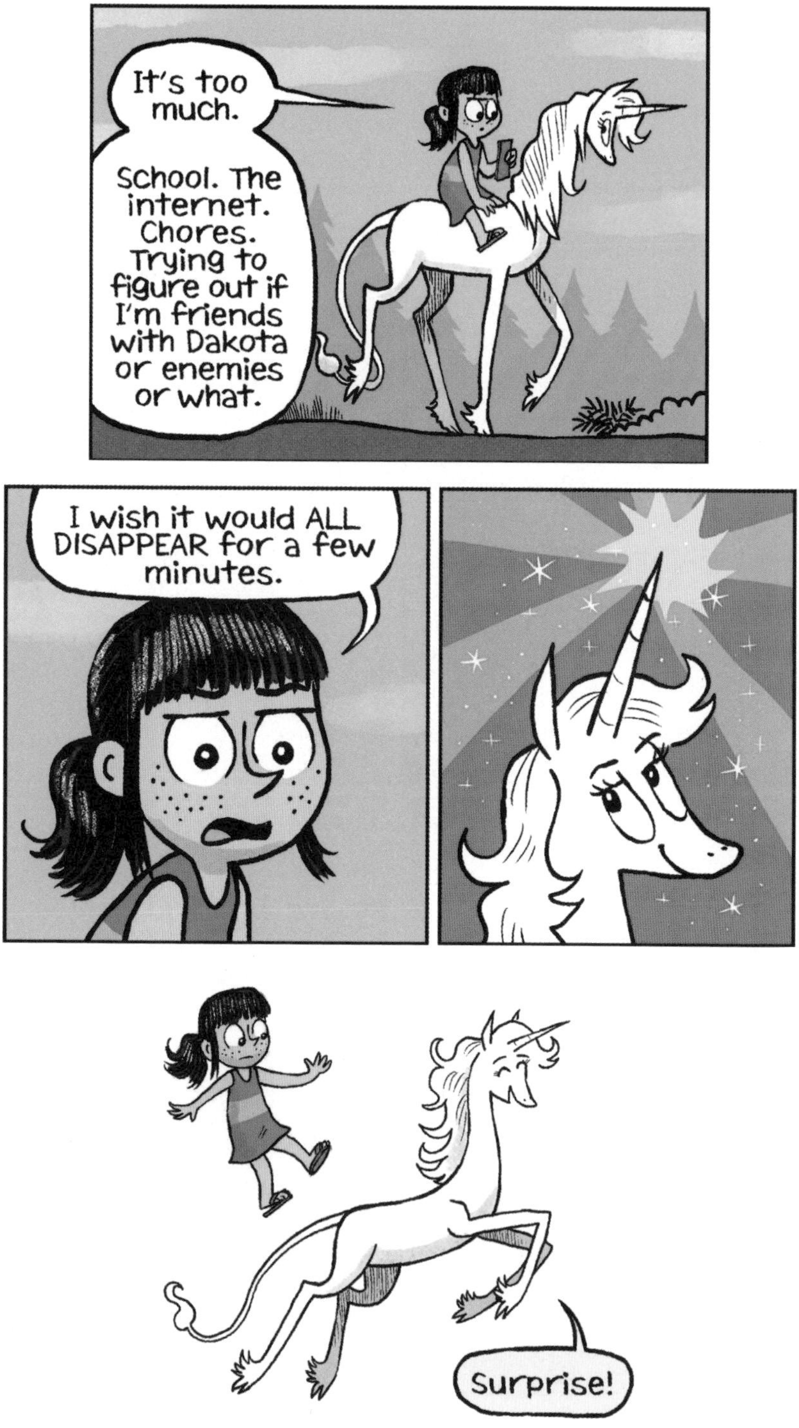
It's too much.
School. The internet. Chores. Trying to figure out if I'm friends with Dakota or enemies or what.
I wish it would ALL DISAPPEAR for a few minutes.
Surprise!

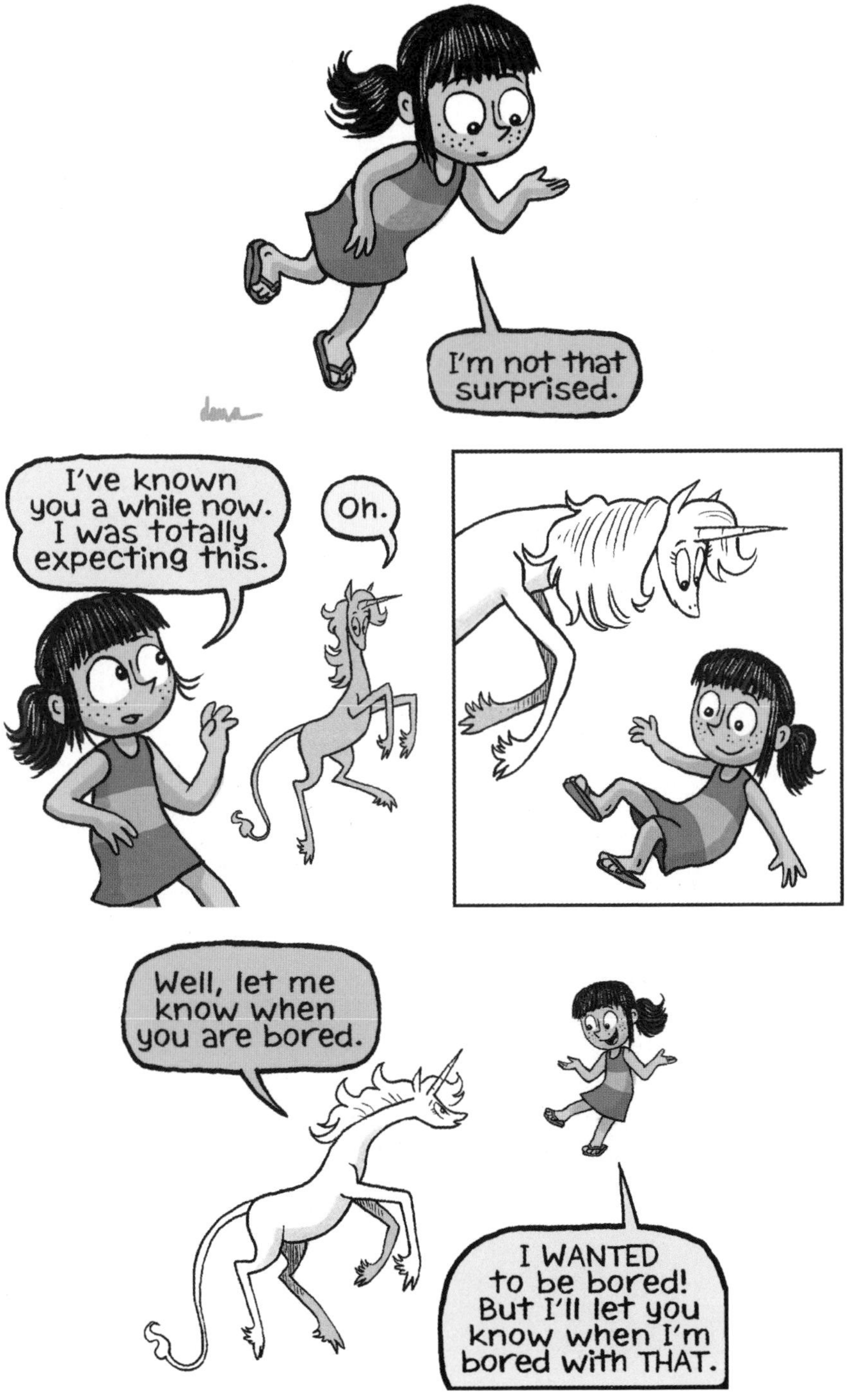
I'm not that surprised.
I've known you a while now. I was totally expecting this.
Oh.
Well, let me know when you are bored.
I WANTED to be bored! But I'll let you know when I'm bored with THAT.

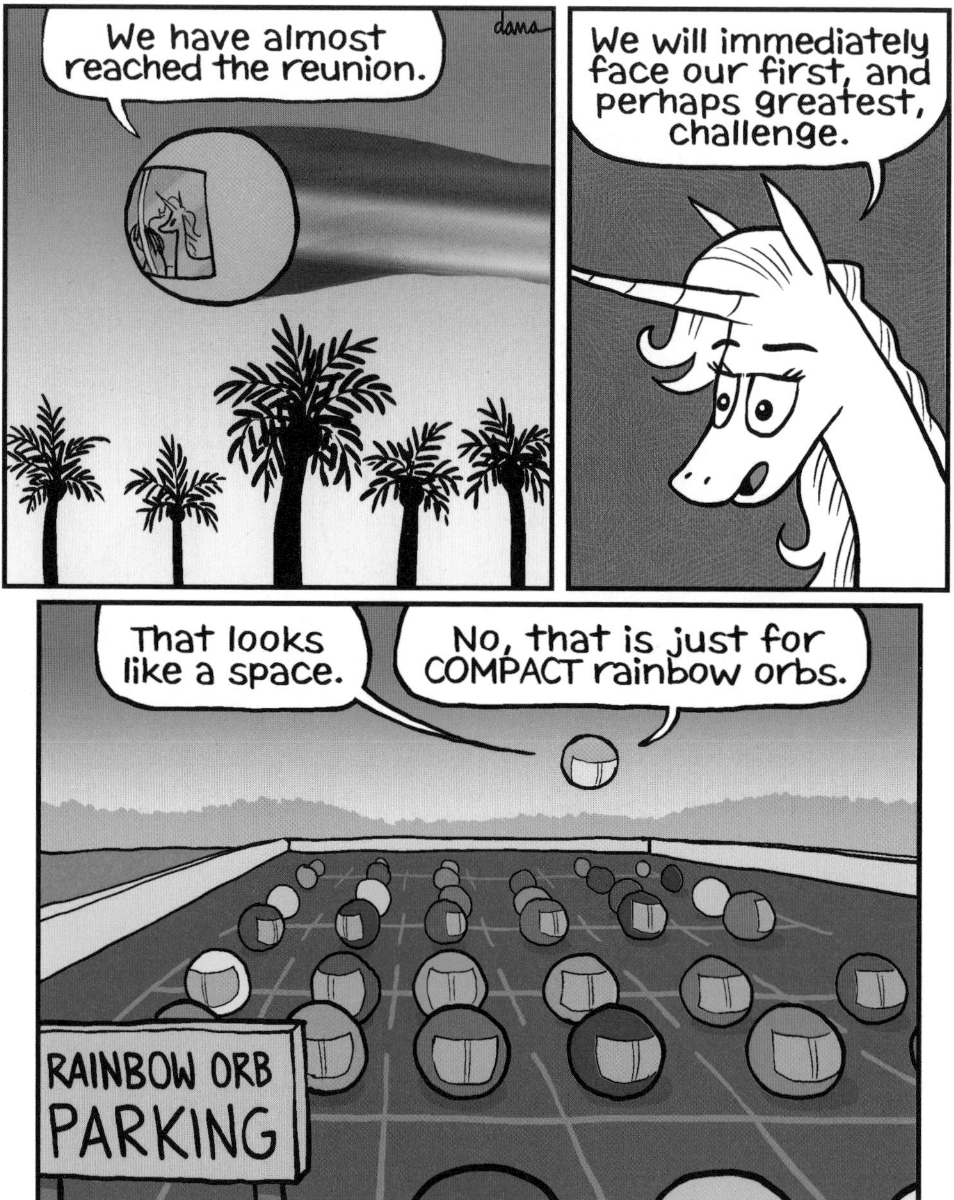

We have almost reached the reunion.
dana
We will immediately face our first, and perhaps greatest, challenge.
That looks like a space.
No, that is just for COMPACT rainbow orbs.
RAINBOW ORB PARKING

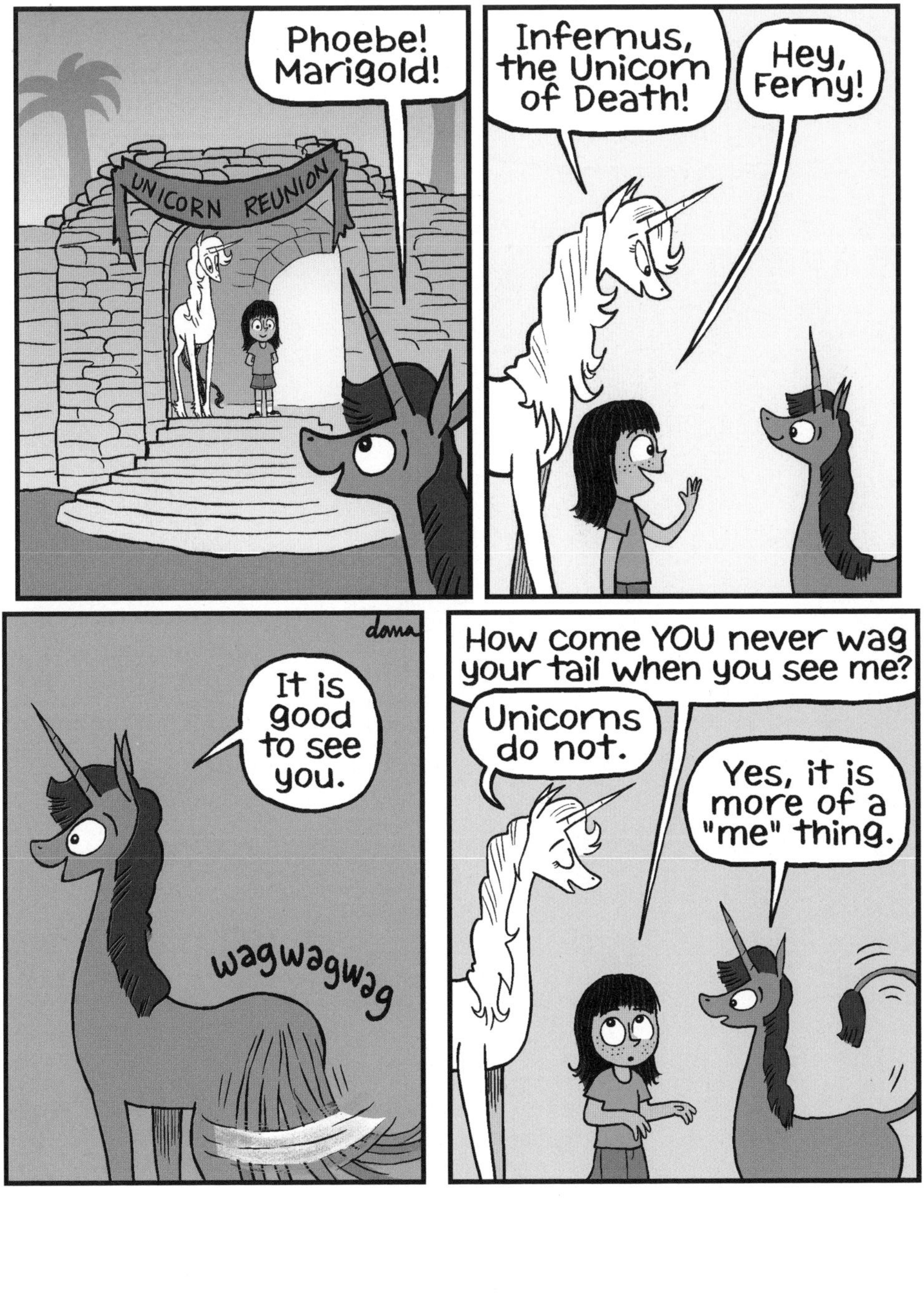
Phoebe! Marigold!
UNICORN REUNION
Infernus, the Unicorn of Death!
Hey, Ferny!
dana
It is good to see you.
wagwagwag
How come YOU never wag your tail when you see me?
Unicorns do not.
Yes, it is more of a "me" thing.

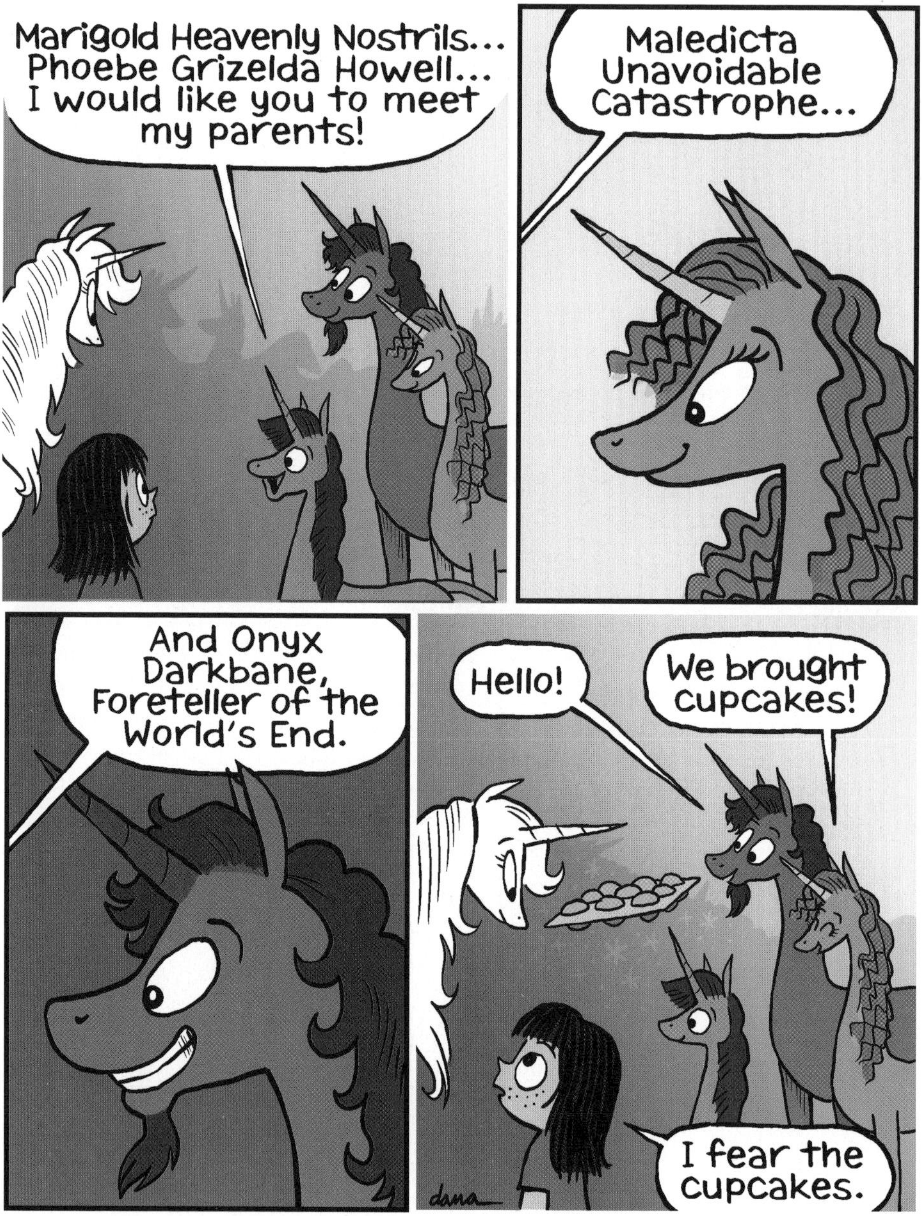
Marigold Heavenly Nostrils... Phoebe Grizelda Howell... I would like you to meet my parents!
Maledicta Unavoidable Catastrophe...
And Onyx Darkbane, Foreteller of the World's End.
Hello!
We brought cupcakes!
I fear the cupcakes.
dana

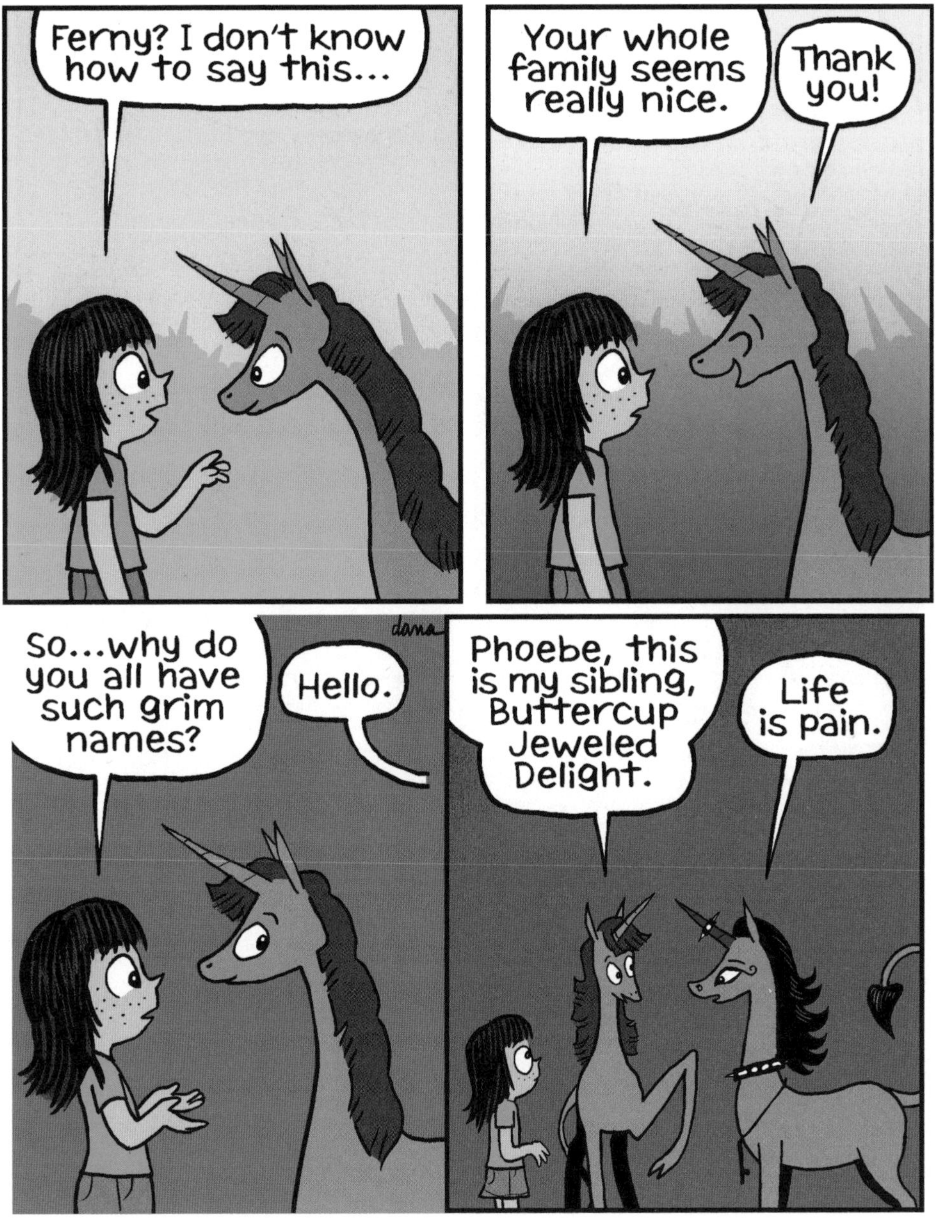
Ferny? I don't know how to say this...
Your whole family seems really nice.
Thank you!
So...why do you all have such grim names?
Hello.
Phoebe, this is my sibling, Buttercup Jeweled Delight.
Life is pain.
dana

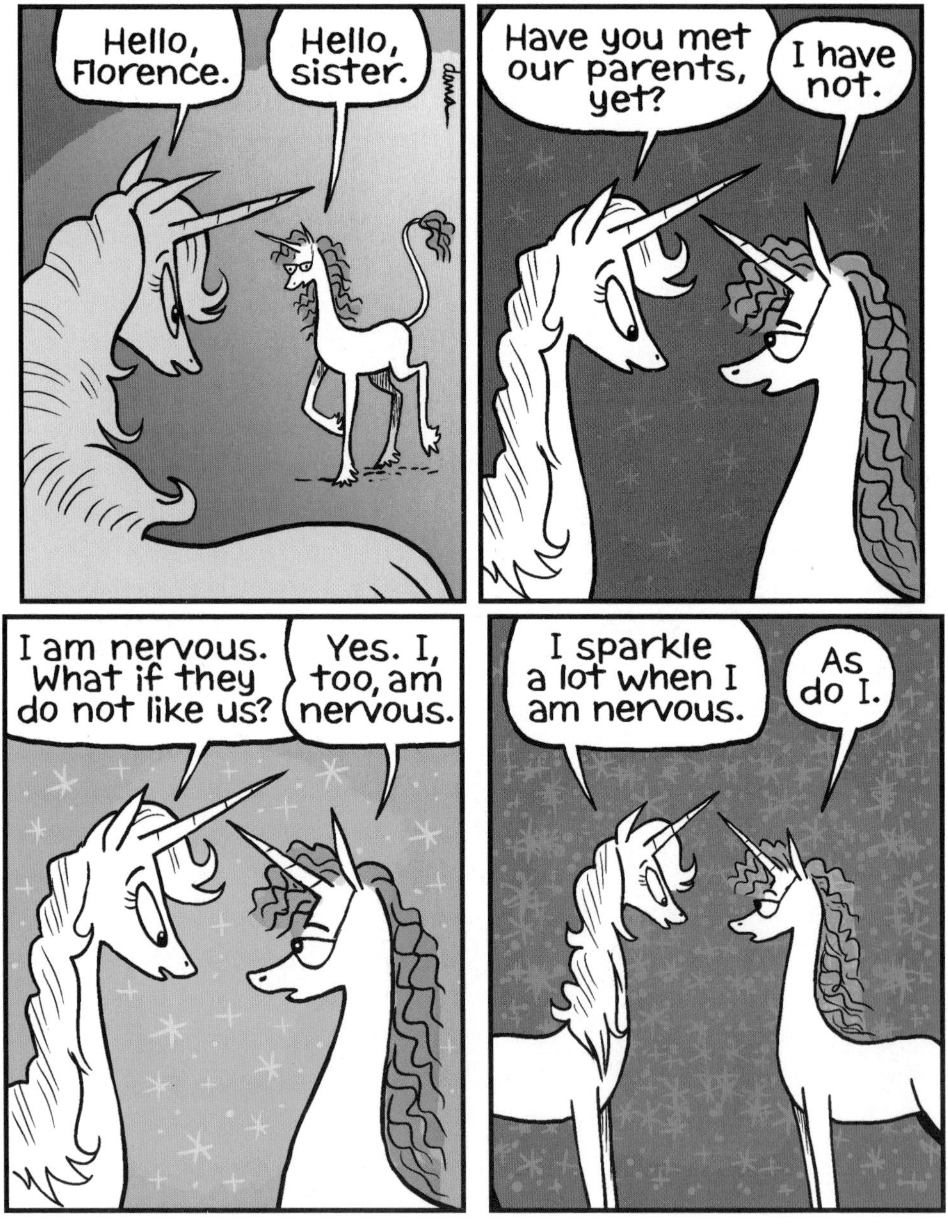
Hello, Florence.
Hello, sister.
Have you met our parents, yet?
I have not.
I am nervous. What if they do not like us?
Yes. I, too, am nervous.
I sparkle a lot when I am nervous.
As do I.

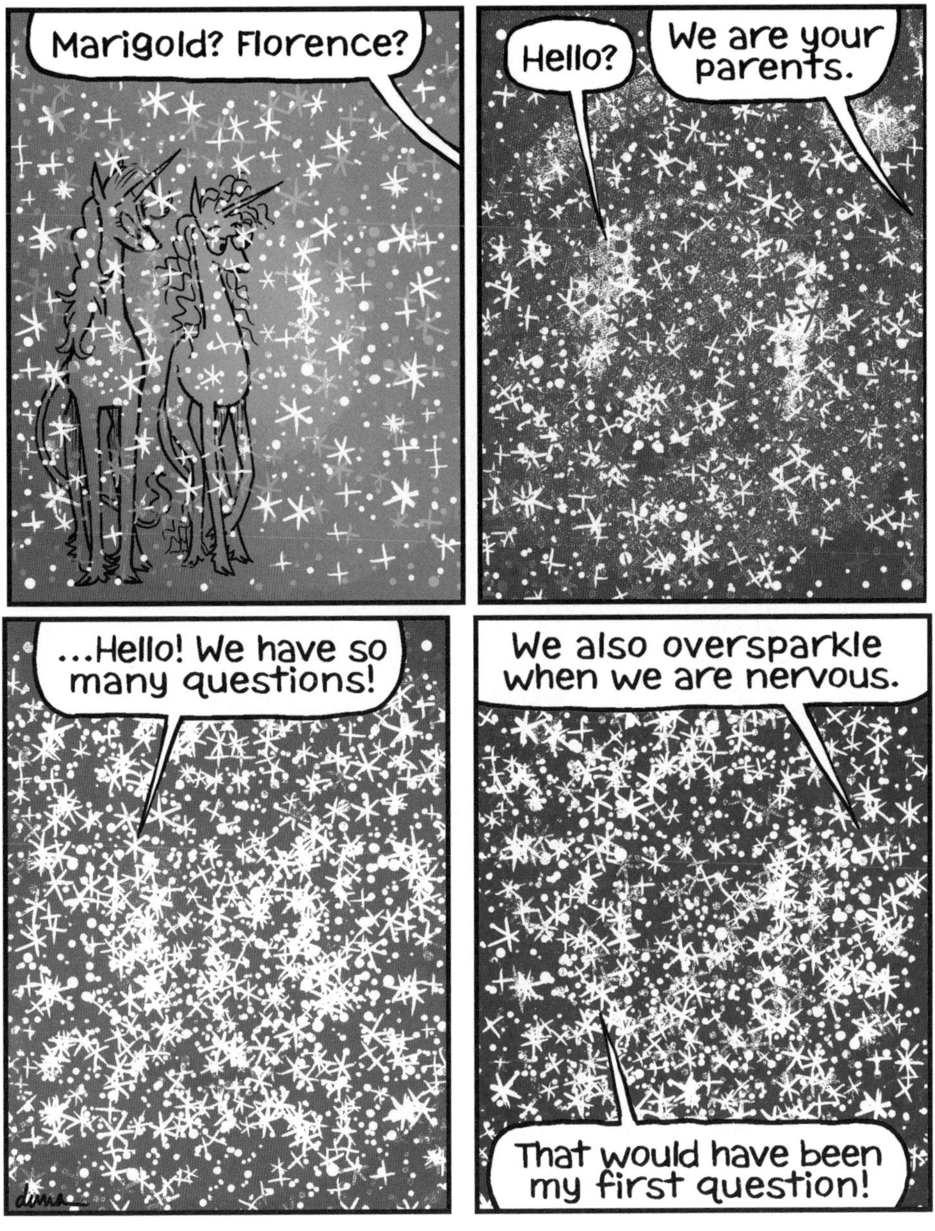
Marigold? Florence?
Hello?
We are your parents.
...Hello! We have so many questions!
We also oversparkle when we are nervous.
That would have been my first question!

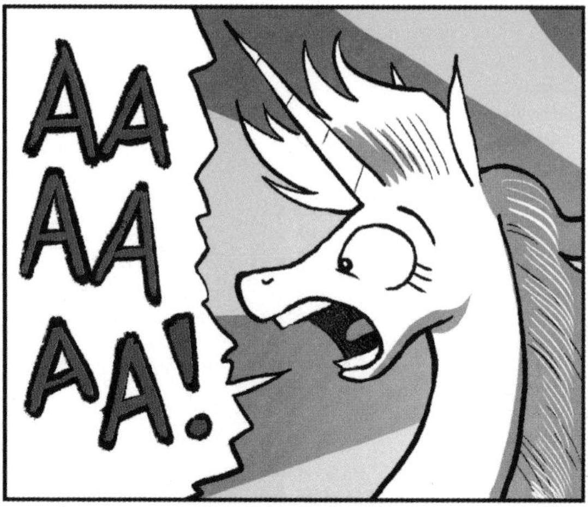
AAAAAA!

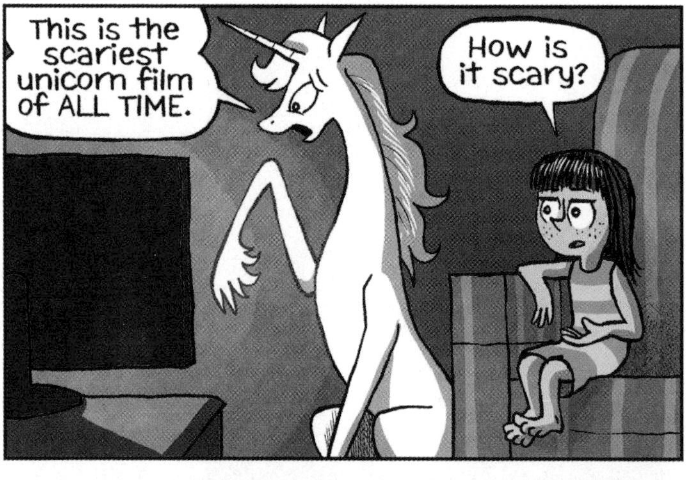
This is the scariest unicorn film of ALL TIME.
How is it scary?

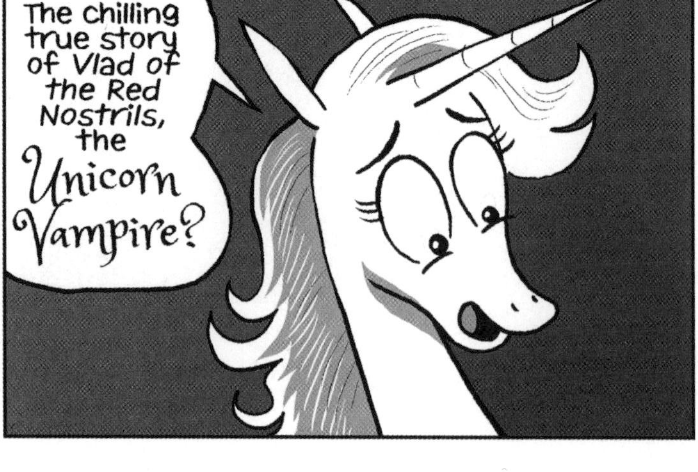
The chilling true story of Vlad of the Red Nostrils, the Unicorn Vampire?

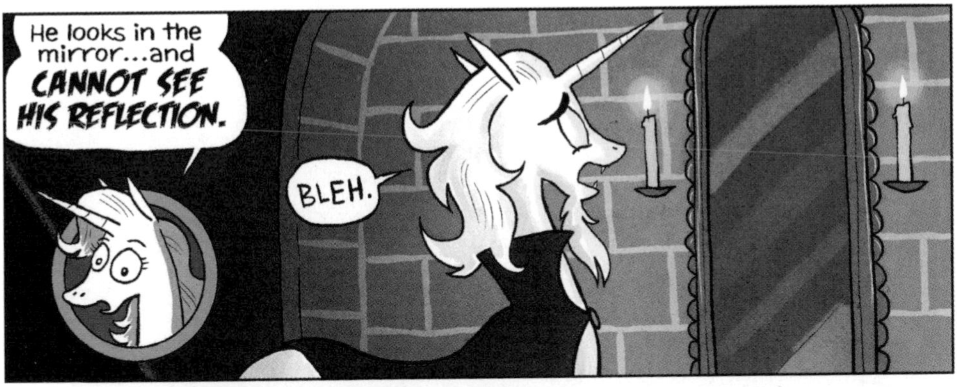
He looks in the mirror...and **CANNOT SEE HIS REFLECTION.**
BLEH.

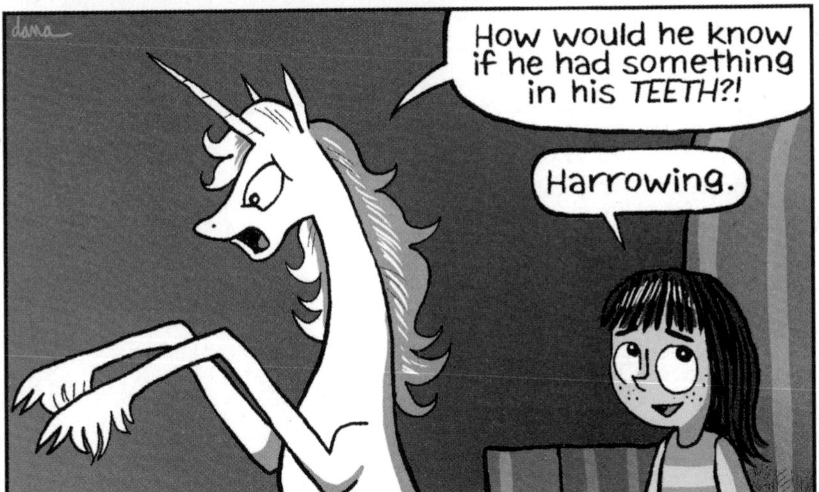
dana
How would he know if he had something in his *TEETH*?!
Harrowing.

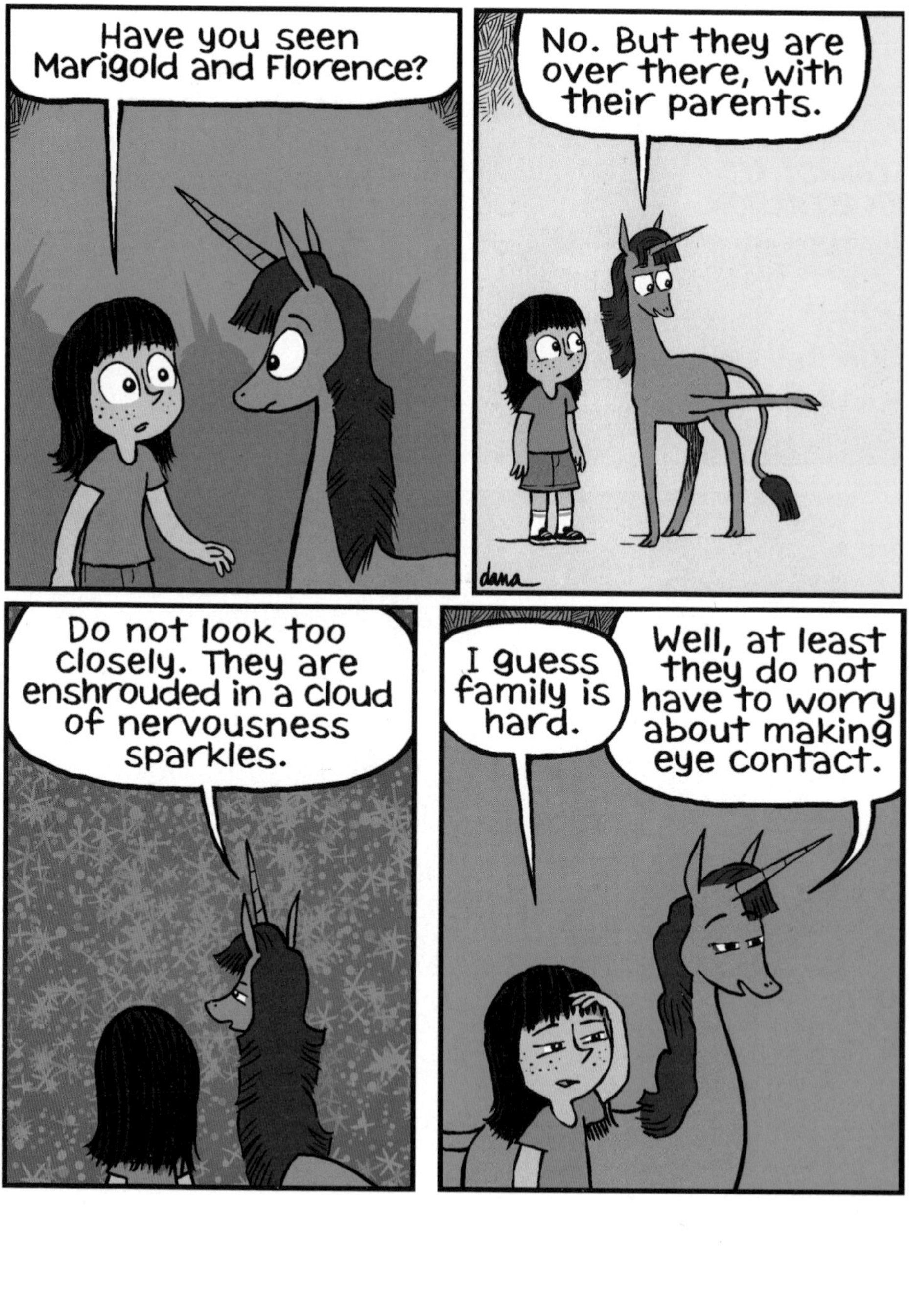
Have you seen Marigold and Florence?
No. But they are over there, with their parents.
dana
Do not look too closely. They are enshrouded in a cloud of nervousness sparkles.
I guess family is hard.
Well, at least they do not have to worry about making eye contact.

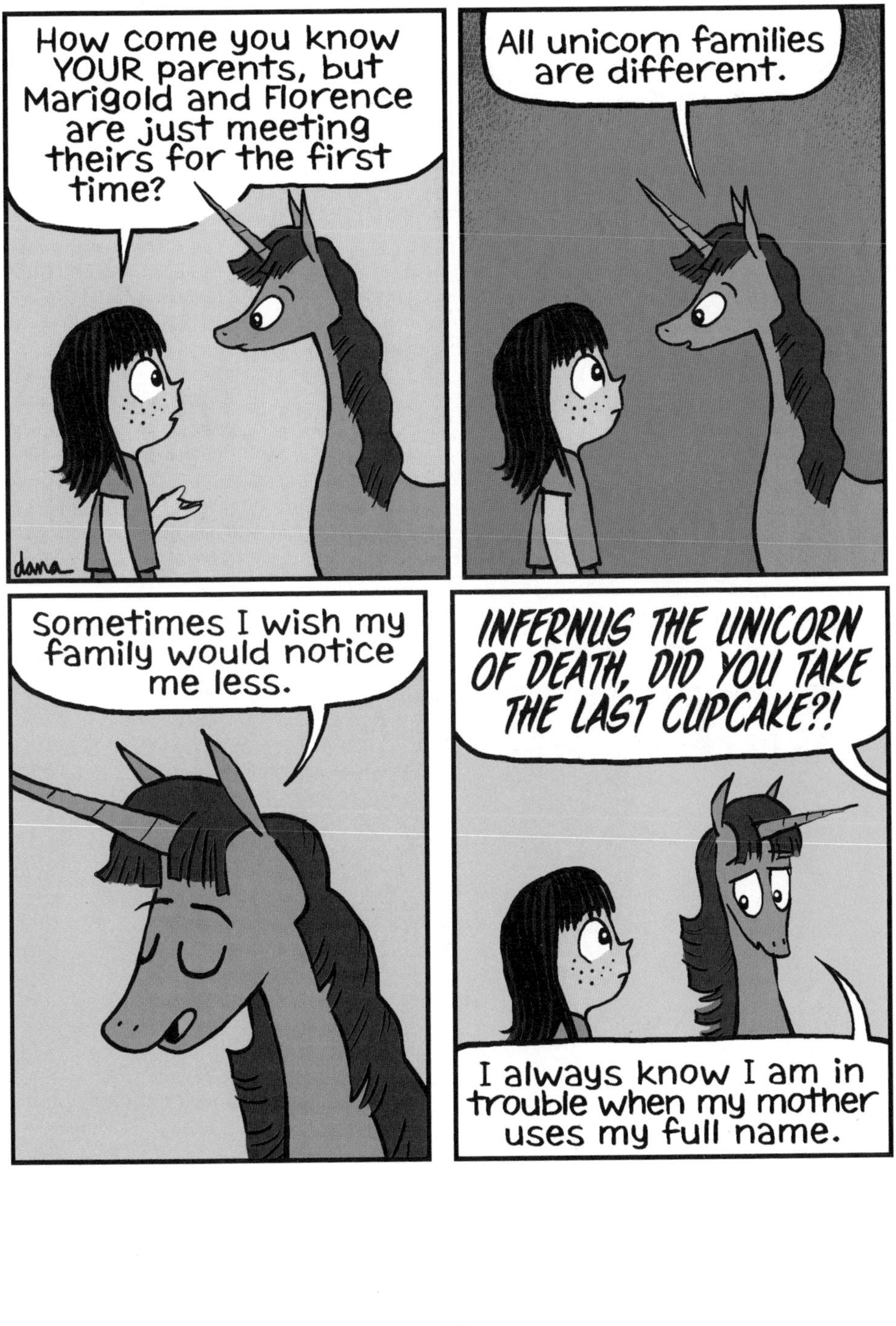
How come you know YOUR parents, but Marigold and Florence are just meeting theirs for the first time?
dana
All unicorn families are different.
Sometimes I wish my family would notice me less.
INFERNUS THE UNICORN OF DEATH, DID YOU TAKE THE LAST CUPCAKE?!
I always know I am in trouble when my mother uses my full name.

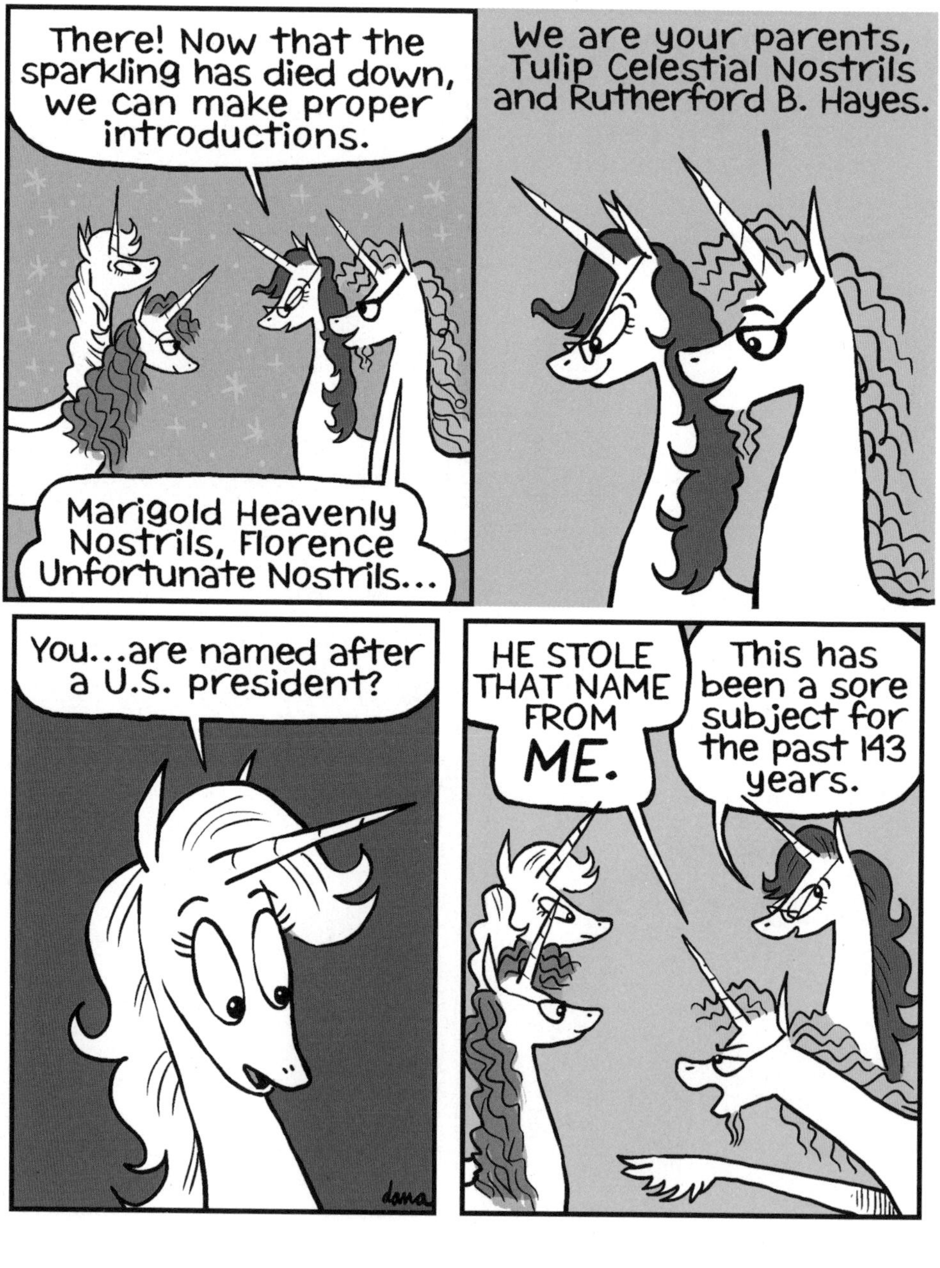
There! Now that the sparkling has died down, we can make proper introductions.
Marigold Heavenly Nostrils, Florence Unfortunate Nostrils...
We are your parents, Tulip Celestial Nostrils and Rutherford B. Hayes.
You...are named after a U.S. president?
HE STOLE THAT NAME FROM ME.
This has been a sore subject for the past 143 years.
dana

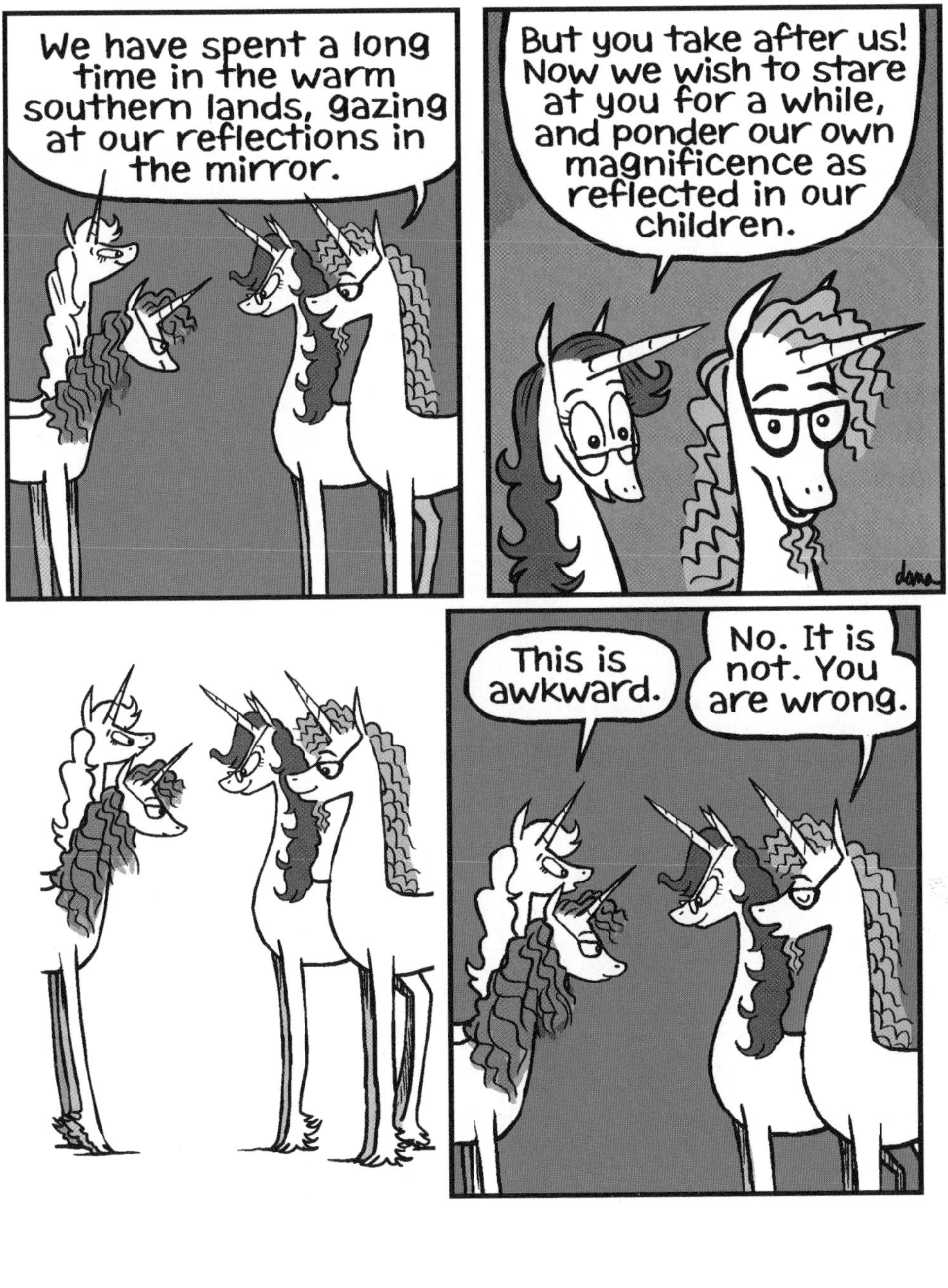
We have spent a long time in the warm southern lands, gazing at our reflections in the mirror.
But you take after us! Now we wish to stare at you for a while, and ponder our own magnificence as reflected in our children.
dana
This is awkward.
No. It is not. You are wrong.

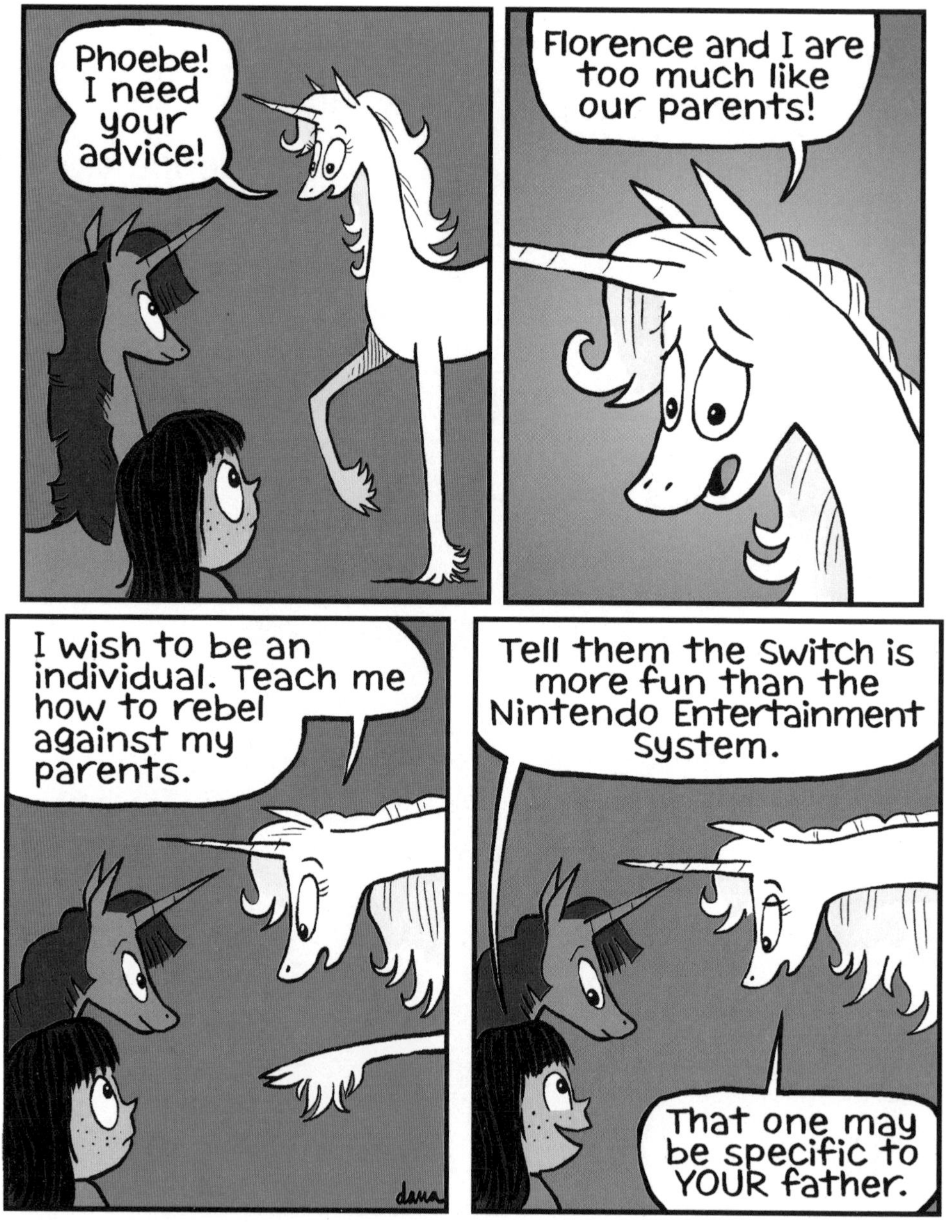
Phoebe! I need your advice!
Florence and I are too much like our parents!
I wish to be an individual. Teach me how to rebel against my parents.
Tell them the Switch is more fun than the Nintendo Entertainment System.
That one may be specific to YOUR father.
dana

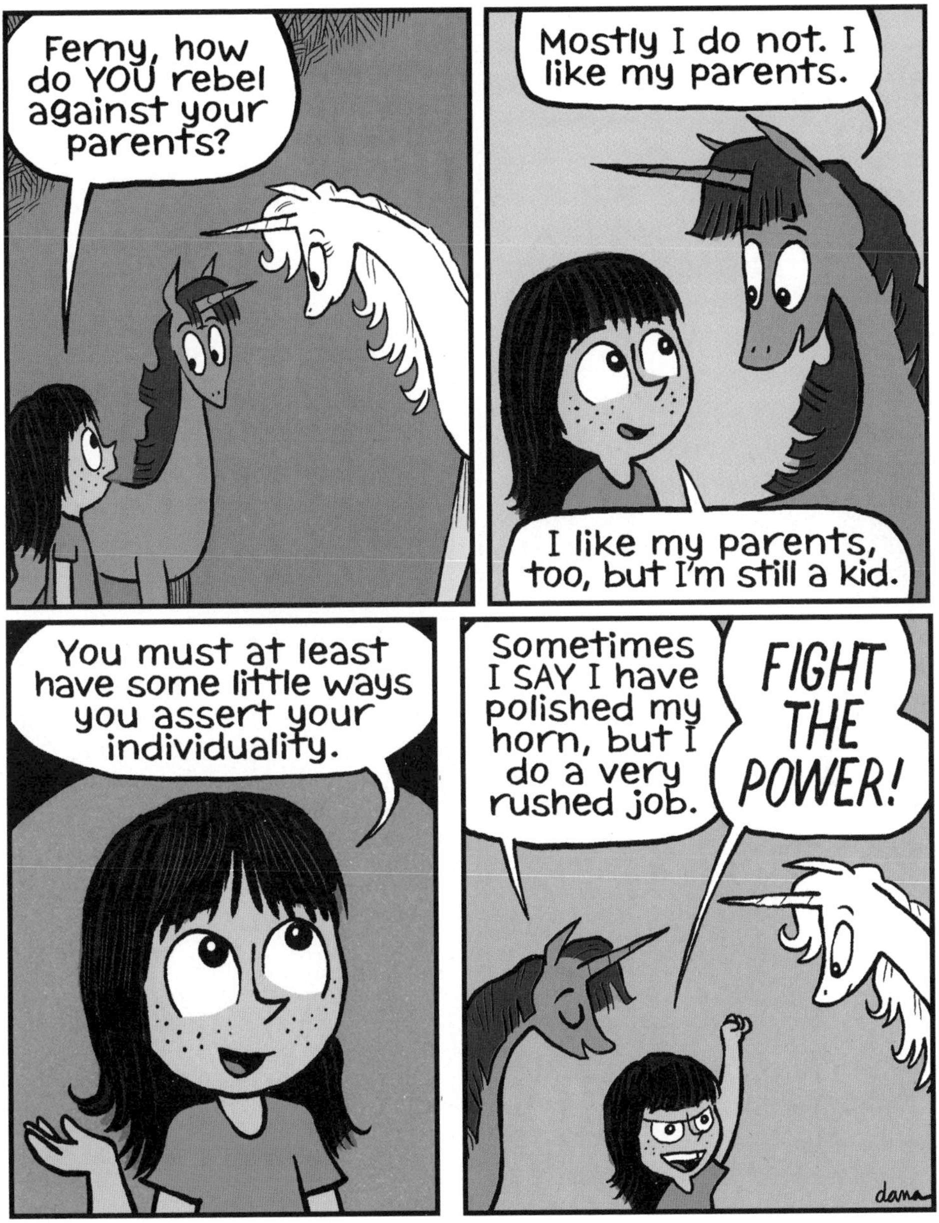
Ferny, how do YOU rebel against your parents?
Mostly I do not. I like my parents.
I like my parents, too, but I'm still a kid.
You must at least have some little ways you assert your individuality.
Sometimes I SAY I have polished my horn, but I do a very rushed job.
FIGHT THE POWER!
dana

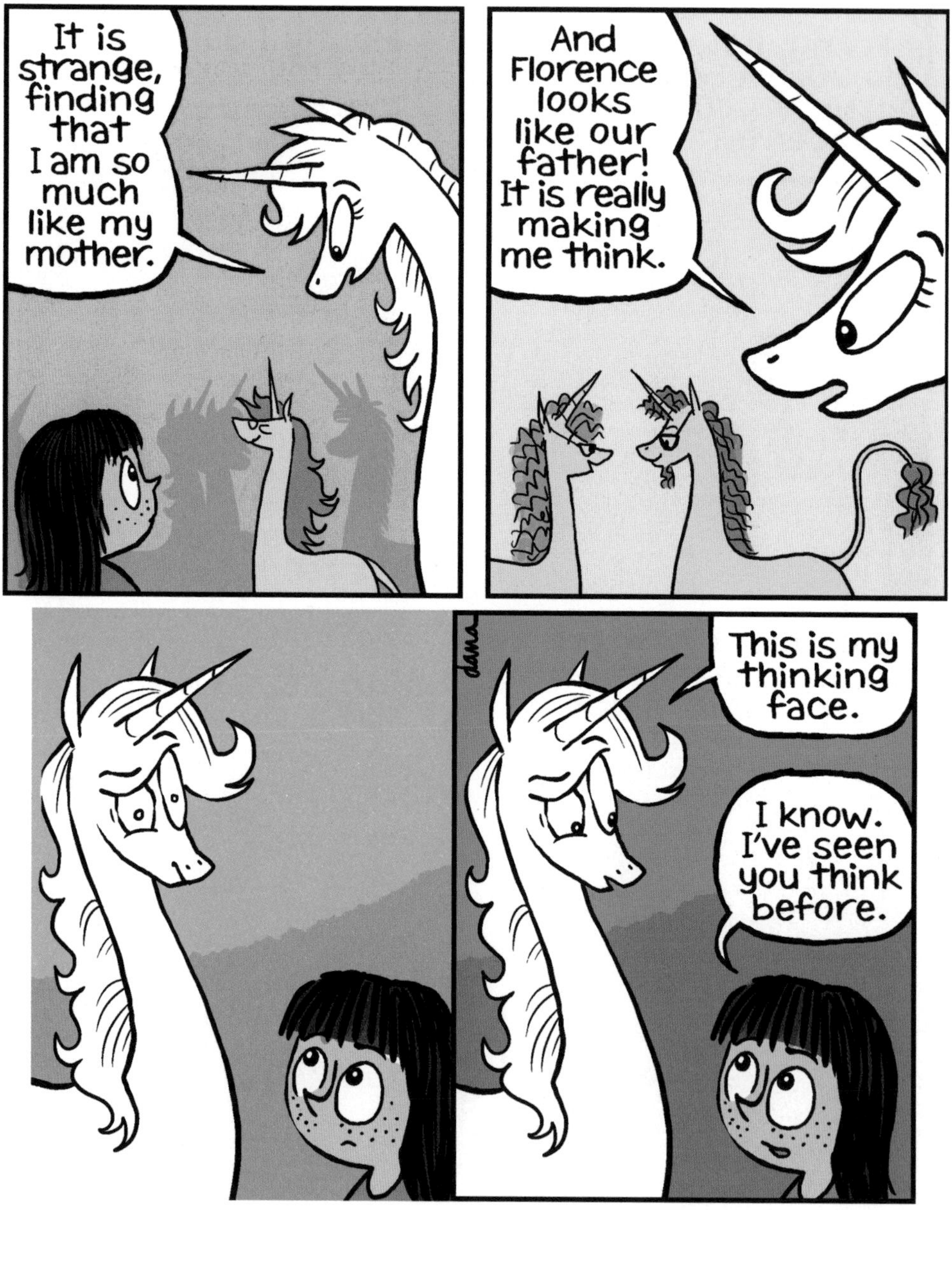
It is strange, finding that I am so much like my mother.
And Florence looks like our father! It is really making me think.
dana
This is my thinking face.
I know. I've seen you think before.

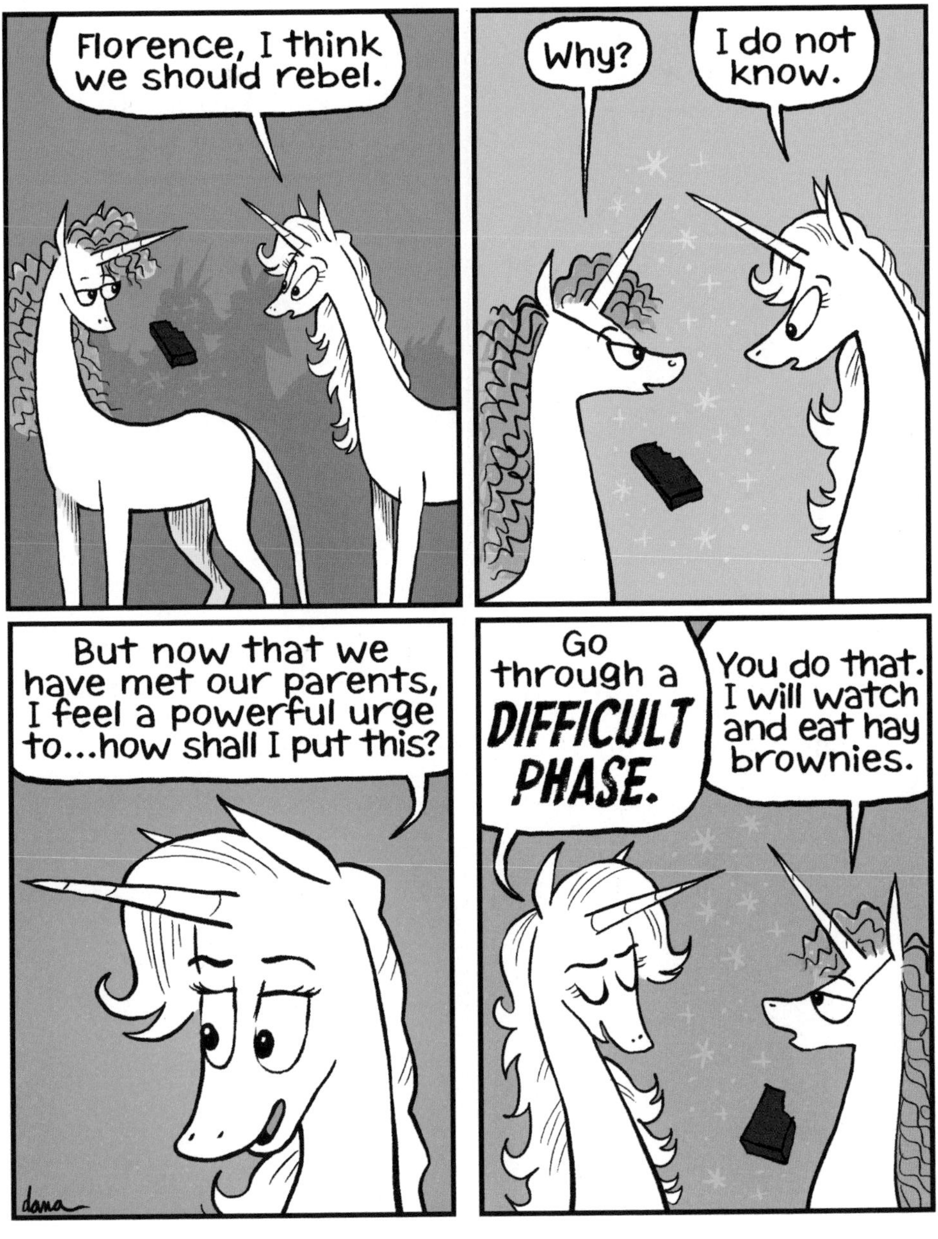
Florence, I think we should rebel.
Why?
I do not know.
But now that we have met our parents, I feel a powerful urge to...how shall I put this?
Go through a DIFFICULT PHASE.
You do that. I will watch and eat hay brownies.
dana

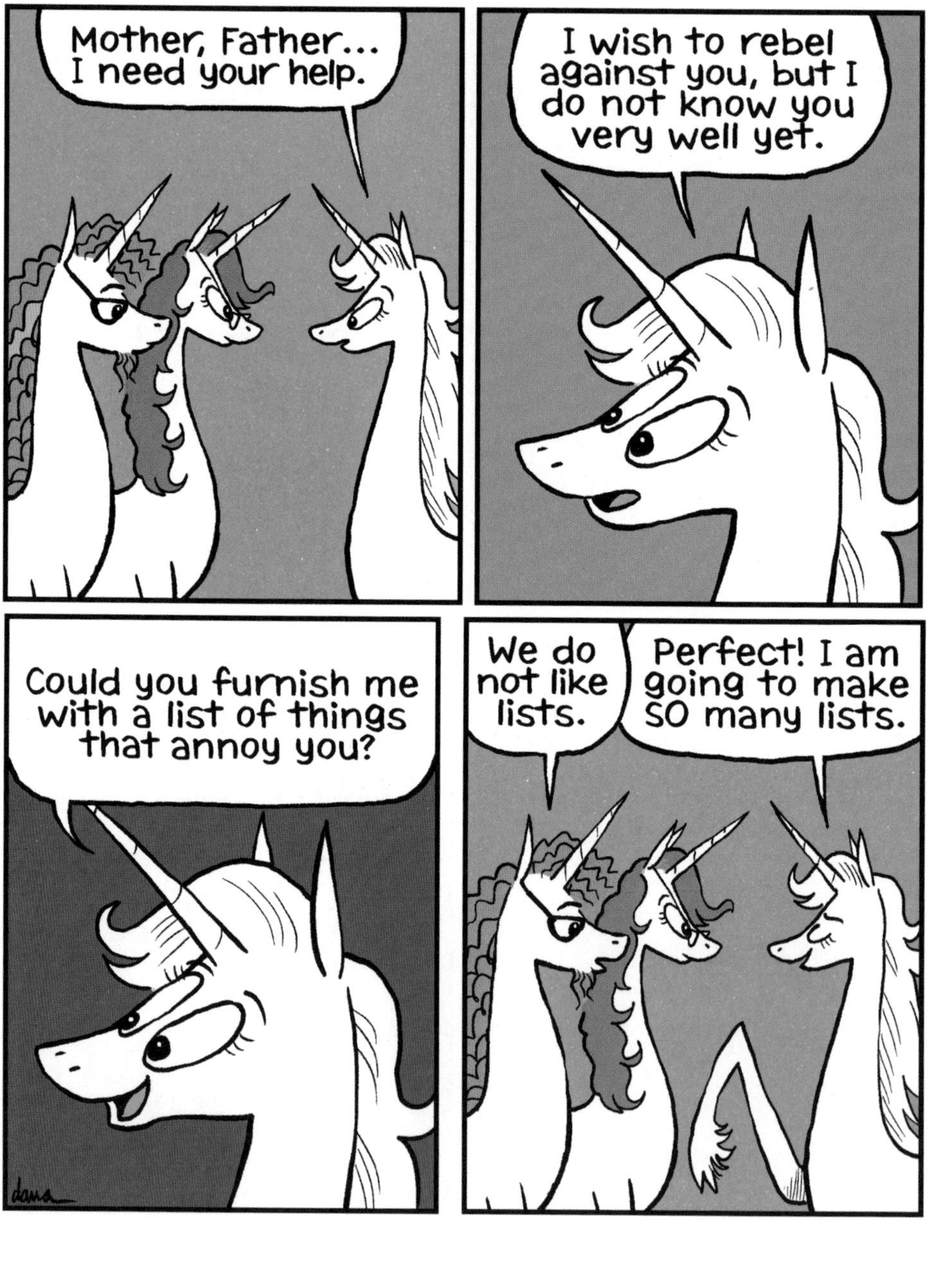
Mother, Father...
I need your help.
I wish to rebel against you, but I do not know you very well yet.
Could you furnish me with a list of things that annoy you?
We do not like lists.
Perfect! I am going to make SO many lists.
dana

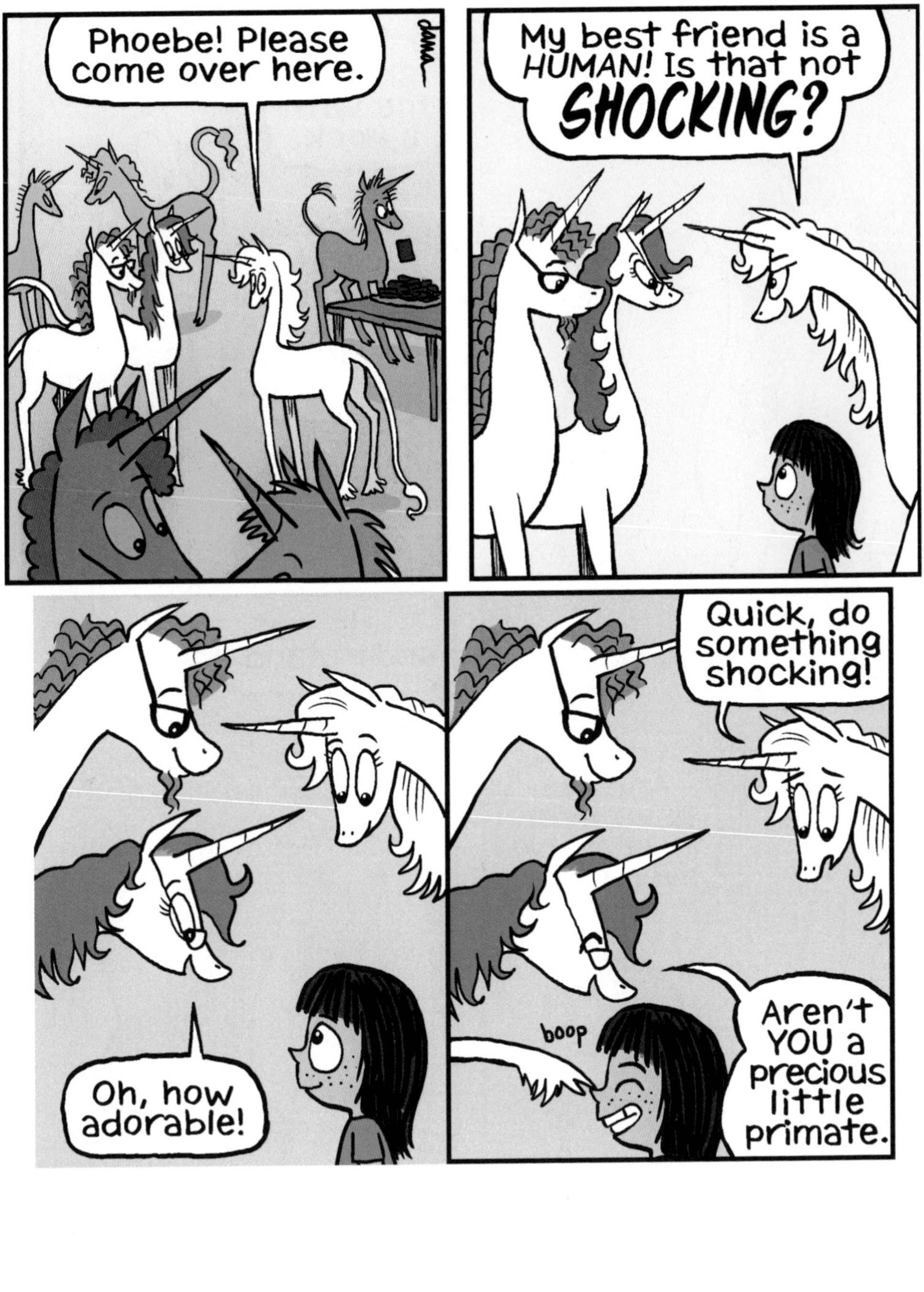
Phoebe! Please come over here.
My best friend is a HUMAN! Is that not SHOCKING?
Oh, how adorable!
Quick, do something shocking!
boop
Aren't YOU a precious little primate.

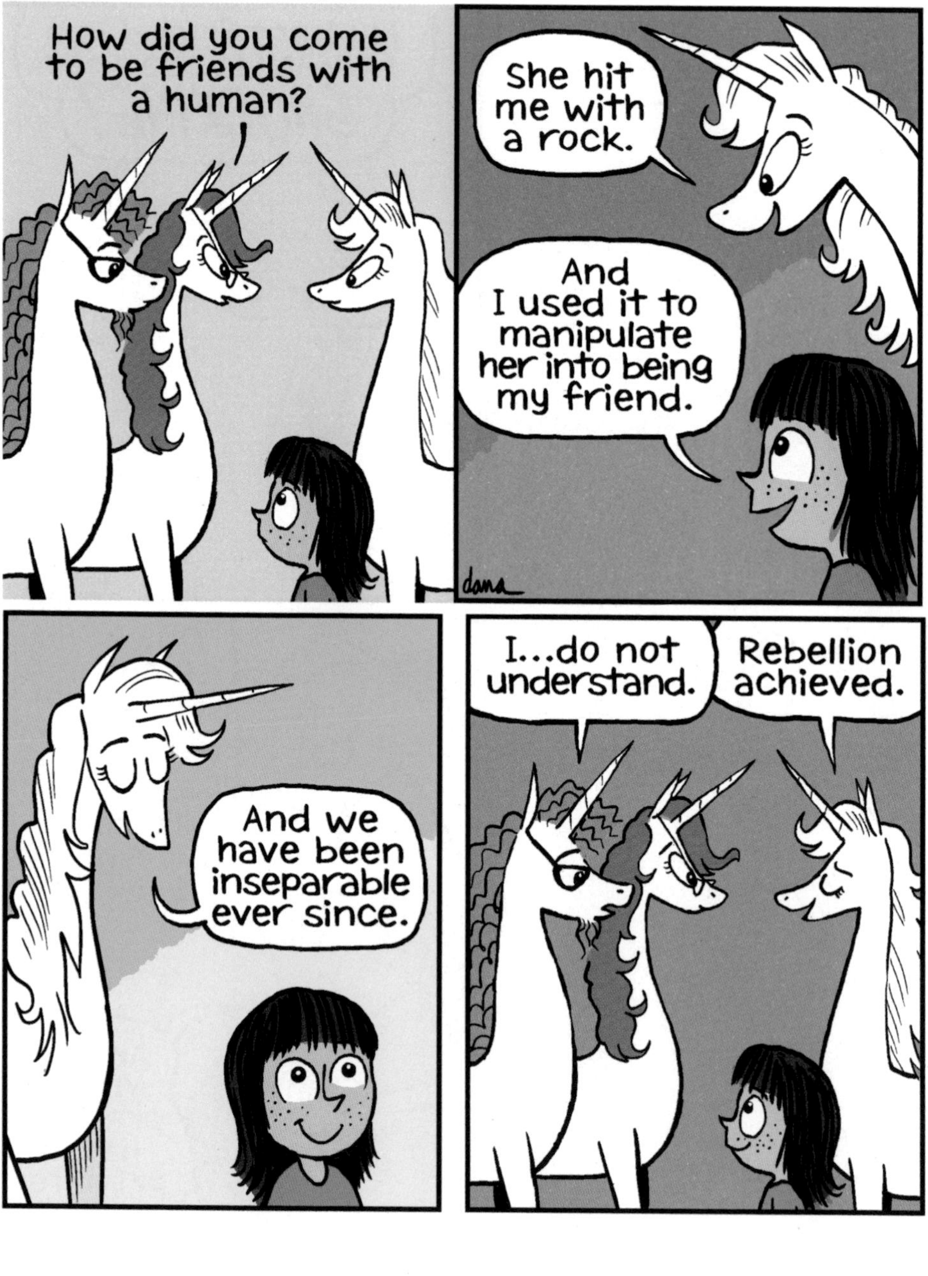
How did you come to be friends with a human?
She hit me with a rock.
And I used it to manipulate her into being my friend.
dana
And we have been inseparable ever since.
I...do not understand.
Rebellion achieved.

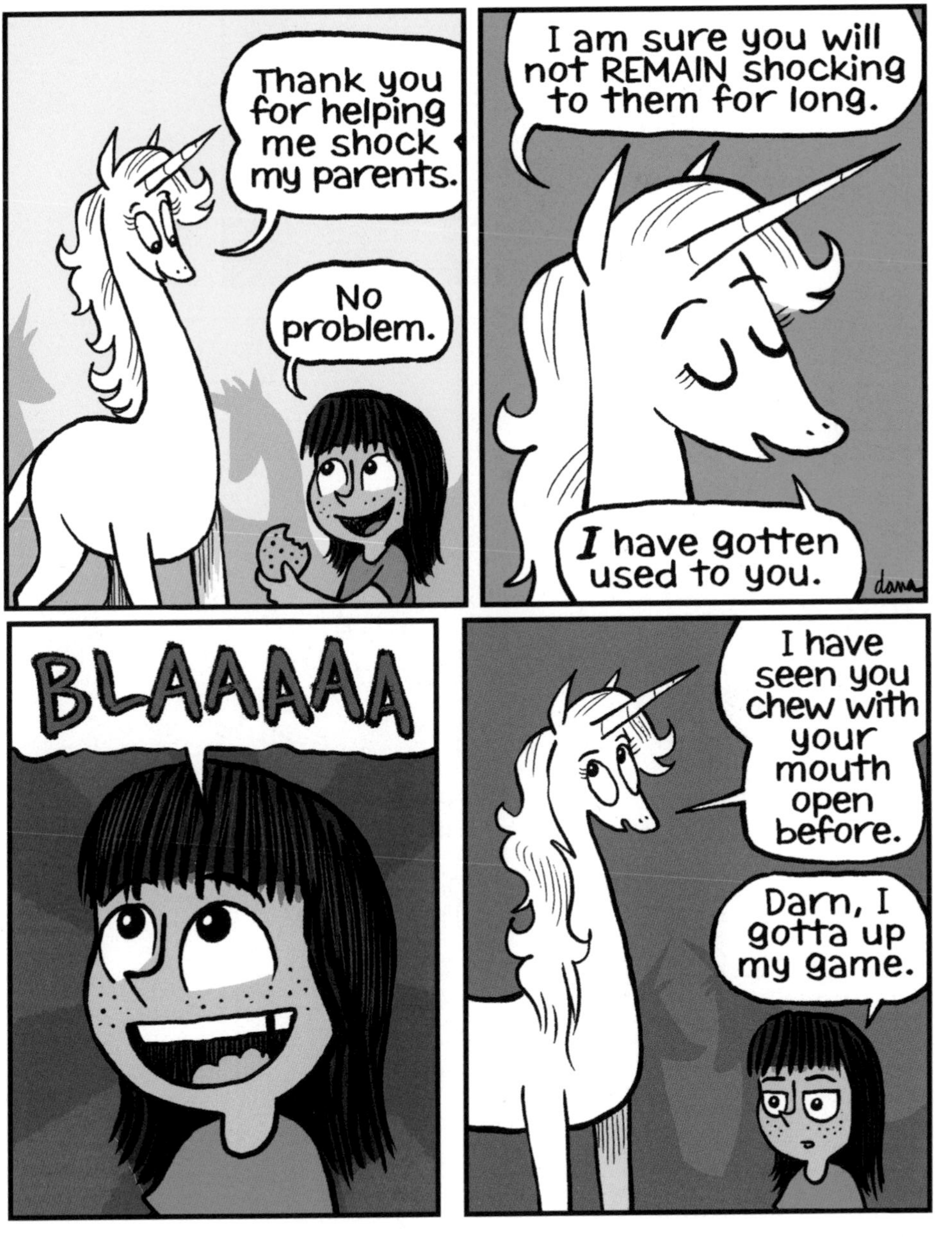
Thank you for helping me shock my parents.
No problem.
I am sure you will not REMAIN shocking to them for long.
I have gotten used to you.
dana
BLAAAAA
I have seen you chew with your mouth open before.
Darn, I gotta up my game.

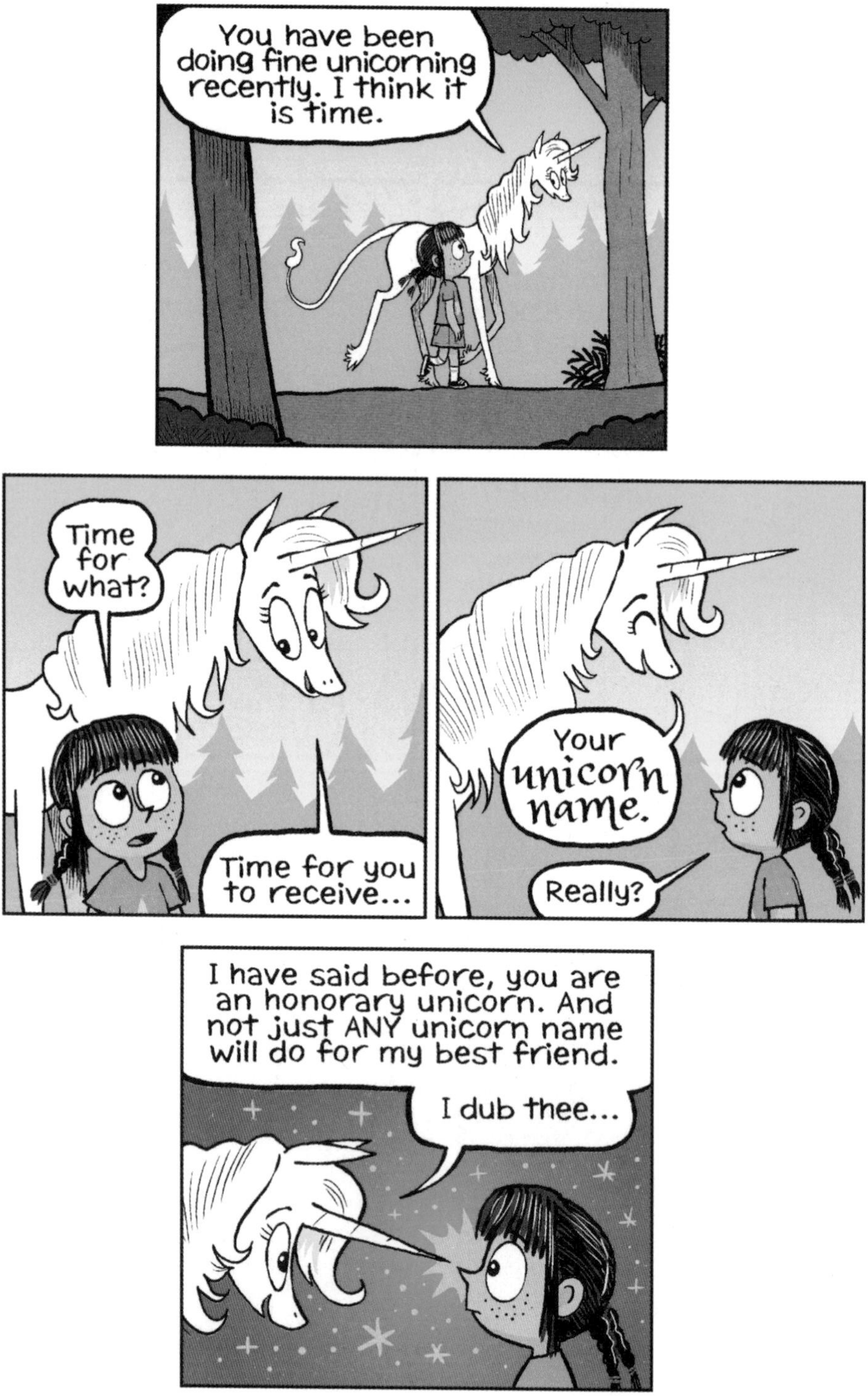
You have been doing fine unicorning recently. I think it is time.
Time for what?
Time for you to receive...
Your unicorn name.
Really?
I have said before, you are an honorary unicorn. And not just ANY unicorn name will do for my best friend.
I dub thee...

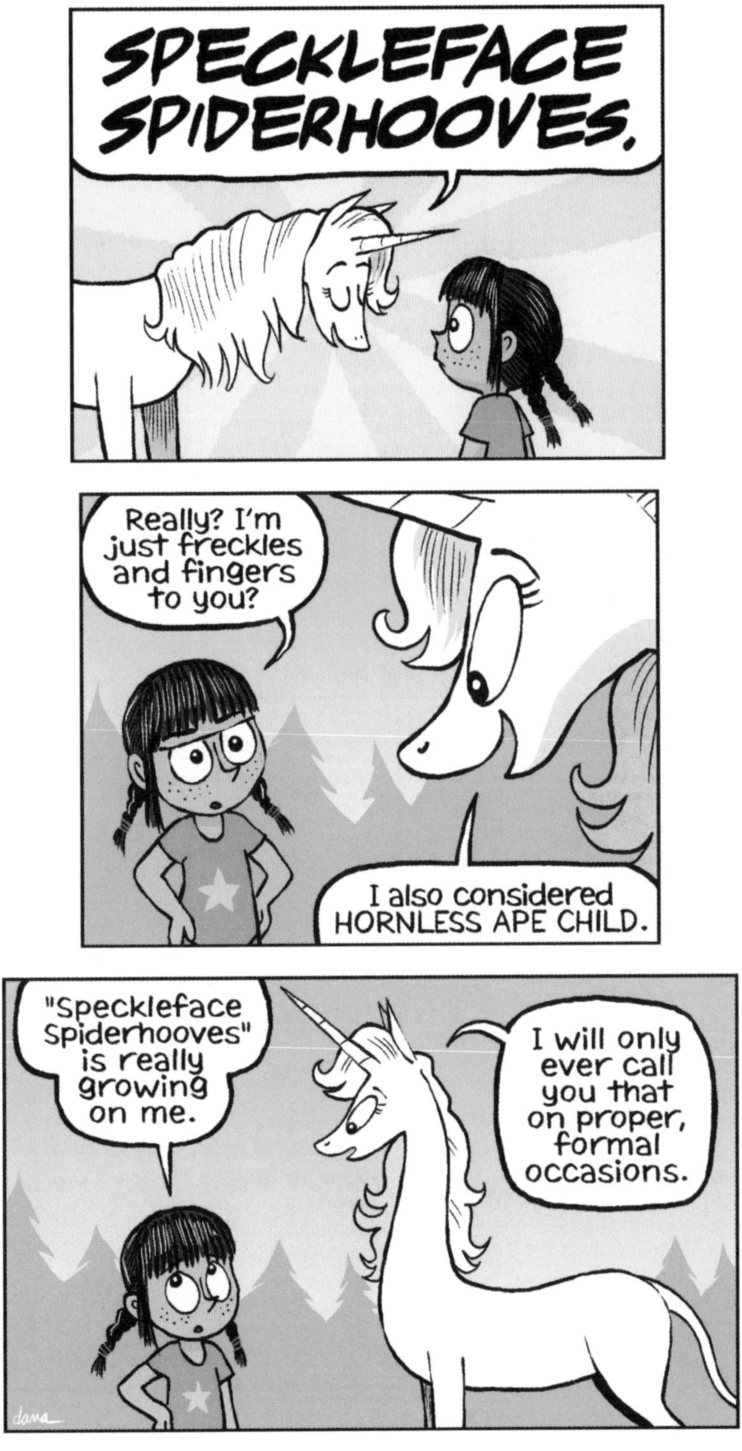
SPECKLEFACE SPIDERHOOVES.
Really? I'm just freckles and fingers to you?
I also considered HORNLESS APE CHILD.
"Speckleface spiderhooves" is really growing on me.
I will only ever call you that on proper, formal occasions.
dana

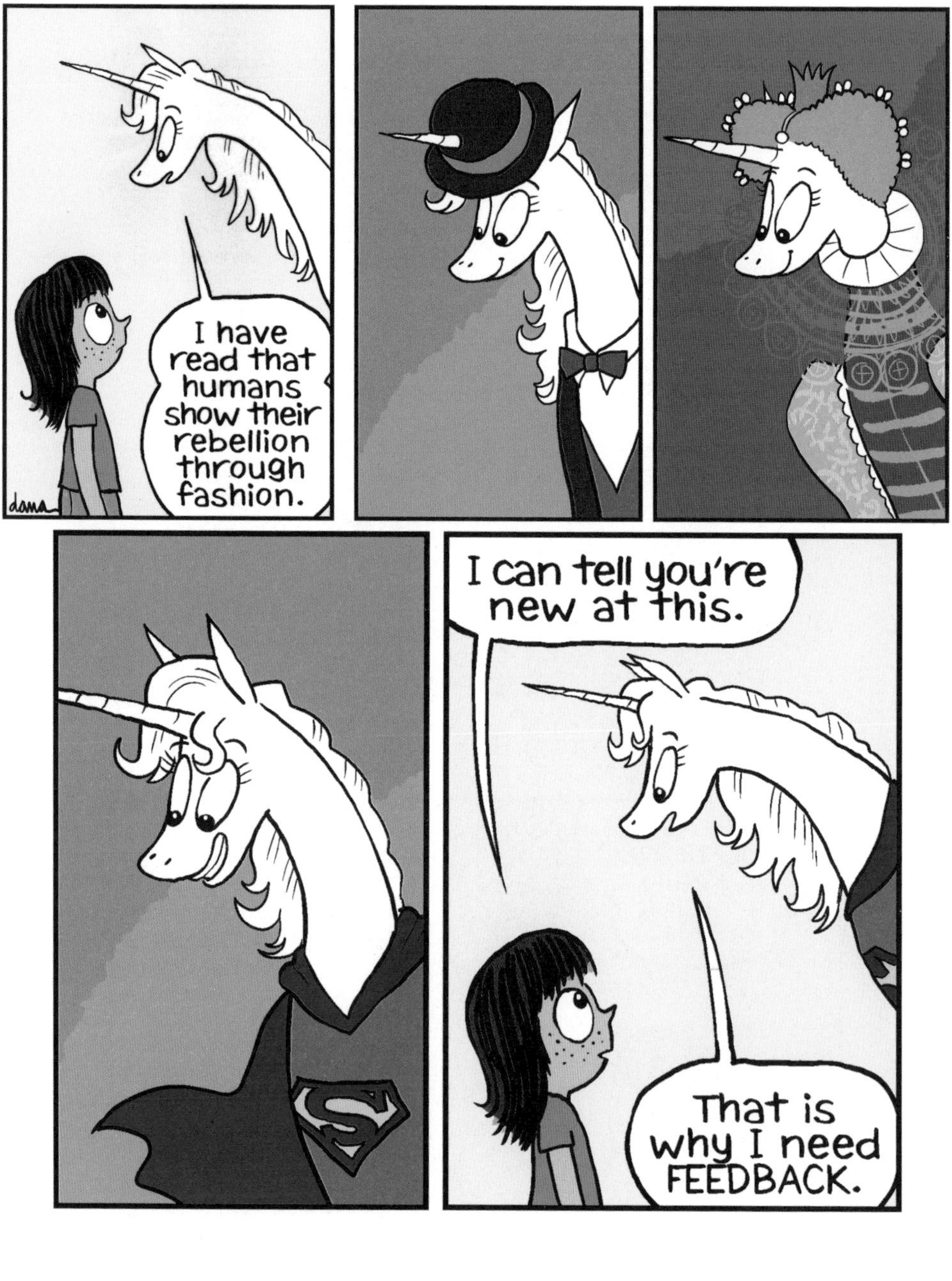
I have read that humans show their rebellion through fashion.
dana
I can tell you're new at this.
That is why I need FEEDBACK.

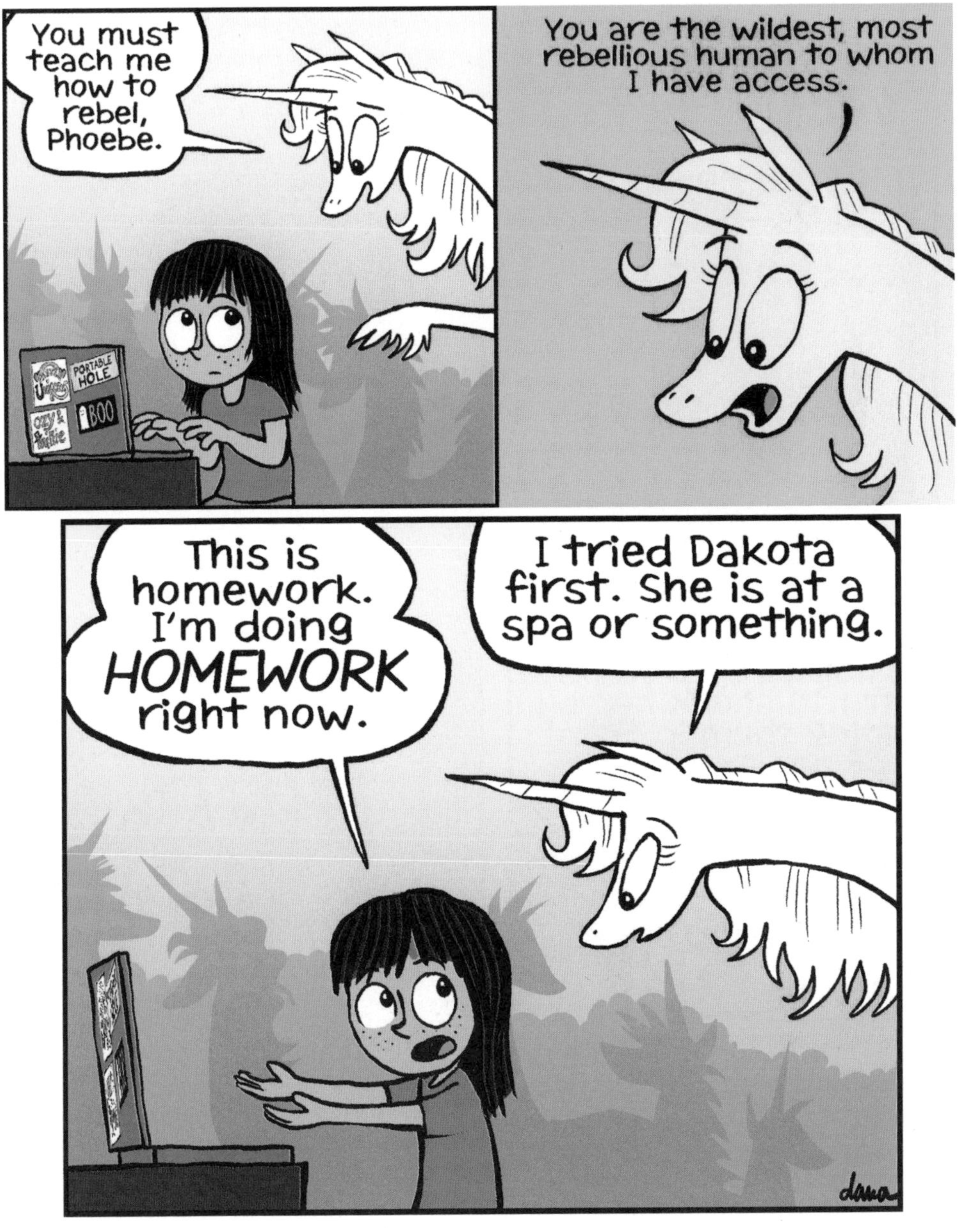
You must teach me how to rebel, Phoebe.
PORTABLE HOLE
BOO
You are the wildest, most rebellious human to whom I have access.
This is homework. I'm doing *HOMEWORK* right now.
I tried Dakota first. She is at a spa or something.
dana

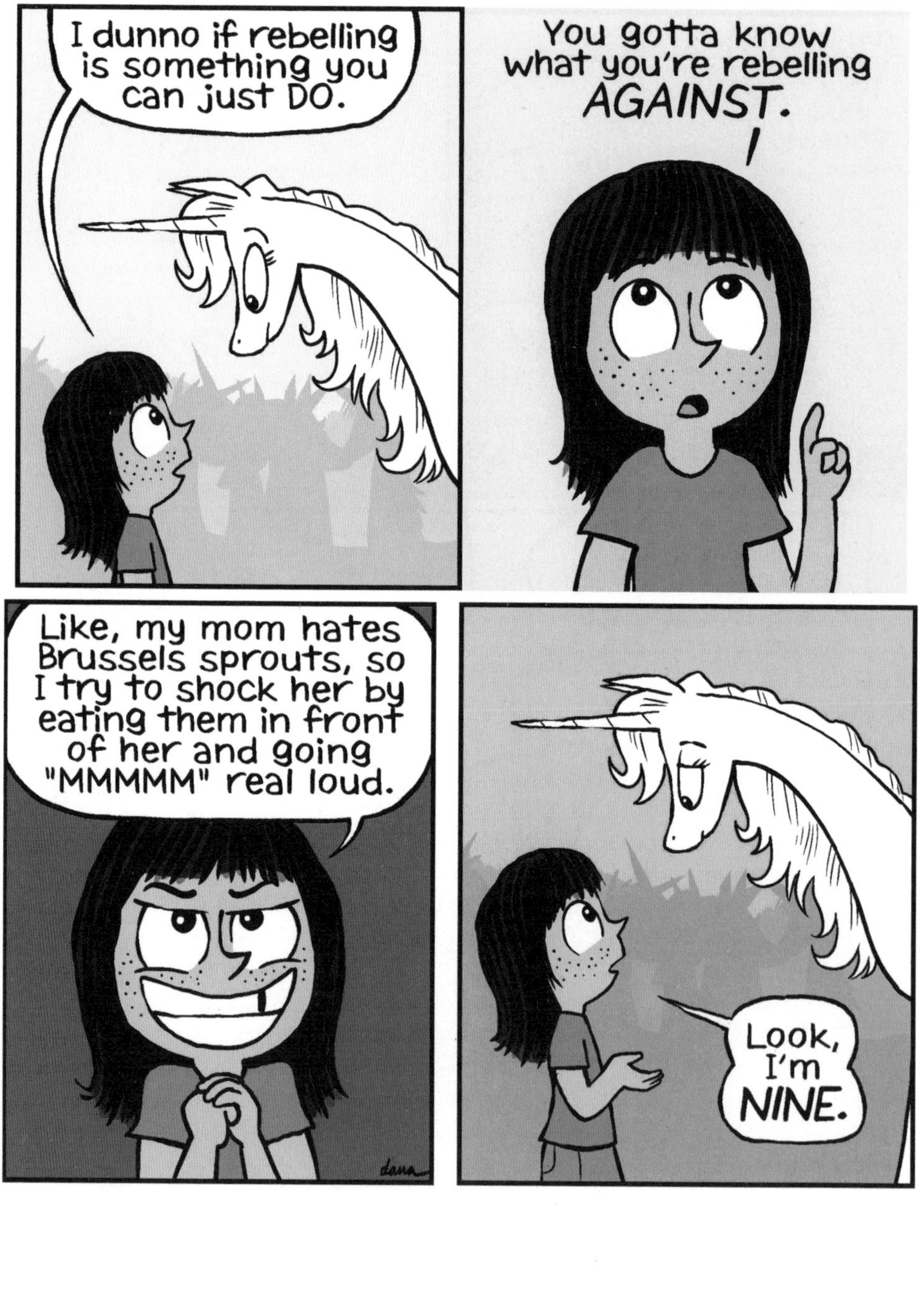
I dunno if rebelling is something you can just DO.
You gotta know what you're rebelling AGAINST.
Like, my mom hates Brussels sprouts, so I try to shock her by eating them in front of her and going "MMMMM" real loud.
Look, I'm NINE.
dana

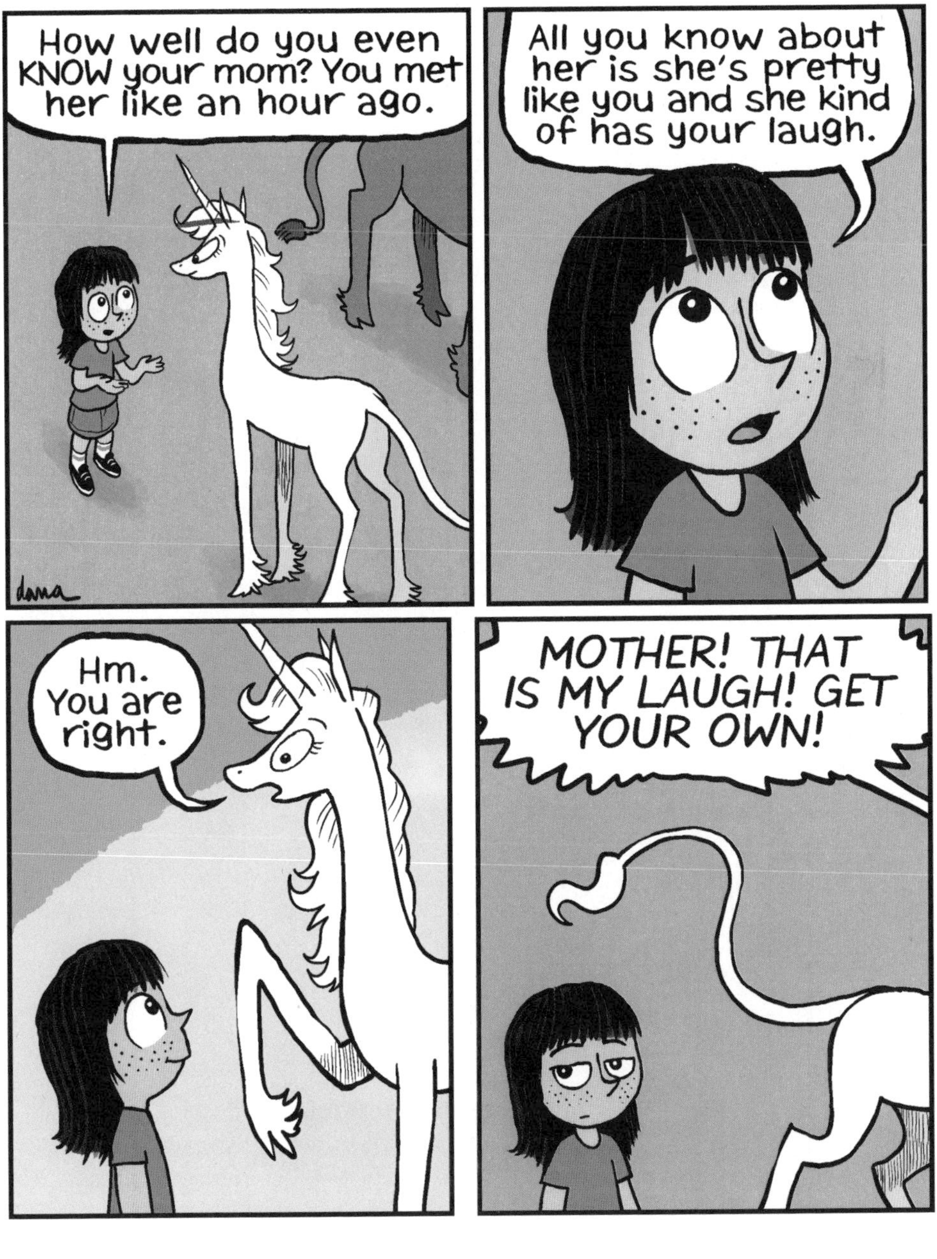
How well do you even KNOW your mom? You met her like an hour ago.
dana
All you know about her is she's pretty like you and she kind of has your laugh.
Hm. You are right.
MOTHER! THAT IS MY LAUGH! GET YOUR OWN!

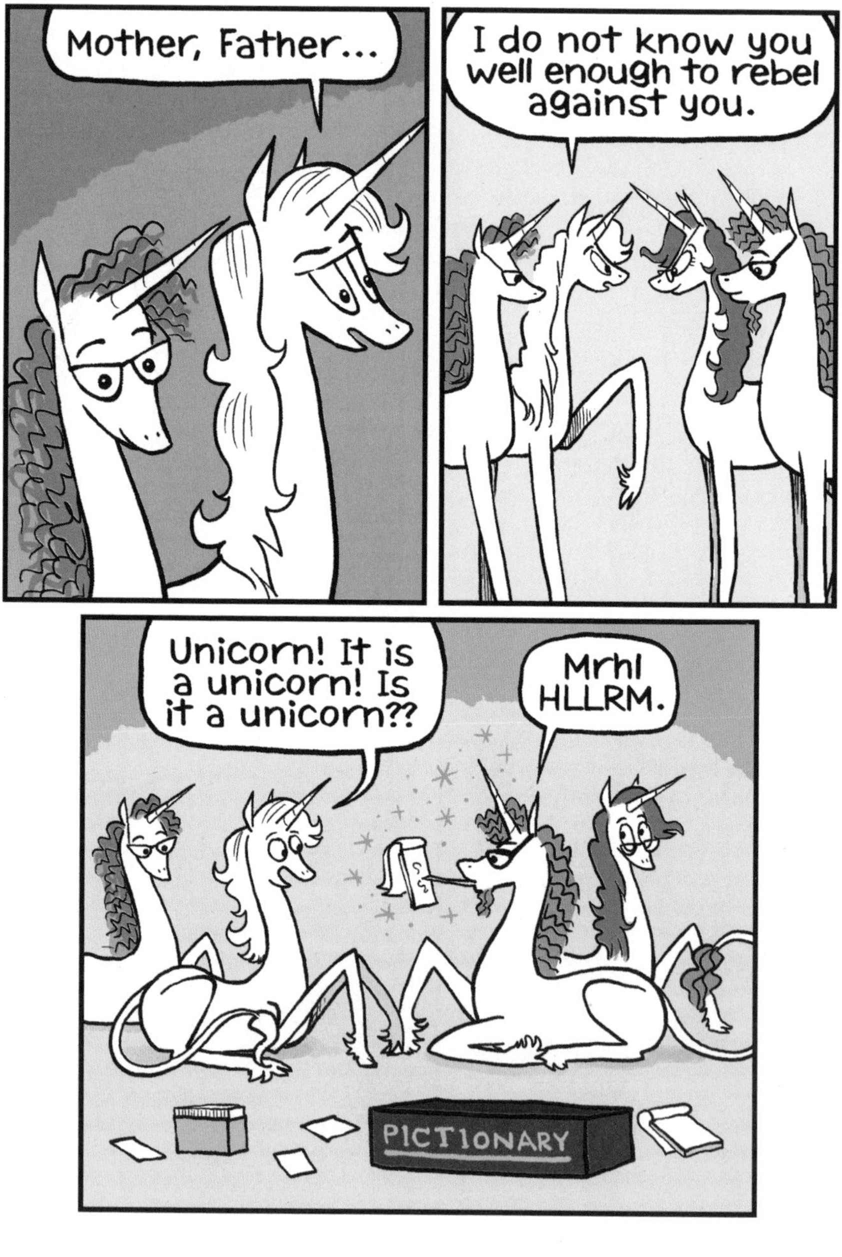
Mother, Father...
I do not know you well enough to rebel against you.
Unicorn! It is a unicorn! Is it a unicorn??
Mrhl HLLRM.
PICTIONARY

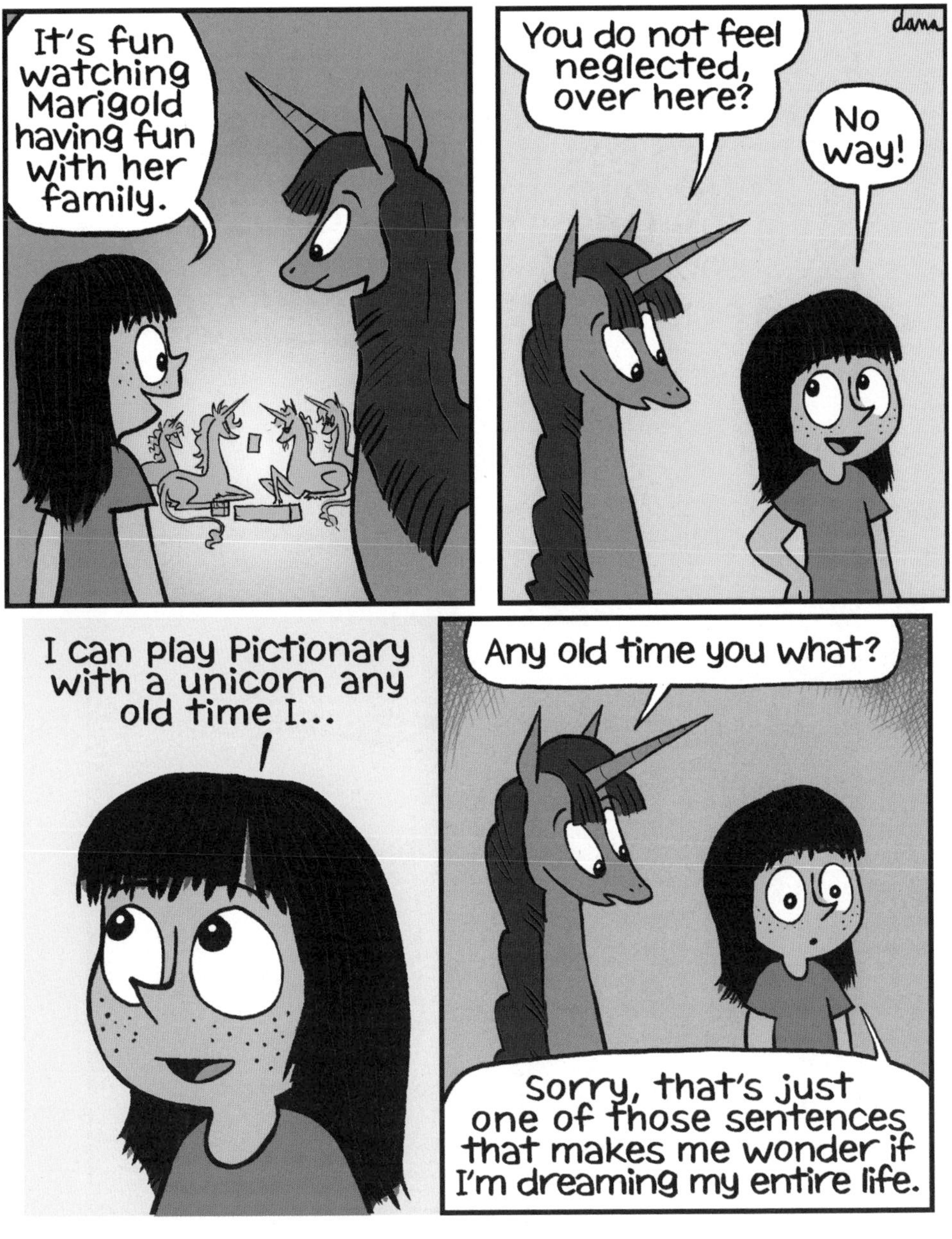
It's fun watching Marigold having fun with her family.
dana
You do not feel neglected, over here?
No way!
I can play Pictionary with a unicorn any old time I...
Any old time you what?
Sorry, that's just one of those sentences that makes me wonder if I'm dreaming my entire life.

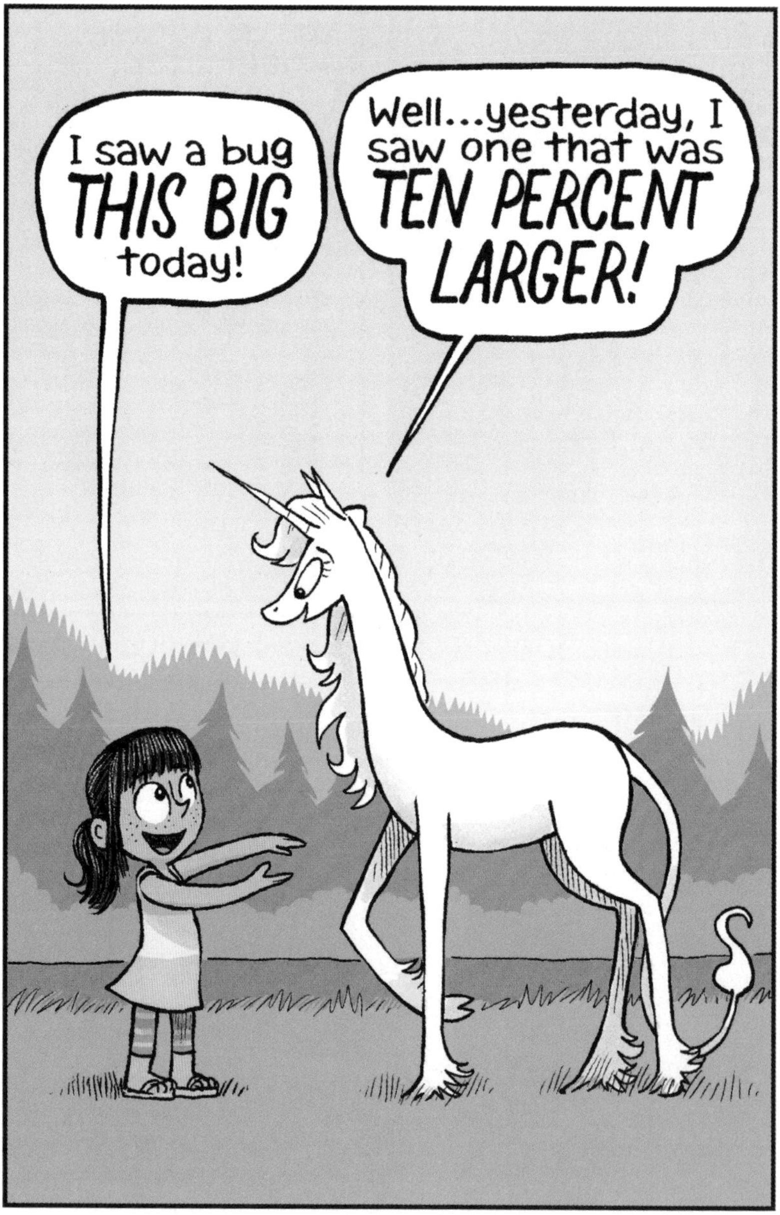
I saw a bug THIS BIG today!
Well...yesterday, I saw one that was TEN PERCENT LARGER!

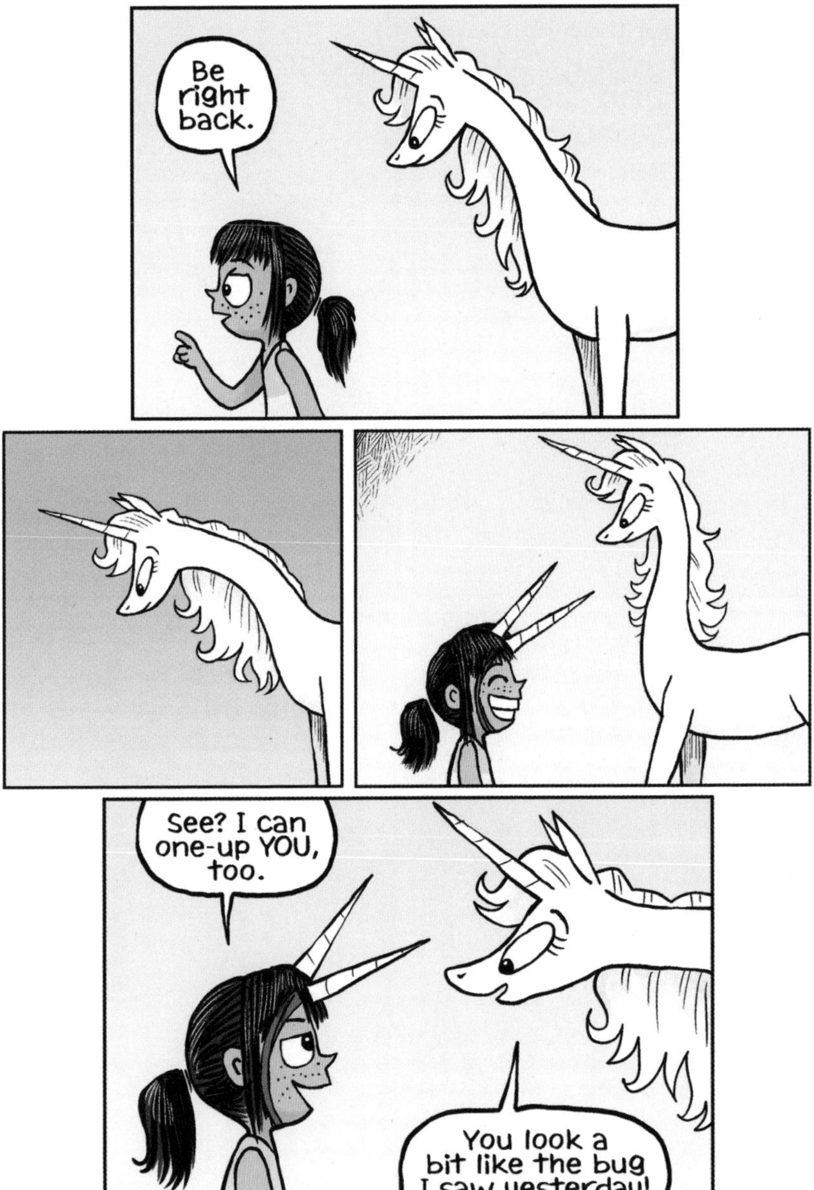
Be right back.
See? I can one-up YOU, too.
You look a bit like the bug I saw yesterday!

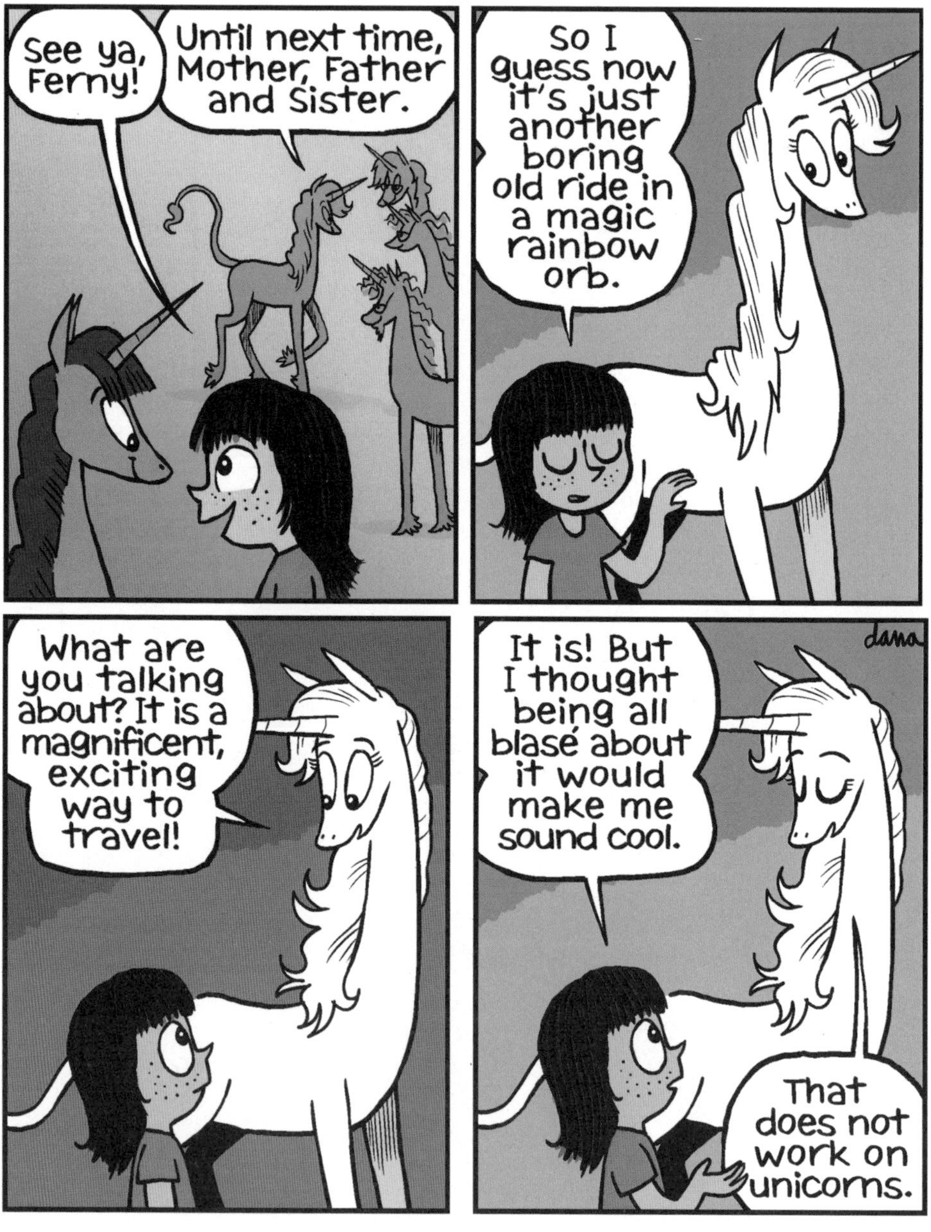
See ya, Ferny!
Until next time, Mother, Father and Sister.
So I guess now it's just another boring old ride in a magic rainbow orb.
What are you talking about? It is a magnificent, exciting way to travel!
It is! But I thought being all blasé about it would make me sound cool.
That does not work on unicorns.
dana

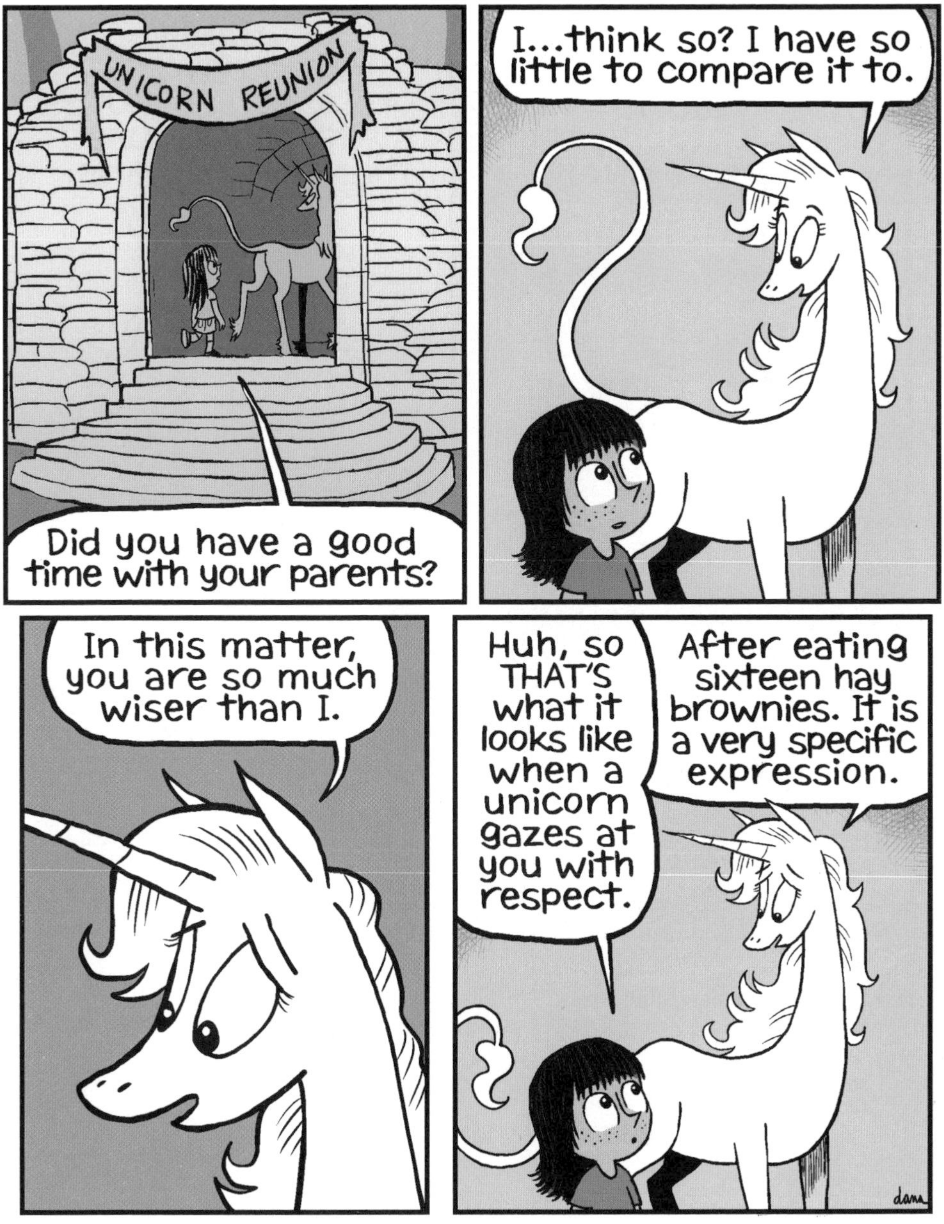
UNICORN REUNION
Did you have a good time with your parents?
I...think so? I have so little to compare it to.
In this matter, you are so much wiser than I.
Huh, so THAT'S what it looks like when a unicorn gazes at you with respect.
After eating sixteen hay brownies. It is a very specific expression.
dana

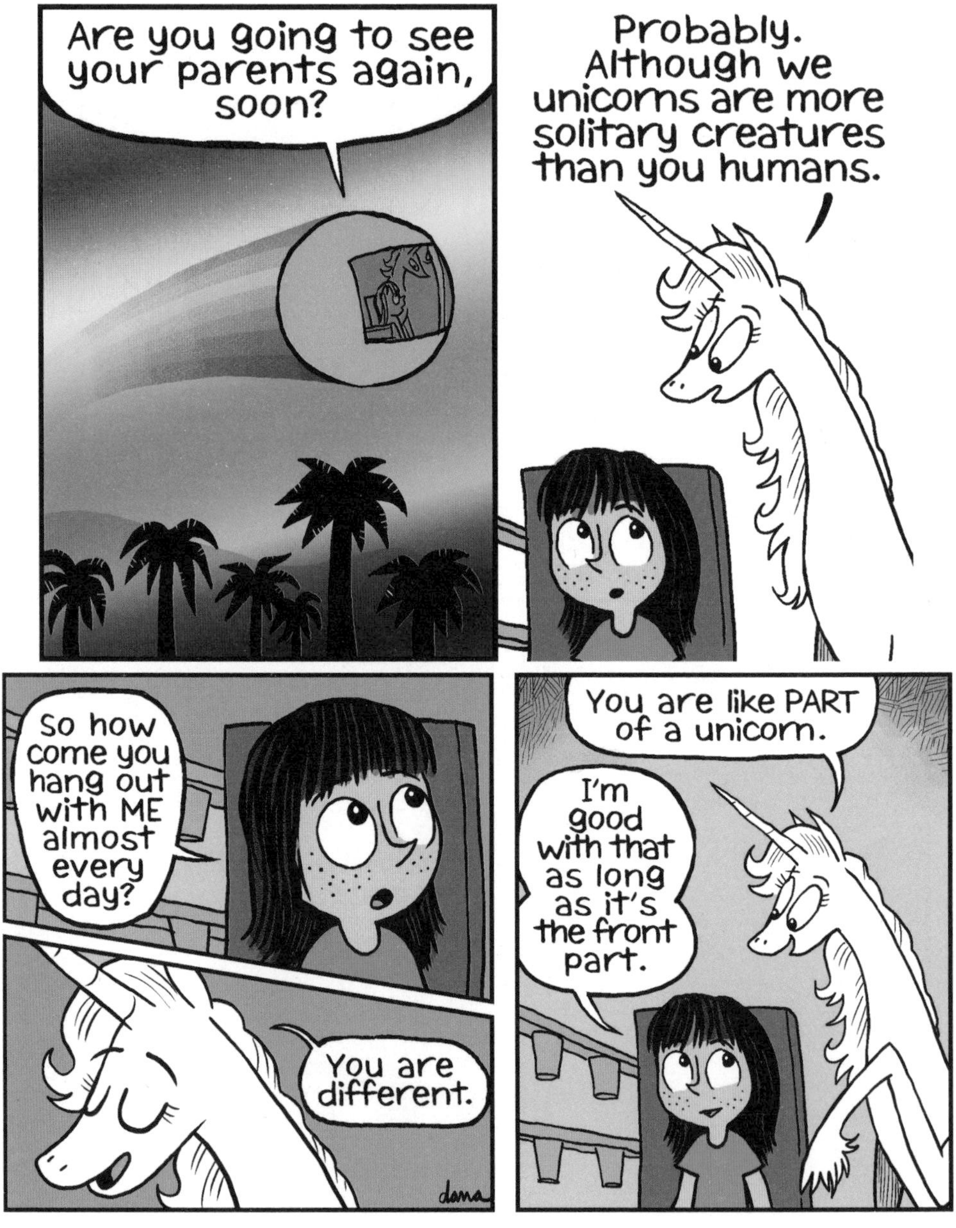
Are you going to see your parents again, soon?
Probably. Although we unicorns are more solitary creatures than you humans.
So how come you hang out with ME almost every day?
You are different.
dana
You are like PART of a unicorn.
I'm good with that as long as it's the front part.

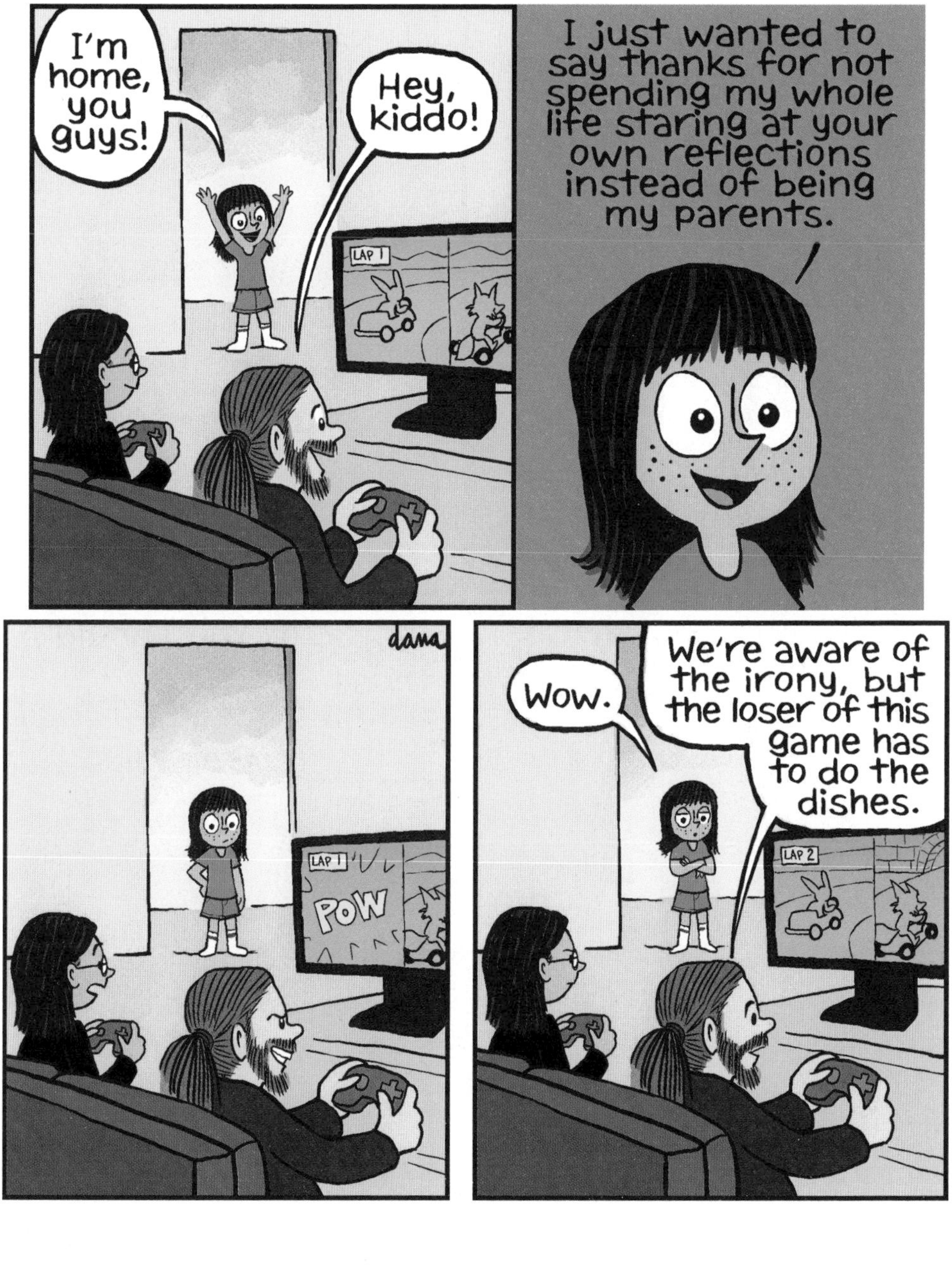
I'm home, you guys!
Hey, kiddo!
LAP 1
I just wanted to say thanks for not spending my whole life staring at your own reflections instead of being my parents.
dana
LAP 1
POW
Wow.
We're aware of the irony, but the loser of this game has to do the dishes.
LAP 2

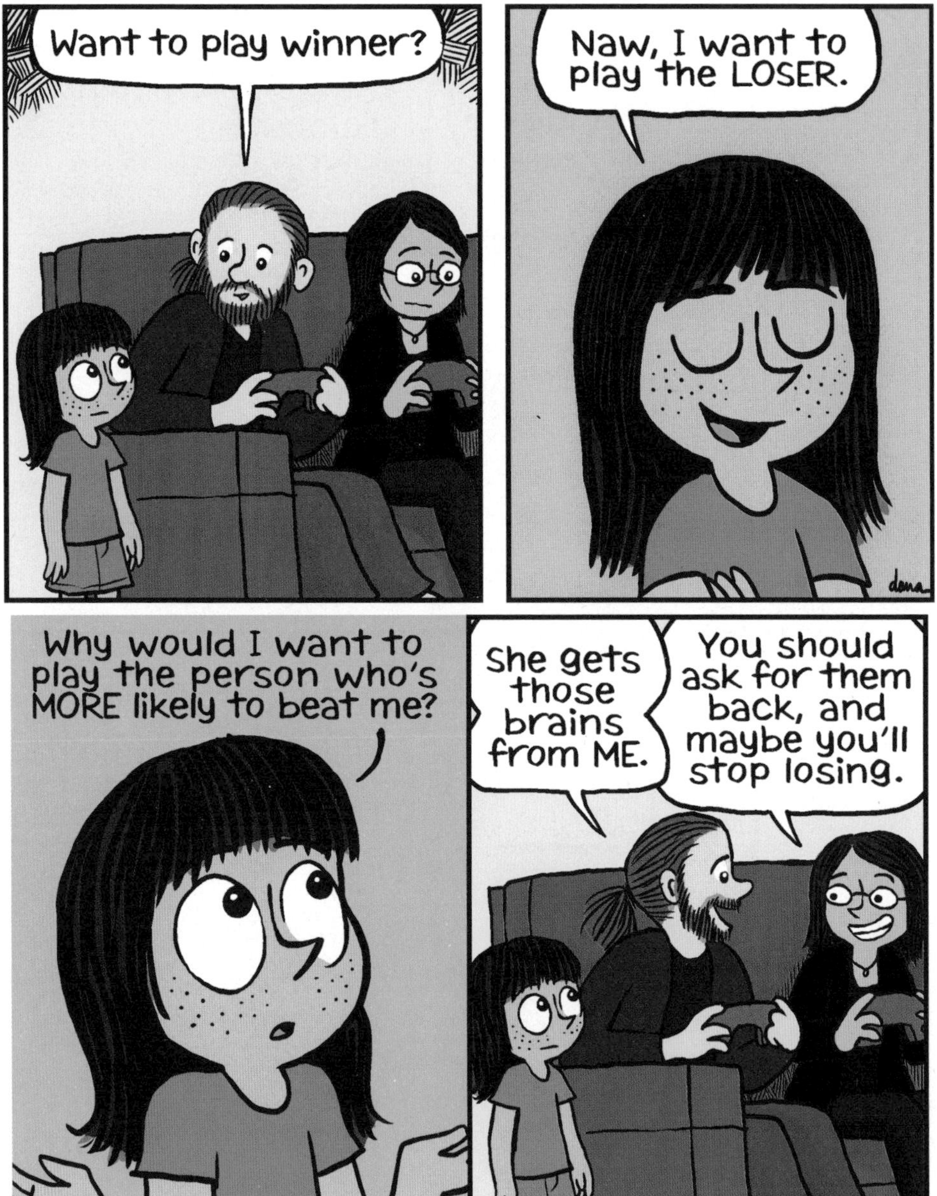
Want to play winner?
Naw, I want to play the LOSER.
dana
Why would I want to play the person who's MORE likely to beat me?
She gets those brains from ME.
You should ask for them back, and maybe you'll stop losing.

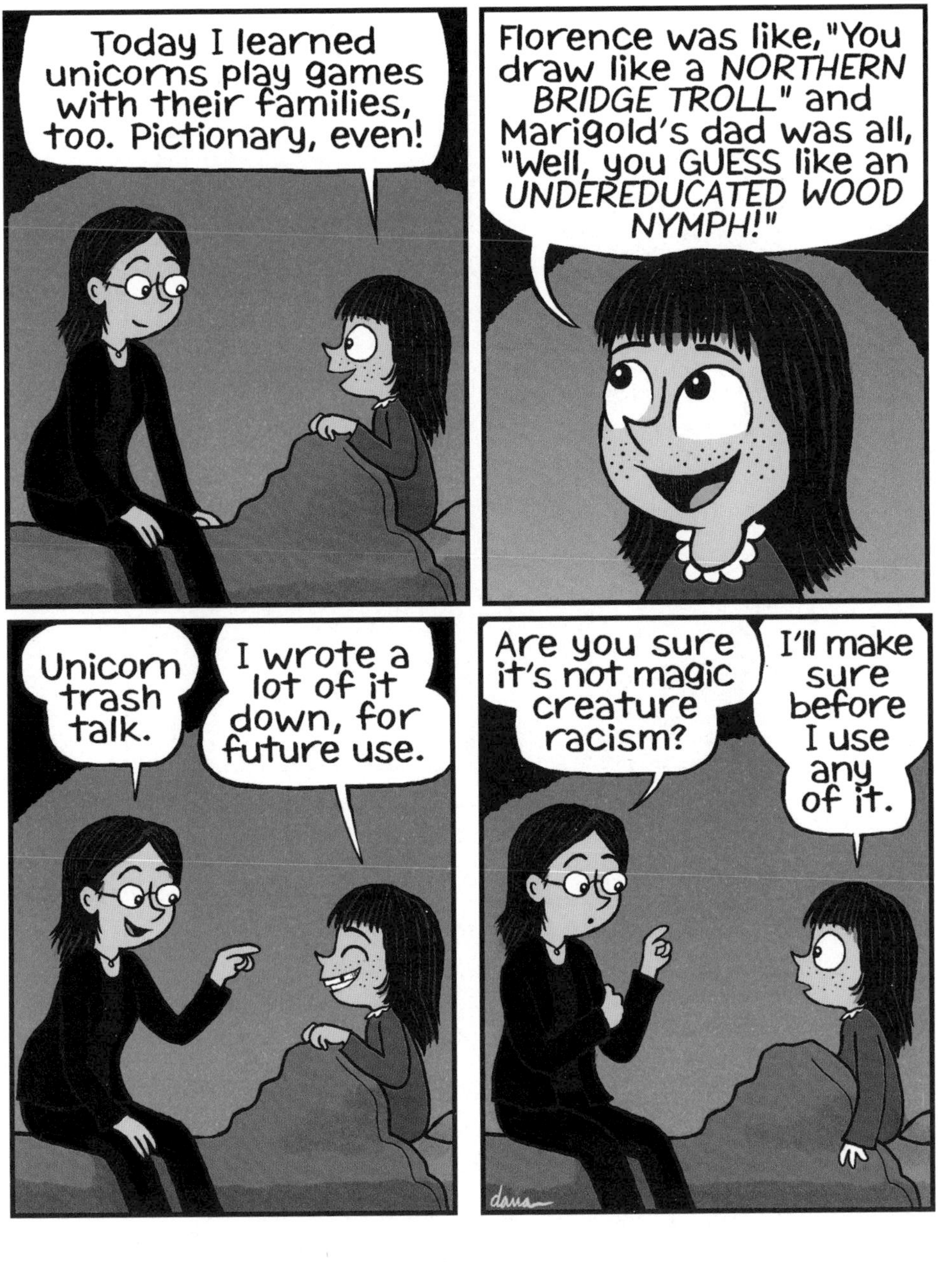
Today I learned unicorns play games with their families, too. Pictionary, even!
Florence was like, "You draw like a NORTHERN BRIDGE TROLL" and Marigold's dad was all, "Well, you GUESS like an UNDEREDUCATED WOOD NYMPH!"
Unicorn trash talk.
I wrote a lot of it down, for future use.
Are you sure it's not magic creature racism?
I'll make sure before I use any of it.
dana

You ever wonder what your life would be like if we'd never met?
Would you be friends with some other human kid?
Possibly, but I doubt I would like her as much as you.
She would not have your smile, or your laugh...

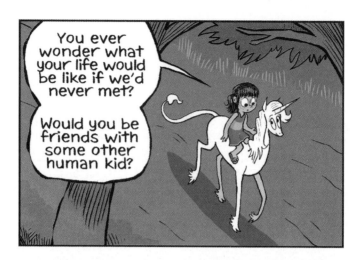

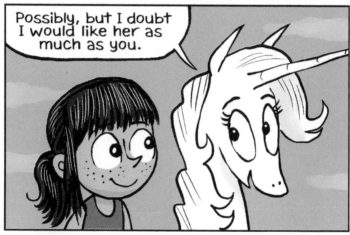

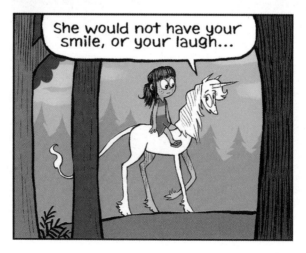

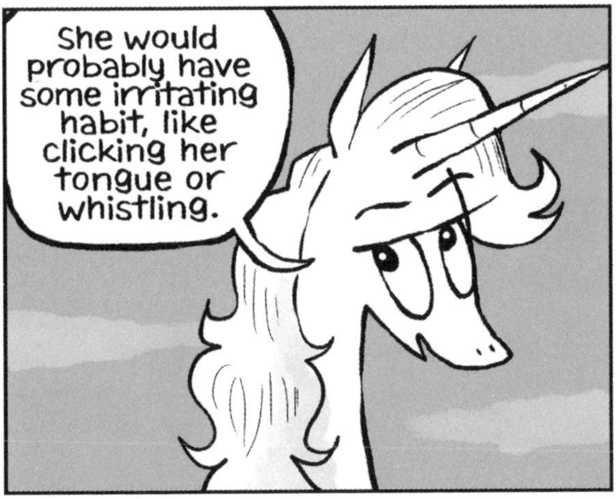
She would probably have some irritating habit, like clicking her tongue or whistling.

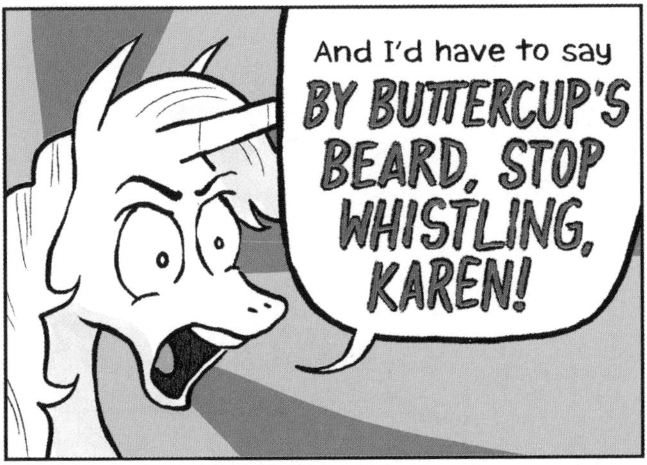
And I'd have to say
BY BUTTERCUP'S BEARD, STOP WHISTLING, KAREN!

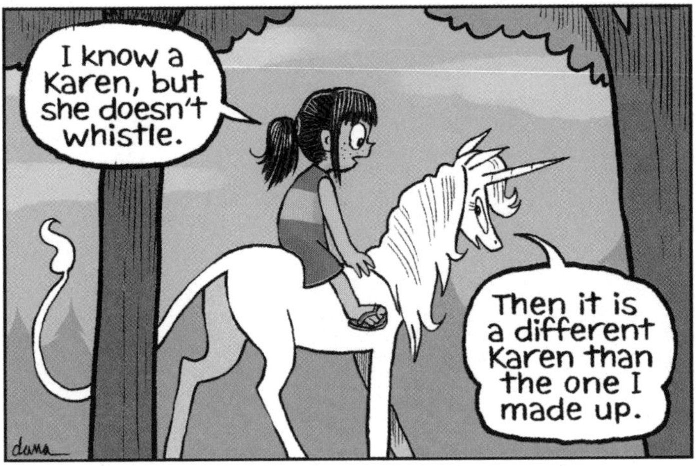
I know a Karen, but she doesn't whistle.
Then it is a different Karen than the one I made up.
dana

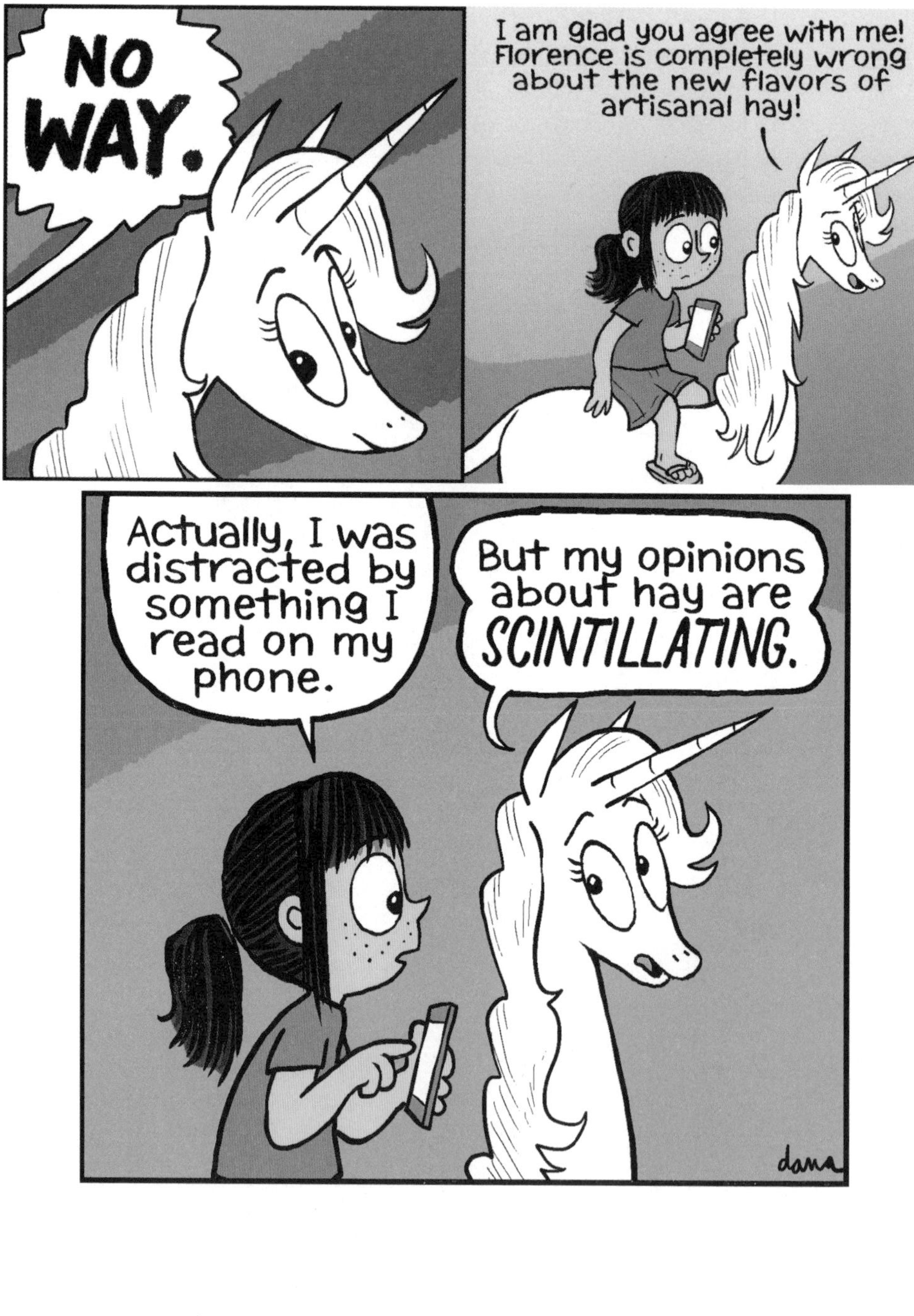
NO WAY.
I am glad you agree with me! Florence is completely wrong about the new flavors of artisanal hay!
Actually, I was distracted by something I read on my phone.
But my opinions about hay are SCINTILLATING.
dana

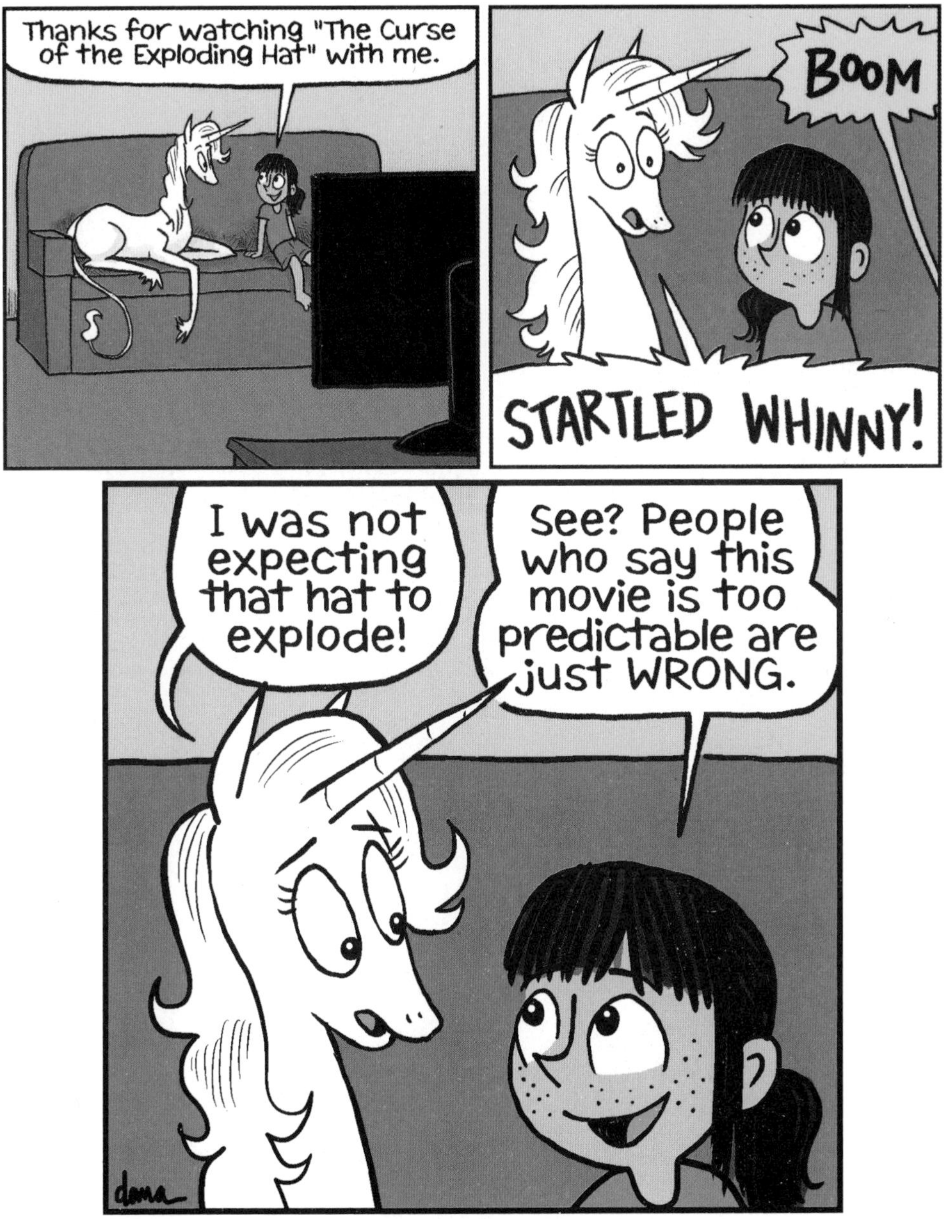
Thanks for watching "The Curse of the Exploding Hat" with me.
BOOM
STARTLED WHINNY!
I was not expecting that hat to explode!
See? People who say this movie is too predictable are just WRONG.
dana

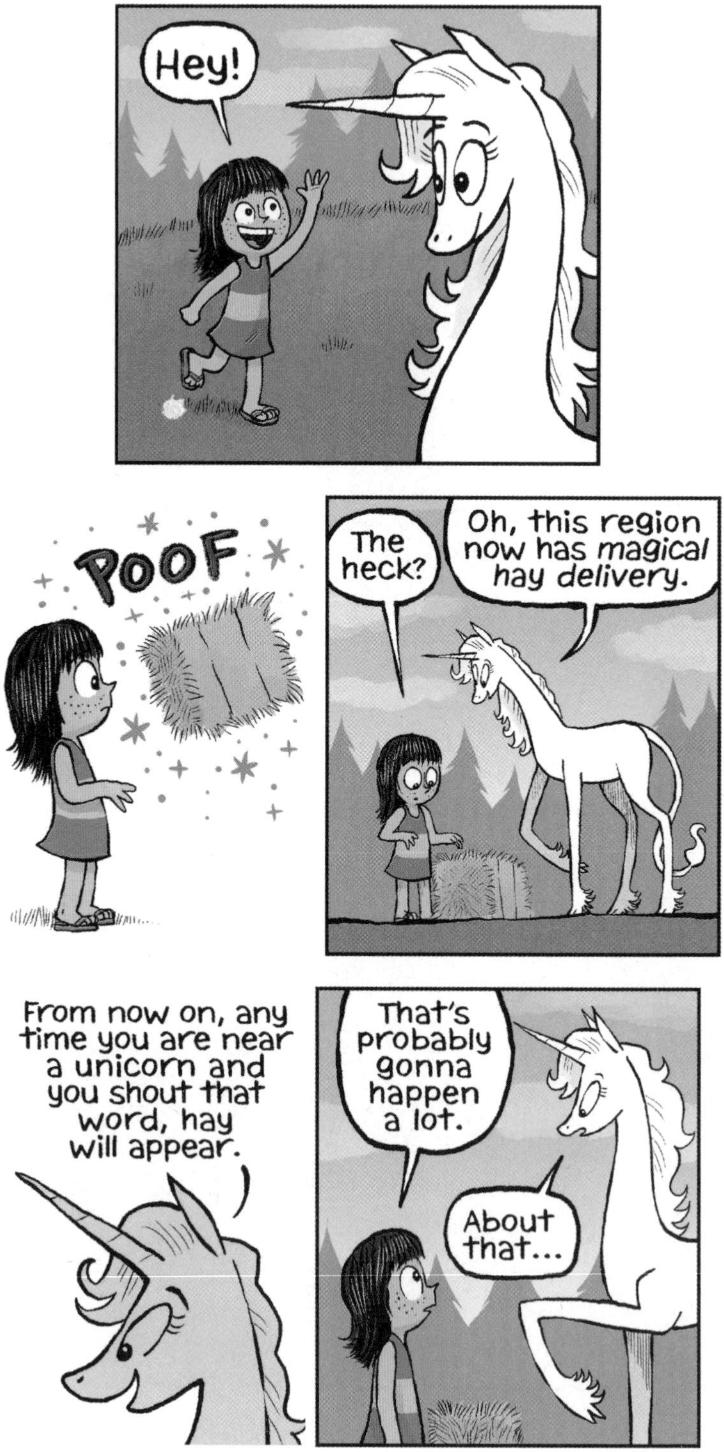
Hey!
POOF
The heck?
Oh, this region now has *magical hay delivery*.
From now on, any time you are near a unicorn and you shout that word, hay will appear.
That's probably gonna happen a lot.
About that...

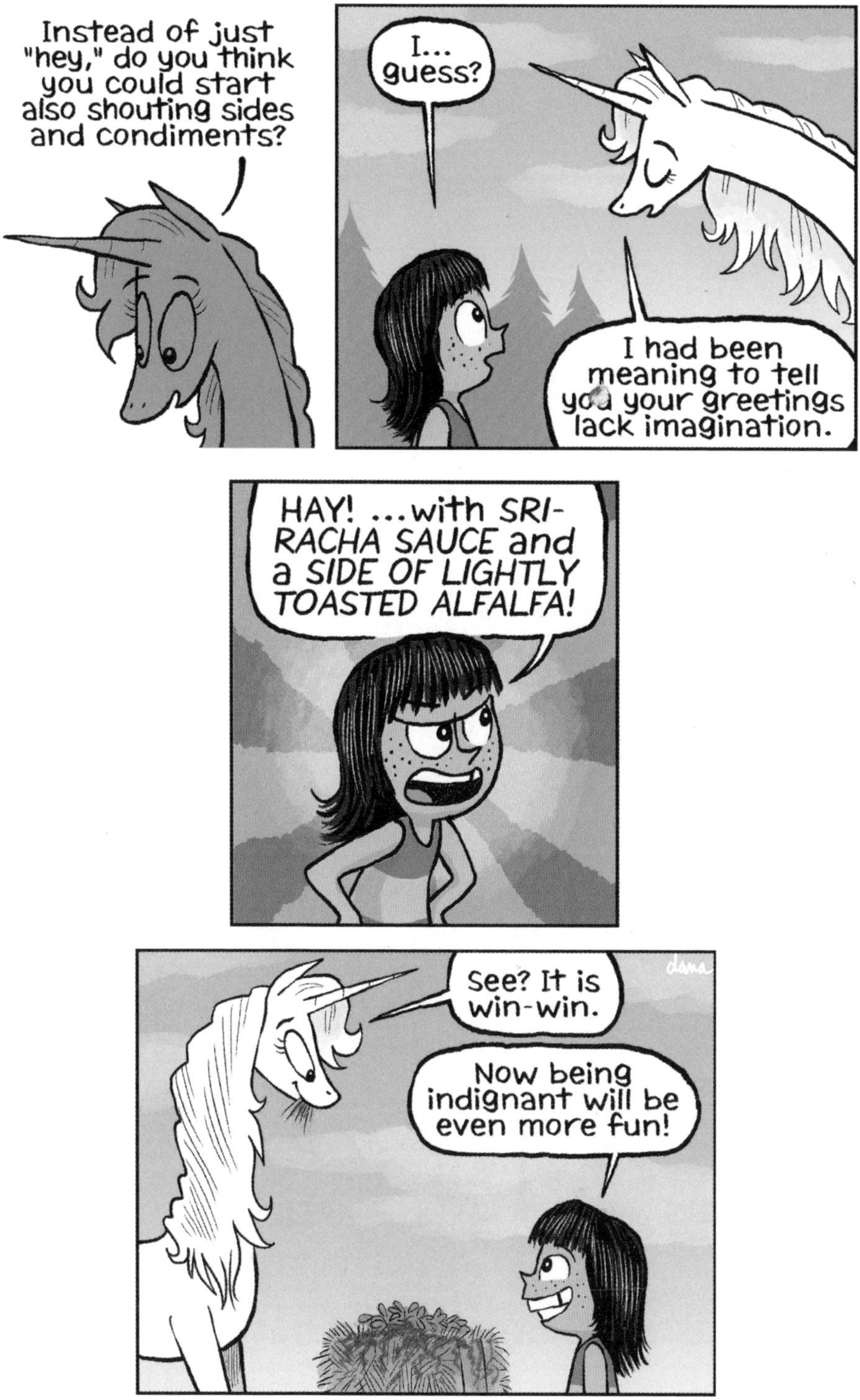
Instead of just "hey," do you think you could start also shouting sides and condiments?
I... guess?
I had been meaning to tell you your greetings lack imagination.
HAY! ...with SRI-RACHA SAUCE and a SIDE OF LIGHTLY TOASTED ALFALFA!
See? It is win-win.
Now being indignant will be even more fun!

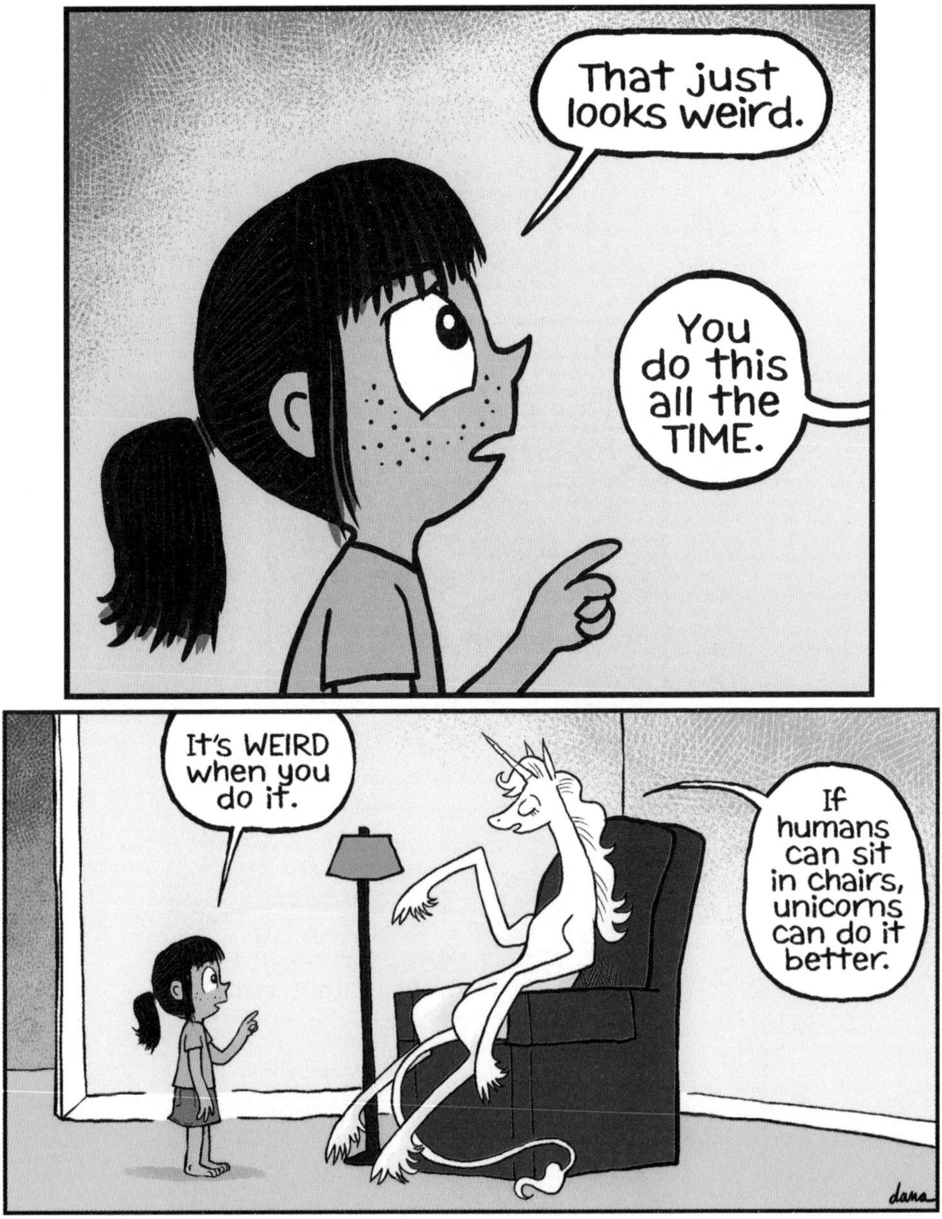

That just looks weird.
You do this all the TIME.
It's WEIRD when you do it.
If humans can sit in chairs, unicorns can do it better.
dana

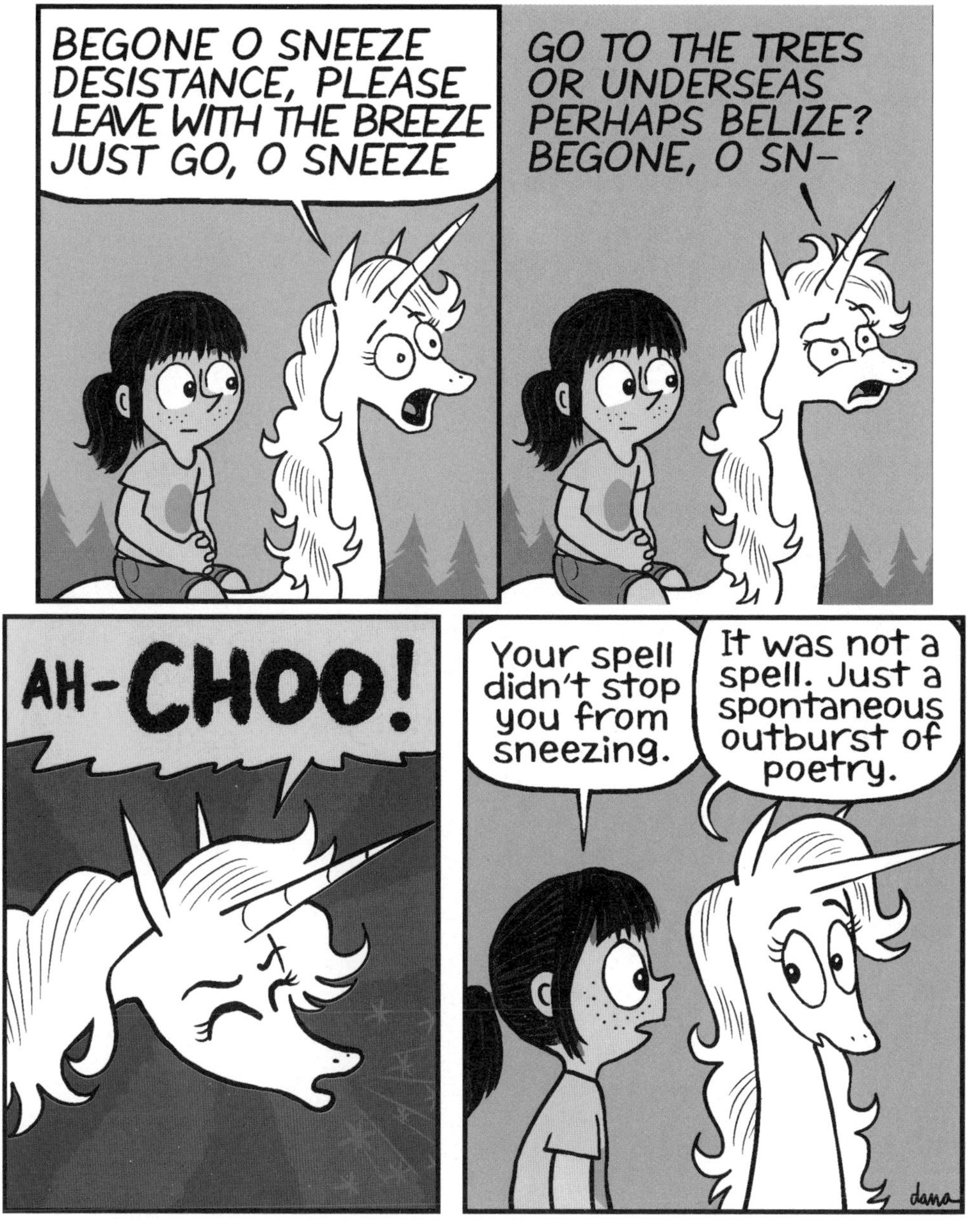
BEGONE O SNEEZE
DESISTANCE, PLEASE
LEAVE WITH THE BREEZE
JUST GO, O SNEEZE
GO TO THE TREES
OR UNDERSEAS
PERHAPS BELIZE?
BEGONE, O SN–
AH-CHOO!
Your spell didn't stop you from sneezing.
It was not a spell. Just a spontaneous outburst of poetry.
dana

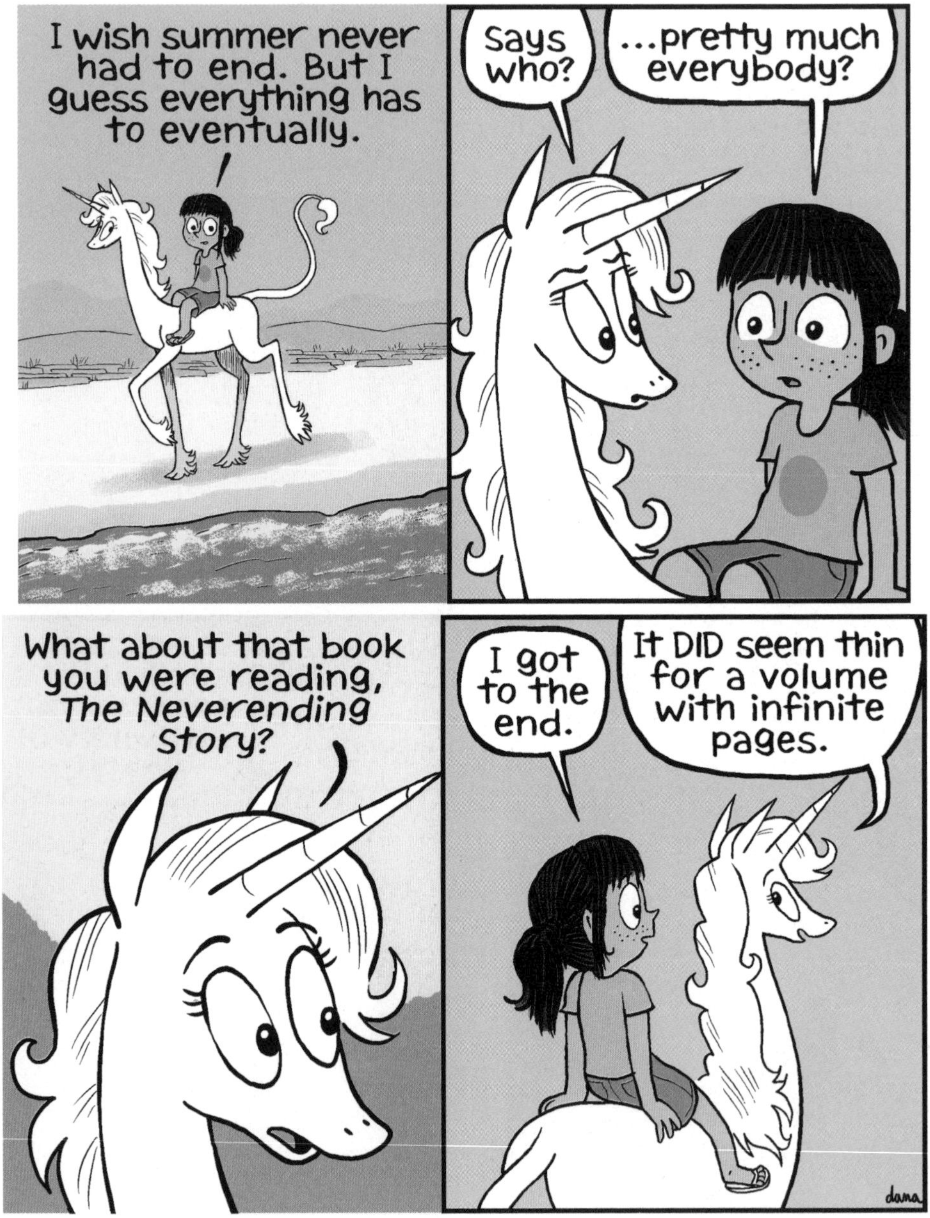
I wish summer never had to end. But I guess everything has to eventually.
Says who?
...pretty much everybody?
What about that book you were reading, The Neverending Story?
I got to the end.
It DID seem thin for a volume with infinite pages.
dana

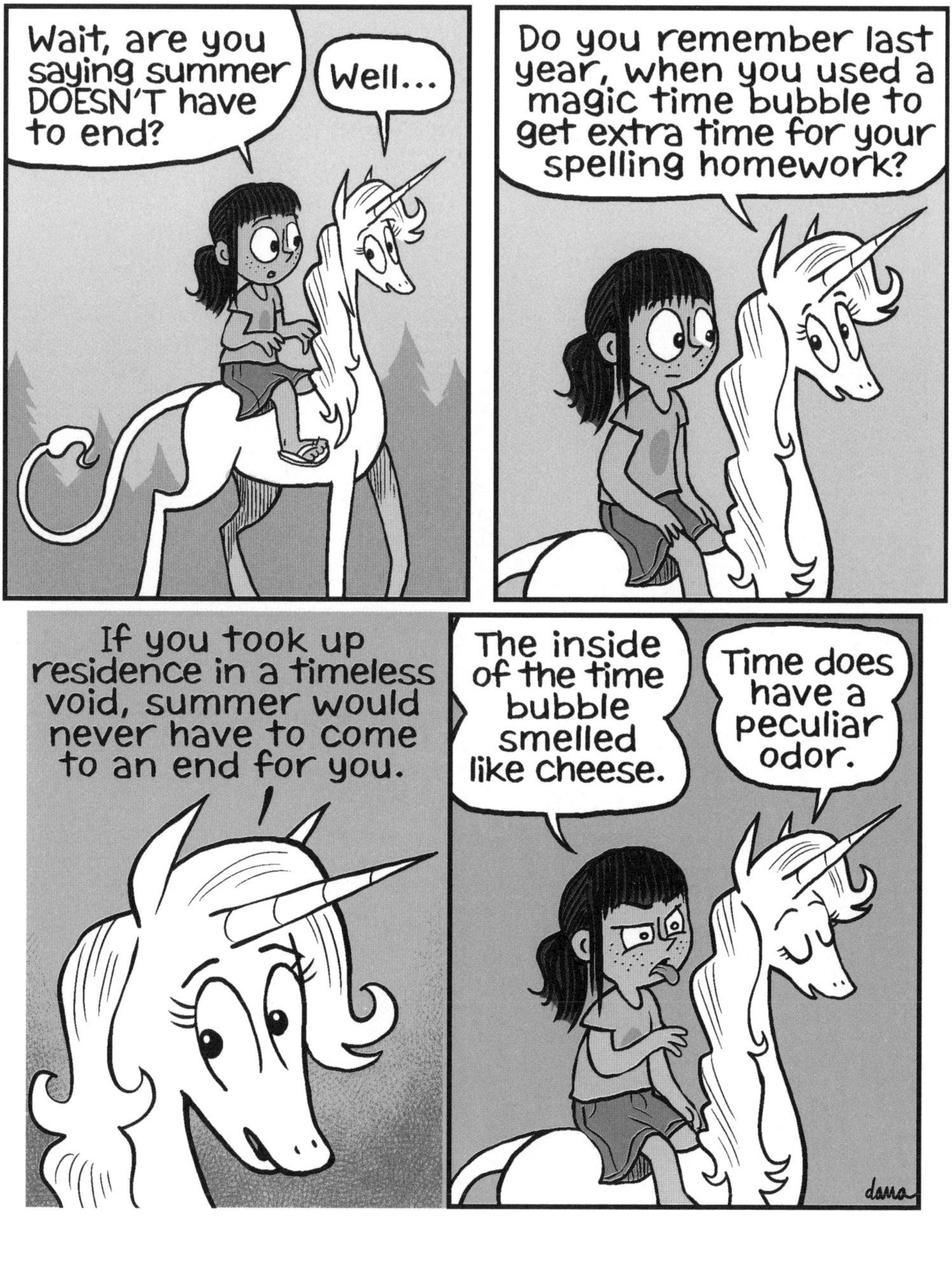
Wait, are you saying summer DOESN'T have to end?
Well...
Do you remember last year, when you used a magic time bubble to get extra time for your spelling homework?
If you took up residence in a timeless void, summer would never have to come to an end for you.
The inside of the time bubble smelled like cheese.
Time does have a peculiar odor.
dana

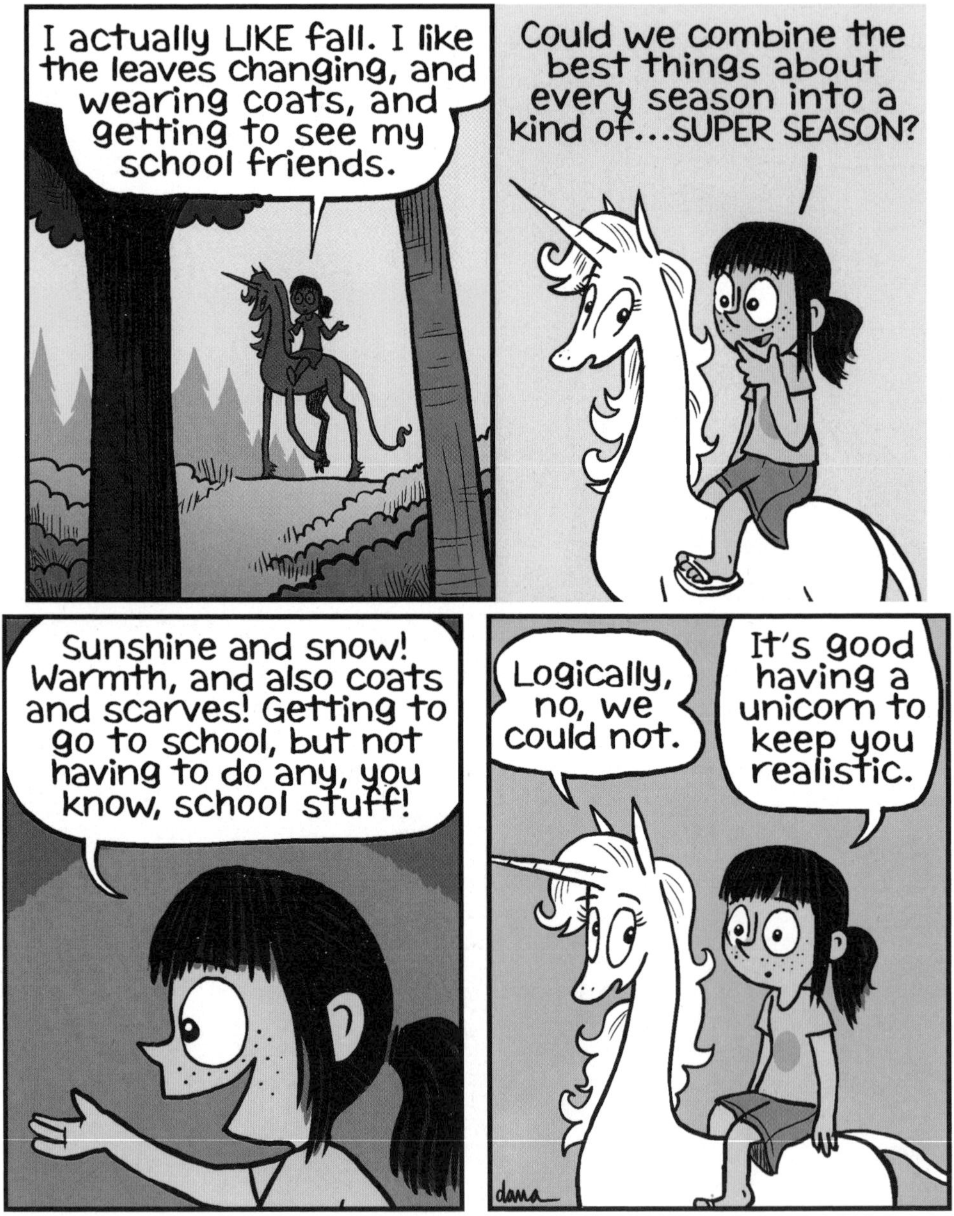
I actually LIKE fall. I like the leaves changing, and wearing coats, and getting to see my school friends.
Could we combine the best things about every season into a kind of...SUPER SEASON?
Sunshine and snow! Warmth, and also coats and scarves! Getting to go to school, but not having to do any, you know, school stuff!
Logically, no, we could not.
It's good having a unicorn to keep you realistic.
dana

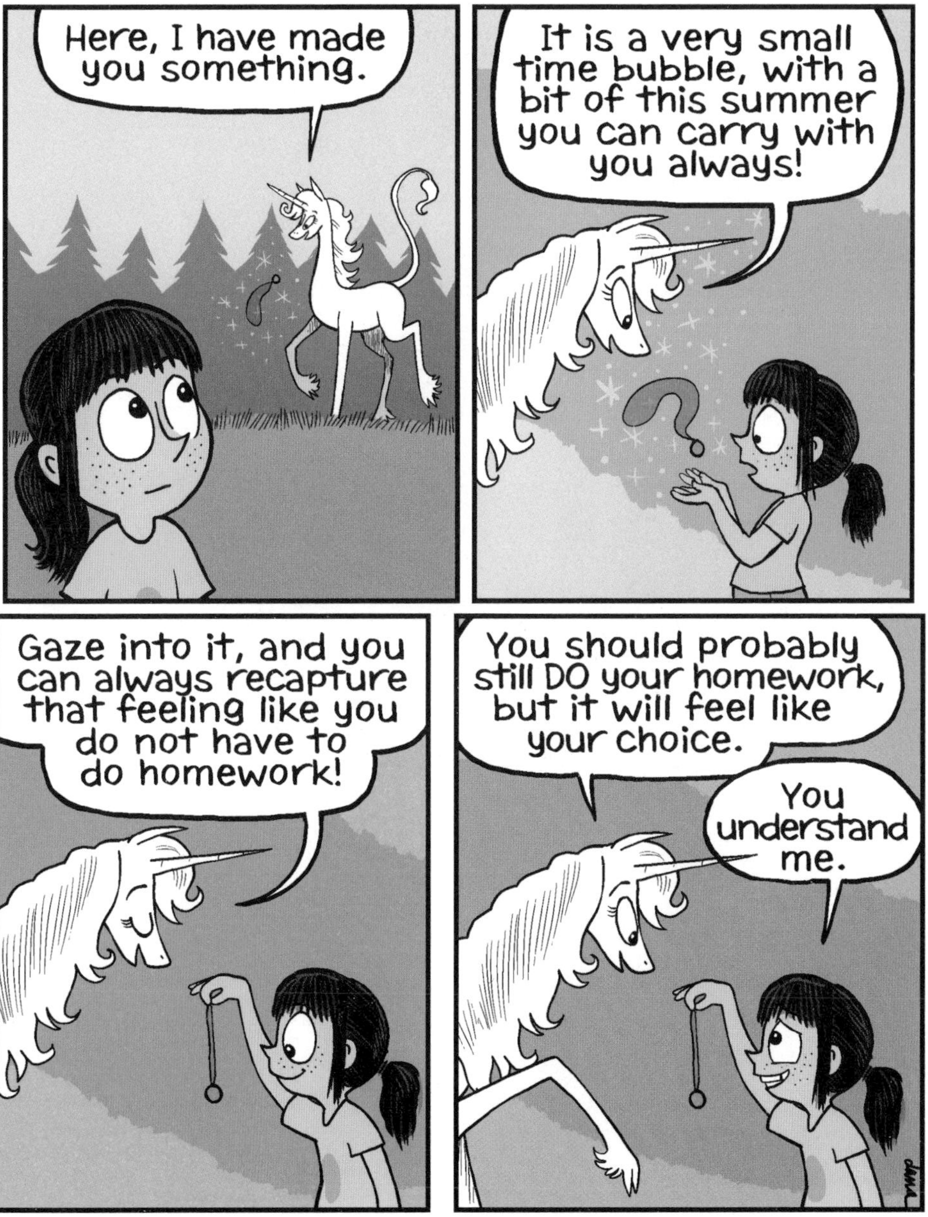
Here, I have made you something.
It is a very small time bubble, with a bit of this summer you can carry with you always!
Gaze into it, and you can always recapture that feeling like you do not have to do homework!
You should probably still DO your homework, but it will feel like your choice.
You understand me.
dana

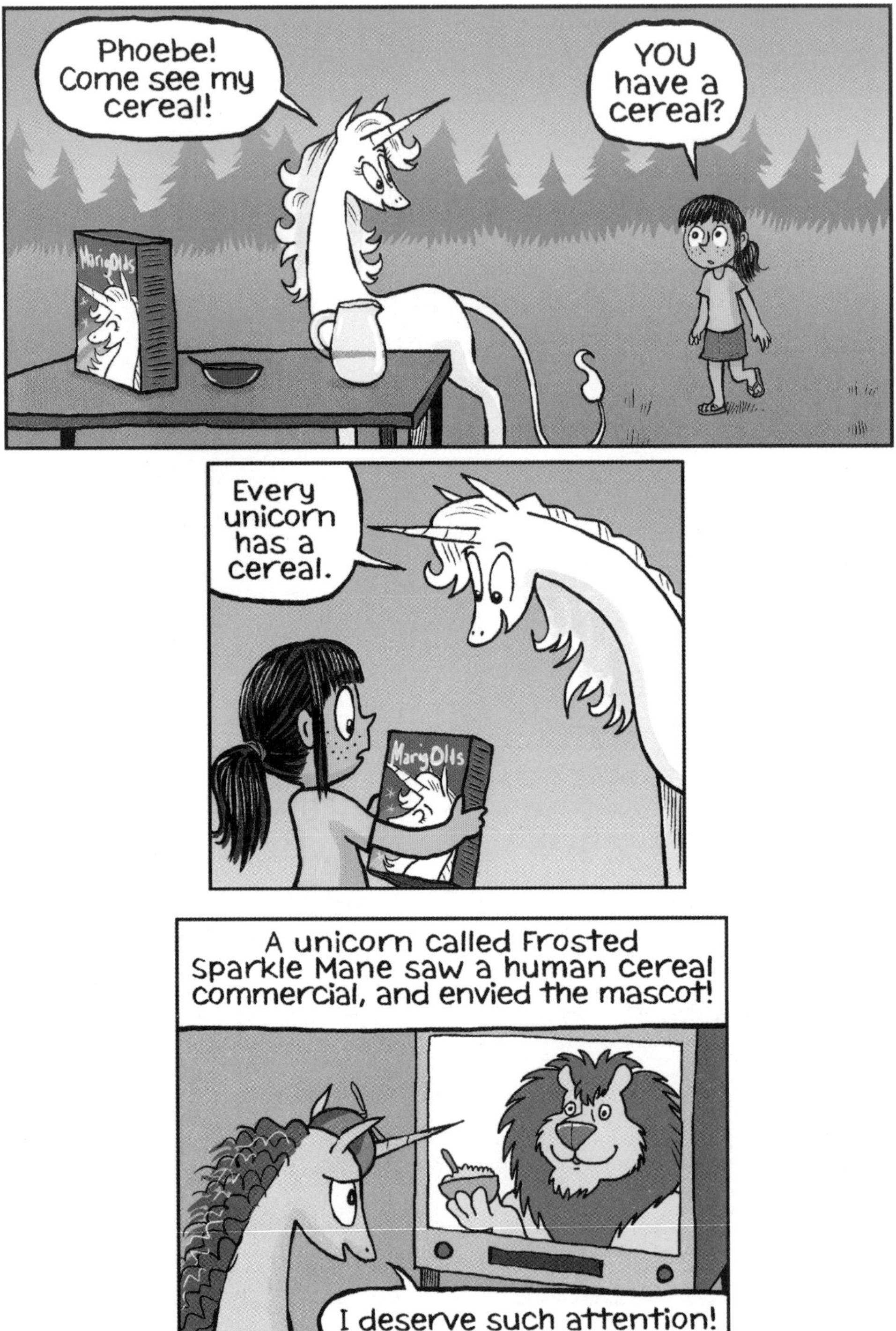
Phoebe! Come see my cereal!
YOU have a cereal?
MaryOlds
Every unicorn has a cereal.
MaryOlds
A unicorn called Frosted Sparkle Mane saw a human cereal commercial, and envied the mascot!
I deserve such attention!

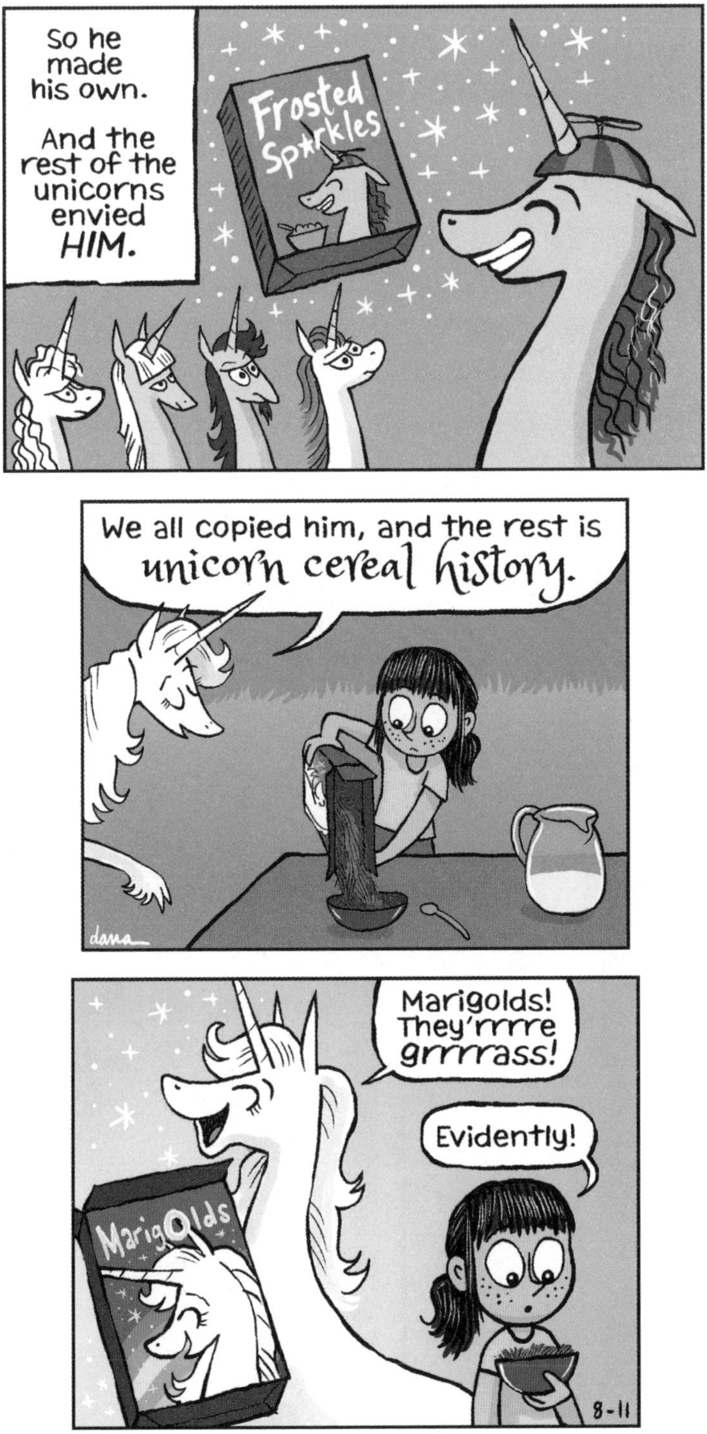
So he made his own.
And the rest of the unicorns envied HIM.
Frosted Sparkles
We all copied him, and the rest is unicorn cereal history.
dana
Marigolds! They'rrrre grrrrass!
Evidently!
Marigolds
8-11

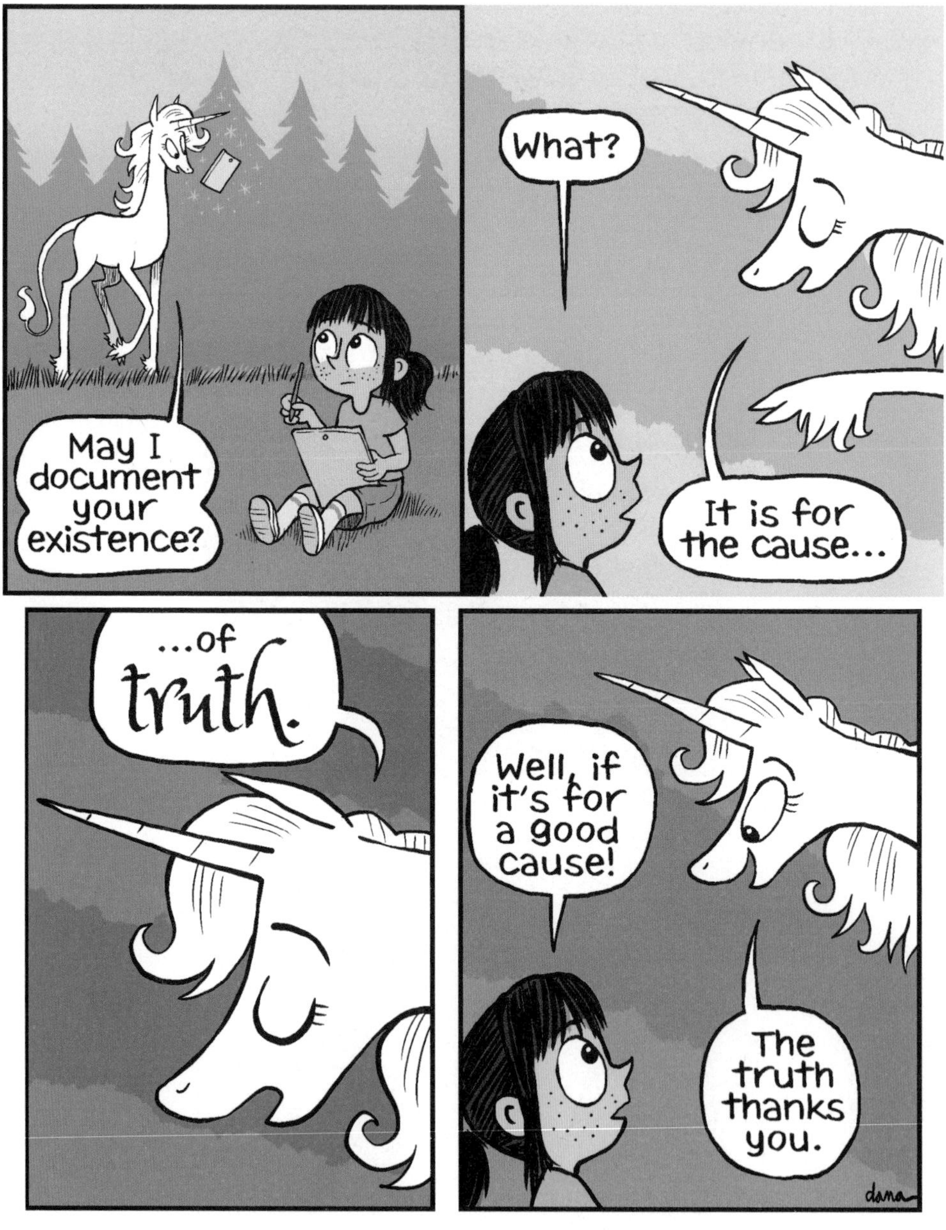
May I document your existence?
What?
It is for the cause...
...of truth.
Well, if it's for a good cause!
The truth thanks you.
dana

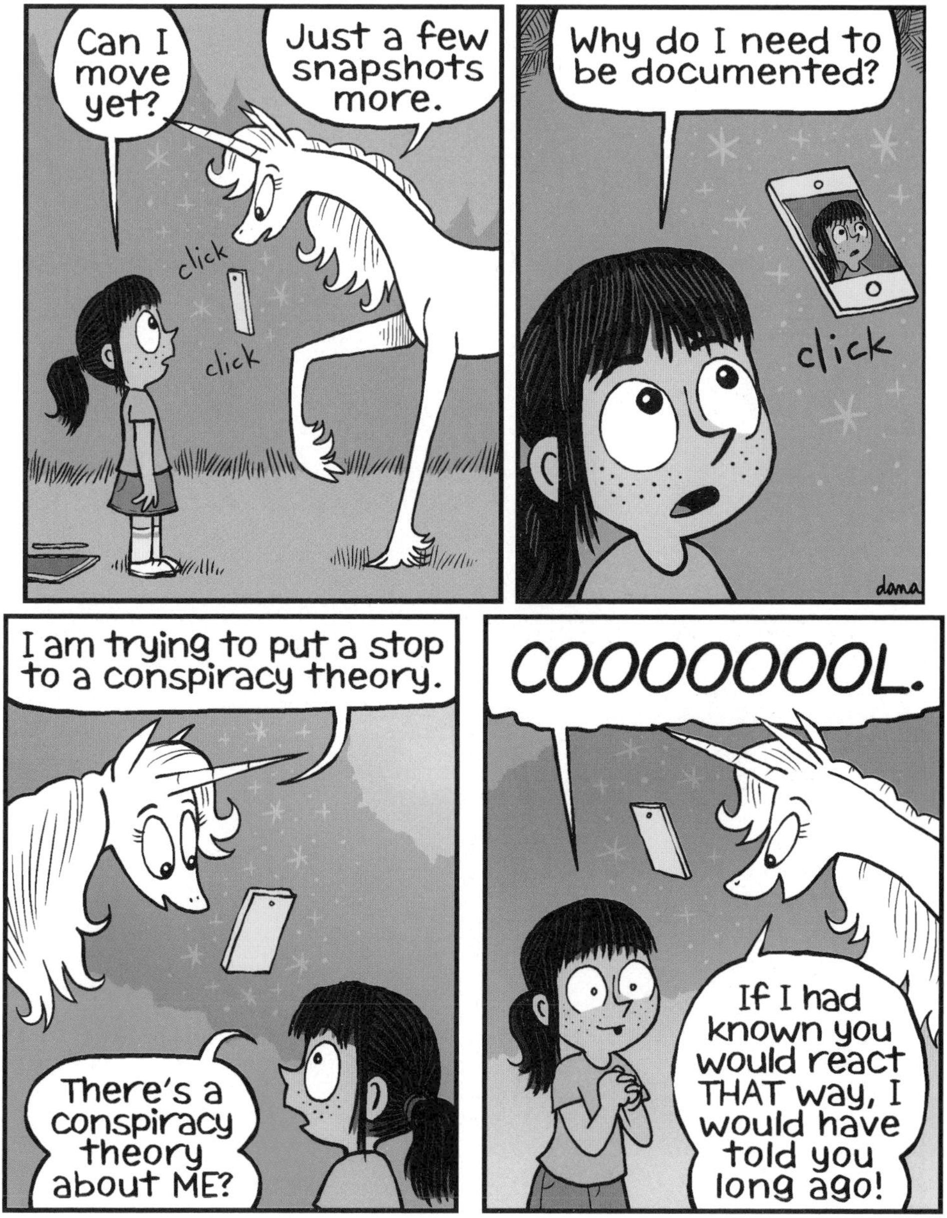
Can I move yet?
Just a few snapshots more.
click
click
Why do I need to be documented?
click
dana
I am trying to put a stop to a conspiracy theory.
There's a conspiracy theory about ME?
COOOOOOOL.
If I had known you would react THAT way, I would have told you long ago!

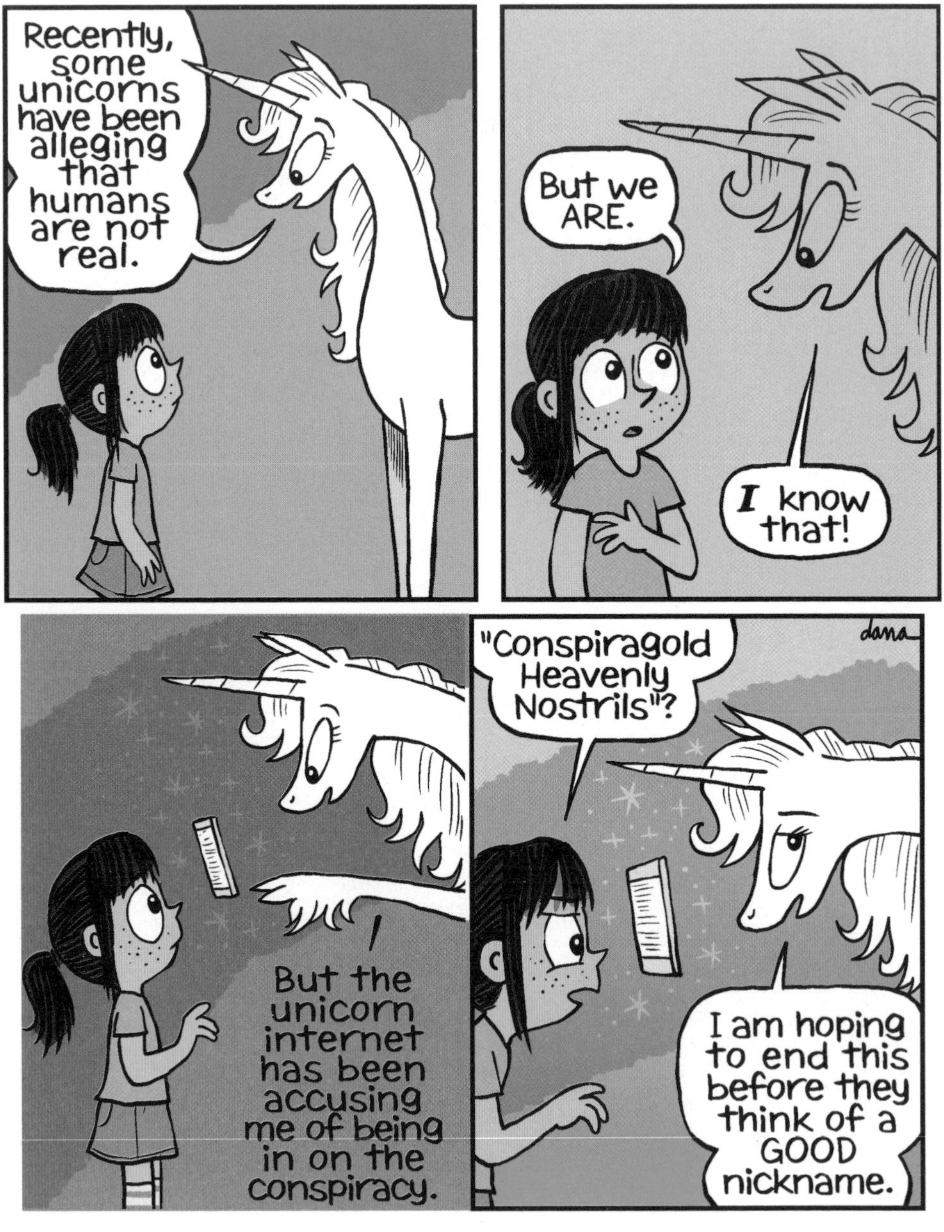
Recently, some unicorns have been alleging that humans are not real.
But we ARE.
I know that!
But the unicorn internet has been accusing me of being in on the conspiracy.
"Conspiragold Heavenly Nostrils"?
I am hoping to end this before they think of a GOOD nickname.
dana

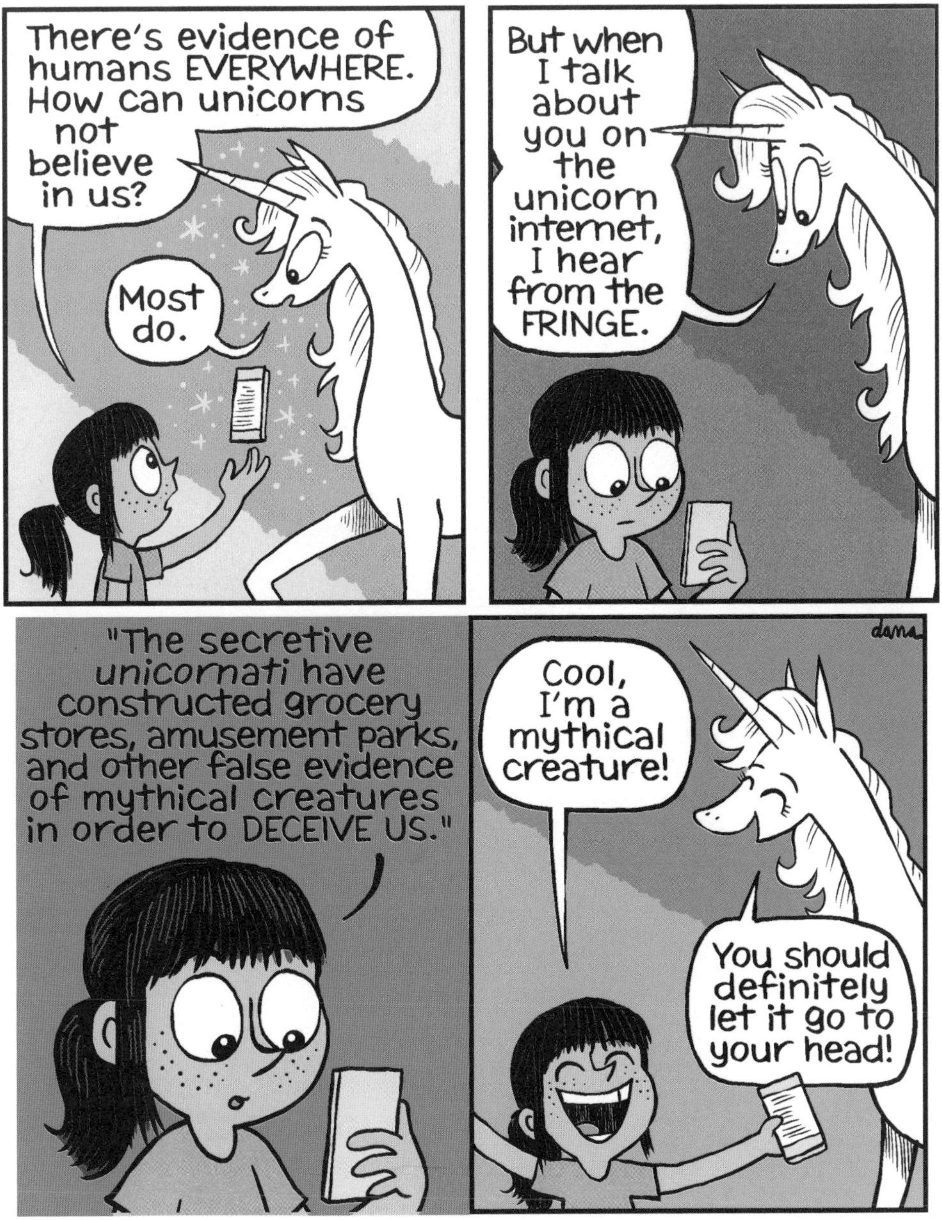
There's evidence of humans EVERYWHERE. How can unicorns not believe in us?
Most do.
But when I talk about you on the unicorn internet, I hear from the FRINGE.
"The secretive unicornati have constructed grocery stores, amusement parks, and other false evidence of mythical creatures in order to DECEIVE US."
Cool, I'm a mythical creature!
You should definitely let it go to your head!
dana

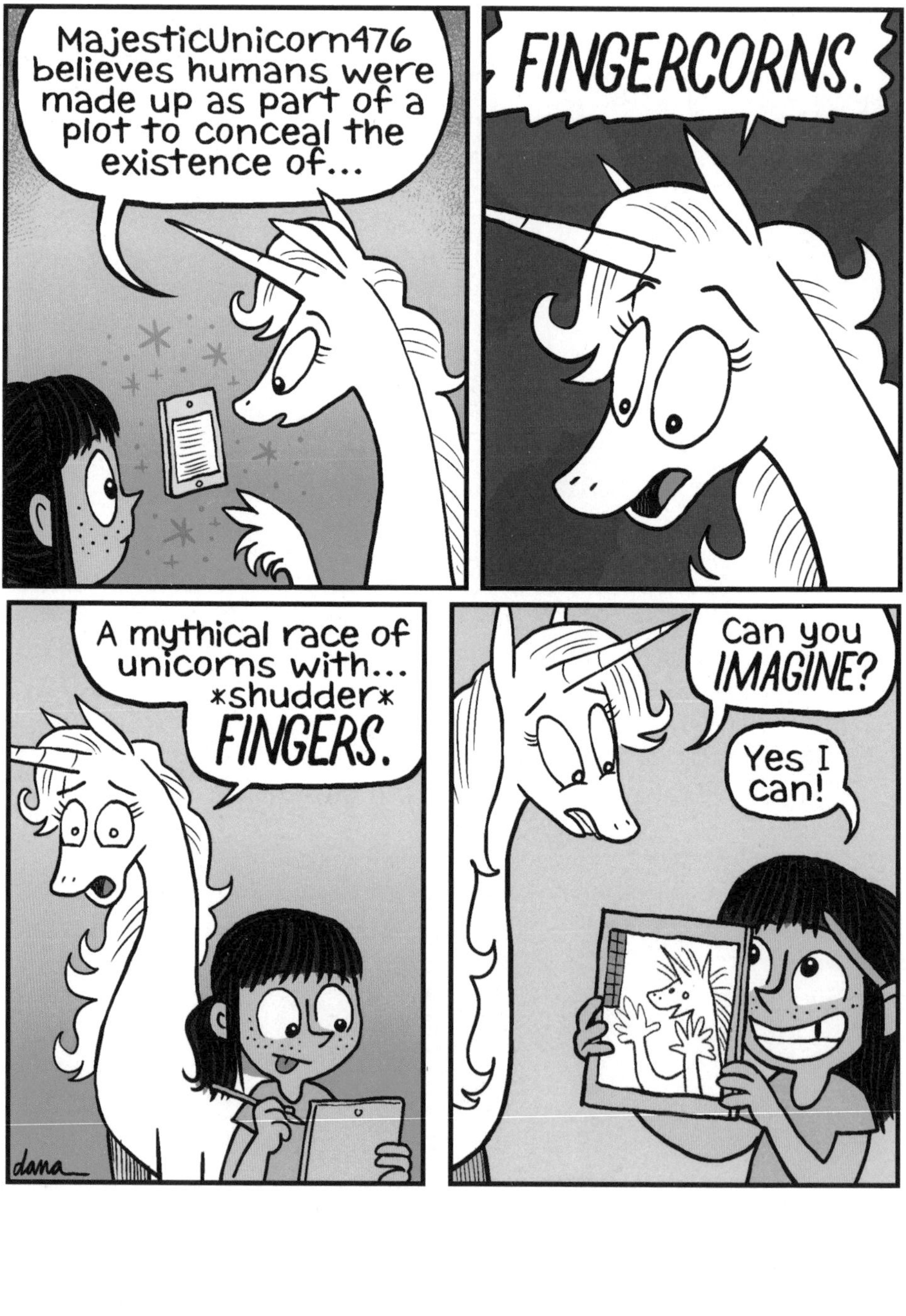
MajesticUnicorn476 believes humans were made up as part of a plot to conceal the existence of...
FINGERCORNS.
A mythical race of unicorns with... *shudder* FINGERS.
Can you IMAGINE?
Yes I can!
dana

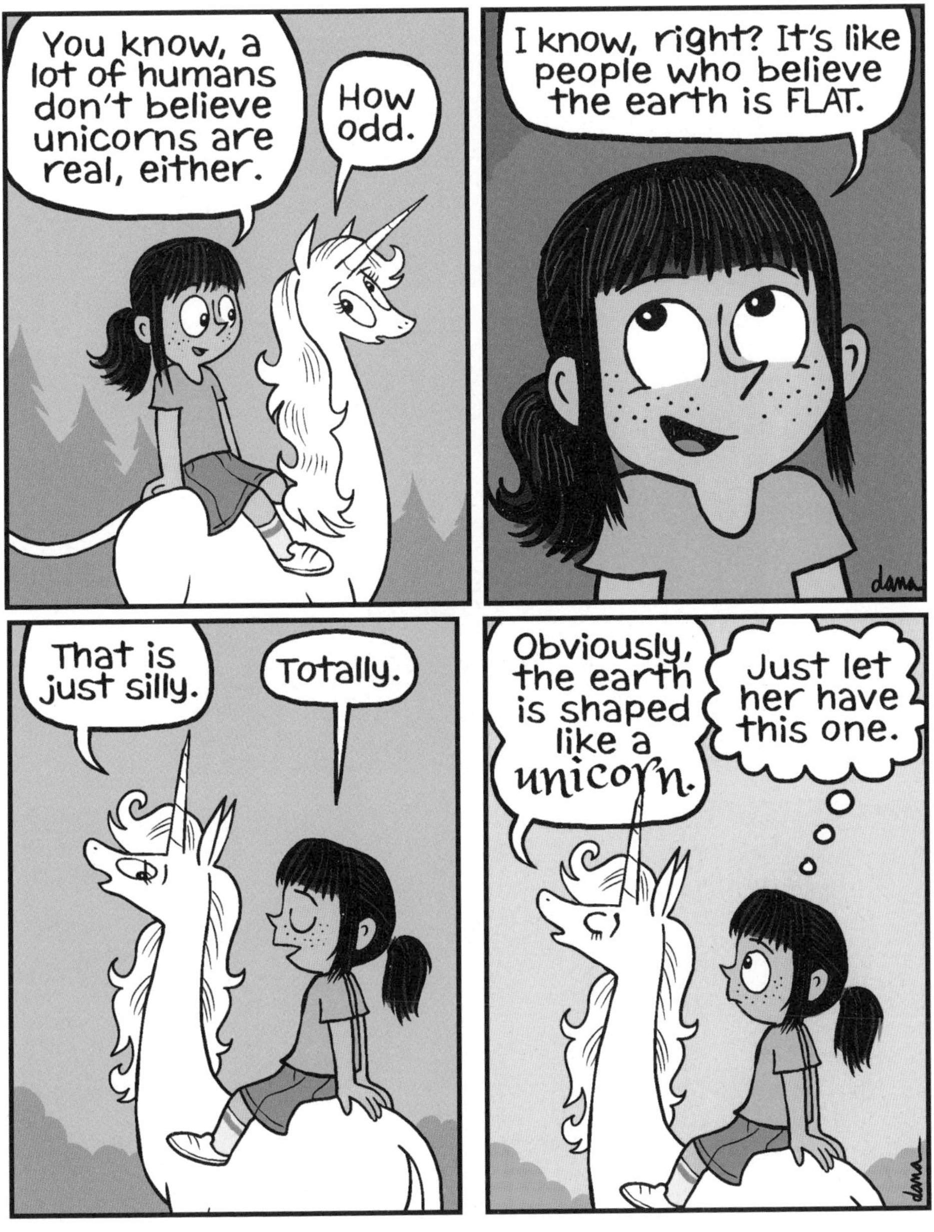
You know, a lot of humans don't believe unicorns are real, either.
How odd.
I know, right? It's like people who believe the earth is FLAT.
dana
That is just silly.
Totally.
Obviously, the earth is shaped like a unicorn.
Just let her have this one.
dana

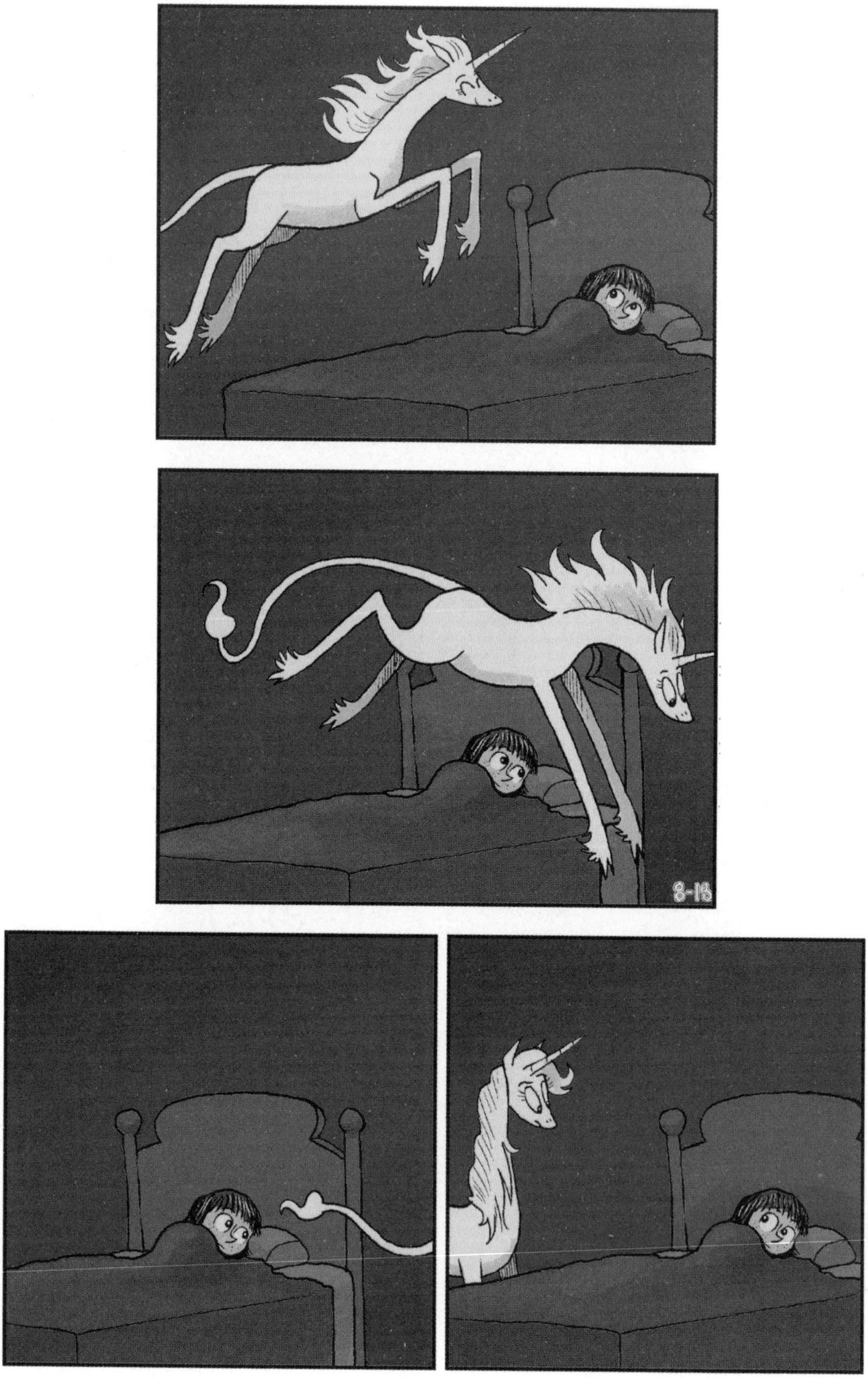
8-18

You are not asleep yet.
This isn't helping me sleep.
If counting sheep works, counting unicorns ought to work even better.
Even if it DID work, I know it's just one unicorn, coming back over and over.
I shall return with my disguise kit.
This is way more fun than sleeping.
dana

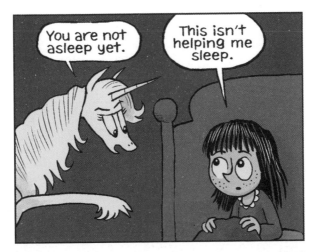

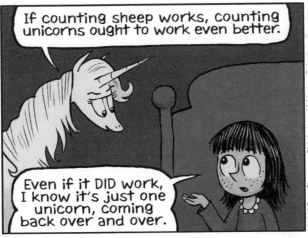

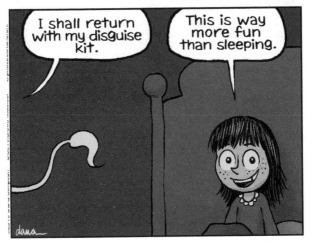

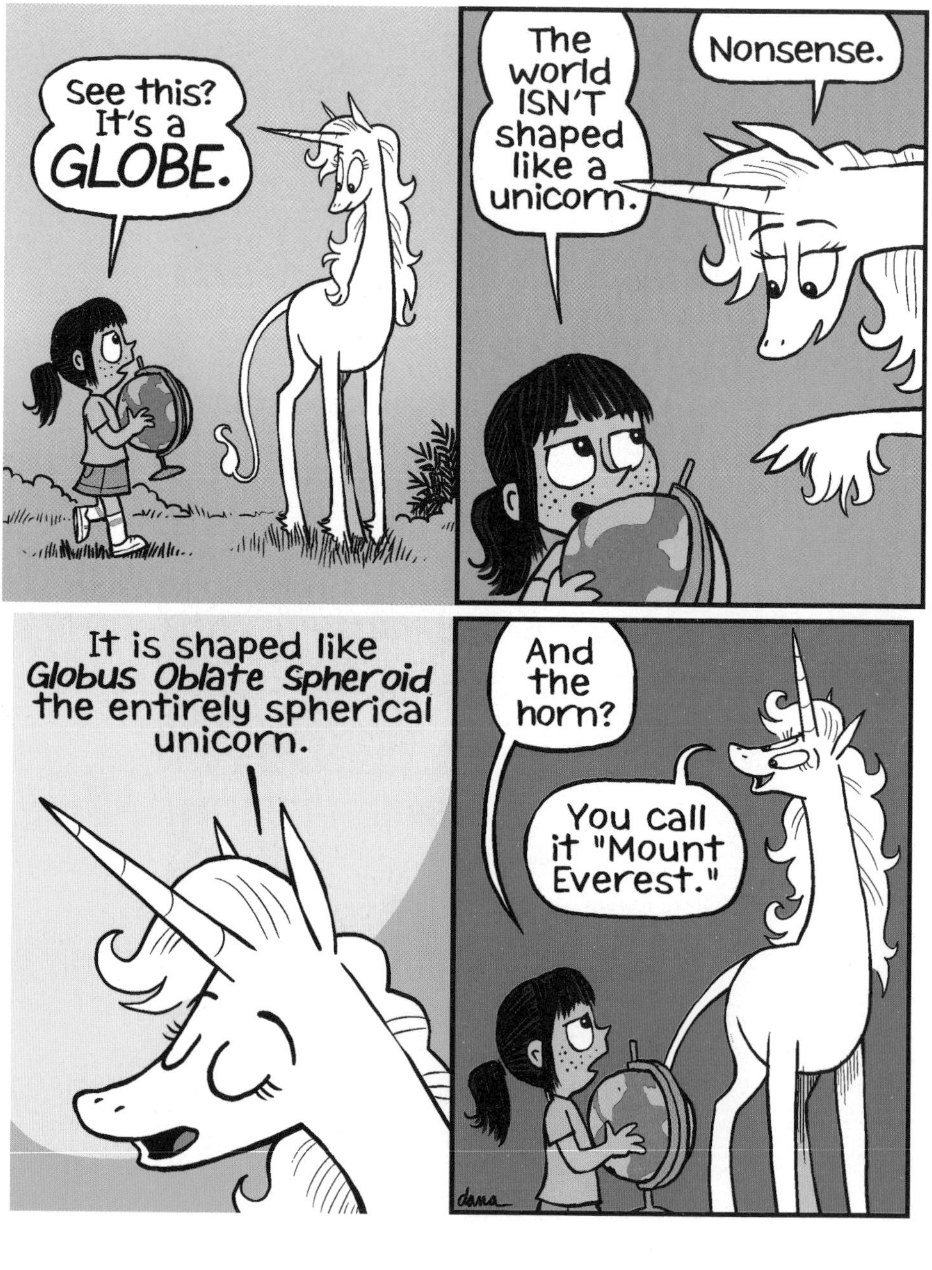
See this? It's a GLOBE.
The world ISN'T shaped like a unicorn.
Nonsense.
It is shaped like Globus Oblate Spheroid the entirely spherical unicorn.
And the horn?
You call it "Mount Everest."
dana

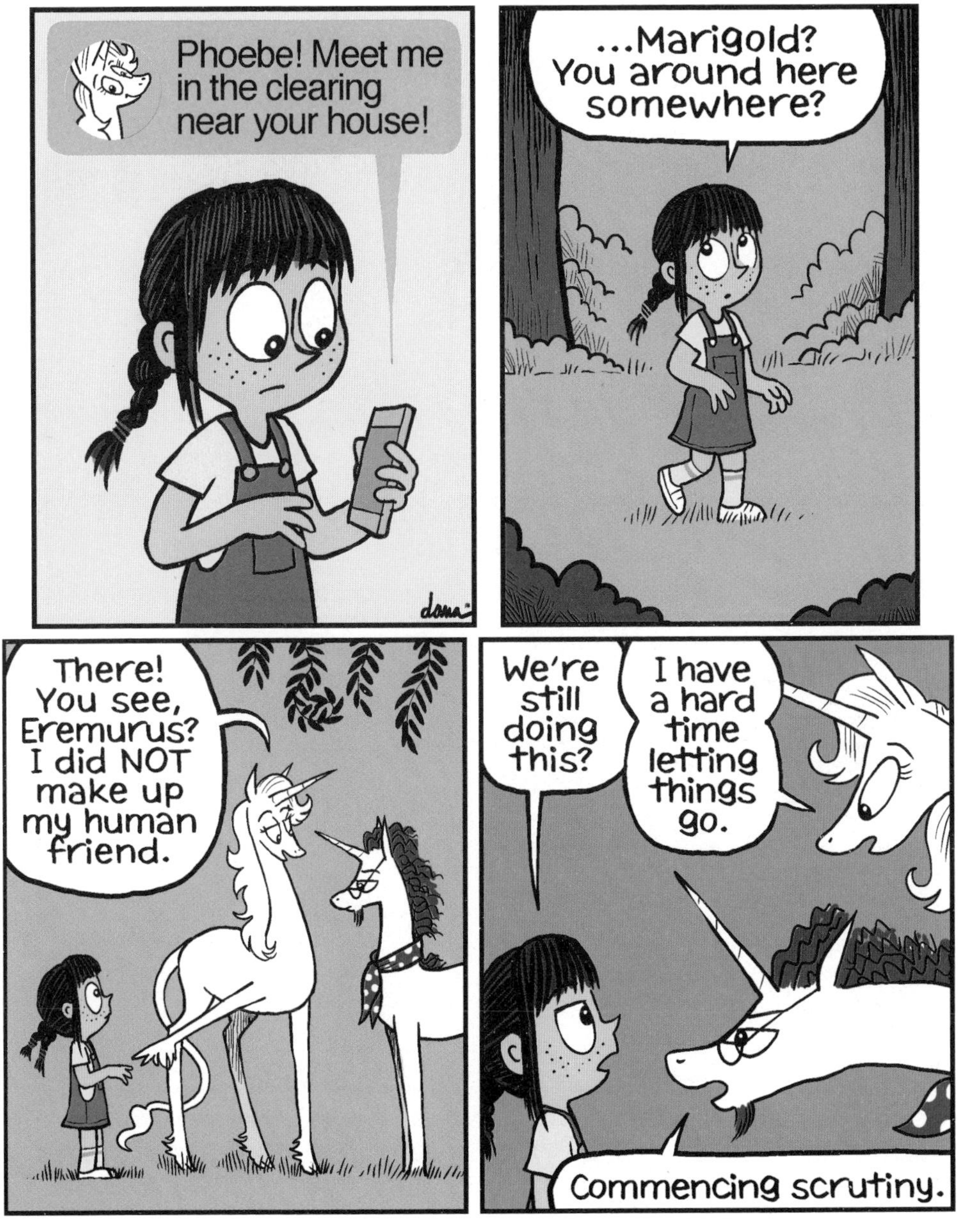
Phoebe! Meet me in the clearing near your house!
...Marigold? You around here somewhere?
There! You see, Eremurus? I did NOT make up my human friend.
We're still doing this?
I have a hard time letting things go.
Commencing scrutiny.

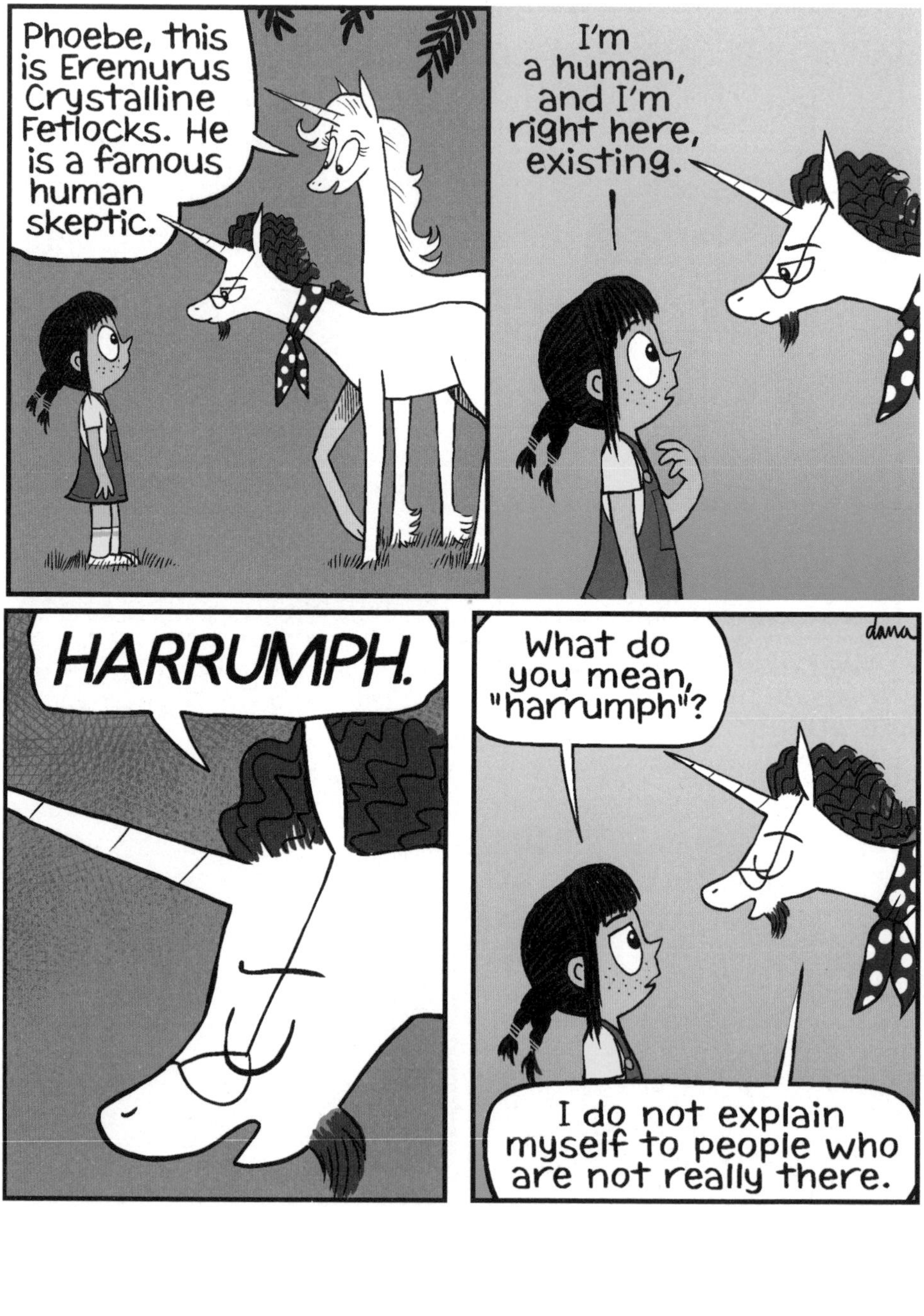
Phoebe, this is Eremurus Crystalline Fetlocks. He is a famous human skeptic.
I'm a human, and I'm right here, existing.
HARRUMPH.
What do you mean, "harrumph"?
I do not explain myself to people who are not really there.
dana

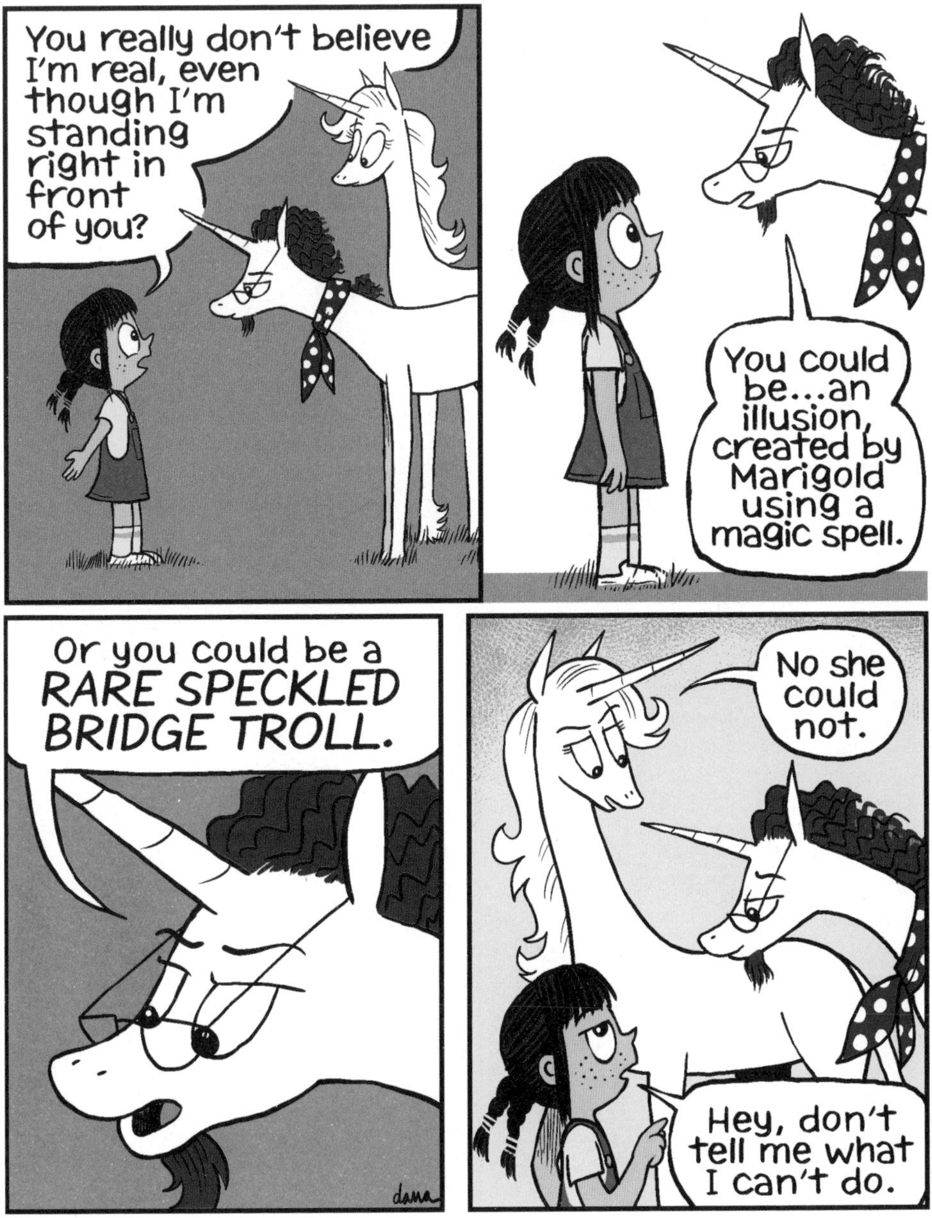
You really don't believe I'm real, even though I'm standing right in front of you?
You could be...an illusion, created by Marigold using a magic spell.
Or you could be a RARE SPECKLED BRIDGE TROLL.
No she could not.
Hey, don't tell me what I can't do.
dana

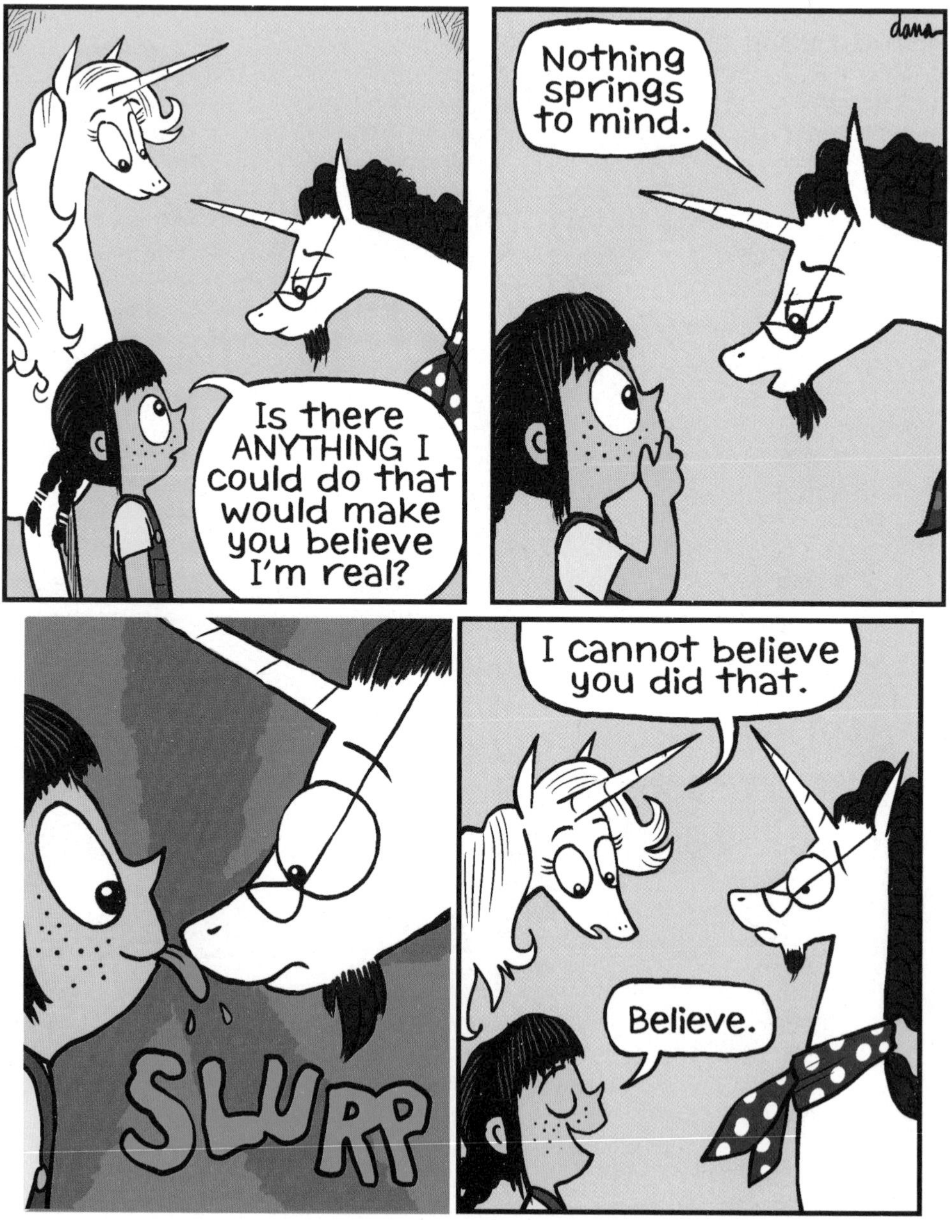
Is there ANYTHING I could do that would make you believe I'm real?
Nothing springs to mind.
SLURP
I cannot believe you did that.
Believe.

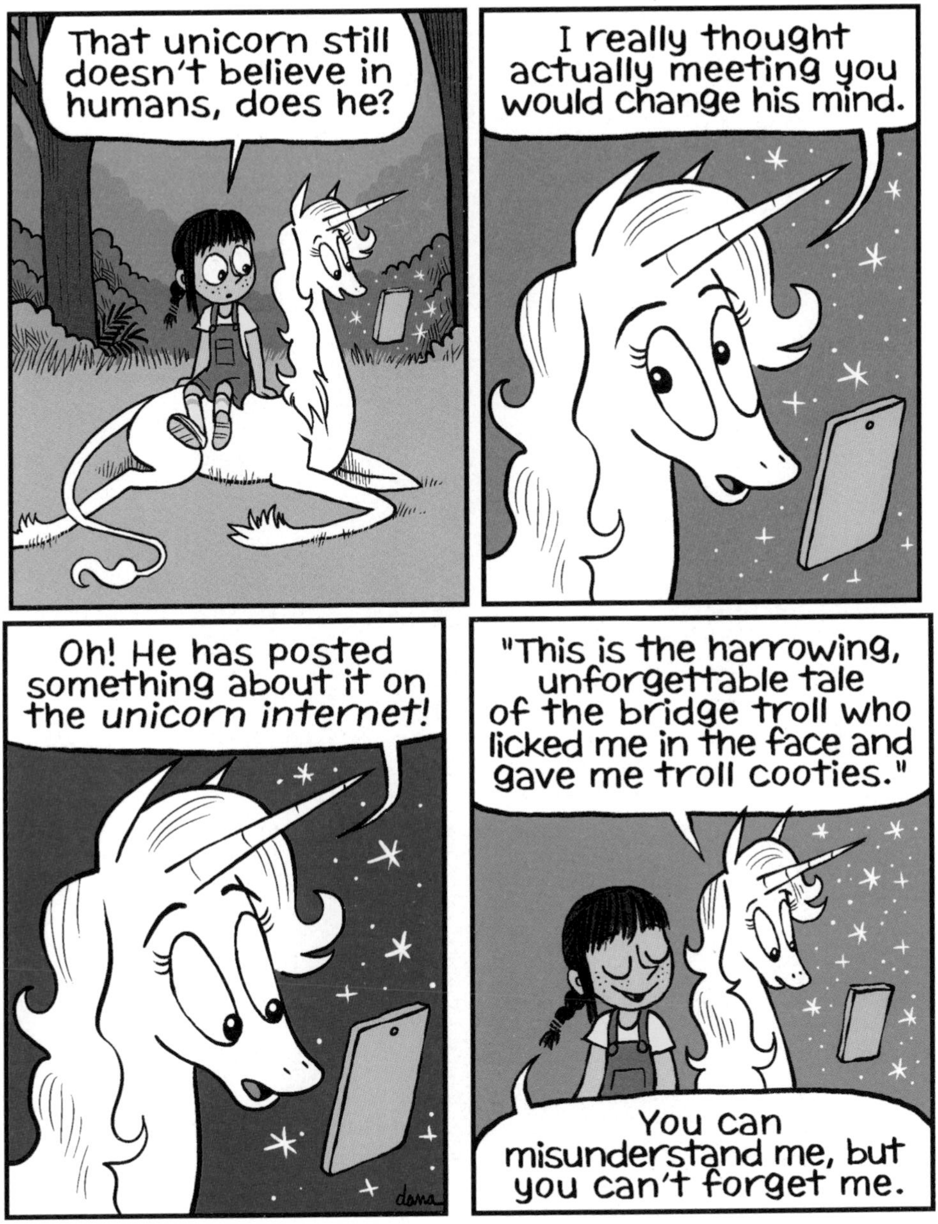
That unicorn still doesn't believe in humans, does he?
I really thought actually meeting you would change his mind.
Oh! He has posted something about it on the *unicorn internet*!
"This is the harrowing, unforgettable tale of the bridge troll who licked me in the face and gave me troll cooties."
You can misunderstand me, but you can't forget me.
dana

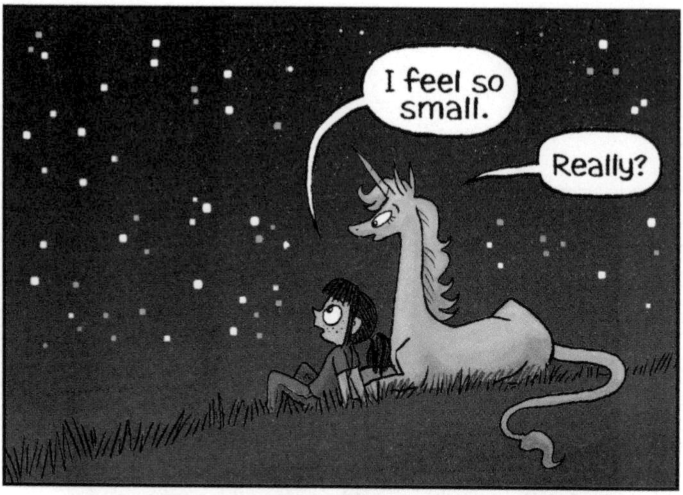
I feel so small.
Really?

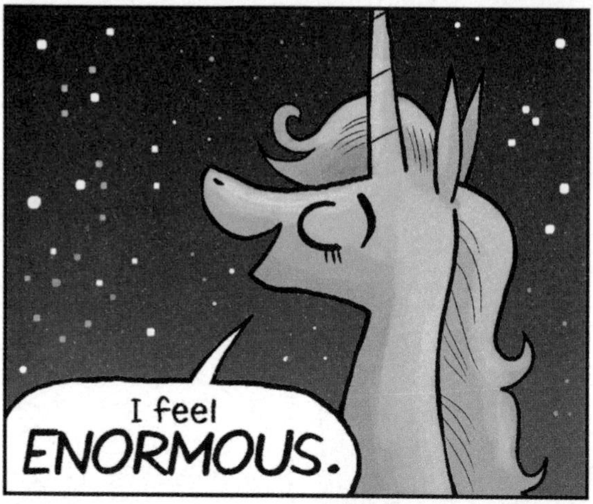
I feel ENORMOUS.

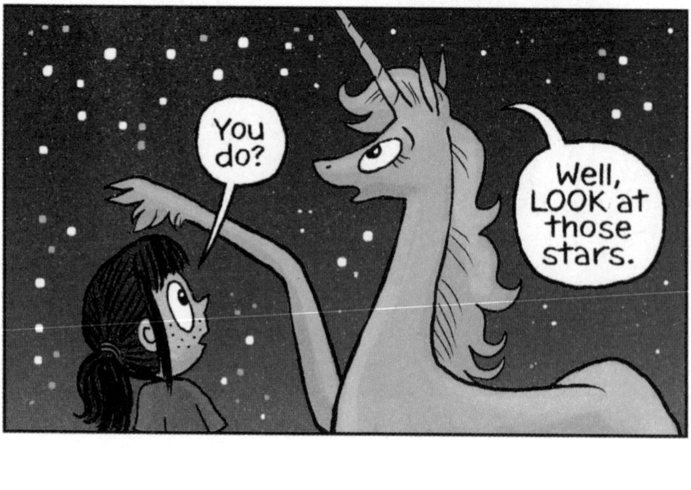
You do?
Well, LOOK at those stars.

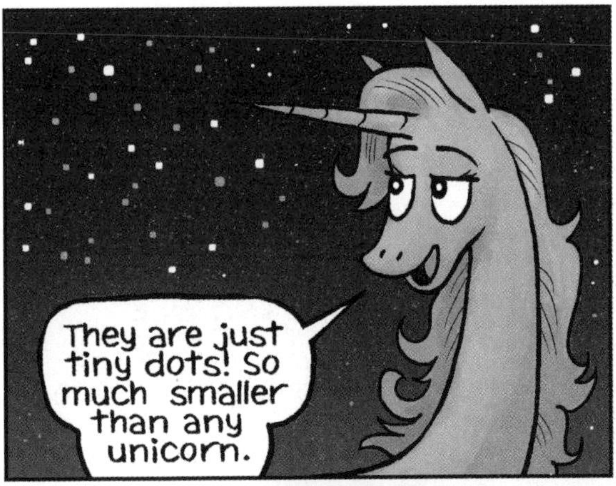
They are just tiny dots! So much smaller than any unicorn.

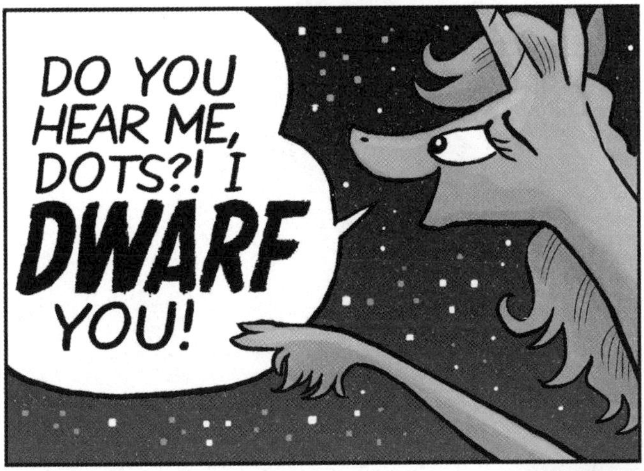
DO YOU HEAR ME, DOTS?! I DWARF YOU!

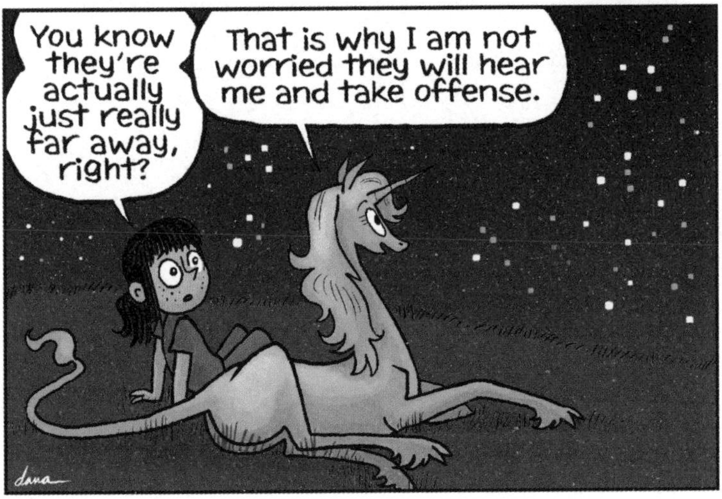
You know they're actually just really far away, right?
That is why I am not worried they will hear me and take offense.
dana

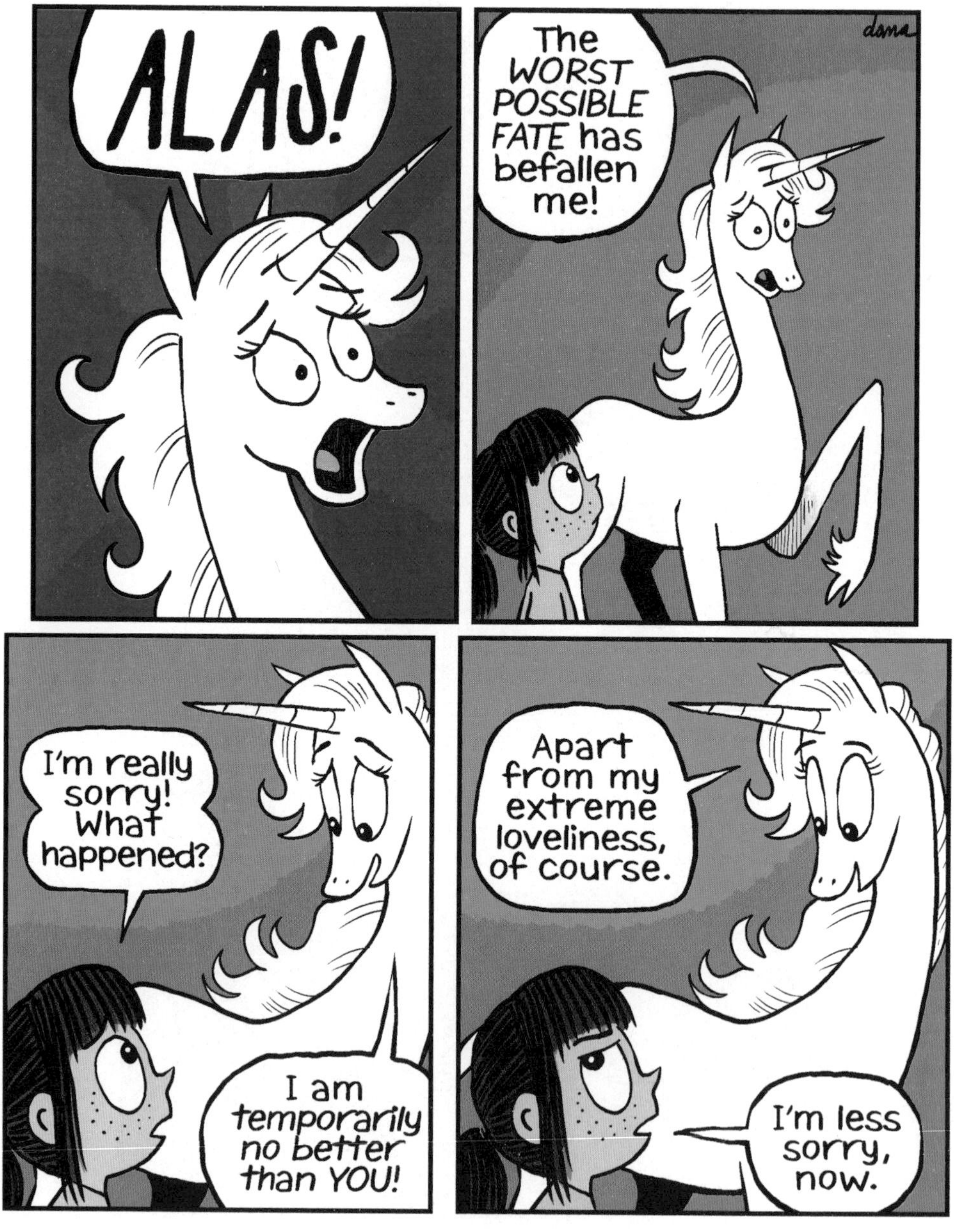
ALAS!
The WORST POSSIBLE FATE has befallen me!
dana
I'm really sorry! What happened?
I am temporarily no better than YOU!
Apart from my extreme loveliness, of course.
I'm less sorry, now.

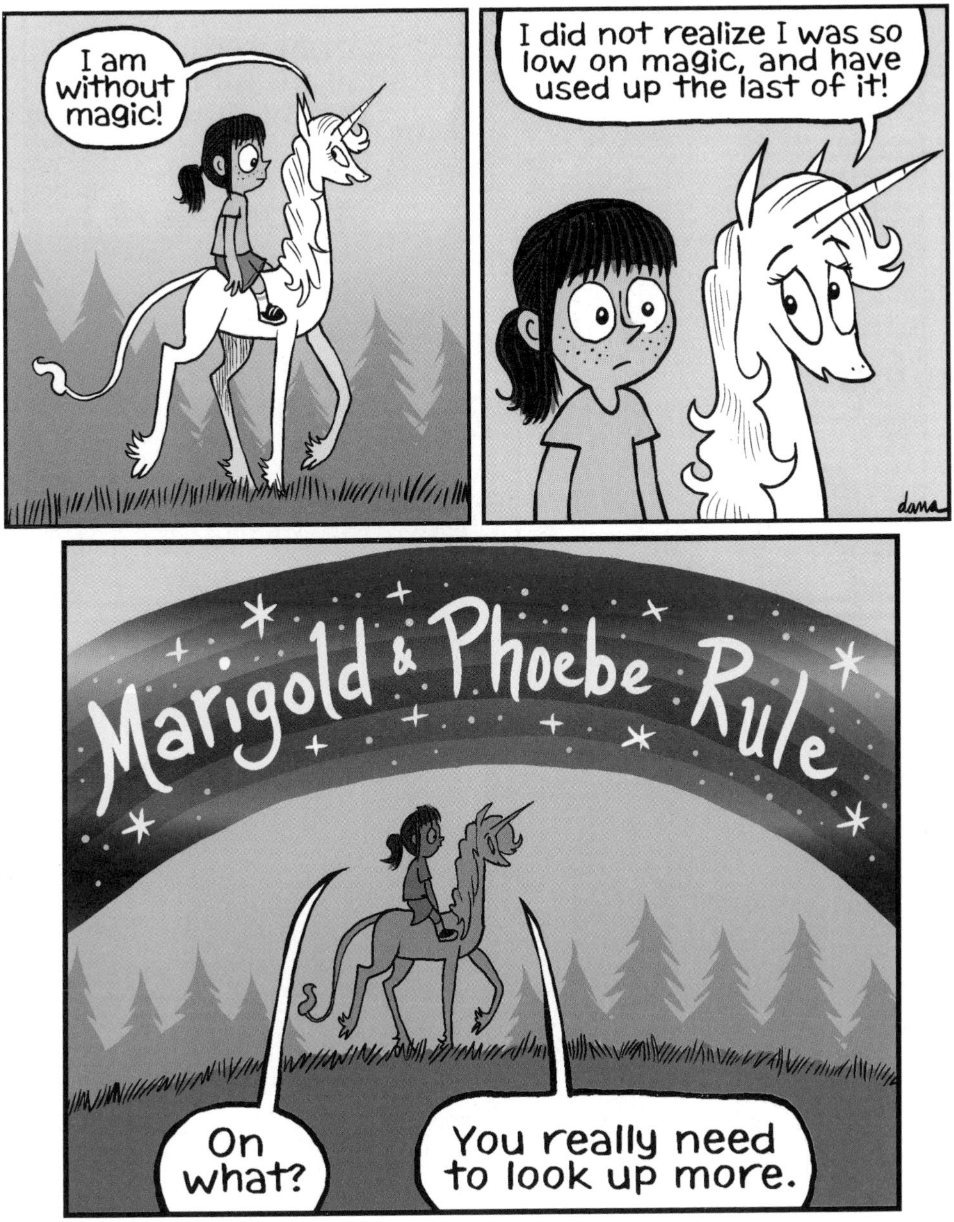
I am without magic!
I did not realize I was so low on magic, and have used up the last of it!
dana
Marigold & Phoebe Rule
On what?
You really need to look up more.

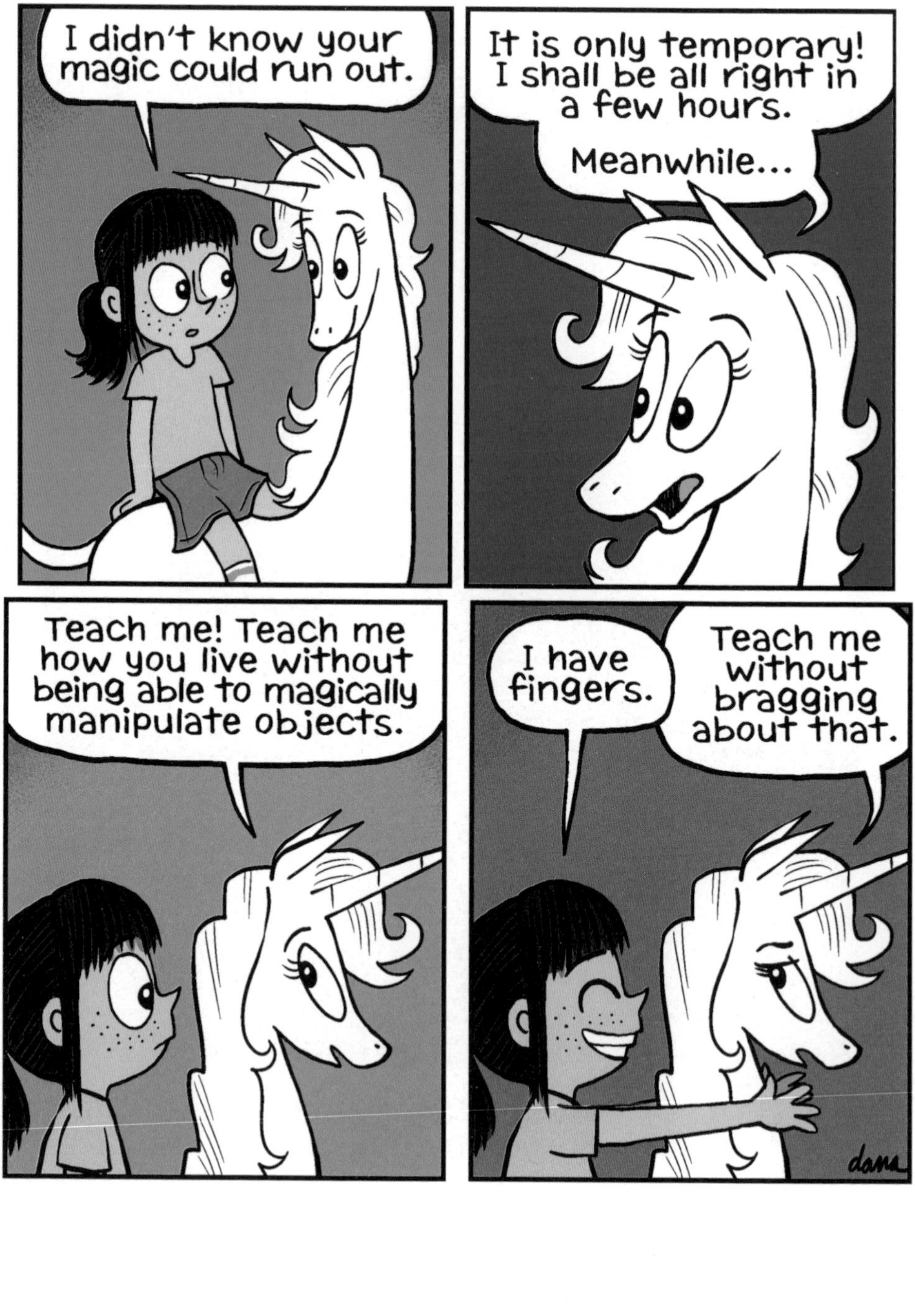
I didn't know your magic could run out.
It is only temporary! I shall be all right in a few hours.
Meanwhile...
Teach me! Teach me how you live without being able to magically manipulate objects.
I have fingers.
Teach me without bragging about that.
dana

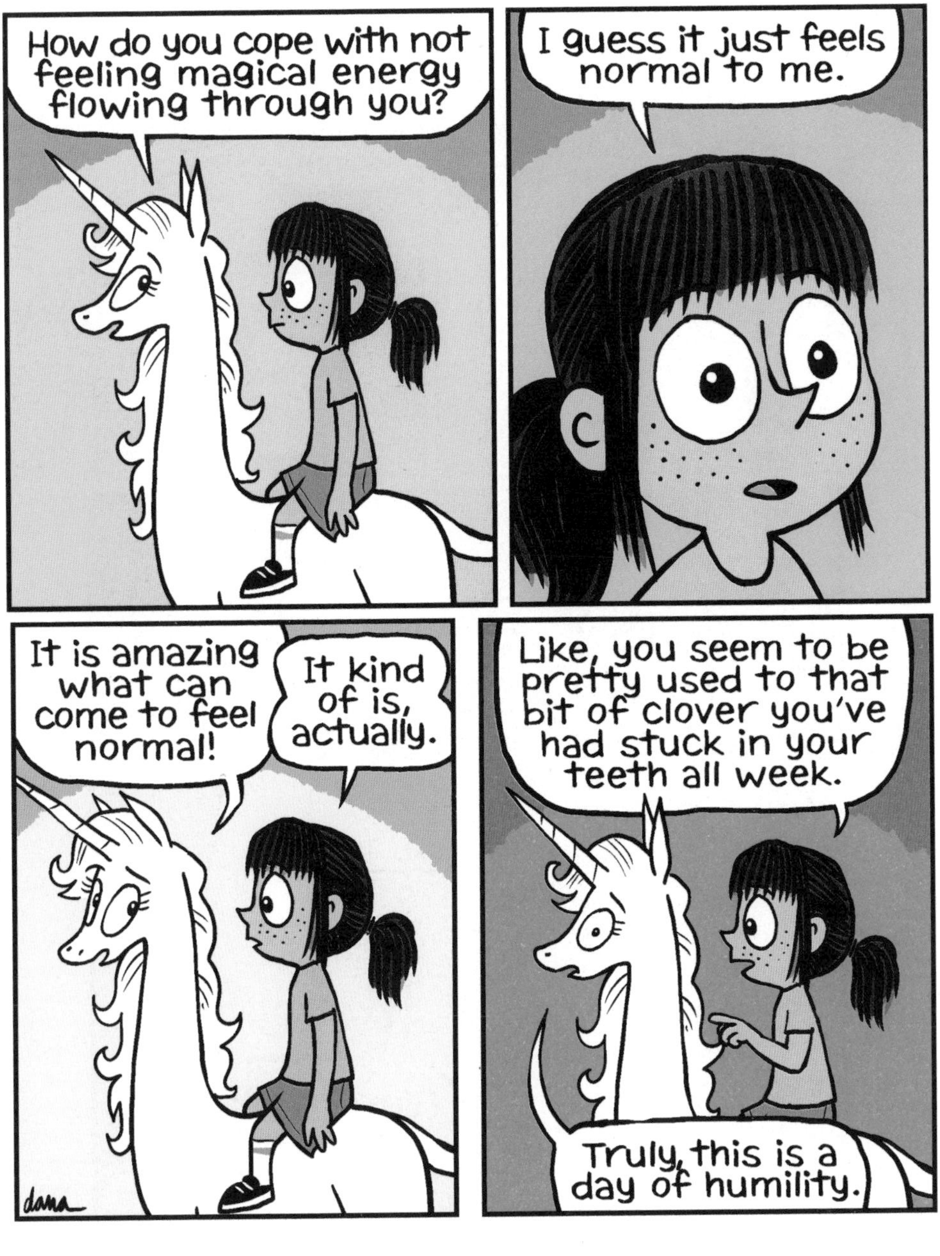
How do you cope with not feeling magical energy flowing through you?
I guess it just feels normal to me.
It is amazing what can come to feel normal!
It kind of is, actually.
dana
Like, you seem to be pretty used to that bit of clover you've had stuck in your teeth all week.
Truly, this is a day of humility.

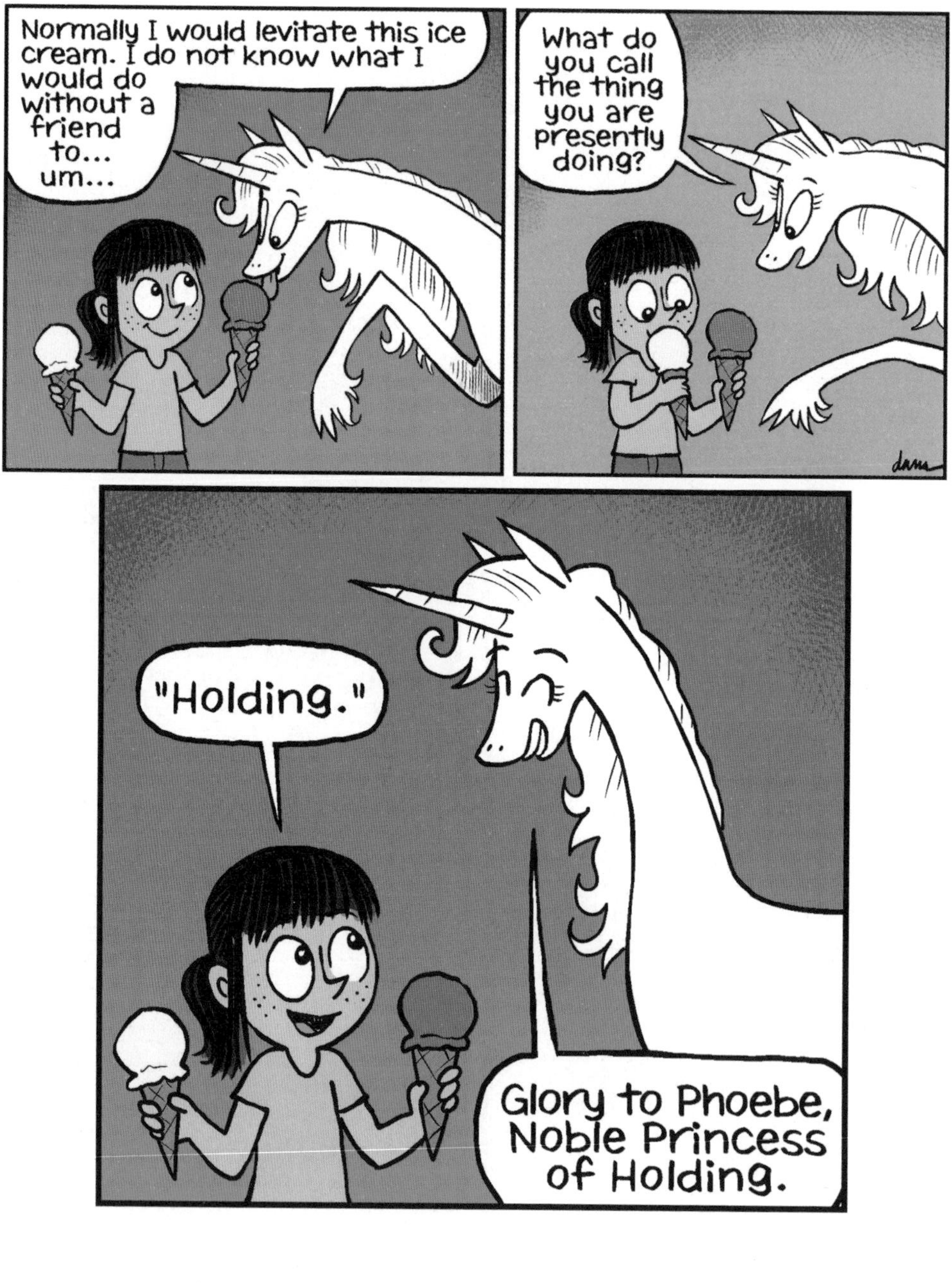
Normally I would levitate this ice cream. I do not know what I would do without a friend to... um...
What do you call the thing you are presently doing?
dana
"Holding."
Glory to Phoebe, Noble Princess of Holding.

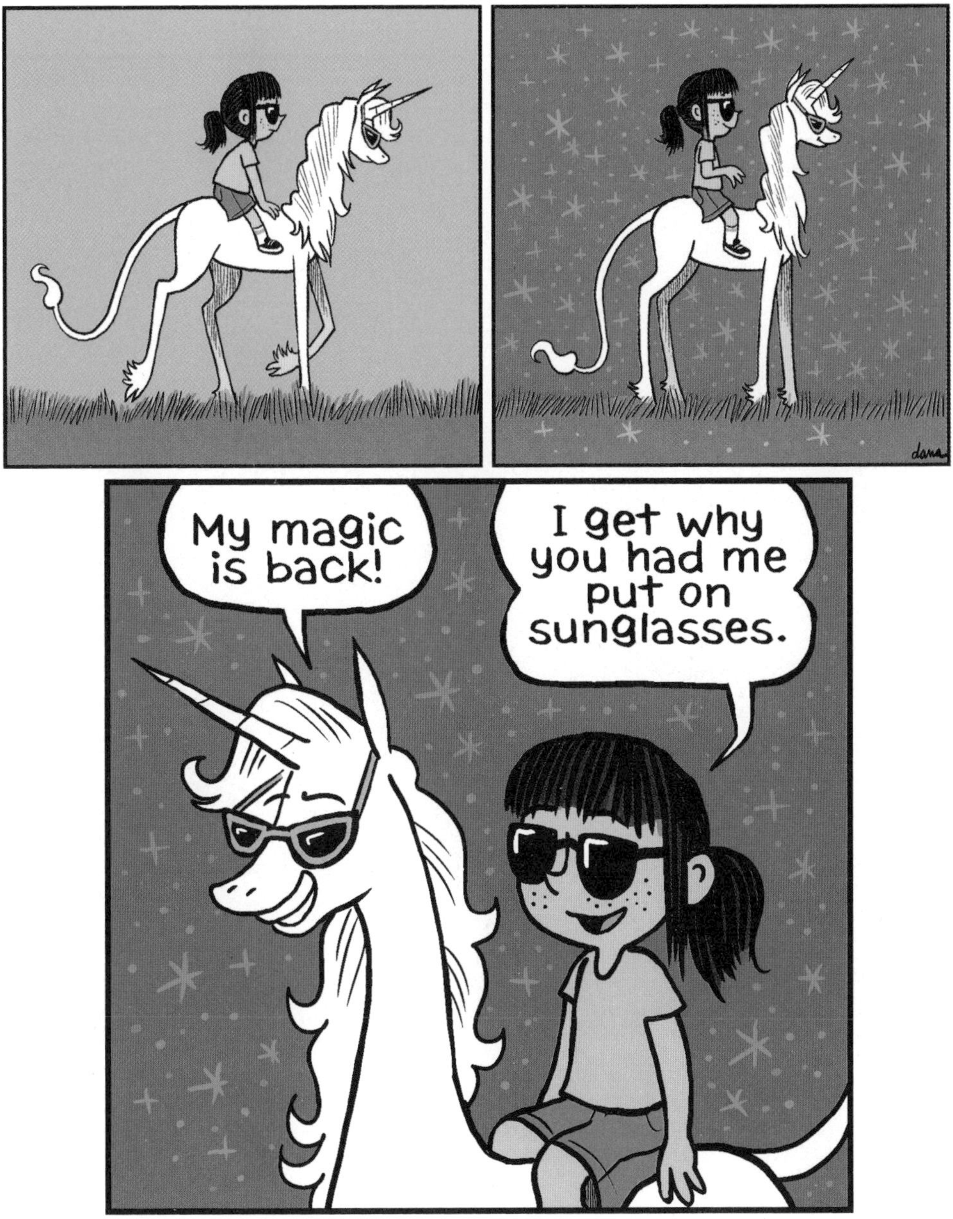
dana
My magic is back!
I get why you had me put on sunglasses.

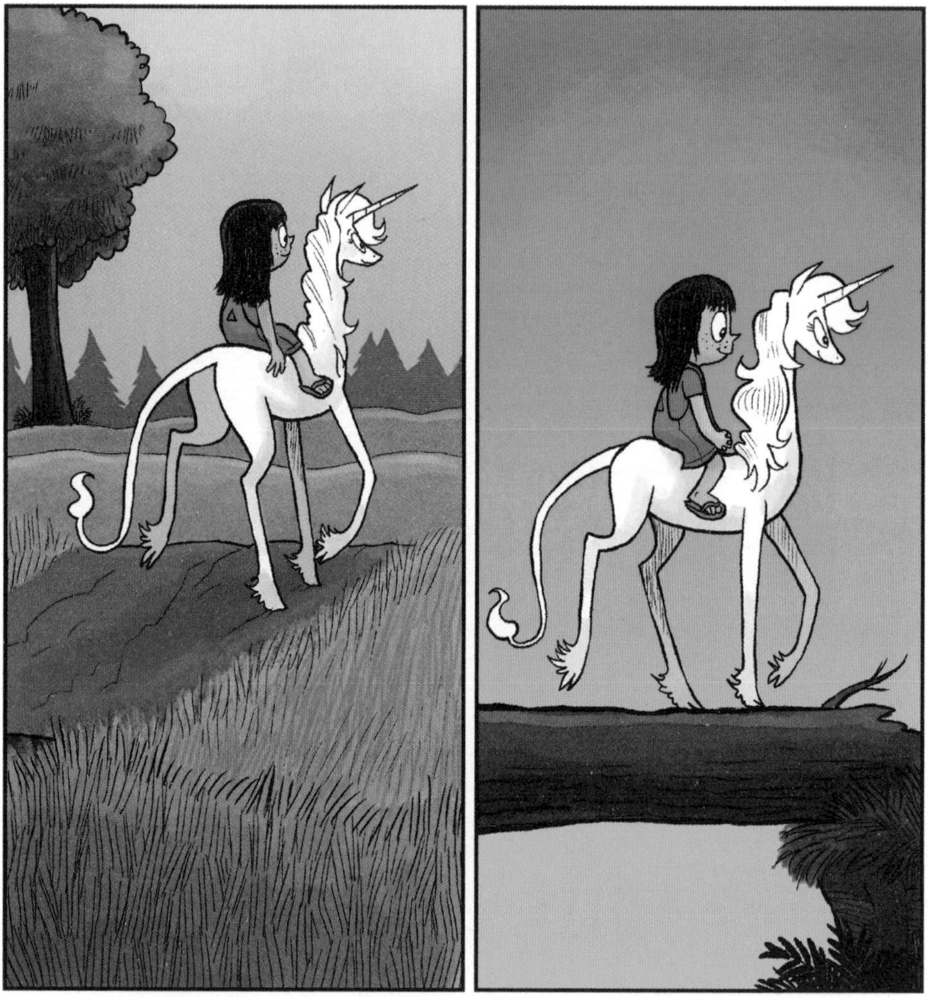

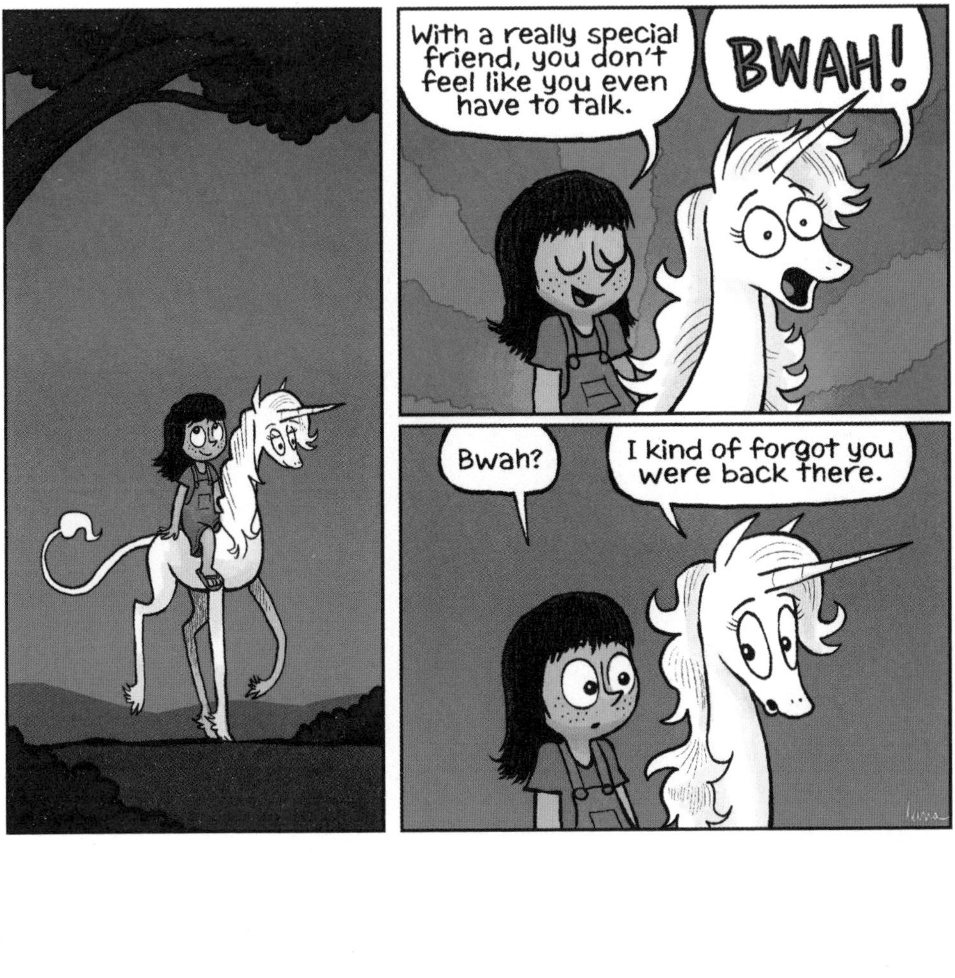
With a really special friend, you don't feel like you even have to talk.
BWAH!
Bwah?
I kind of forgot you were back there.

MORE TO EXPLORE! A special section featuring words to learn!

GLOSSARY

artisanal (arr-tiz-un-uhl): pg. 132 – adjective / something that is hand-crafted or made to high standards by an artisan or craftsperson

conspiracy theory (kun-speer-uh-see theer-ee): pg. 149 – noun / an idea that goes against science or established belief, such as the idea that the moon is made of cheese

contractors (kon-trak-ters): pg. 5 – noun / someone who leads a project, often home repair or construction, and hires people to do specific jobs in order to complete the larger project.

enshroud (in-shrowd): pg. 102 – verb / to cover up in something so as to be fully or partially hidden from view

harrowing (hair-oh-ing): pg. 101 – adjective / stressful, distressing, and highly uncomfortable

humility (hew-mill-ih-tee): pg. 167 – noun / a state of feeling humble and not proud (unicorns are not known for their humility)

irony (eye-run-ee): pg. 127 – noun / A form of speech in which the real meaning is concealed or contradicted by the words used. Irony is used for humorous effect, to help tell a story, or in order to deliver a message.

manipulate (muh-nip-you-layt): pg. 112 – verb / to influence someone in order to control them or make them do something that you want

photosynthesis (foe-toe-sin-thuh-sis): pg. 42 – noun / the process by which green plants use sunlight to create food, using carbon dioxide and water to produce oxygen

primate (pry-mayt): pg. 111 – noun / a member of a group of mammals with highly developed brains, including humans, monkeys, and apes; most primates have opposable thumbs (thumbs that can bend), and all except for apes and humans have tails

racism (ray-sih-zum): pg. 129 – noun / a negative and unfair view or opinion of another race of people based on their outward characteristics and belonging to that race

resplendence (rih-splen-dince): pg. 63 – noun / impressively colored or remarkable in appearance

obsessed (ub-sessd): pg. 136 – adjective / to be fixated with a specific topic or interest that you can't stop thinking about

orb (ohrb): pg. 89 – noun / a round object in the shape of a ball, also known as a sphere

rebel (rih-bell): pg. 109 – verb / to act out against someone or something, such as a ruling government, institution, or parent

scintillating (sin-tuh-lay-ting): pg. 132 – adjective / shining and brightly reflecting light, shimmering

spoiler (spoy-lerr): pg. 54 – noun / any bit of information that gives away the plot or story of a book, movie, or other work of art before someone has a chance to experience themselves

Andrews McMeel Publishing
a division of Andrews McMeel Universal
1130 Walnut Street, Kansas City, Missouri 64106

www.andrewsmcmeel.com

22 23 24 25 26 SDB 10 9 8 7 6 5 4 3 2 1

ISBN: 978-1-5248-7158-1

Library of Congress Control Number: 2021947499

Made by:
King Yip (Dongguan) Printing & Packaging Factory Ltd.
Address and location of manufacturer:
Daning Administrative District, Humen Town
Dongguan Guangdong, China 523930
1st Printing—12/27/21

ATTENTION: SCHOOLS AND BUSINESSES
Andrews McMeel books are available at quantity discounts with bulk purchase for educational, business, or sales promotional use. For information, please e-mail the Andrews McMeel Publishing Special Sales Department: specialsales@amuniversal.com.

Look for these books!

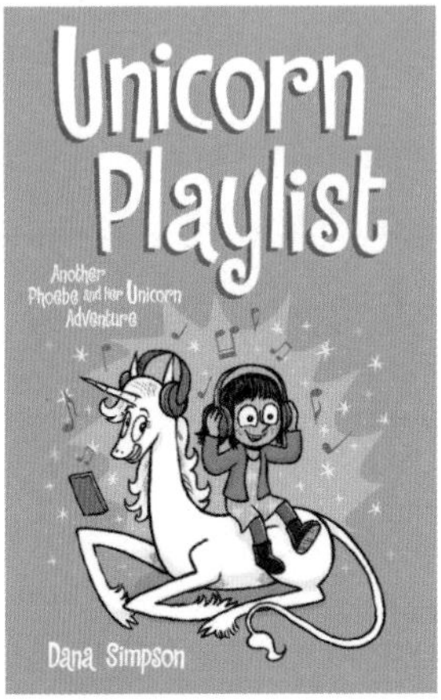
Unicorn Playlist
Another Phoebe and her Unicorn Adventure
Dana Simpson

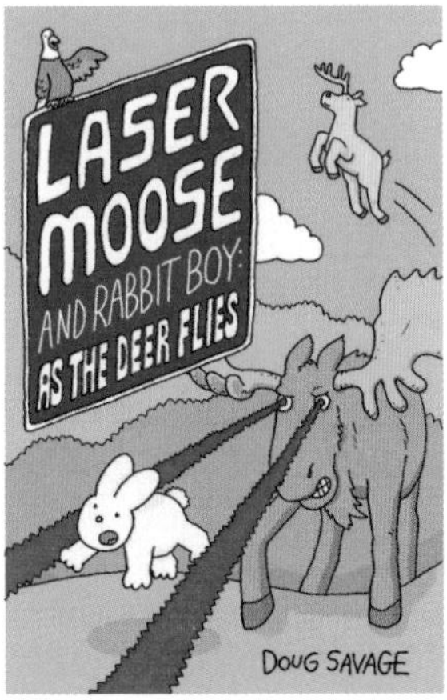
LASER MOOSE AND RABBIT BOY: AS THE DEER FLIES
DOUG SAVAGE

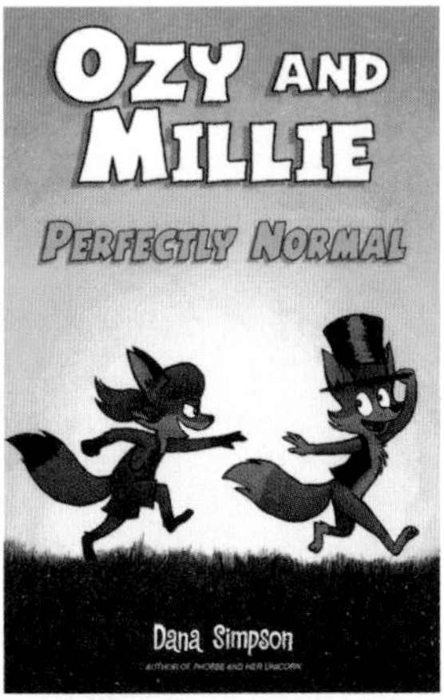
OZY AND MILLIE
PERFECTLY NORMAL
Dana Simpson

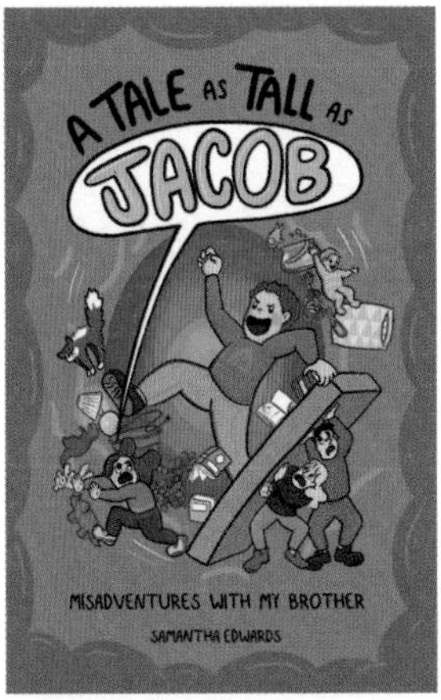
A TALE AS TALL AS JACOB
MISADVENTURES WITH MY BROTHER
SAMANTHA EDWARDS

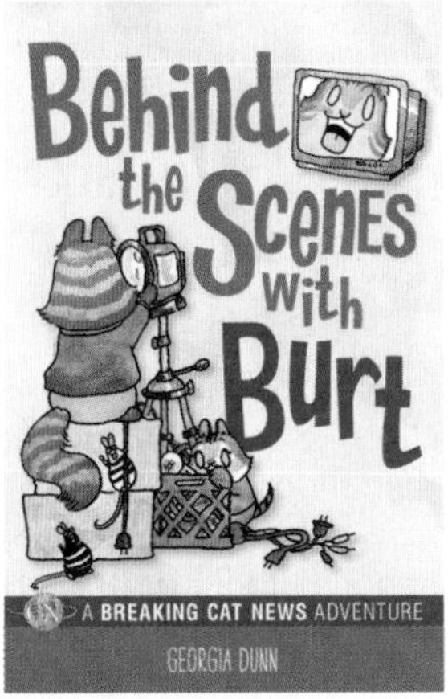
Behind the Scenes with Burt
A BREAKING CAT NEWS ADVENTURE
GEORGIA DUNN

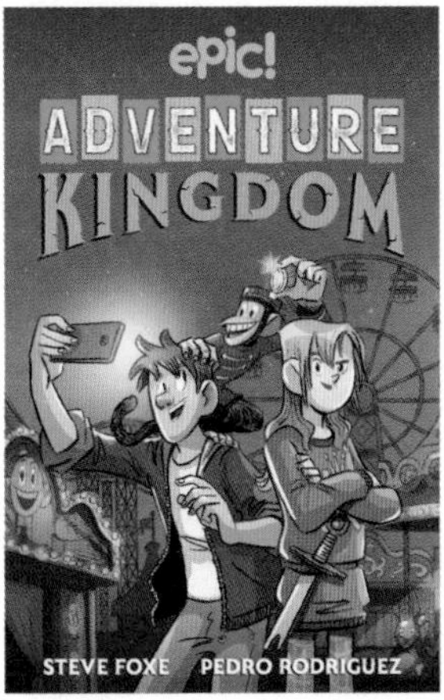
epic!
ADVENTURE KINGDOM
STEVE FOXE
PEDRO RODRIGUEZ

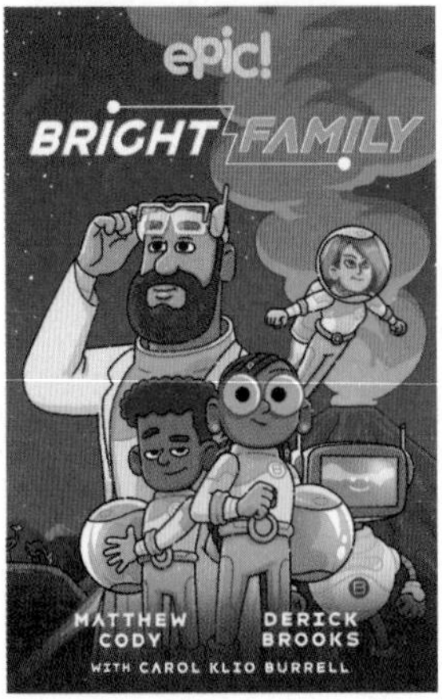
epic!
BRIGHT FAMILY
MATTHEW CODY
DERICK BROOKS
WITH CAROL KLIO BURRELL

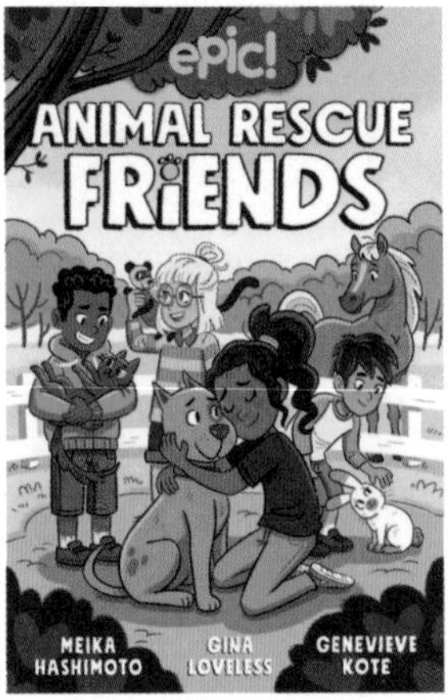
epic!
ANIMAL RESCUE FRIENDS
MEIKA HASHIMOTO
GINA LOVELESS
GENEVIEVE KOTE

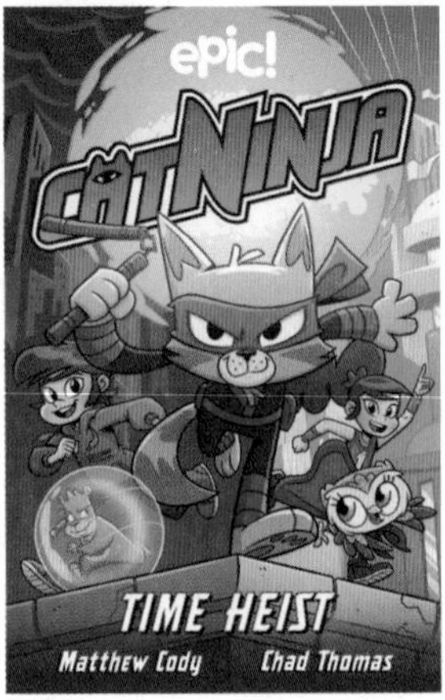
epic!
CAT NINJA
TIME HEIST
Matthew Cody
Chad Thomas